ISLAND OF GLASS

By Kathryn Le Veque

Printed by Dragonblade Publishing in the United States of America

Library of Congress Control Number 2014-032

Kathryn Le Veque Novels

Medieval Romance:

The de Russe Legacy:
The White Lord of Wellesbourne
The Dark One: Dark Knight
Beast
Lord of War: Black Angel
The Falls of Erith

The de Lohr Dynasty:
While Angels Slept (Lords of East Anglia)
Rise of the Defender
Spectre of the Sword
Unending Love
Archangel
Steelheart

Great Lords of le Bec:
Great Protector
To the Lady Born (House of de Royans)

Lords of Eire:
The Darkland (Master Knights of Connaught)
Black Sword
Echoes of Ancient Dreams (time travel)

De Wolfe Pack Series:
The Wolfe
Serpent
Scorpion (Saxon Lords of Hage – Also related to The Questing)
Walls of Babylon
The Lion of the North
Dark Destroyer

Ancient Kings of Anglecynn:
The Whispering Night
Netherworld

Battle Lords of de Velt:
The Dark Lord
Devil's Dominion

Reign of the House of de Winter:
Lespada
Swords and Shields (also related to The Questing, While Angels Slept)

De Reyne Domination:
Guardian of Darkness
The Fallen One (part of Dragonblade Series)

Unrelated characters or family groups:
The Gorgon (Also related to Lords of Thunder)
The Warrior Poet (St. John and de Gare)
Tender is the Knight (House of d'Vant)
Lord of Light
The Questing (related to The Dark Lord, Scorpion)
The Legend (House of Summerlin)

The Dragonblade Series: (Great Marcher Lords of de Lara)
Dragonblade
Island of Glass (House of St. Hever)
The Savage Curtain (Lords of Pembury)
The Fallen One (De Reyne Domination)
Fragments of Grace (House of St. Hever)
Lord of the Shadows
Queen of Lost Stars (House of St. Hever)

Lords of Thunder: The de Shera Brotherhood Trilogy
The Thunder Lord
The Thunder Warrior
The Thunder Knight

Time Travel Romance: (Saxon Lords of Hage)
The Crusader
Kingdom Come

Contemporary Romance:

Kathlyn Trent/Marcus Burton Series:
Valley of the Shadow
The Eden Factor
Canyon of the Sphinx

The American Heroes Series:
Resurrection
Fires of Autumn
Evenshade
Sea of Dreams
Purgatory

Other Contemporary Romance:
Lady of Heaven
Darkling, I Listen

Multi-author Collections/Anthologies:
With Dreams Only of You (USA Today bestseller)
Sirens of the Northern Seas (Viking romance)

Note: All Kathryn's novels are designed to be read as stand-alones, although many have cross-over characters or cross-over family groups. Novels that are grouped together have related characters or family groups.

Series are clearly marked. All series contain the same characters or family groups except the American Heroes Series, which is an anthology with unrelated characters.

There is NO particular chronological order for any of the novels because they can all be read as stand-alones, even the series.

For more information, find it in **A Reader's Guide to the Medieval World of Le Veque**.

To my muse, Lee Reherman
Who was surely Kenneth in another life

TABLE OF CONTENTS

CHAPTER ONE

Kirk Castle
The Welsh Marches
October, 1333 A.D.

"YOU CANNOT KNOW my pain," the woman wept. "I do not understand where I went wrong in raising my only child. She has had the best education that my husband and I could provide for her. She has wanted for nothing. I do not understand why she rebels against me."

The man seated opposite the woman had heard this tale before. It was difficult not to yawn in the face of her agony. He had stopped offering his advice long ago, mostly because he had no children and was therefore not an expert on their rearing. But he knew where his sister had gone wrong, experience or not. A fool could have realized it.

"You have spoiled her," he said simply.

The woman's weeping grew louder. She muffled it in her expensive kerchief, held tightly to her nose. "What have I done that you would not have in my place?"

Garson Mortimer, cousin to Roger Mortimer and the First Earl of Wrexham, was not a normally patient man. His only sister was trying him sorely to the point where he wanted to rip out what was left of his thinning hair. She never listened to him as it was, only using him to vent her frustrations.

He leaned back against his chair, a sturdy piece of furniture built by Welsh craftsmen. So close to the border of Wales, English and Welsh cultures seemed to blend together in a calliope of disciplines ranging from food to architecture. His opinions on women and childrearing, however, were strictly English.

"Do we truly need to revisit this subject?"

"We do!"

"Then I would not have sent her to receive her education at a monastery," he said flatly. "I told you that was a mistake. St. Wenburgh is far too unconventional."

"But her father…!"

"God rest his soul, he wanted the best for Aubrielle, but she does not have the countenance to gracefully accept the privilege that has been given her. The more she is given, the more she wants."

Graciela Mortimer de Witney sniffled into her kerchief again, the tears in her dark eyes lessening as she thought on her brother's words. "Aubrielle is merely curious for knowledge, Garson. Since the monks taught her to read…"

"A sin!" Garson slapped his hand on the arm of the chair. "Tevor should never have allowed it. Imagine, a woman knowing how to read!"

"My husband was only doing what he thought best for her. He believed that a lady with education would be an attractive asset to a potential husband."

"An asset, *pah*," Garson snorted. "Education has only put ideas into that inherently fertile mind she possesses. And what has it reaped? Only grief."

Graciela was feeling like a scolded child, not at all receiving the sympathy she had hoped for. "She has been a joy at times."

"Then why are you here?" When his sister faltered in her reply, Garson stood up and began to pace the rough wooden floor of his solar. The joists creaked beneath his weight. "You are here because you cannot handle her. She has become unruly and unless something is done, she will shame the entire family with this wild dream she pursues."

Graciela's tears had faded. "She is spirited and intelligent."

"She is out of control. Any young lady that would set off from her home on a journey, without escort or thought to her care and safety, is idiotic."

"I would not call her idiotic."

Garson emitted a grunt of frustration. "Graciela, do you hear yourself? Your daughter set off from Highwood House en route to Glastonbury because the monks at St. Wenburgh told her that the Holy Grail of Christ was buried there."

"She simply wanted to prove them right."

He threw up his hands. "Not to glorify God, but to prove a myth."

The woman fidgeted with her hands, the golden tassels of her belted dress. "She has always had a fascination to verify the legend. She believes the discovery of the Grail would be a boon for the entire country, especially with its war against Wales and Scotland."

Garson stared at her a moment before running his hand over his face. Why his sister attempted to justify her daughter's psychosis was beyond him. "Of all the wonderful things she learned, out of everything she had been told, the only item that sticks in her mind is the Quest for the Holy Grail. Where Arthur failed, the Lady Aubrielle Grace de Witney will succeed? How arrogant."

"She would try."

He couldn't continue with the conversation. It was making him crazy. "If you have not come for my help with Aubrielle, then why are you here? To lament your woes and aggravation with a daughter who is headstrong without compare?"

Graciela lifted her pale face. Soft gray light from the lancet windows fell upon her fine, pretty features. "I am afraid, Garson."

"Of course you are. So am I."

"I cannot manage my own daughter. I am afraid tragedy will befall her if she continues on this quest."

"What do you want me to do about it?"

"She needs someone stronger than she is. Since the death of her father, that duty must fall to you. You are all that I have that stands between me and the destruction of my child."

Garson exhaled heavily. "I am not a nursemaid," he said. "Moreover, I have enough battles on my hands. As we speak, half of my army is in Wales at Dinas Bran Castle in retaliation for the raid against one of my villages six days ago. People were killed and the food stores raided."

"I am sorry for your troubles, brother, truly, but there is much at stake with Aubrielle," she pleaded. "Please, Garson. You are my only hope."

He knew he shouldn't. But he could not stomach her pleading. "If I agree, then it will be done my way. I want no interference from you."

"Of course."

"If she so much as sets foot outside this castle, I will lock her in the vault and throw away the key."

"Whatever you feel necessary."

He cast her a condescending look. "You do not mean any of it."

"But I do! Perhaps you can convince Aubrielle of the error of her ways. She respects you."

"She does not. And she fears nothing, either." Garson shook his head with regret. "Not even her dazzling beauty will overcome her character flaws. There is no man on earth that will want a wife he has to do battle with on a daily basis."

Graciela toyed with the fine kerchief in her hand. "Will you… will you perhaps consider finding a husband for her? She brings an attractive dowry of the Lordship of Tenbury. And then there is Highwood House…."

Garson waved his hands irritably. "I know very well what my own niece brings to a husband and if I die without an heir, she will also inherit Wrexham."

"Do you intend to remarry soon, Garson?"

His flustered manner fell dramatically. "My widower status is not at issue," he muttered. "We were discussing Aubrielle."

"Of course, Brother."

Garson tried not to linger on thoughts that his sister's question provoked. Five years after the death of his beloved wife in childbirth, the pain was still fresh.

"I will do what I can for Aubrielle," he struggled to shift focus. "But I can promise nothing."

Graciela rose from her chair and went to her brother. "My thanks," she put her cold hands on his fingers. "I know she will be in good hands. Pray be understanding with her."

He cocked an eyebrow. "You swore not to interfere."

Graciela smiled. "That is not interfering, simply a mother's request."

Garson knew even as he agreed that he was going to regret it. He kissed his sister on the cheek all the same, resigned to the fact that he was a fool for her troubles. The door to the solar creaked opened and a small man with gray hair appeared, bowing profusely in the presence of his lord.

"My lord," he said. "I beg pardon, but we have a… problem."

Garson knew he shouldn't ask; he probably already knew the answer. "What is it, Arbosa?"

The Majordomo of Kirk looked between the earl and his sister. "The Lady Aubrielle has gone missing."

"What?" Graciela exclaimed softly. "I left orders that she be watched!"

"We did watch her, my lady," the man assured her. "She said she wanted to gain some fresh air and wandered into the bailey. We've not seen her for some time."

Garson left Graciela in the musty solar. If he was to be in charge of his niece's redemption, then it would start at this moment.

CHAPTER TWO

Dinas Bran Castle
Powys, Wales

For early June, the weather was typical. The rain had fallen so heavily that it had been like walking through sheets of crystalline silver. Spoiling the effect was the mud that it created, churning like black rivers as it rolled down the sides of the motte. Men in chain mail, bearing the seal of Wrexham, had struggled up the slick, sloping sides en route to the keep at the top to do battle. From beginning to end, the entire deed had been a nightmare.

The clash had lasted nearly two days, not particularly long where battles were concerned. Dinas Bran Castle had been held by Dafydd ap Gruffydd, brother of Llewellyn the Last, though no one had actually seen the man leading his men to battle. Mostly, it seemed to be held by raiders disguised as Welsh soldiers. It hadn't taken tremendous effort to breach the wooden gate and penetrate the castle. Rather than fight, most of the Welsh had fled. Kirk's army had come away with little more than exhaustion and minimal satisfaction.

On the way back to Kirk Castle, the rain had washed away the layers of mud accumulated from mounting the enormous Welsh motte. The men-at-arms were on foot, tired, marching on muddy roads that had them sloshing up to their ankles. The chargers were wet, filthy beasts with bad tempers, handled by knights that were equally filthy and bad tempered. Armor rusted in the rain, creating problems with comfort and movement. The closer they drew to Kirk Castle, the more evident their misery.

Kenneth St. Héver was one of those knights with the filth and bad temperament engrained into his skin. Wet and exhaustion were nothing new to him, as he had been in the knighthood since his twentieth year. Eighteen years later, it had completely taken over his nature. He had a reputation for being exceptionally unfriendly though never unfair. He commanded one hundred and twenty five retainers, men personally given to him by King Edward for Kenneth's service against Roger Mortimer.

Kenneth's relationship with his fellow knights was an agreeable one but he was very reluctant to form friendships; he only had two true friends, men he had served with since he had been knighted, and both of them were tied up in wars with the Scots. Kenneth, in fact, had only recently returned to the Marches after helping Tate de Lara, Earl of Carlisle, and Stephen of Pembury, Guardian Protector of Berwick, subdue the Scots at Berwick-upon-Tweed. He was back on the Welsh Marches now because the king wanted him here and was not particularly happy about it. He wanted to be back at Berwick with his friends. Yet he had no choice; he had a job to do on the Marches.

So his mood was consistently clouded these days. Kenneth paid little attention to the men marching in distress beside him; his focus was diverted to the countryside in search of threats. Over the years, scanning his surroundings had become habit. Somehow the landscape was always threatening, rain or shine, and he was not one to be caught unaware. As he scrutinized the trees, a knight on a large bay steed rode up beside him, lifting his visor to reveal brown eyes set within an unshaven, dirty face.

"We'll be seeing the turrets of Kirk over the crest of this hill," the knight commented. "I can already taste the cool ale and a knuckle of beef."

Kenneth's visor was down, but not to shield his face from the rain. He simply didn't like others looking at him, studying his face, perhaps reading his thoughts.

"Had these lazy fools moved faster, we would be seeing those turrets sooner," he growled.

"The men are tired."

"Then they are women. To be exhausted after a small skirmish is an insult."

The brown-eyed knight grinned. Everett l'Breaux was a congenial man and hardly offended by Kenneth's brusque manner.

"If you'd lift that visor, I am sure I would see exhaustion written all over your face as well," he commented. "There is no shame in that."

Kenneth flipped up his three-point visor, of the latest style for ease and protection. Eyes of the palest blue, like a sea of ice, gazed steadily at Everett. "All you will see on my face is boredom."

"You are a hard man, Ken."

A massive gray stallion jogged up between them, shoving Everett's horse aside. Kenneth's animal, muzzled after the battle, snapped its teeth and swung its big head at the intrusion. Only Kenneth's phenomenal strength kept the beast at bay.

Lucius de Cor was the captain of Wrexham's army. He was an older man that had seen many battles for a succession of English kings. Close to retirement, he was nonetheless fully in charge of the men under his command. But he looked to Kenneth, his second, to make sure his orders were enforced. St. Héver was the only man in the corps who inspired that kind of fear and respect. Only an idiot would argue with him.

"Have the men pick up the pace, Ken," he ordered. "I want to be cleaned and seated by sup."

Kenneth moved into action before the command left Lucius' lips. He spurred his beast back along the lines of marching men. His armored arm was lifted, commands bellowing from his throat. Immediately, the block of three hundred men picked up into a steady trot. Somewhere in the back of the lines, a few of the men seemed to be exchanging an inordinate amount of conversation. Kenneth spurred his charger around the rear of the column and came upon them.

"What goes on?" he demanded.

When St. Héver demanded, men listened. These soldiers were not

Kenneth's retainers; they belonged to another knight who had stayed behind at Kirk, Sir Reid de Bowland. But they responded with more attention to Kenneth than they would have to their own liege.

"A soldier's disagreement, m'lord," one man replied. "We didn't mean to disrupt the march."

Kenneth's gaze was so piercing it could have cut steel. "What kind of disagreement?"

The two men arguing looked at each other, fearful to speak. The second man finally spoke. "I lost my crossbow on the slopes of Dinas Bran Castle, my lord," he said. "Malf found it and will not give it back."

"So he has stolen from you."

Malf's eyes widened. "No, my lord, I didn't steal it."

"Then return it to him."

"But this isn't his weapon," the soldier was almost pleading, afraid of what was coming. "I know of Sheen's weapon. This is not it."

Kenneth continued to look between the two men, a heavy silence filling the air. By this time, Lucius had come upon them.

"What is the issue, St. Héver?" he demanded.

"Sheen lost his weapon on the slopes and tells me that Malf found it. Malf insists it is not the lost weapon but another."

Lucius frowned impatiently. "There is no time for this foolery. Perhaps you both need to be reminded on the value of weapons and camaraderie." He glanced at Kenneth. "Ten lashes each when we return. Perhaps next time, Sheen will be more careful about his weapon and Malf will be more apt to share his found one if he sees that his comrade has none."

It was swift justice designed to send a message to all of the soldiers. Kenneth nodded, knowing it was expected that he would deliver the blows. That was his position, as second in command of the army. He followed Lucius back to the front of the column just as they crested the hill.

Kirk loomed ahead, a massive fortress with her green, gold and scarlet Wrexham banners waving in the wind. But something else caught their attention: a lone figure moving off of the road and into the trees. It was at some distance, a black little spot with legs. Kenneth focused in on it, as did Lucius and Everett. As they drew closer, it appeared to be a figure on a small palfrey or donkey. The little beast's legs were moving furiously, making haste for the shelter of the forest.

Lucius frowned. "Go see what that is," he told Kenneth.

Kenneth spurred his unruly animal into a gallop. He knew it would be no time before he overtook the figure on the palfrey. He entered the border of trees nearly the same time as the figure did.

"Halt," he ordered.

The figure kept going. Kenneth rode up beside it and gave a shove to the shoulder, sending it tumbling to the wet ground. He heard a high-pitched cry, indicating to him that the figure was a woman. As he brought his horse around, the lady came to her feet and took off through the bramble at a dead run.

Kenneth spurred his charger after her. His prevailing emotion was irritation; the woman was small, dodging through some bushes that he couldn't get through on his big horse. A savage game of cat and mouse was afoot as the two of them plowed deeper into the forest.

He followed her, closer at some times, further away at others. She was fast and she was clever. The more she ran, the angrier he became. At one point, he fell in directly behind her and she ducked into a cluster of close-knit trees. He should have known better; he was too close and going too fast when she led him through some heavy branches. Unable to respond fast enough, a big branch caught him and knocked him off his charger.

Rising from a supine position in full armor was no easy task, but Kenneth managed to do so quite ably. Aggravated, he suspected the woman was somewhere out of the trees, well ahead of him and well rid of him. He couldn't remember the last time someone, especially a woman, had bested him. In fact, there had never been a time to his recollection. His anger grew, but more at himself. As he considered which direction to take, something heavy struck him on the back of the head.

The blow pitched him forward onto his knees. Dazed but not senseless, he rolled onto his back, away from the follow up strike he knew was coming. It also brought him face to face with his attacker and, for a moment, he could not believe his eyes. The woman he had chased all over Creation had a large piece of wood in her hand, swinging it at him with the intent to kill him.

But she made a mistake that would cost her. She was too close as she came in for another hit. Kenneth lashed out with a massive leg and took her feet out from under her, reaching out to disarm her as she fell. He tossed the wood far off into the trees, pinning the woman to the ground in the same motion. She was small and no match for his strength.

"Get off me!" she fought and grunted. "Let me go!"

Kenneth's vision was still muddled from the blow, but it wasn't so muddled that he couldn't see what lay beneath him. A woman with the most astoundingly beautiful face he had ever seen lay there, her sea-colored eyes blazing and her rich brown hair spread over the ground like angel's wings. Before he could utter a word, she thrust her head forward and smashed him in the nose with the top of her head. It was a brutal move. Blood spurted but he didn't let go; he let it drip down onto her soft white neck.

"Oh!" she shrieked. "You are bleeding on me!"

"That is your misfortune."

She stopped squirming and glared at him. "If you do not release me, I swear I shall do more than bloody your nose. I shall wring your neck!"

He had no idea why that statement made him want to smile. It was a struggle not to react. He leapt off of her with the agility of a cat and grabbed her by the wrist, pulling her up with him in the same motion. "I would sincerely like to see you try," he said.

The woman twisted and pulled. "Let me go, you brute."

"What is your name?"

She pounded at the hand that held her. "That is none of your business!"

"I beg to differ."

She flew at him, all fists and feet, but he caught her, turned her around, and trapped her against him. It was dangerous to have her head near his face where she might head-butt him again. As it was, the blood from his nose was dripping down onto her hair. She struggled ferociously as he leaned down.

"Now," he growled in her ear. "You will tell me who you are."

"Never!"

He tightened his grip, squeezing the air from her. "Name, woman."

"N-no!"

His response was to pick her up, legs dangling, and carry her in the direction of his charger. The muzzled animal was attempting to graze a patch of wet grass several feet away. The woman kicked and struggled. As he passed by a birch tree, she thrust her legs out, kicked off against the tree, and sent him off balance. Kenneth recovered and made a mental note not to get close to any more trees.

They were at the horse and Kenneth was trying to decide how, exactly, he could maintain his hold on her and mount the horse at the same time. Pounding thunder in the distance signaled catching his attention.

He turned to see Everett approach. The knight's brown eyes widened when he saw the woman, the blood. "Jesus," he breathed, focused on the struggling woman. "Lady Aubrielle…."

Somewhere in the back of Kenneth's mind, the name sounded familiar. Everett dismounted his steed.

"Lady Aubrielle, are you all right?" he asked.

Kenneth wasn't sure what to say. But he knew he was not going to release the woman lest she attack him again. "You know this wildcat?" he asked Everett.

Everett looked rather pale. "I have forgotten you've only been at Kirk a couple of years," he said. "You've not yet met the earl's niece, the Lady Aubrielle Grace de Witney."

The information sank in. *The earl's niece.* Kenneth released his grip and, true to his fear, the lady swung around with a fist. He put his hand up, catching her wrist before she could strike his face. They glared at each other, each one completely unwilling to bend to the other.

"Brute," she hissed at him. "Fiend!"

Everett was making a fool out of himself in his effort to ease the situation. "Can I assist you, my lady? What are you doing out on the open road?"

"That is none of your affair, Everett l'Breaux," she snapped. "Give me your horse so that I may be on my way."

Everett shook his head. "Alas, I cannot, my lady. My horse responds only to me. He is far too much for you to handle."

The woman seemed to back off somewhat, but only by necessity. Kenneth could see it was temporary; she was simply re-thinking her strategy. *Aubrielle Grace de Witney.* He had heard the name before, several times. As Everett mentioned, however, he had never seen the earl's only niece. He knew that her father, the earl's brother-in-law, had passed away about the time Kenneth had come into the earl's service and it was up to the earl to help manage his widowed sister's estates. Other than that, he knew little about her. He'd certainly never heard she was such a spitfire.

He would not take his eyes from her, but there was more to it than the fear that another fist would come flying at him. As he had observed before, she was unquestionably beautiful; her wide sea-colored eyes and long lashes were set against a sweet oval face of porcelain skin and rosebud lips. Her dark hair fell straight and silken to her waist. When she reached up to smooth the strands in her face and tuck them back, he could see that her delicate little ears stuck out ever so slightly. In truth, it was a delightful feature. He could see nothing unappealing about the woman other than the fact that she behaved like a wild animal.

"Then I shall find my mount and be on my way," she was trying desperately to stay in control of the situation.

Everett and Kenneth looked at each other.

"I am afraid we cannot allow you to go," Everett was reluctant to deny her but sensibilities dictated he should. "Perhaps we should return to Kirk and see about procuring you an escort for your journey."

Her pretty face darkened. "I am not going back," she growled. "You cannot force me."

"But...."

"No!"

By this time, Lucius had come upon his missing knights. Wondering what had befallen them, he set out to discover for himself. He saw the lovely young woman, immediately recognizing her. Being closer to the earl than the others, he had heard stories of the Lady Aubrielle Grace and he had met her on a few occasions. He knew what a burden she had been to her mother. Whatever she was doing out here, in the middle of the wild country, could not be good. He did not relish the confrontation that was undoubtedly to come.

"My lady," he greeted her evenly.

Aubrielle looked at the captain with little tolerance. "Ah, the fearless Captain de Cor," she said with a hint of sarcasm. "Three knights against one small lady? That hardly seems fair."

"What are you doing out here, my lady?"

She lifted a well-shaped eyebrow defiantly. "As I have told your henchmen, it is none of your affair."

Lucius scratched his chin. He knew the earl would be angry if he simply left her out here, alone. He already suspected they were well beyond the negotiating stage. He looked at Kenneth, his nose bloodied, and sighed with resignation.

"Take her."

Kenneth grabbed her again before she could run. She screamed and yelled, struggling as Kenneth mounted his charger with Everett's assistance. At one point she tried to flip herself off the horse, kicking Kenneth in the side of his helmed head in the process. Stoically, Kenneth maintained both his temper and his grip on her. She kept fighting, and he kept holding.

It was thus the entire way back to the castle.

ᏅᏰ

THE DOOR WAS locked and there was little chance escaping. Aubrielle had spent a long time pouting, alternately sitting in the only chair the chamber had to offer and stomping about the floor. When she would grow weary of one, she would do the other.

Night was falling and still, her mother had not come to tell her farewell. She knew that it had been her mother's intention all along to leave her with her uncle, though the woman had camouflaged the truth in the guise of a family visit. Soon her anger gave way to disappointment, and then sadness. As the sun set, she knew that her mother was never coming. Disappointment gave way to tears.

Aubrielle's tears eventually faded and she wiped her eyes, trying to be callous to the fact that her weakling mother had abandoned her. She consoled herself with the knowledge that she would have escaped Kirk also had it not been for the big blond beast that had caught her. Her mind wandered to the knight they called Kenneth; all she had been able to see of him was his eyes, so blue that they were nearly silver. He had thick blond lashes, too. His body was enormous, much larger than any man she had ever seen, and he had easily used that strength against her. The more she had struggled against him, the easier it seemed to become for him. He'd never raised a sweat or uttered a word of pain in all of the struggles they had been through.

She was singling out a particular hate for him at the moment. Mostly, she was feeling hurt and abandoned and needed someone other than herself to blame. Rising from the chair, she paced over to the hearth, watching the embers burn low. The night would be cold; she could feel the breeze passing through the lancet windows. Glancing around her chamber, she noted that it was a large room with a big bed. It was then she noticed her trunks in the corner. Her tears sprang fresh, realizing this place was to be her prison.

Her foot was sore where she had kicked the big knight. She sat on the bed and removed her slipper, rubbing her sore toes. It had been stupid to kick armor, but she had done it anyway. As she was rubbing, the door to her chamber rattled and her heart leapt, startled by the sound. The panel finally opened and the earl entered, followed by a serving woman with a tray in her arms. Behind the woman came Lucius.

Aubrielle hadn't seen Lucius in a few years. He was a tall man, nice looking, his dark brown hair now tinged with gray at the temples. His dark beard was neat and trimmed. When he smiled apprehensively, she gave him a hateful look and focused on her uncle.

"So you bring food to the prisoner," she said. "I suppose I should thank you for your humane treatment."

The earl's pleasant expression faded. "You are as lovely as ever, Aubrielle. A pity I cannot say the same for your manner."

She lifted an eyebrow at him. "What would you know of my manner? You make it a point of not being around me whenever my mother and I visit. In fact, I would say this is the first time in years you have addressed me civilly."

The earl rubbed a hand over his face, glancing at Lucius, wishing to God he had never agreed to his sister's plea. The serving girl set the tray down before Aubrielle and quickly vacated the chamber. As the woman left, another figure entered the room.

Aubrielle knew it was the knight who had captured her simply by his eyes. The rest of the man meant nothing to her, even though he was without his armor. His enormous size gave him away as well, arms the size of tree limbs and legs as thick as a horse's neck. His hair was a pale shade of blond, the thick curls close cropped against his scalp. He met her gaze, feeling her hatred clear across the room. His only reaction was to plant his thick legs and cross those massive arms across his chest. If she were hoping to intimidate him, she would be sorely disappointed.

Aubrielle felt as if she was being ambushed. She pointed at Kenneth. "So you bring him to fight with me again?" she looked at her uncle. "Why have you brought them both? To punish me?"

"No one is going to punish you, Aubrielle," the earl sat in a chair, slowly. "Everything in your life does not have to be a battle. If you would only stop your belligerence, you would see that."

She didn't know what to think. "Then why have you come? Why are they here?"

"Can I not come and visit my own niece?" the earl asked. "You are a guest in my home. Am I not allowed to visit with my guests?"

She fixed him in the eye. "Where is my mother?"

"She has gone home."

Aubrielle knew that, but still, the truth hurt. She felt like an orphan. For the first time, her aggressiveness slipped.

"So she has left her burden with you," she murmured.

Garson could see she was wavering and he welcomed the opportunity for rational conversation.

"She had hoped that a change would do you good," he said. "Your mother is not a strong woman. She is weary."

"Weary of me," Aubrielle said. "I know the truth, uncle. You need not spare me."

The earl tried not to validate her too much. "I wasn't aware I was sparing you anything," he said casually. "Aubrielle, your mother is tired. The death of your father has taxed her sorely and she needs time to rest and recover. At this moment, your headstrong manner and determination is simply too much for her to bear. She hopes that…."

"She hopes that you will somehow conquer the shrew that has made her life miserable and drove her husband to an early grave," Aubrielle stood up from the bed. "Do not assume that I am oblivious of the truth, uncle. I know that she has left me here for you to put some sense into my head. She cannot control me and bears the hope that somehow you can."

Garson crossed his arms, formulating his words. "You have had an unconventional upbringing, Aubrielle. Though you are as beautiful as a new morning, you are without a doubt the most unusual woman I have ever known. Your father permitted you to read and write, and the liberal monks at St. Wenburgh filled your head with such nonsense as I cannot comprehend. Do you not understand how odd you are, child? Do you not understand our frustration?"

Aubrielle looked at him, hurt on her face. "I am sorry if my learned mind is considered an oddity. I am not ashamed of my upbringing."

"I know you are not. But the time has come for a more conventional education."

"What do you mean?"

The earl rose wearily from his chair. "I mean that your mother has asked me to domesticate you. She would like you to learn to behave more as a proper woman should."

"You mean she wants me to become another stupid sheep in fine silks and lace."

"I mean that you are to put foolish ideas like searching for the Holy Grail out of your mind," Garson wagged a finger at her. "It means that you learn to act like a lady so that a potential husband will approve of you."

Aubrielle cast a long glance at Lucius, then Kenneth. "And you have brought my trainers, is that it?"

"They will help," he admitted. "Between the three of us, I think we can handle you. Perhaps we can teach you something from a male perspective."

Aubrielle focused on Lucius. "How noble, being reduced to a nursemaid."

Lucius merely smiled. "I can think of a worse task, my lady."

It was meant as flattery, but she mocked him. "Really? Perhaps you'll be assigned to cleaning the stables next."

Lucius did not let the comment bother him. He maintained his smile and his composure. The earl, knowing nothing would be settled in one night, decided to end the conversation at this juncture. Aubrielle was still too brittle to rationally handle. He indicated Kenneth as he moved for the door.

"I am told you have already met, but allow me to formally introduce Sir Kenneth St. Héver, second in command of Wrexham's army," he pronounced the last name "*Saint Hay-ver*". "Get used to him. He seems to be the only one strong enough to deal with you."

"What about dear Lucius?" she asked, contemptuously sweet.

Lucius and the earl were heading out the door. "You shall see enough of him," the earl said. "Try not to eat Sir Kenneth alive, Aubrielle. I need him."

The door slammed with grim finality. Aubrielle stood there a moment, thinking on the entire conversation, aware that the massive blond knight was still standing there. She looked at him, more closely this time. He really was a big brute, though not unhandsome. In fact, if she thought on it, he was really quite pleasant to behold if one liked that type. She couldn't have cared one way or the other.

"So," she turned away, moving back to the food that was cooling on the tray. "You lost the wager, I take it."

Kenneth hadn't moved since he had first entered the room. He watched her inspect a piece of white bread. "What wager would that be, my lady?"

She picked at the crust. "You drew straws to see who would have to tend me this first night. I assume you lost."

"I won."

She looked at him, a piece of crust halfway to her lips. Much to his surprise, she laughed softly. "Of course you did. You won a sleepless night, wondering if I am going to kill you as you sleep."

Kenneth wondered why he suddenly felt so strange. The very instant she laughed, he felt as if all of the wind had been knocked out of him. She had a delicious smile that curved delicately over her straight white teeth, changing the entire countenance of her face. He'd never seen anything so lovely.

He shifted on his thick legs, unwinding his arms. "I believe I can defend myself."

"You barely held your own this afternoon."

"Fortunately for you I did not fight back."

She put the bread in her mouth, cocking her head as she chewed. "I have never seen you before. You are new to Kirk."

"I came into the earl's service two years ago, my lady."

"I see. Whom did you serve before?"

"The king."

Her eyebrows lifted. "You left the king's service to swear fealty to a mere earl?"

"I was a gift from the king to the earl for his support during the battle for the crown."

No matter how unconventional Aubrielle was, she knew that St. Héver must be a great knight to warrant such respect from young King Edward. The gifting of a knight was a great honor. Her respect, and fear, for the man took root.

"Are you going to stand there all night or are you going to sit?"

Kenneth took the chair the earl had been seated in. Aubrielle picked at her bread, eyeing him as she did so.

"Are you married?"

"Nay, my lady."

"Why not?"

"Because I am not."

She puckered her lips. "You are not the friendly type, are you?"

He would not dignify her question with a response. She returned to her meal in silence. Kenneth watched her, thinking he might have been able to warm to her had she not been so disagreeable. Their first meeting earlier in the day had fairly negated that possibility. He did, however, admire her cunning and fighting ability. She was a surprisingly tough woman and he respected that.

Aubrielle was bored with her meal after only a few bites. She pushed the tray aside and went to stand before the fire. She yawned and stretched, peering out of the corner of her eye to see if Kenneth was watching her. He was, but pretended he wasn't.

"I think I should like a walk before retiring for the night," she said.

Kenneth shook his head. “The rules have been established, my lady. The earl has dictated that you may not leave this chamber, for any reason, without his permission. Any attempt to do so will result in imprisonment in the vault.”

She stopped mid-yawn. “He wouldn’t dare!”

“I am afraid he would, my lady”

She marched over to him, her little fists resting angrily on her hips. “And just who are you? The enforcer of this ridiculous rule?”

“One of them.”

“Is that so? How do you intend to stop me? I can slip out and you’ll never know it. I invite you to try.”

“I wish you wouldn’t.”

She scowled at him, torn between the undeniable attraction to prove her point and the undeniable knowledge that he would be forced to prove his. Bullying hadn’t worked with the man. Perhaps another tactic would.

“Fine.” She turned on her heel, stomping towards the bed. Clothes and all, she lay down upon it. “I would retire now.”

“As you wish.”

She rolled over on her side, her mind racing in a hundred different directions. Her ears were painfully attuned to St. Héver’s movement, but there was none. He was apparently still seated, as silent as a ghost. Her determination grew that she should out-last the man, wait for him to fall asleep, and then slip from the room. She had no doubt that she could accomplish this.

What Aubrielle didn’t anticipate was how exhausted she was. The strain of emotions and the physical exertions of the day took their toll. She awoke with a start, unaware of how long she had been asleep, or even when she had fallen asleep. She only knew that she had that heavy groggy feeling, as one does when one does not sleep nearly enough. But no matter; she had a plan and needed to act on it. She listened for any sounds in the room but heard nothing. If St. Héver was still there, he was asleep. Perhaps her falling asleep hadn’t been a bad thing after all.

She debated a moment as to whether or not she should roll over and take a look. Curiosity won over. Slowly, she turned onto her back.

The fire in the room was dim. St. Hévér was still in his chair, sitting like stone, his ice-blue eyes staring into the dying embers. Not strangely, fury swept Aubrielle. She had waited for the man to weaken, had fallen asleep over the turmoil of it, only to awaken and see that he hadn't moved a muscle. Was the man not human? In a huff, she put her feet on the ground and stood up.

Kenneth turned his attention away from the fire, watching her as she took the coverlet and the linen covering the down mattress and tied the ends together. He remained silent as she ripped one of the canopies off the bed and tied it on the other end of the coverlet. He knew quite clearly what she was doing. He also knew that he was going to let her waste all of her effort and then tie her up with her own creation. If she wanted to push him, then he would push back.

It was past midnight as she pulled her makeshift rope off the bed and marched to the lancet window, ignoring Kenneth altogether. He hadn't tried to stop her so far. The cold air blew in from the north, running icy fingers through her silken hair; she shivered. A support post stood near the door, several feet from the window, and she tied the end of her rope to it. Still, St. Hévér hadn't said a word. Aubrielle's first test of her rope unraveled the end; slightly chagrinned, not to mention concerned, she retied the end, more firmly this time. Testing it again, it held. She took the other end and tossed it out of the window. Peering from the sill, she could see that her rope fell several feet short of the bailey below. In fact, she would be dropping about twelve feet before hitting the ground. The odds weren't good.

She took the second and last canopy off the bed, reeled in her rope, and tied the canopy to it. It was amazing and methodical to watch her work, so dedicated and well processed in her endeavor. Tossing it out of the window again, the drop to the ground was now down to five feet. Much better odds. Without a word, Aubrielle gathered her skirt and prepared to leap onto the windowsill. She'd almost forgotten that St.

Héver was in the room until his powerful arms suddenly grabbed her. It was an instant fight.

"Let me go!"

Aubrielle kicked as he pulled her away from the window. Because of their first bloody encounter, Kenneth was aware of her skills and took no chances. He had her around the torso, her arms pinned, her body dangling as he took her over to the bed. As they reached the stripped mattress, Aubrielle somehow got a foot in behind his knee and tripped him. They crashed onto the bed.

Aubrielle grunted as his weight came down on her. Because she was struggling so much, Kenneth had landed half on her, half on the mattress. She tried to kick him so he clamped an enormous leg over her thighs, trapping her in a human vise.

Aubrielle shrieked in frustration, realizing she was effectively corralled. Kenneth's mouth was by her ear.

"Time to sleep, my lady," he said as casually as if he was talking about the weather. "Relax and go to sleep."

Aubrielle was grinding her teeth. "Let go of me, you beast," she growled. "Let me go or I swear you'll regret it."

"I have heard those threats before," he said steadily. "Go to sleep, now. 'Tis late."

She was more than frustrated that he had let her go through the motions of rigging an escape route, only to thwart her efforts. Deep down, she knew that he would stop her eventually, but it had been cruel of him to let her get her hopes up. She wasn't used to being impeded, but she had experienced an entire day and night full of St. Héver's preventative presence. She hated everyone, as they hated her.

Her fury dissolved into hot tears. Her struggles came to a halt and huge, painful sobs shook her small body. The more embarrassed she became, the deeper the sobs. Kenneth felt the weeping that shook her body, wondering if it was another ploy, yet instinctively knowing that it was not. Her sorrow was real. Her body was limp, a warm soft mass against him, and he loosened his grip on her. It was difficult to be so severe with her in her moment of weakness.

Kenneth had never been good with words or emotions. His mother had died when he was still an infant, leaving him to be raised by his father, a knight, who had been crushed by his wife's death and buried himself in alcohol to avoid the pain. Consequently, Kenneth had hardly known a compassionate or loving touch. Being sent to foster at age five, raised by the knights of Warwick Castle, had left him little concept of what emotion was. Years of being forced to repress any feeling he had left him numb to anything other than what his sworn duty dictated; if it dictated compassion, then he would mechanically give it. If it dictated mercy, then he grasped the concept well enough to deliver it. But he'd forced himself long ago to stop truly feeling anything. In his experience, it had always been too painful.

Which was why he was genuinely surprised to feel a strange tugging in his chest as Aubrielle wept. She was crying and it was his doing. But he had only been doing his duty. Could she not understand that?

"Why do you weep?" his voice was husky, commanding.

Aubrielle wept softly. "Leave me alone."

"As you wish."

She sobbed, sniffled, wiping her nose on her hand. "Why am I treated as if I am a mindless animal, meant to be caged?" she apparently wished to tell him in spite of her earlier retort. "God has given me a sharp mind, eager to learn, yet no one understands my needs. I have been educated but unable to further my knowledge."

Kenneth put a hand up, smoothing the brown strands of hair that had drifted across his cheek. The softness of her hair didn't escape his notice.

"Is that why you are attempting escape?"

"Of course. Why else did you think I was trying to leave?"

"A lover."

"I do not have a lover. Only a love of knowledge."

He fell silent a moment, contemplating. "What is it that you must discover?"

She sniffled again. Her sobs were lessening. "Something Man has been seeking for a thousand years."

"What is that?"

"The Grail."

Kenneth fell strangely silent. When he finally released her, Aubrielle realized she was sorry to see him go. She had enjoyed the warmth of his arms, even if he had been subduing her. She sat up on the bed, watching him as he went to the window to remove the make-shift rope.

His manner was stiff and cold. She sensed something more than his usual demeanor.

"So you are shocked by my answer?" she ventured.

He untied the knot on the column. "You speak blasphemy, lady."

She had heard that before. "Why?" she demanded. "Why must everyone that knows of my quest say that? Do you know that the only people who did not call it blasphemous were the monks of St. Wenburgh, the only men who would truly have the right to say so? If they do not believe it, why should you?"

He reeled in the rope. "Suffice it to say that now I know of your reasons for attempting escape, I shall do more than my diligence in ensuring that you do not."

Her brow furrowed. "Why do you have such bias and determination against me?"

Kenneth paused, rope in hand. He looked at her, stricken above all other thoughts with those of her beauty. He was a knight of the realm and all of the rigid requirements that went with it. Weakness of any kind had never been part of his nature. Now was not the time to start.

"I am a knight and I have a duty," he said simply. "Moreover, when I swore my oath of fealty, I vowed to God to protect the Faith, and that includes holy relics like the Grail. They are not meant to be sought like common treasure. They are not meant for mortals to touch, but to be revered and protected always."

She cocked her head. "Protect it from me?" He didn't say anything and she continued. "But you do not understand. It is my intention to bolster the Faith by the discovery of this most precious relic of Christ. I will do this for God's glory, and for England's."

He began to untie the knots of the linens so he could put them back on the bed. "I will not argue this point with you, lady. I have no interest in your logic or explanations, so you can save them for those who would listen."

Aubrielle could see that he would not be convinced. He was the coldest man she had ever met.

"Are you always so indifferent?" she asked softly.

His eyes were like ice. "If you will rise from the bed, I will replace these linens. 'Tis late and you should be asleep."

The softness in Aubrielle's voice was quickly replaced by hardness. "I do not require a nursemaid, knight. Other than your orders from my uncle, you'll do nothing else for me and you'll certainly not issue commands. Is that clear?"

"Aye, my lady."

She yanked the linens from him, placing them on the mattress as the monks at St. Wenburgh had taught her. Her lines were straight, her corners tight and perfect. Resigned to the fact that she would not be escaping this night, she removed her shoes and silently slipped under the coverlet.

As she lay there, facing the wall, she wondered what thoughts ran through St. Héver's mind. There was something to his coldness that ran beyond mere knightly training. All knights were supposed to be even tempered, chivalrous, and deadly to the enemy. It was as if St. Héver was somehow dead inside. She wondered why.

For the first time in weeks, she slept the entire night and well into the dawn.

CHAPTER THREE

KENNETH HAD WATCHED her sleep until Everett came to relieve him after sunrise. He relinquished his post with some reluctance, unsure if Everett could handle the lady. He would never have admitted that he did not want to relinquish guard duty because he had found watching the lady sleep a pleasant experience. But he left Everett with Lady Aubrielle and went down to the great hall where the earl was having his morning meal.

There were dogs everywhere fighting for the scraps. The hearth wasn't working correctly and smoke billowed up into the rafters as the steward and a couple of servants tried to clear the blockage. Garson sat at the long table, chewing on his bread with rotted teeth and wondering if he would ever find a meal pleasant again. His dour expression lifted when he saw Kenneth.

"Ah," he motioned the knight to the table. "And how is my niece this morning? She didn't give you too much trouble, I trust?"

Kenneth shook his head. "None at all, my lord."

The earl cocked an eyebrow. "I am sure you are being generous, Kenneth. Do you mean to tell me that she behaved like a princess and went right to bed without incident?"

Kenneth couldn't lie to him; he shrugged his big shoulders. "She was determined to escape at one point, but I was able to convince her that lowering herself four stories to the bailey on a rope of bed linen would not be the wisest decision."

"A rope of linen?" the earl almost spit his bread onto the table. "Surely you jest?"

"Hardly, my lord. She would have broken her neck had I not intervened."

Garson shook his head, taking a large gulp of watered wine. "Not only is she determined, she is reckless. A dangerous combination."

Kenneth didn't reply; his silence was agreement enough. He stood there a moment, waiting patiently as the earl swirled his wine. It seemed as if there was much on his mind.

"I am sure you are exhausted," he finally said, without elaborating on his thoughts. "Take your leave. I do not require your services the rest of the day, as I am sure you could use the rest. And do not lie to me and tell me that you do not need to sleep."

Kenneth fought off a grin; it was a joke between them that Kenneth never slept. The earl accused him of being a nocturnal beast, ever watchful, always vigilant. Dipping his head respectfully to his liege, he quit the hall and made his way to the knight's quarters.

The two structures that serviced the upper class warriors were built against the outer wall. As he traversed the bailey, he crossed paths with Reid de Bowland and Sir Bradley Trevalyn. The two knights rounded out the earl's five-man knight corps, seasoned men with retainers and power of their own. Reid was a tall, congenial knight with copper-colored hair, while Bradley was shorter, stockier, and more rugged in appearance. They saluted Kenneth as their paths merged.

"My lord," Reid greeted him. "I see you've returned from both battles unscathed."

"Both battles?"

Reid grinned as Bradley spoke up. "Everett told us about Lady Aubrielle. If Dinas Bran wasn't enough, you had to take it on the chin from her as well."

Kenneth grunted. "Hardly a battle, I assure you. Properly handled, she's quite manageable."

"It helps when you employ ropes and shackles, Ken," Bradley muttered.

"I did nothing of the sort." He cocked an eyebrow. "The weight of my body and brute strength were sufficient.

"Aye, but barely," Reid offered.

"Barely."

He left Reid and Bradley with snorts of humor as he completed his trip to the knight's quarters. Entering the larger of the two buildings, he made his way to the room at the end of a long, narrow hall. It was a dingy room with a small slit window for light and ventilation. If he stopped to think about it, it was a depressing little room, but it was something he was used to. There was comfort in the dreariness. Removing his armor, he arranged it carefully on the rack in the corner. When he finally lay upon the hard bed, he found that he could not sleep at all.

For a man whose only physical contact with women had been an occasional whore, his thoughts lingered around the soft sweetness of Aubrielle in his arms. She hadn't been like any other woman he'd ever had contact with. She smelled sweet, and her hair was silken and clean. Her skin, from what he had touched whilst grabbing her wrists, had been baby-soft. No, she certainly wasn't like any woman he'd ever been with. It was like comparing a priceless wine against rancid ale.

She was a beautiful, fine woman, no doubt. But it was her mind that he questioned. Her quest had him puzzled; the search for the chalice of Christ was the root of her attempts to escape. There was no lover, which strangely relieved him, and her only reason in wanting to flee Kirk was to travel to Glastonbury. That's why she had run from him in the forest, and why she had made her foolish attempt to escape her chamber. But to seek what Arthur and his knights could not find was not only arrogant, it was sacrilegious. He couldn't believe she had such a lofty goal. If God had meant it to be discovered, He would have arranged for such an event by those far more worthy than Aubrielle Grace de Witney.

He somehow managed to fall into a fitful sleep. As a trained warrior, he always slept lightly, but the noise from the bailey didn't bother him in his exhausted state. He slept through all of it.

The scuffling of feet in the late afternoon awakened him, however. He was just sitting up as a knock fell upon his door. He grunted a word of entry and the panel opened. Kenneth's squire, a lad of nineteen years, stuck his head into the room. His dark, handsome features were wrought with concern.

"My lord," he said. "Captain le Cor says you should come."

Kenneth passed a weary hand over his face before reaching for his boots. "What is it, Max?"

"The earl's niece, my lord," the boy said. "She is in the vault."

Kenneth wasn't surprised. "What happened?"

"She hit Sir Everett across the head with a fire poker."

He didn't let the lad see the smile that tugged at his lips. He didn't know why he found it so humorous. He simply nodded his head and pulled on his other boot. The lad preceded him from the knight's quarters, leading him across the busy bailey. Kenneth plowed a straight path while Max dodged soldiers and animals; he had yet to acquire the commanding presence that his liege had. Eventually they reached the vault that was lodged on the two lower levels of Kirk's enormous gatehouse.

Kenneth descended the narrow spiral steps into the dungeon, his bulk barely fitting down the passage. Widely spaced torches lit the way. On the first level below the main ground level, they found the earl, Lucius, Reid, Bradley and Everett. One look at Everett with a huge welt across his forehead and a cut lip, and Kenneth cocked an eyebrow.

"I told you to watch your back."

Everett gave him an intolerant look. "It wasn't my back she struck."

"What happened?"

"You wouldn't believe it; she simply walked to the fireplace, picked up the brass poker, walked right up to me and slugged me across the face."

"What did you say to upset her?"

"I told her that she could not leave."

"Even when she cried and pleaded?"

Everett rolled his eyes. "That woman is incapable of crying. She sat like a stone, all day, hardly moving and not speaking a word. Then, she asks if she may leave. I told her, regretfully, that she may not, so she smacks me on the face with the poker."

"That's it?"

"That's enough."

Kenneth looked at the earl; he was curious how the man would react to the latest incident. Garson was leaning against the wall, his expression weary. His focus was on Kenneth.

"It would seem that you are the only one able to control her," he said.

Kenneth shrugged modestly. "I am not sure if you would call it control, my lord. I literally had to sit on her. And I didn't let her get near the fire poker."

Reid and Bradley fought off varying degrees of smirks. Everett looked disgusted. Lucius held no discernible expression. The earl, however, cast Kenneth a penetrating look. "I cannot have her attacking my knights."

"Understood, my lord."

"Then consider her your problem until the problem is solved."

Kenneth didn't like the sound of that. "My problem, my lord?"

It was apparent that the earl was tired of dealing with his niece. She had only been at Kirk one day and, already, he was done with her. He should have never consented to having her in the first place.

"Since you are the only one who can handle her, I henceforth leave her to you. But if you come to the conclusion that she cannot be controlled, you have my permission to commit her to a convent, or a prison, or whatever else you deem necessary." Garson pushed himself off the wall, heading for the narrow steps. "I am finished with this. I wash my hands of the girl. Do what you will with her, but I do not want to hear any more about her. Is that clear?"

Kenneth knew he could not protest the decision, much as he wanted to. He was, frankly, stunned. "It is, my lord."

Lucius gave him a long look as he followed the earl up the steps. Everett, not wanting to be sucked into being a party to Kenneth's task, followed shortly and took Max with him. Reid and Bradley were the last to leave, offering some semblance of assistance that was politely refused. They felt sorry for Kenneth, but were nonetheless glad it wasn't their problem.

When everyone had fled, Kenneth stood there a moment, thinking the earl most cowardly for his actions. As an obedient knight, however, he prepared to fulfill his requirements. He had no choice.

It was dark in the dungeon, smelling of mold and rot. It was a hellish place for a man much less a woman. There was a cell several feet in front of him and a second cell off to his right. He peered into the second cell; it was empty. Looking into the first, he could see Aubrielle seated against the far wall, a heavy iron shackle around her ankle. Her arms were scratched and bleeding, and her gown was torn.

She caught movement and looked up, meeting Kenneth's icy gaze. She was trying very hard to be brave. Slowly, he entered the cell, looking down at her cuts and bruises. Knowing Everett, there was no possibility that the man had beaten her. Whatever was on her had happened in the ensuing struggle to get her into the cell. He could have only imagined the battle.

He didn't quite know what to say. He crouched down, several feet away. Aubrielle met his gaze steadily.

"So," she said quietly. "I see that they have called for you. And how are you to punish me for my actions this time?"

As he continued to gaze at her, his most prevailing thought was how beautiful she was. He'd spent all last night gazing at her beauty and it had managed to disrupt his normally steady mind. Now, looking at her, he realized to his horror that the feelings of fascination were growing stronger. But he had no time to indulge his foolishness.

"You will listen to me carefully, lady, for I will only explain this one time," he said in a low voice. "The earl wants nothing more to do with you. For all intents and purposes, you are no longer a consideration or a burden to him. He has entrusted your welfare to me entirely, to see to and to do with as I see fit and necessary. In simple terms, you are now my ward. Do you understand what I have said so far?"

Aubrielle stared at him, confused. "Your ward?"

"Aye."

"What does that mean, exactly?"

"That you belong to me."

Her look of confusion grew into one of outrage. "So the term 'ward' is a kind word for a concubine?" She rattled her chains violently. "I shall have none of it, do you hear me? I shall not be your whore!"

He remained cool. "You misunderstand. Our agreement does not entail physical or emotional terms. The earl has ordered me to either subdue you or commit you. Your choices are to either learn to conduct yourself as a proper lady, with all of the behavior modifications related thereto, or to be committed to a convent where you'll never again know freedom or leisure. The earl is unwilling to indulge your current behavior a moment longer. You have pushed him to the limit of endurance and a decision must be made."

She stared at him before turning away. "Are you asking me to make that choice now?"

"You have no alternative."

It was clear she was attempting to hold back hot, angry tears. The shackle around her ankle had rubbed a bloody welt and she touched it distractedly as if trying to ease the pain. "Do you think a convent can hold me?" she murmured. "I can escape far easier there."

"If that is your intent, then I have your uncle's permission to throw you in prison."

Her head snapped up. "You wouldn't dare!"

"If there is no other choice."

"On what charge? I have done nothing!"

"I am sure your uncle would swear that you've done something. Stealing, perhaps. Or perhaps you owe him money and refuse to pay. Believe me when I tell you that it doesn't matter what charge. You will go to prison if that is the decision."

Her mouth was hanging open in disbelief. "All of this simply to keep me from following my dream?" she whispered. "I am not a criminal, sir knight. I am a lady of noble birth, highly educated and worthy of respect. I have never done anything even remotely evil or subversive in my entire life. Why is there such a set against me?"

Kenneth could feel her pain; it was radiating from her eyes, reaching out to touch him. He had a strange sensation, suspecting it was weakness but unsure how to react to it.

"It was evil to hit Everett," he said simply.

She averted her gaze. "I do not like the way he looks at me."

"What do you mean?"

"He stares at me. Strangely. I do not like it."

"Is that why you hit him?"

She shrugged. "I hit him because he touched me."

Kenneth stood up from his crouch, so fast that the movement startled Aubrielle. He was standing over her, his eyes like shards of glass. "You will tell me now. How did he touch you?"

Aubrielle had found herself in many confrontational situations with St. Hėver, but she had never been truly frightened of him until now. There was something in his voice that was inherently terrifying.

"When I tried to leave," she hated the quiver in her voice. "He put his hand on my arm to try and force me to stop. So I hit him."

Kenneth's mercurial fury abated. In fact, when he thought on it, he was surprised at how venomous he had felt at the thought of someone other than himself laying a hand on her. Of course, it was perfectly all right for him to physically restrain her, even lay on her if necessary in order to control her, but in his mind he was apparently the only one allowed to do so. He realized he would have killed Everett had the man's intentions been anything other than chivalrous. He looked down at the frightened woman as his anger cooled, feeling like an idiot.

"He should have spanked you," he muttered.

"What was that?"

"I said that he should have spanked you," he repeated, loudly. "No, you are not evil or subversive in the conventional sense, but I have never in my life seen such a headstrong female. A good spanking would do you a world of good."

Her expression hardened. A hand drifted up to her shoulder, fingering the material of her gown. "If you are thinking of beating obedience into me, do not bother." She yanked the top of her sleeve down, exposing a good portion of the top of her left shoulder blade. "The monks of St. Wenburgh already tried."

Kenneth could see the montage of faded scars on her back. Someone had obviously taken a branch to her. He'd seen flogging many a time; he'd delivered more than his share. As a child, he'd been the recipient of one or two rounds. It was a painful, ugly act. He didn't know why he was suddenly coming to regret being so harsh with her.

"How old were you?" his voice was husky.

She pulled her garment back up on to her shoulder, torn between embarrassment and indifference. "I was nine years of age the first time."

"The first time? There were more?"

"Three."

For the first time since they'd met, his icy façade faltered. He exhaled slowly as he reclaimed his crouched position. He'd never before seen such stubbornness, yet he found himself admiring her for her determination.

"And still you dream," he murmured. "Will nothing short of death convince you to change your path?"

A smile spread across her lips. "Have you never had anything that meant so much to you that you would brave fire and brimstone to attain it? We are mere mortals, Sir Kenneth. Our lives are finite. All we have are our dreams before our lives are quickly ended. If I must endure tribulation in the pursuit of my dream, it is of little consequence. I could never live with myself had I not tried."

He understood, somewhat. But the concepts of dreams did not come easily to him. He'd never been allowed to have them. "Whatever you feel you must pursue and however you feel you must achieve it, you must understand that your ideas are unconventional."

"I understand that. But unconventional does not necessarily mean wrong."

"Agreed. But it has taken many hundreds of years to achieve the civility and society that we have now. Unconventional ideas threaten the order of our world."

She thought a moment, seeing an open door for debate. "But did we not achieve such civility by pursuing thoughts and dreams that, perhaps at one time, would seem unconventional? Did we not learn by trying and by making mistakes?"

He could see where she was leading. "Aye."

"But still we forged on, with bizarre notions and half-witted schemes that, perhaps when the time was right, blossomed into fruition." She smiled at him, sensing that he was open to her logic. "All I ask is to be a part of that discovery process, to advance our ideals of religion and the heights of our knowledge. I know that going to Glastonbury to find the chalice of Christ must seem strange, but perhaps believing in a man who preached the love of his enemy seemed strange a thousand years ago to those people who eventually formed the basis of Christianity. But it doesn't seem strange now."

Kenneth didn't care that he was actually listening to what she had to say. She was passionate and articulate, and made a great deal of sense. But his inner demons began to fight him and it was difficult to resist.

"Your reasoning is sound, lady," he said softly. "But there were also those crucified for those unconventional beliefs. Even now, heresy is punishable by death. No matter what your dreams or beliefs, you must tread carefully."

"I know," she said bravely. "Those marks you see on my back tell the tale. But it did not stop me."

"What would?"

"Finding the Grail or die trying."

He sighed. "What makes you believe that you can find this Grail that the great Arthur and his knights could not?"

She seemed to back off. He could see she was hiding something. "I simply believe that I can, that's all."

He lifted an eyebrow. "That's *not* all. Tell me why you believe you can find it."

"I just do," she leaned back against the stone wall, coated with green growth. "May I ask you a question, sir knight?"

"Perhaps."

"Do you intend to leave me in this place all night?"

He thought a night in the vault might help her see the error of her ways. But then again, maybe not. No matter his indecision, she had to be punished for striking Everett.

"I do," he replied steadily. "Do you require anything to make your stay more palatable?"

It was a foolish question; the woman had absolutely nothing but the clothes on her back. She wasn't even wearing shoes.

"No. I am quite content."

She was lying, but it was a commendable lie. Without a word, Kenneth quit the cell. He returned shortly with a lit torch; night was falling and the weak light that strayed down the stairwell was fading rapidly. Soon it would be pitch black. He propped the torch in the iron wall sconce.

"I shall return with your supper."

"Do not bother." She shifted, laying down in an attempt to get comfortable. "I am not hungry. I simply want to sleep. It's been a busy day of thrashing knights."

It was a humorous statement. Kenneth looked at her as if she was mad, but inside, he was grinning. There was no possible way that he was going to allow her to see him crack a smile.

He left the cell and returned a nominal amount of time later carrying bread, a knuckle of beef, and a cup of ale. Aubrielle still lay on the ground, her eyes closed, presumably asleep. He stood there a moment, watching her quiver. It occurred to him that it must be terribly cold on the hard stone. He simply couldn't stand by and observe her discomfort. If she would not allow him to bring her anything to see to her comfort in her time of punishment, perhaps she wouldn't object to what comfort he could offer her.

He set the tray down and went to sit against the wall, next to her head. Carefully, he put his hands underneath her shoulders and gently lifted. She was limp, like a sleeping cat, as if she had no bones at all. She became lucid as he settled her head atop his right thigh.

"What…?" she muttered.

"Shh, quiet," he put his hand on her head to silence her. "Be still now. Go back to sleep."

The trauma of the day must have been exhausting, for she fell back asleep without another word. Kenneth settled back against the stone, his hand still on her head, wondering if he was going above and beyond the call of his knightly duties. Was he overstepping his bounds? Perhaps he wasn't doing enough? She was his charge, after all. He'd never had a charge in his life, especially not a woman. He didn't want one, even now, but he was strangely pleased by it. It was a peculiar situation.

Aubrielle shivered again and he moved his hand from her head and put it on her arm; it was cold. In fact, the whole dungeon was cold. He moved his hand back and forth, rubbing some warmth back into her slender arm. Damn her for not allowing him to bring her a coverlet. Now he would have to spend all night rubbing her flesh to make sure she didn't freeze. It would be a very long night.

The dawn came too soon as far as he was concerned.

CHAPTER FOUR

HIGHWOOD HOUSE WAS in flames. Embers erupted into the night sky, dancing a macabre waltz with great clouds of black smoke. The mixture lifted up to the stars until both smoke and spark faded into oblivion. Also accompanying this ghastly symphony was the scent of charred wood and flesh.

Four men stood in the fortified courtyard of what had once been a fine manor. Now it was ash. There were several other men on horseback, patrolling the perimeter of the house, making sure no one was left alive. The four men in the courtyard watched the last of the blaze; three of them were unrepentant about their deadly act, while the fourth cowered. His ragged priestly robes contained a strange mixture of body odor and incense, and his pale face wrought with grief. He was out of place and nearly out of his mind with fear. He had begged the others not to commit this foul crime, but to those who would kidnap a man of God, anything else was a minor misdeed.

"Brother Grendel," the man on a massive black steed spoke to him. "Reclaim your mount. We ride to Kirk Castle."

Grendel de Vais turned to face the man who had ripped him from St. Wenburgh as one would have extricated a rotted tooth. St. Wenburgh was protected, holy ground, but these men from the north had not heeded that inherent safeguard. They had ridden into the monastery, making demands and brutalizing the monks. They stopped short of murder, but had used it as a threat. St. Wenburgh was a learning institution. The men had been searching for something the monastery had in its possession.

Grendel, being a brother and not a fully consecrated priest, had tried to reason with him as the others cowered. Being in a protected environment for a length of time left men fearful to defend themselves, unused to the realities of the world. But Grendel had stood his ground, even when the men had beat on two of his colleagues.

They called themselves *A Ordem do Anjo Preto*. The Order of the Black Angel. A man named de Gaul was their leader. Grendel never heard the names of the others, men who covered their head with black hoods and wore mail that was rusty and broken. Their chargers were big animals, emaciated, yet exhibiting an unearthly strength. The only way for the monks to rid themselves of the terror was to give the men what they were seeking. It came to a decision; the monks of St. Wenburgh betrayed another to save themselves. They were feeble men, unused to fright, and said many a litany to beg God's forgiveness for their faults.

But God's forgiveness did not help Grendel's situation. He was in dire straits. Though Highwood House had been burned to the ground with the occupants inside, still, the men did not have what they sought. Grendel closed his eyes when he thought of the lady of the House pleading for her life just before they cut her throat. He could not erase it from his mind. After that, it occurred to him that he saw his own life coming to a sudden end and saw no point in remaining quiet about his predicament. If they could kill a helpless woman, imagine what they would do to a useless friar.

"Do you intend to attack Kirk Castle, then?" he asked.

De Gaul snorted. "Not attack, brother. But we have our ways."

"What ways?" Grendel asked. "Your quest has come to an end. As I have told you many a time, I am not entirely sure that the girl even has it. But she had always shown great interest in reading it. One day it was in our library, and when she left, it went missing."

The dark warrior looked at him with eyes full of fire and wickedness. "Logic is the better part of progression, brother. If it is possible it went missing because she stole it, then by all means, we must find out."

"She will be protected at Kirk."

"As I said, we have our ways. You needn't worry. Once you verify that we have indeed located the Scroll of Munsalvaesche, your part in this shall be complete."

Grendel had known the Lady Aubrielle de Witney for many years. She had studied under him, a voracious student of learning. He thought of her, a delicate beauty with an iron will. He didn't doubt for a minute that she had taken the Scroll of Munsalvaesche. She had been fascinated by it. King Titurel, Lord of Munsalvaesche Castle, had authored the parchment during the Dark Ages, times long ago where man and beast roamed in realms of witchcraft and mystery. St. Wenburgh possessed many such parchments from kings and scholars long dead. Some were in languages lost to the ages.

The scroll spoke of the Holy Grail, the priceless object used during the last supper and eventually used to capture the blood of Christ as he was dying upon the cross. Lady Aubrielle had been fascinated by the old Latin script, spending many long hours reading and translating the contents. How the Order of the Dark Angel knew of the scroll, he did not know. He was only aware that they knew of it, and that Lady Aubrielle was in grave danger.

☙

"YOU ARE POSITIVE?"

"There is no doubt. The physic says he has been dead for several hours. He more than likely passed away some time during the night."

Kenneth exhaled slowly. The news was devastating. It was dawn and Max had summoned him from the dungeon with no hint of what he was about to fall privy to. Garson de Montgomery de Mortimer, 1st Earl of Wrexham, was dead. Kenneth felt as if the wind had been knocked out of him.

Lucius knew the feeling well. He, too, was stunned. Though the earl had been inordinately exhausted yesterday, they had all assumed it had been because of the Lady Aubrielle's escapades. They hadn't considered that it was something more serious. Now the reality was upon them.

"You realize what this means?" Lucius whispered.

Kenneth knew. "Lady Aubrielle is his heiress. The castle and titles pass to her now."

Lucius let out a hiss. He was trying to keep his voice down so the household servants didn't hear, but it was difficult. "Christ, of all the..." he could hardly contain himself. "Kirk is far too powerful for her to govern. The girl has been locked up in a monastery for the majority of her life. What in the hell does she know about governing?"

"It doesn't matter what she does, or does not, know. She has now inherited the Wrexham earldom and whatever her bidding, we must comply."

Even more shocking than the earl's death, the thought of submitting to Lady Aubrielle's commands was horrifying. Lucius was beside himself.

"She is in no position to govern this castle, nor this land," Lucius countered. "I will send world to the king immediately. He must know of the situation."

Kenneth couldn't argue, but somehow, he felt as if he was betraying Lady Aubrielle by undermining her inheritance. "It will take time for the king to assess our needs and send aid. He may even come himself to evaluate the situation. Kirk governs a critical portion of the Welsh Marches. She is strategic and strong." He crossed his arms, lifting an eyebrow at his captain. "So what do we do? We can no longer keep her in the vault. She is our lady and must be informed of the situation."

Everett, Reid and Bradley entered the second floor at that moment. Lucius had summoned the knights and quickly, and quietly, informed them of the earl's passing. Their faces registered different phases of shock as the gravity of the situation settled. Not only was the Earl dead, but Kirk was a mighty castle with a mighty army, now without a leader. There was an entire world of implication Wrexham's death had opened the floodgates to.

"What are we going to do?" Everett directed the question more at Kenneth. "We have over one thousand men-at-arms. Who will lead us now?"

"Lady Aubrielle has inherited the earldom," Kenneth replied steadily. "Kirk is now her holding."

The knights were aware of the logical confusion, but still, the truth was shocking. A glance at Lucius told them that the man was stricken. He was the captain and should have been able to hold himself in check, but his control was shaken. Since no one seemed to have anything more to say, Kenneth took charge and went to free Lady Aubrielle from the vault. He suspected she might be interested in what he had to say.

☙

"BUT YOU DO not understand. I do not want it."

Kenneth stood in the small, cramped chamber that Lady Aubrielle had occupied when she had first arrived at Kirk. He was facing off with a surprisingly angry young woman.

"Want it or not, you have inherited it nonetheless. Kirk and the earldom are yours."

Aubrielle scowled at him. Dirty and disheveled from her night in the vault, she was in an awful mood. News of the earl's death had momentarily saddened her, but the additional news of her inheritance had sparked a rage.

"Not if I refuse," she said. "No one can force a title and lands on me."

Kenneth didn't understand her reluctance. "Anyone in England would be pleased and privileged to inherit this earldom. Do you understand the power and wealth you now have? One thousand men await your bidding, my lady, including me."

She knew that, but the thought truly hadn't occurred to her until he mentioned it. She looked at the big blond knight, remembering his comforting presence in the vault, struggling against the pleasant thoughts it provoked. He wasn't the pleasant type. The thought of commanding him, though not disagreeable, was nonetheless interesting.

She forced herself to calm and take in the situation. Arguing with

St. Héver would not change facts; she was now Countess of Wrexham. Although she'd always known that, for lack of children, she was by rights Garson's heir, it never occurred to her that someday she would actually inherit everything. It wasn't something she had ever wanted or dreamed of. Now, she realized it would make her a hugely marriageable prospect, as her husband would inherit the earldom by marriage. She wanted a man to have this place, a great warring fortress with a thousand man army. She had no use for it. All she wanted was to go to Glastonbury and complete her quest.

Marriage. It would be the only way to be rid of her burden, for she simply couldn't sign over her inheritance. The laws of the land prohibited it. Out of the corner of her eye, she could see St. Héver's silent form. She knew he was waiting for her to start fighting with him again. But fighting was the last thing on her mind.

"May I ask you a question?" she said.

"Of course, my lady."

"What is your lineage?"

His ice blue eyes clouded with confusion. "My lineage?"

"Aye, your family. Where do you come from?"

"I come from Northumberland, my lady."

"That is where you were born. But what of your father and mother? Who were they?"

He did not answer right away. He was attempting to figure out why she was asking personal questions. Aubrielle saw his hesitation.

"If you are to serve me, I must know about you."

He conceded her request. "My father was a knight for the Earl of Northumberland. My family has served Northumberland for four generations."

"Was he from noble blood?"

"On his mother's side. She was a cousin to the House of Lancaster."

"And your mother?"

His hesitance seemed to grow stronger. "I never knew my mother. She perished in childbirth."

"But what of her lineage? Was she of noble blood, too?"

It was apparent she would not give up. In fact, he knew from experience that she would be quite persistent until he told her what she wanted to know.

"Her name was Cassandra. She was a granddaughter of Princess Blanche, eleventh daughter of Henry the Third. That also makes me a cousin to the Earl of Carlisle, Tate de Lara, who is the illegitimate first-born son of Edward the First.

Aubrielle's eyes widened. "You are Plantagenet?"

"Three generations removed."

The idea that had occurred to Aubrielle earlier suddenly took full bloom. But she had to be clever about it; St. Héver was no fool.

"Sir Kenneth, may I ask you another question?"

"If you must, my lady."

She smiled at his reply; he seemed so resistant. "You said that anyone in England would be pleased and privileged to receive this earldom, did you not?"

"I did, my lady."

"And you are sworn to obey my commands, as your lady?"

He knew instantly where she was leading. Or, at least, he thought he did. "You cannot give me this earldom, my lady."

"But I can order you to marry me and thereby transfer title and power to you."

He didn't see her proposal coming until she had said it. Instead of instant refusal, he actually stopped to ponder the idea. It was entirely out of character that he should even remotely entertain it. As much as the thought of being married to her enticed him on too many levels to acknowledge, he knew that he could not.

"Out of the question, my lady."

"But why?" She moved towards him, her lovely face anxious. "You are perfect. You are descended from royalty. In fact, you are a distant cousin to the king. He would not refuse the match. Is the means by which you inherit the earldom so unattractive to you?"

For some reason, he was having difficulty looking at her. He turned away, pacing towards the hearth simply to have some breathing room. "The means by which to achieve this is perhaps the most attractive aspect of it, have no doubt."

"Then why do you refuse? Do you not want to be the second Earl of Wrexham?"

He crossed his arms and looked at her. "Why do you offer this? Surely you do not wish to marry me."

She couldn't tell if he was angered by the idea or pleased by it. She was careful to explain. "It would be a marriage of convenience, I assure you. I would not expect you to perform the duties of a husband, physically or emotionally. The marriage would be in title only, simply so I would not have to shoulder the burden of this vast earldom. I would not interfere with your rule or your life."

He didn't know why her words disappointed him so. He had thought he had made it clear that the marriage aspect did not distress him. Obviously, it distressed her. He was ashamed that he had revealed his thoughts on the matter, embarrassed that she had not responded in kind.

"I shall not be a convenience for you." He moved for the door. "If that will be all, my lady, I shall beg my leave."

"No, wait," she pleaded.

He paused at the door, his eyes like ice. "What is your wish, my lady?"

Her expression softened. In spite of their rough beginnings, Kenneth St. Héver had shown an inordinate amount of kindness to her. Even when she was in the vault, he had never berated her or been cruel. He had spent the entire night by her side, making sure she was comfortable. All she had ever shown him was spitefulness. She was coming to feel very sorry for her actions.

"Please do not go," she asked softly.

The ice in his gaze melted somewhat. "What do you wish?"

"I wish for you to marry me and inherit the earldom. You may consider it a reward for all of your years of service. You may consider it my gift to you for the kindness you have shown me. If I said this was a marriage of convenience, I simply meant that you should feel no obligation towards me."

Her gentleness surprised him. He had no idea she was capable of it. He knew he should have stuck to his instincts and left the room, but he couldn't bring himself to do it.

"I was always under the impression that it was a man's duty to offer a proposal of marriage, my lady," he said quietly. "I have never heard of a woman offering."

She smiled faintly. "As you have said, I am somewhat unconventional."

He gazed at her, studying her fine features. He was attracted to her, of that there was little doubt. He was coming to see that, when properly handled, she could be sweet and gentle. The fact that he would inherit an earldom if he married her was of little consequence; he had no great aspirations. It was strange for a knight not to have any and he knew that. If he married her, it would be because he wanted to, not because he was attempting to gain an empire.

But the fact remained that although he admired her and found her attractive, she was eccentric, bold and headstrong. He was used to complete order in his life and Aubrielle's proposal had come too fast, too unexpectedly. It was disruptive to that order.

"My lady, though your offer is most flattering and generous, I am not sure it is right or even appropriate for me to accept," he struggled to be tactful. "Wrexham is a large and strategic earldom. The king may have other ideas for a marital match, someone of higher ranking and power."

The smile on Aubrielle's face faded. She turned away from him. "Of course, you are correct," she said quietly. "Contrary to what you may think of me, Sir Kenneth, I am not a fool. I am fully aware of the responsibilities I have inherited. I suppose my offering marriage is simply a way for me to discard the responsibilities that I do not want by forcing them on you. You, however, have a choice in the matter and are fully justified in rejecting that which you do not want."

"It is not a matter of what I want," he said. "It is a matter of the correct course of action in this situation."

She stopped by the hearth, looking into the hypnotic gyrations of the flame. She didn't have an answer for him. The shock of the situation had abated, leaving her disheartened and weary.

"No matter how I resist my inheritance, I cannot refuse," she murmured. "It is thrust upon me whether or not I want it."

"That is true, my lady."

She shook her head sadly. "I do not want this. I have never wanted it."

He had been standing by the door. Slowly, he made his way back into the room. Though he'd never in his life felt pity, at this moment, he realized that he did. It was an awkward situation in that he wanted to comfort her, but did not know where to begin.

"I have no words of reassurance for you, my lady," he said quietly. "But I can tell you that you have my fealty and I will assist you however I can, to the best of my abilities."

She smiled weakly. "From what I have seen, your abilities are substantial. My uncle obviously placed a good deal of faith in you."

The corners of his lips turned upward as if his mouth possessed a mind of its own. Kenneth wasn't the smiling type. It was a strange, warm moment.

"So you do know how to smile," Aubrielle observed. "I was sure that your ability had been lost a long time ago."

Her remark made him self-conscious, but the warm expression remained on his face.

"So was I," he admitted.

Her smile broadened, her teeth white and straight. She had a very lovely smile. "And I am equally certain that all of this pleasantness between us is placing an undue strain on your senses."

"Undue strain?"

"Aye. We always seem to be at each other's throats. Perhaps all of the nicety will cause you to lose all consciousness from the shock of it."

Kenneth did something then that he hadn't done in years. He laughed. It was an awkward, short burst, but a laugh nonetheless. He looked so surprised afterwards that Aubrielle burst into gales of laughter. She clutched her stomach, struggling to catch her breath.

"That was wonderful," she gasped. "I had no idea you were capable of such a thing. You have made me very happy in a situation where I have not felt much happiness nor hope."

He watched her, the way she giggled, the lines of her pretty face. He felt as he had never felt in his entire life. It was as if the curtain of gloom that had covered his world since the dawn of his age suddenly lifted. He could see light on the other side.

"I will be here as you need me, my lady," he said. "Until the end of my life, I shall serve you and only you."

It was a bold statement. He should have been embarrassed by it, but oddly, he was not. He meant every word.

Aubrielle's smile faded as the impact of his declaration sank in. There was something more than simple loyalty behind it.

"If that is true, then why do you not agree to marry me? 'Twould be far easier to serve me until death if you were my husband."

A twinkle came to his eye. "That is true. But did you ever consider that, as your husband, you would be equally obligated to obey me?"

She lifted an eyebrow. "Leave it to you to see the negative aspect of the situation."

"It is not a negative aspect to me. In fact, the more I think on it, the more appealing it becomes."

"Then forget my offer. I can see that you would take far too much delight in commanding me to your will."

He stroked his chin. "You cannot take back your offer. I forbid it."

There was light-hearted humor in the air. Aubrielle stomped a foot. "You cannot forbid me. I forbid it."

Kenneth had not felt so much levity in years. It was a wildly uninhibited sensation, completely foreign, completely wonderful.

"You have no choice," he said pointedly. "You will understand your place or there will be no marriage."

"Then are you consenting?"

"Only if we have an understanding, my lady."

The conversation took a serious turn. Aubrielle observed Kenneth for a long moment, attempting to determine how sincere he was. He had refused her moments earlier. Had he so quickly changed his mind? If so, why?

"My offer is the same as it has always been," she said. "Marry me and the earldom is yours. I do not intend to interfere with your rule or your life."

"What does that mean?"

"It means that I will leave Kirk and continue on my quest. 'Tis a long way to Glastonbury. You will not be troubled by me again."

He rested his big fists on his hips. "That is something we will make clear here and now. As my wife, you shall remain with me. You will be involved in my life as I will be in yours, for I do not intend that our marriage will be in name only. I would be ashamed to have my wife cavorting across the whole of England unattended. Your behavior would be a direct reflection on my abilities as a husband and as a man."

She hadn't thought of it that way, as her expression suggested. She also knew from experience that arguing with him would be to no avail.

"I would not want to bring shame to you," she said. "But my mind has not changed. I am going to Glastonbury."

He, too, knew from experience that arguing would change nothing. Marriage would not alter her plans. But he could not have her traipsing about by herself. As a sworn servant, he was not in a position to forbid her. As her husband, however, he would be in a supreme position of control. Yet she would fight him and their entire marriage would be one marathon battle. Perhaps the only way to manage her would be to let her do what she must and be done with it so they could get on with their lives.

"Then I have a counter proposal for you, my lady."

"And that is?"

"I will escort you to Glastonbury myself. I will give you one month to do what you must, to search however you must. But at the end of one month, you will return to Kirk, we will marry, and we shall hear no more of your quest to find the Holy Grail. You will become Lady St. Héver and accept your destiny."

It was a fair offer, she knew. He was giving her the opportunity to fulfill her dream in a logical fashion. It wasn't a perfect proposal, for she could see that becoming Lady Wrexham would offer her little opportunity to pursue other dreams she may entertain in the future, but she had to be realistic. If she did not agree to compromise, an offer like this might not ever come again.

"Two months," she countered. "I want two months."

"Agreed," he said. "And the rest?"

She sighed heavily. "As you wish. I will do my best to become a proper lady wife."

"Do I have your word?"

"Aye."

Kenneth realized that, with one simple word, he had become a betrothed man. It wasn't as dismal a prospect as he had imagined it would be. In fact, he was strangely looking forward to it. Without anything more to say, as all had been spoken of, he nodded his head to silently acknowledge their understanding and turned for the door. Aubrielle's voice stopped him.

"Is this how you take your leave, then?" she demanded. "You simply walk away without a word of farewell to your intended?"

He looked at her, truly ignorant of what she meant. "What would you have me do, my lady?"

She put her hands on her hips angrily. "Good Lord, St. Héver, must I explain everything? I am your betrothed now. I expect to be treated as such."

Kenneth came back into the room, fully intending to right his boorish behavior. He thought to shake her hand or salute her, but he reminded himself that it was inappropriate to do either of those things with a lady. By the time he reached her, he couldn't think of anything other to do than to take her hands. Bringing them to his lips, he kissed them both softly. It was an enchanting moment, more than he could have anticipated.

"Is that sufficient, my lady?"

Aubrielle's sea-colored eyes glittered. "That will do, sir knight. That will do."

He gave her hands another kiss, gently. He smiled at her, but the truth be known, he didn't know exactly what to feel. Events had occurred with blinding rapidity. All he knew was that he might, quite possibly, feel the most happiness he had ever experienced in his life and he was at a loss to understand why. The best thing to do at the moment was for him to leave and collect his thoughts, which he did. He found he couldn't think when she was looking at him.

After he was gone, Aubrielle sat for a long time staring into the hearth, watching the dance of the fire and wondering at the path her life had abruptly taken. More than traveling to Glastonbury, her thoughts revolved around the man she was to marry. Her mother, she was sure, would be pleased at the prospect. All Graciela had ever wanted was for her daughter to marry a strong man, one who could control her. Kenneth St. Héver was quite capable of that, as he'd proven many a time. For the first time in her life, Aubrielle was doing exactly as her mother had wanted and not displeased about it.

❧

"SHE'S IN THE courtyard, Ken. She says that she is leaving for Glastonbury today and that you promised to take her."

It was well before dawn. Kenneth rubbed the sleep from his eyes as he leapt out of bed, finding his clothing in the dark, cold room. Reid handed him a big leather boot.

"I did promise to take her, but I did not say when," he muttered, pulling on his shoes. "So she intends to leave today, does she?"

Reid had been on night watch when Lady Aubrielle had appeared in the gloom with her story. He stood back as Kenneth pulled on a heavy woolen tunic, covering his muscular chest. It was cold outside, the fog and chill deep before sunrise. They all knew of the impending marriage, as Lady Aubrielle had informed them last eve at supper.

Their reactions had varied; Everett had been pleased, Reid and Bradley had dutifully toasted the match, Kenneth seemed unaffected, and Lucius appeared strangely detached. If the others hadn't known better, they thought the man might be jealous. But the lady had explained her reasoning; that she felt herself unequal to the task of ruling the earldom and had offered the marriage contract to Sir Kenneth based on his lineage. It all seemed perfectly logical and sound.

"I do not envy the task you have ahead of you, my friend," he told Kenneth. "She may be a beauty, but she is as willful as a wild horse."

Kenneth pushed past him, into the dark corridor of the knight's quarters. He would not comment on Reid's statement, mostly because the same dilemma had kept him up most of the night. His euphoria from their engagement had cooled, leaving him muddled for the rest of the day. This morning, the situation was not much clearer.

It was misting outside. He could see Aubrielle standing in the courtyard, wrapped in a heavy cloak with a hood that concealed her face. She heard his footfalls as he approached and she turned to him, her sea-colored eyes luminous. She smiled, completely unsettling his building annoyance.

"Good morn to you, sir knight," she sounded uncommonly congenial. "I am surprised to see that I am ready before you are."

"Ready for what, my lady?"

Her smile faded. "To travel to Glastonbury, of course. Do you mean to say that you have already forgotten our bargain?"

"I have not forgotten at all. We do indeed have a bargain. But we did not specify when this trip to Glastonbury was to take place."

She gazed at him, the pleasant twinkle leaving her beautiful eyes. He could see all of the excitement drain from her. After a moment, she turned away and headed back to the keep. Kenneth watched her go.

"My lady," he called to her in a low voice. "A trip of this magnitude takes some planning. We could perhaps discuss this after your morning meal."

"I have already eaten," she grumbled.

She continued walking and Kenneth, though he was loathe to do it, followed. "Then we shall discuss it now."

He entered the keep on her heels, sending a servant for watered ale and bread. Aubrielle went into the great hall and removed her heavy cloak. Kenneth stole a glance as she settled into a chair near the hearth; she had a delightful figure with full breasts and a slender torso. He went to the fire and stoked the blaze until the flames were as tall as he was.

"Now," he leaned the poker against the stone. "We cannot leave until the earl is in the ground. Did you not recollect there is a funeral to be had?"

She shrugged. "I thought not to attend because my darling uncle had washed his hands of me. Why should I pay respects to his memory when he clearly cared nothing for me or my welfare?"

"Be that as it may, as his heiress, it is your duty to tend him."

She looked away from him, having nothing to say to that. He leaned against the wall, crossing his big arms and watching her face. She was such a lovely creature who had moments of perfection in character, but they were infrequent. He wanted very much to see more of the sweetness beneath.

"You are highly educated, of that there is no doubt," he said quietly. "But you still have much to learn."

She cast him a long glance. "What do you mean?"

"You have much to learn about patience and of self-sacrifice, and of general manners. Did the monks teach you any of that, or did they simply give in to your spoiled character and petty whims?"

Aubrielle flared. "You saw the marks on my back. The monks indulged me nothing."

"Perhaps not. But you did not learn anything from their beatings. You continue to be headstrong and selfish."

"How dare you speak to me that way."

"Have I said anything that is untrue?"

She leapt out of the chair, her cheeks flushing pink. "How would you know if what you say is true? You do not know me at all. How do you know that I am impatient and selfish?"

"You forgot spoiled and petty."

The poker was closer to her than it was to him. She picked it up and hurled it at his head. Kenneth ducked easily, turning to watch the poker clatter against the wall.

"And you forgot violent," she hissed. "Simply because I am giving you an earldom, do not think for a moment that it gives you license to insult me."

Kenneth knew she could be demonstrative with her anger. That was a kind way of putting it. He also knew that, one day, she might put out his eye were he not careful. If he was going to subdue this type of behavior, it would have to start now.

"I have said nothing untrue," he growled. "But I can guarantee you that if you ever again so much as entertain the thought of physically assaulting me, my retribution shall be swift."

The sea-colored eyes were stormy. "You'll not threaten me."

"Be assured, it is not a threat."

He knew she was going to test him. He could tell by the expression on her face. She was angry enough to spit nails. Grasping a pewter candlestick on the carved stone mantle, she hurled it at him. Kenneth reached out, grabbed it before it could hit him, and set it carefully on the table near him. With a heavy sigh, he moved towards her.

"You will regret your actions."

Aubrielle was so furious that she was barely rational. She was so used to having her way that to run into an obstacle only inflamed her. She was, however, aware that Kenneth was coming towards her. It was a temptation to run, but she refused. It was a mistake. Kenneth grasped her gently but firmly by the arm, took the chair she had been sitting in, and promptly threw her across his lap.

Aubrielle gasped with shock as his open palm came down on her bottom. Though padded from the blow by her heavy skirts, it was nonetheless a sting. With the second strike, she shrieked like a banshee.

"St. Hével!" she hollered. "Let me up!"

He didn't react other than to spank her again. Two more blows followed as Aubrielle twisted and yelped. When he was finished, he pulled her up the arms and planted her feet on the floor. Aubrielle was so overwhelmed by the entire experience that she was, for the moment, speechless. She rubbed her bum, casting Kenneth the most hateful expression he had ever seen.

"Do we understand one another?" he asked in a low voice.

Her reply was to take a swing at him. He dodged the flying fist, tossed her over his lap again, and proceeded to spank her four more times as she writhed and growled. When he was finished, he pulled her up by the arms again to stand. Aubrielle's face was positively red with shame and anger.

"I can do this all day if it pleases you, my lady," he said calmly. "The sooner you learn to control yourself, the sooner we can move forward with plans for Glastonbury."

She backed away from him, rubbing her backside. "You are a contemptible brute, St. Héver," she muttered. "God help me forever thinking to marry you."

She was closed to tears; he could see it. He was coming to think that perhaps he had spanked her too hard and it was a struggle not to regret his actions. He'd only meant to teach her a lesson, to prove that he would not fall victim to her tantrums. In a completely uncharacteristic turn, he felt himself folding like an idiot.

"Come here," he said to her softly.

She eyed him as if he was the Devil. "No."

Kenneth patiently held up a hand to her, motioning with his fingers. "Please. I promise I have no ill intentions."

Aubrielle continued to stand there, studying him. She didn't know what to think. She was angry, true, but she was also hurt. Not only had he seemingly forgotten their bargain, but he had chided her for neglecting the earl's funeral. Perhaps just the smallest part of her knew that he was right, and it was difficult to maintain her anger.

It seemed like an eternity before she took a step towards him. It was very slowly, so he would know that she wasn't easily ordered about. But when she came within range, he gently grasped her wrist and pulled her to him. He seated her upon his lap and his thick arms wrapped around her waist. For a moment, they simply sat and stared at each other. Kenneth was becoming so swept up with her splendor that he almost forgot what he had intended to say.

"I am sorry if I hurt you," he said quietly. "But if you are to behave like a child, then I will treat you like one."

Her anger abated, leaving ripples of sorrow in its wake. She gazed into his ice blue eyes, thinking somewhere in the back of her mind that the man was growing increasingly handsome. He had a very square jaw and a rugged beauty, but somewhere in his face lay a gentleness just below the surface. She had seen it before and was seeing it now. It was a gentleness that could instantly become terrifyingly hard.

"I was not aware that I was behaving like a child," she replied. "It is my opinion that you were being unfair. Naturally, I reacted."

His arms tightened around her. "Unfair? How?"

"By forgetting our bargain. You promised to take me to Glastonbury."

"Did I say when?"

"Logically, I believed it would be immediate. You know that I am anxious to go. Why in the world would I expect any delay?"

"You went on a weak assumption. All you had to do was ask when we would make the trip, not force my hand by appearing in the bailey and demanding that it be this day. You knew that we had to bury the earl, yet you conveniently overlooked that in lieu of your own wants. Polite requests are honored much more willingly than imperious commands, my lady. Have you not heard the old saying that it is much easier to catch flies with honey than with vinegar?"

She understood his meaning, and she further understood that he was completely correct. It was difficult to swallow her pride, but something in his manner made it a far easier to let it go.

"I have."

"Then know that I will move heaven and earth to fulfill your polite requests. A sweet word will bend me to your will far more easily than an overbearing command. And I can promise you that the same will be said for every man, woman and child at Kirk." His blue eyes glistened. "We all want to love and respect our new lady. Give us a reason to."

So much of what he said was prudent and true. Aubrielle couldn't help it; she smiled at him, thinking there was far more to this man than the hard façade and brute-force manner. Although she considered herself the more conventionally educated one, she knew that she could learn much from him.

"Well said, sir knight," she murmured. "I shall do my best to remember that."

"Good." Even though their conversation was coming to a close, he did not let her go. He liked the feel of her upon his thighs. "The priests have announced funeral mass for the earl at vespers. My day will be dedicated to the preparation of that. But when it is complete, I will organize a party to escort you to Glastonbury that will leave the following day. Will that be acceptable?"

"Completely," she said.

His response was to smile faintly, glad she was being agreeable, glad she was sitting on his lap, and generally glad that they weren't locking horns anymore. She could be quite captivating when she wasn't throwing temper tantrums. They continued gazing at each other until Aubrielle's cheeks began to turn a charming shade of pink and she discreetly stood up. Kenneth stood as well, wishing he could spend more time talking to her, but he had duties awaiting him.

"Can you keep yourself occupied today?" he asked her. "Most everyone will be busy with preparations for the funeral and unable to attend you."

"Posh. I do not need to be entertained. I have much preparation for our journey that will keep me busy." She cocked her head as a thought occurred to her. "Did anyone think to send word to my mother about his passing? She is his sister, after all."

"I sent a messenger last night."

"But we will not wait for her to attend?"

"It is June, my lady. It is imperative we lay your uncle to rest so that his body will not putrefy in this moist air."

It was a blunt way of putting it, but she nodded her agreement. As they moved for the door, Kenneth bent down and picked up the infamous poker. Aubrielle looked sheepish as he put it back against the hearth.

"You certainly have a liking for fire pokers as your weapon of choice," he commented. "But at least I did not suffer Everett's fate."

She attempted not to appear too ashamed. "His reflexes are not as quick as yours. I hadn't meant to hit him, only frighten him."

He lifted an eyebrow. "I am sure I do not need to worry over the speed of my reactions any longer because we will never again have such a display."

She wished he would get off of the subject. "As you say, my lord."

He was amused at her chagrin. Aubrielle paused by the doorway as he continued through, into the foyer. When he realized she hadn't followed him, he turned to look at her, thinking perhaps there was something more on her mind. She stood there, looking at him impatiently.

"Already, you have forgotten," she sighed. "Men are so forgetful."

He retraced his steps. "What have I forgotten, my lady?"

She put her hands on her hips. "That as your intended, I am due a word of farewell before you go about your day. 'Tis the polite thing to do, you know. Were you not, just a moment ago, instructing me in the convention of proper manners?"

He grinned; he couldn't help it. "Of course," he said quietly. "How could I be so foolish?"

She smiled in return; in fact, St. Héver seemed capable of drawing more smiles out of her than anyone ever had. His great hands came up and gently cupped her face. It was an amazingly tender gesture and her heart began to beat wildly against her ribs. He leaned down and softly kissed her forehead, each cheek, and finally took both of her hands again and laid delicate kisses upon her fingers. Aubrielle was so overwhelmed that she was having difficulty breathing. He'd never touched her lips, but he didn't have to. The pure tenderness of his farewell said far more than any single kiss to the lips could have ever conveyed.

At least, that was what she thought. Kenneth was apparently unsatisfied with his chivalrous farewell and clamped down over her mouth in a deeply passionate kiss. It took her breath away. But just as quickly, he released her and quit the foyer, leaving her seeking the wall behind her for support. It was several moments yet before she could stand unaided, much less walk.

She may have started the battle, but St. Héver had definitely won the war.

CHAPTER FIVE

THE PAST TWO days had been muddling. That was the best way to describe the state of Aubrielle's mind. Her entire life had followed a distinct path, one she never thought to vary from. But the past several hours had seen that path take a sharp detour, as if she were riding on the back of a runaway horse. She seemed to have no control at all.

After her skirmish and subsequent reconciliation with Kenneth, she had retreated to her chamber and spent the morning making sure she was prepared for their journey. She was, in truth, wildly excited. But other emotions had her within their grip, strange and unsettling though they might be. Over and over, she relived the events of the last two days; she had come to Kirk with her mother. Her mother had abandoned her. Her uncle, in turn, had also abandoned her, though he'd had the audacity to leave her to one of his knights. Just as the situation turned from bad to worse, her uncle died and, lo and behold, she inherits an earldom. In a panic, she coerced a knight into marrying her so that the responsibility of the rule would fall to someone who had a notion of how to justly administer said rule.

Yes, yes, that was how she remembered it. They were dizzying events. But the most recent strains to the Disorientation Symphony were those of emotion. They were both wonderful and terrifying, and not coincidentally, they seemed to rise and fall with Kenneth St. Héver's presence. Standing by the lancet window, where sounds from the bailey trickled freely, Aubrielle gently banged her forehead against the wall when all thoughts seemed to converge on Kenneth. Maybe if she banged long enough, she could jolt them right out of her head.

A husband had never been in her plans. 'Twas not that she never planned to marry; it was simply that she had never actively sought to marry. Her entire life had been her father, St. Wenburgh, and the knowledge she had acquired there. Sometimes her mother entered her world, but never long enough. Graciela was too weak to sustain herself.

Graciela's feeble character had hurt Aubrielle. She had always wished she had been blessed with a mother who had loved and supported her. Graciela had simply cowered to her, and when she could not handle her, she cast her off. In her stronger moments, Graciela said she understood Aubrielle's desires. She had understood them so well, in fact, that she had fled from them.

Aubrielle moved away from the window, wandering over to the bed where her satchels rested. There were two; one was completely full of clothing, cloaks, gloves and the like. The second also held clothing, but it also held parchment, quill, ink, and several vellums that she had taken with her from St. Wenburgh. This was her most valuable bag.

She ran her fingers over the leather. The bags had belonged to her father. She felt the pangs of longing for him, but quickly chased them away. She could no longer waste her energy on grief, though it had been long years since she had felt it fresh. But one death reminded her of another and she knew that vespers was approaching. It was her duty, as Kenneth had said, to pay respects to the man who had left her a vast empire and fortune to match. She didn't really care about the money, though it was a good thing to have. Perhaps St. Héver would be so kind someday to inform her of how much Garson had passed to them. Perhaps she would buy more books and items of learning. That was about the extent of her concern for the riches she had inherited.

A serving woman had been in and out of the chamber all day, helping her pack, making sure she took toiletries with her. She was a small woman with missing teeth and a pale face. The next time she came around, Aubrielle asked for some warm water to wash in. The servant returned with a big copper tub and buckets of hot water. Not remembering the last time she bathed, Aubrielle enjoyed a long, hot bath. The serving woman had managed to stir up violet-scented soap and washed her hair with flat ale. Not strangely, there were still clumps of St.

Hėver's blood in her locks from when they had met two days before.

Aubrielle was cleaner than she had anticipated by the time the water was cool. The sun was lowering and the serving woman had stoked the blaze in the hearth so that she could dry herself. She thought it odd that, as she sat on the small three-legged stool while the servant brushed out her hair, her thoughts were centering more around St. Hėver than their impending journey. She felt a small amount of guilt that her thoughts weren't centered around her dead uncle at all, but that could not be helped. She was selfish just as St. Hėver said she was. Suddenly, different dimensions of her life were coming into focus and she was greedily fixated on them.

A soft white linen sheath was the first thing to touch her newly-dry, violet-scented skin. Tender-soft pantalets followed. The serving woman then helped her into a heavy brocade gown of rich black, woven on the sleeves and the neckline in filigree silver. If Aubrielle had one vice other than her hunger for learning, it was for pretty clothes. Her mother had started her early with that. She appreciated the craftsmanship of a finely made gown and an interesting fabric. This garment was no exception and was gloriously made and with a whalebone girdle of black and silver, her slender torso was emphasized and the overall picture, magnificent.

When the gown went on, she sat back down on the stool as the serving woman put on her woolen hose and garters. She pulled her shoes on herself as the servant went back to brushing her long, silky hair. The ale had brought out the natural wave and the woman formed loose curls with her hands as it dried. All the while, Aubrielle sat with a distant look on her face, wondering why she couldn't seem to focus on anything in particular. It occurred to her that she was looking forward to the funeral because she knew that Kenneth would be there.

A foolish thought, but a true one. She felt like an idiot. Her hair was almost completely dry by the time a knock at the door came. Aubrielle stood up from the stool, light-headed with excitement. Kenneth had come for her. But her anticipation was shot when Everett appeared.

Everett was unable to conceal his delight at so beautiful a lady. He stood in the door, dressed in his finest, looking fit and handsome. He smiled warily at Aubrielle.

"Sir Kenneth thought to give me the opportunity to escort you to the chapel, my lady," he said, "provided that you do not take a poker to me again."

Aubrielle lifted an eyebrow. "Not tonight, Sir Everett. I have no desire to end up in the vault again."

His smile broadened and he held out his forearm, indicating it was time to go. "If my lady pleases."

She pulled on a black glove, holding her other glove in that hand as she put her uncovered one on Everett's forearm. She knew she looked plausibly stunning, and smelled sweetly of violets. The expression on Everett's face told her he was fairly impressed with her ability to look like a lady when it was required.

The keep was dark and quiet but for a few servants moving about. Everett escorted her down the stairs carefully, admonishing her more than once to watch her step. He led her out of the keep and down the retractable wooden stairs to the bailey below. It was still and reasonably quiet in the cavernous yard, the night cool with a hint of moisture to it. They drew near the small circular chapel located near the towering outer wall.

The warm glow of candlelight emitted from the thin lancet windows that were carved into the walls of the stone edifice. The ancestral burial place of the Mortimers was able to seat nearly thirty people, but as they entered, the only people inside were three priests, a couple of altar boys, Lucius, Reid, Bradley, Max the squire, and Kenneth.

Aubrielle's attention was drawn to Kenneth, standing on the opposite side of the dimly lit chapel. Their eyes met and she could feel the heat from his gaze. She watched him as he made his way towards her; he, too, was dressed in his finest ceremonial armor bearing the seal of Wrexham. Somewhere during the day he had shaved and washed, lending weight to his handsome appearance. The more she studied the man, the more attractive he became.

"We are ready to commence, my lady."

"Is this all?" she whispered, looking around. "No more to attend?"

Kenneth shook his head. "The earl did not want a large funeral. In fact, he was rather adamant about it. He wanted to be put in the ground, as he so eloquently stated, and be done with it."

He escorted her to the front of the chapel where the crypt bearing her uncle's body had been opened. Next to his effigy was another feminine one. Aubrielle recognized her aunt, Isobel, Garson's beloved wife. Lucius was there, and he bowed to Aubrielle as she approached. She could smell the stale rank of alcohol on him.

"My lady," he greeted her tightly.

She looked at Lucius but wasted no time analyzing his manner. He had been strange since the betrothal had been announced, but she had no desire to burden herself with his reasons. She had known Lucius for many years and they had never been compatible. Lucius was the type of man who, at times, was more concerned with making himself a shadow of his liege to gain favor rather than doing his job.

"Do you require a chair, my lady?" Kenneth asked quietly.

She shook her head. "I doubt I'd be able to sit with the licking you gave me earlier."

Kenneth cleared his throat loudly as she spoke, hoping it would drown out her words to anyone listening. "Much is your misfortune, my lady."

She looked at him, smiling knowingly as their eyes met. Kenneth was trying to pay attention to the priests as they prepared to begin, but it didn't stop him from giving her a wink. He hoped she had learned a lesson from this morning. Time would tell if she was truly giving thought to her behavior or merely trying to fool him into believing so.

The funeral mass began with a short prayer. If one thing was as strong as his devotion to his knighthood, it was Kenneth's devotion to the Faith. He was deeply religious. Perhaps that was why it was so hard for him to understand Aubrielle's quest to locate the Grail. It was sacred to him, and to most Christians, and his opinion of her search was torn between blasphemy and approval.

The priest made the sign of the True Cross and lapsed into the first reading, chosen by the earl himself. It was relayed in the traditional Latin. For Aubrielle, it was a second language and she easily understood it. The priests at St. Wenburgh had conversed and taught in the language.

"O Lord, see how my enemies persecute me! Have mercy and lift me up from the gates of death, that I may declare your praises in the gates of the Daughter of Zion and there rejoice in your salvation."

There were more verses after that, followed by a prayer and a short homily. The topic of the homily was, not strangely, the importance of humility to God's Will while on Earth. The conclusion was set with the liturgy for all in attendance, the sacred communion of Christ. The priest blessed the congregation by making the sign of the True Cross once again, to which Aubrielle and the knights responded by also crossing themselves.

The funeral for Garson Mortimer, 1st Earl of Wrexham, had taken less than a quarter of an hour. It had been oddly unfulfilling. When it was over, Lucius vacated the chapel without a word. He was followed by the rest of the knights and the squire. Only Kenneth remained behind, standing quietly as Aubrielle passed a final glace over the crypt bearing her aunt and uncle's effigies. It was unclear what she was thinking; perhaps she was contemplating her future. Together, they walked from the chapel.

The ambiance of the bailey was bright with moonlight and the silence between them was comfortable. Aubrielle gazed up at the stars, finding the constellations that the monks had taught her. Astronomy had been a favorite subject, one usually forbidden to women. She had, not surprisingly, insisted upon instruction.

"Do you know anything about the stars, sir knight?" she asked.

Kenneth noticed her focus and he, too, looked up to the sky. "Nay, my lady," he said, although it wasn't the truth. He actually knew a great deal about them for navigating travel but he didn't want to sound as if he knew everything. "My focus has always been on warfare."

As they walked, they were unconsciously wandering closer and closer to one another. Aubrielle pointed up into the sky. "The word 'astronomy' is a Greek word. It literally means 'law of the stars'. There is a document called the Rig-Veda that is thousands of years old and identifies many of the star clusters we now know."

"I see," he strolled casually. "Did the monks teach you that?"

"That and more. The Rig-Veda is a Hindu writing, the earliest known scripture from that religion. It is part of a bigger group of writings called the Mandalas. Have you ever heard of them?"

"I have not. But, then again, my formal education was confined to those subjects related to my vocation."

Aubrielle could have gone for hours about astronomy. She was fascinated by it. But for the first time in her life, she was hesitant to reveal her knowledge. She did not want Kenneth to think she was displaying her intellectual superiority.

"I have not read them myself, only about them," she said. "If you would ever like to know about astronomy, I could tell you what I have learned."

"By all means, tell me." He didn't sound threatened by her offer in the least. They had wandered so close together that he took her hand and tucked it into the crook of his elbow. "I cannot promise to be a good student, but I am willing to try."

"Did you never complete formal education?"

He nodded. "As every young lad does. During the time I fostered, I was schooled in reading, writing, mathematics, military tactics, the art of warfare, weapons, military history and theory, and other subjects related to the knighthood."

He was seriously downplaying the fact that he was quite brilliant in just about every subject, but his modesty prevented him from telling her that. The woman prided herself on being highly educated and he would allow her to believe that between the two of them, she was the smartest. It meant a great deal to her, he suspected.

Oblivious to his chivalrous thoughts, Aubrielle smiled knowingly at him. "Let me guess," she lifted an eyebrow. "You excelled in military tactics, warfare, weapons, and military history and theory."

"I did," he conceded humbly. "In fact, those subjects came too easily to even categorize them as a study. To me, they simply flowed. I was also quite good in mathematics."

"Well," she said thoughtfully, "then I believe we are even. Those subjects do not flow easily to me, but the others do. Perhaps somehow we will balance one another out."

He liked that thought. "I shall teach you about battle tactics and you can teach me about the stars. On second thought, I'd better not teach you about battle tactics. Knowing your history as I do, you may use them against me."

She pretended to be offended by his comment, jutting her chin into the air and looking away from him. Kenneth simply grinned, placing his free hand over her fingers and clasping the warm digits.

"Does your backside really hurt that bad?" he asked.

"I am surprised you didn't break your hand beating me as you did."

He laughed. It was the second time in as many days that he had done so. At this rate, he'd laugh more in the next few days than he had in his entire life.

"My apologies if I bruised you."

"How clever. I noticed that you do not apologize for spanking me."

"Nor will I. You deserved it."

They fell into silence as they mounted the steps for the keep. In the great hall, supper had been laid out and there were several senior soldiers already seated and eating. Lucius, Reid, Bradley, Everett, Max, and a couple of young squires were also present. Kenneth seated Aubrielle between himself and Lucius. Everett, seated across from them, did most of the talking, as was usual. A normal evening would have Kenneth watching the room, Lucius drinking, Reid and Bradley engaging in some sort of gambling vice, and Everett chatting. All that was missing was the earl, and tonight, the men were somewhat humble in his memory.

Aubrielle picked at her fowl, not particularly hungry. Besides, the bird was dry. It occurred to her that what she really wanted to do was be alone with Kenneth so that they could converse more about anything that came to mind. He seemed to be sitting so still and so silent. Once, she stole a glance at him to see what he was up to; he had been gazing out across the sea of men. He had caught her look and a brief wink ensued. But that was all, and not enough to satisfy her. He certainly would not talk to her.

The soldiers were growing loud with their drink. They were throwing scraps to the dogs, placing bets on the ones they believed able to fight for the biggest piece. Everett was attempting to impress Aubrielle with his knowledge of construction engineering where it pertained to castle building, but Aubrielle was focused on a small dog in the writhing, snarling group of canines. It was a little gray dog that kept getting shut out of the scrap fight. Finally, the little dog dejectedly wandered away from the crowd and sat politely by the fire. The pup was smart enough to know he was outmatched and patiently wait for his moment to clean up after the big dogs.

Aubrielle stood up in the middle of Everett's conversation. Kenneth watched her walk from the table and towards the fighting mass of dogs. She gave them a wide berth and came around to the massive stone hearth where the little gray dog sat. She crouched down, holding out her hand to the pup. The dog, thrilled with the attention, licked her fingers happily. She promptly picked up the puppy and brought him back over to the head table.

Kenneth moved over as she sat the dog down between them. Without a word of request from her, he handed her the knuckle-bone from his trencher. He knew instinctively what was on her mind. She accepted the bone and gave it to the dog, which hungrily gnawed on it.

"Poor creature," she stoked the dog's back and was rewarded with a wag of the tail. "He was being ignored. He'll never get anything to eat."

"I think you underestimate him, my lady," Kenneth replied. "He's survived quite some time around here."

She continued to pet the dog, wondering why Kenneth's manner had grown hard. His tone was not the same one she knew when they were alone. She had noticed the change in his conduct when they had been in the chapel, too, in front of his men. He hadn't even come for her himself; he had sent Everett to escort her. The apparent pattern was that he showed very little interest in her when it was in front of his men. He was always polite, yet cold. It was a baffling occurrence, one she did not understand. But she knew that she did not like it.

To her left, Lucius had evidently had enough to drink and begged his leave from the table. Aubrielle glanced at him, weaving his way across the great hall and disappearing into the darkness of the shadowed foyer. The other knights didn't seem concerned with his departure. Kenneth remained as silent as the grave and Everett had all but given up trying to carry on a conversation with her. Dejected at Kenneth's behavior and weary from the day, Aubrielle rose from her seat with the little dog in her grasp. She'd had enough.

"I shall take my leave as well," she said to Kenneth. "I believe I shall take my little friend with me."

Kenneth stood up. "I shall see to you, my lady."

"No," she said pointedly. "You will stay here with your men. I can find my own way."

Kenneth didn't respond; he simply followed her as she walked across the hall and into the foyer. She turned to him as they reached the darkened stairwell.

"I am quite capable of finding my chamber, sir knight," she said. "You need not be bothered with me."

"It is no bother."

"I beg to differ. Please go back to your men."

He cocked his head. "What ails you, my lady?"

So he had picked up on her confusion. Aubrielle recognized that she was having a difficult time controlling her feelings and struggled not to let it show.

"Nothing ails me, I assure you," she said evenly. "I simply want to… be alone."

"Have I done something?"

She growled before she could stop herself. "Of course you have, you dolt. You have ignored me all through dinner. You sent Everett to escort me to the chapel, and every time we are together in front of your men, 'tis as if I cease to exist." Her eyes widened with dismay as she realized what a fool she was being. "Please. Just… leave me alone."

She turned and raced up the steps, dog in hand. Kenneth stood there at the base of the stairs, her words spinning in his head. He realized that she had picked up on something not even he had been aware of. When he was in front of his men, his behavior was always the same. There was no variation. He was Kenneth St. Héver, and the perception of his fierce and unyielding manner must always be apparent.

She was right. He ignored her when they were in public. He didn't want his men to see any other façade but the hard knight. With Aubrielle, he knew he would act like a sotted fool. He was afraid to show weakness, afraid she was playing him for a fool. With a sigh of regret, he turned back to the hall. Perhaps after he'd had a chance to sort it out in his own mind, he could explain it to her.

Aubrielle reached her chamber in a flurry. She raced inside, her cheeks flushed, and stood in the middle of the room like a fool. She could not believe she had said what she did, acting as if she and Kenneth had something more than just an arranged convenience. She had acted as if there was something of emotion involved, and that it had already been established between them. She was acting as if she had a claim to him.

She groaned softly, setting the pup down. He sat right at her feet and wagged his tail as she stood there, her hand on her face, wondering if throwing herself from the window would be a quick end to her humiliation. Perhaps after she'd had time to sort it all out, she could come up with a good explanation so he would not think she actually harbored feelings for him. The mere idea was preposterous, she told herself. She was an intelligent woman; surely she could come up with something believable.

The dog yipped and something very heavy struck her on the side of the face. Dazed, nearly incapacitated, Aubrielle fell to her knees and received another blow, this one to her stomach. With a flash of pain, her world suddenly went black.

ଓ

KENNETH HAD SPENT a solid hour trying to think of something to say to Aubrielle about his behavior. Everything he could think of sounded foolish, so he was leaning strongly towards telling her the truth. He simply didn't know how else to behave when in front of his men. Even as he repeated it in his head, he knew she would reject it. But it was the truth, for better or worse. He didn't want to wait until the morning to tell her. He would tell her now and hoped she had calmed down enough not to try and take the poker to him again.

The feast of drinking and gambling was rolling well into the night as he excused himself from the hall. Sounds of laughter and music followed him as he mounted the dark stairs to the third floor of the keep. There were three rooms on this level; one for the earl, an empty chamber once used by the earl's wife, and Aubrielle's chamber. Once clear of the steps, he passed the empty chamber and came to Aubrielle's door. He noticed immediately that the panel was slightly askew. Knocking softly, he received no reply. Pushing the door open, he entered.

The room was dark but for the fire burning low in the hearth. As his eyes adjusted to the room, he noticed the bed was empty. It was not only confusing, it was alarming. He was halfway into the chamber when he noticed a pile of clothing on the floor.

It was no ordinary pile of clothing. Aubrielle lay crumpled somewhere in it. Kenneth fell to his knees beside her, feeling a surge of terror as he had never felt in his life. He put his fingers to her neck and, feeling her strong pulse, relief flowed through him.

He didn't want to move her for fear of aggravating whatever injury she had, so he shifted to gain a better look at her. He could see a welt on her cheekbone, bruised and bleeding. He could not have imagined what had happened to her. He put his hands on her shoulders and ever-so-gently rolled her onto her back.

"My lady," he whispered. "Aubrielle, can you hear me?"

She moaned a little and he gathered her up, cradling her head in the crook of his arm. He smoothed the loose hair away from her face so he could get a better look at her.

"Aubrielle," he shook her as gently as he could. "Sweetheart, wake up. Open your eyes and look at me."

After a moment, she seemed to become more lucid. Then, her features twisted with pain.

"Oh," she gasped. "I… I…"

Her fist balled up and her entire body tensed. Kenneth could feel the fight in her and he held her steady.

"Aubrielle, 'tis me," he grasped her hand to keep her from striking him. "You are safe, I swear it."

Slowly, the sea-colored eyes lolled open. They were unfocused. "St. Héver?" she whispered.

"I am here. Do not fear."

She blinked and her vision became clearer. "What… what happened?"

He smoothed her forehead, like a mother soothing an ill child. "That is what I intended to ask you. Do you not recollect anything?"

She took a deep breath and instantly doubled over in pain. Had Kenneth not had a good grip on her, she would have tumbled back to the floor. Aubrielle was gasping and weeping.

"Aubrielle, tell me," he demanded softly. "Where does it hurt?"

"My… my stomach."

Kenneth swept her easily into his arms and laid her upon the bed.

She was crying softly, trying to be brave, but the pain was intense. He knew something of injuries from his years on the battlefield and tried to straighten her out so he could better assess the area of injury.

"The first thing we have to do is unlace this girdle," he made small talk, trying to distract her from her agony. The laces came loose and he tossed the accessory to the floor. "Now, let's see what we can discover."

Aubrielle had her hand on her face. "Someone hit me," she murmured. "I remember… someone hit me."

A spark of anger, such as he had never known, began to burn deep in his belly. He tried to focus on helping her for the moment rather than his murderous thoughts of vengeance. The gown would not come off easily and every movement seemed to cause her pain. Taking hold of a seam, he gave a sharp tug and ripped the seam from her armpit to her ankle. A few more rips and the gown peeled away like the skin of an orange. Laid open to her shift, he could now gain better access.

"Show me where it hurts," he said gently.

Aubrielle put her hand to the middle of her belly. Kenneth barely touched her and she yelped. Even though there was no external bleeding, he did not want to take any chances. She needed a physic. Fear began to make strange company with fury in his mind.

He summoned the toothless serving wench and sent her running for the knights. Aubrielle's tears had calmed and he pulled the coverlet over her, hoping to make her more comfortable until the surgeon arrived. He hated feeling so helpless.

"The physic will come soon," he murmured. "Try to rest now."

Her sea-colored eyes were unnaturally bright against her ashen face. "I never heard anything. One moment I was standing, and in the next, I was falling to the floor."

He sat on the bed, his arms braced on either side of her slender body. He pulled the coverlet tighter.

"Did you catch a glimpse?" he asked. "Anything at all? Perhaps a flash of clothing or a weapon?"

She thought a moment, licking her colorless lips. "I… I thought I smelled something."

"What?"

"Ale." She looked at him, a mixture of dread and anger on her face. "I smelt it earlier today, too."

"Where?"

"You will not believe me."

"Of course I will."

"I smelled it on Lucius tonight in the chapel."

"Le Cor?" Kenneth was baffled. "Are you sure?"

She nodded, weakly. "Positive. I remember thinking that he smelt like old ale. And…"

"What?"

"I thought I heard him say something, too."

"What did you hear?"

She fell silent, reluctant to tell him. When she spoke, he barely heard her.

"I cannot be sure. But it sounded like 'whore'."

Kenneth was having a difficult time controlling his reaction. He caught movement out of the corner of his eye and would have bolted into action had he not realized, almost too late, that it was the little gray dog. The creature wagged its tail at him, and Kenneth noticed something in the dog's mouth. He reached down, pulling out a small strip of wet black cloth.

Kenneth held up the cloth, studying it. Aubrielle watched him curiously.

"What's that?" she asked.

He sighed heavily, glancing down at the pup. "Something your little friend has given me."

"What do you mean?"

His jaw ticked as he studied the cloth again. "I am not sure, but I intend to find out."

He wadded the scrap into a closed fist after that, refusing to let her see it. With his free hand, he inspected the lump on her cheek to distract her.

"You've quite a lovely mark," he said. "A rare beauty indeed."

Her fingers flitted over the bruise self-consciously. "'Tis enormous."

He smiled, letting her know it wasn't all that bad. "Not to worry, my lady. You are still the most beautiful woman in all the land."

A hint of a smile creased her lips. "You are mad."

"Not at all. I am quite sane."

"But you should not say such things."

"Why not? 'Tis the truth, with God as my witness."

Her pale pallor turned a soft shade of pink. Kenneth was glad to see that she wasn't so horribly injured that she could not respond to his gentle humor. Still, he wondered what was keeping the knights. He was particularly curious to see if Lucius would show. In fact, he hoped he would.

Everett was the first to arrive. His young face was full of curiosity when he entered, but quickly turned to concern. The barber-surgeon arrived a few moments later. His name was Argus, a dwarf of a man with thin gray hair and quick reflexes. He carried with him a big box of implements and medicaments that resembled a carpenter's toolbox. Reid followed behind him, carrying another box of mysterious supplies.

The little man knew Aubrielle Grace de Witney. He'd been at Kirk for three generations. There wasn't much he didn't know. He took one look at Aubrielle and cast a long glance at Kenneth.

"So," he said. "I see that she finally pushed you over the edge."

Kenneth lifted an eyebrow. "Whatever injuries she has are not of my doing."

The physic changed places with Kenneth and hopped onto the bed beside Aubrielle. He peered at the lump on her cheek. He then proceeded to inspect the rest of her face, running his fingers over her skull to see if there were any angry bumps. As Kenneth and the knights watched, the physic investigated her arms, fingers and shoulders. Then he paused.

"You have a nice crack on the cheek, m'lady," he said. "It could have been worse. Where else do you hurt?"

"My stomach."

Argus made the knights leave the room so that he could examine her torso. The door to the chamber closed softly behind the men and they congregated in the musty darkness of the third floor corridor. Kenneth turned to the others.

"Where is the captain?"

Everett shook his head. "Asleep in his room. I knocked, but he did not answer. He's probably still too drunk to move."

Kenneth digested the information. "And Bradley has the night watch. He's been up on the battlements since sundown."

"Correct," Everett said. "Ken, what's this about? What happened to her?"

Kenneth was again besieged by anger. "Someone attacked Lady Aubrielle when she retired for the evening. You saw her face, and I am deeply concerned about the injuries suffered to her belly."

"Jesus," Everett breathed. "Who would do such a thing?"

Kenneth didn't voice his suspicion right away. He held up the scrap of black material. "That little dog that Lady Aubrielle took from the hall seems to have given us a clue."

Everett and Reid peered closely at the swatch. "Woolen material," Everett fingered it. "Feels rough."

"Does it feel familiar?"

Everett thought a moment. "Like hose." His features suddenly took on a suspicious countenance. "Like the kind of hose we wear into battle to protect against the mail."

Kenneth merely nodded, watching realization dawn slowly in the faces of his men. It was apparent by their expressions that, to different degrees, they were beginning to follow the same trail that Kenneth himself was already well set upon. It was an ominous concept.

"Everett," Kenneth put the material in the knight's palm. "Find Lucius. If his door is bolted, break it down. See if he is missing a portion of his hose."

"Captain le Cor?" Everett was torn between shock and disbelief. "Do you really think…?"

"Lady Aubrielle said she that her attacker smelled of alcohol. Stale ale were her exact words. Who does that sound like?"

Reid hissed a curse and looked away. They all knew the answer, but Everett spoke the obvious. "The captain. He always smells like week old rot."

Kenneth's eyes were like ice. "Find him. I shall be with you shortly."

The knights were gone. Kenneth stood there a moment, wondering what chaos was about to envelope Kirk. With the earl gone and le Cor staging drunken attacks, he was determined not to see it all unravel. This world meant too much to him. It was his duty to take control and secure the safety of the earldom for all their sakes, especially Aubrielle's. She had endured what no one should have to, and he felt phenomenally guilty that he had not been there to protect her.

He took a moment to collect his thoughts. He needed to settle himself and relax. Thoughts of revenge and murder were new to him in the present context and it was imperative that he control himself. When the physic finally opened the door to the chamber once more, he found a very calm knight leaning casually against the corridor wall. The old man waved him in.

"Come, come," he motioned. "Close the door so the draft does not get in."

Kenneth followed him into the room. The toothless servant had built the fire into a nice blaze, and the room was almost too warm. Aubrielle lay upon the bed with a large bandage on her left cheek.

The little gray dog lay peacefully by her head, like a sentinel. His head came up, ears perked, when he saw Kenneth. But just as quickly, he lay back down again as if satisfied the knight meant his lady no harm.

"What is your diagnosis?" Kenneth's gaze lingered on her.

The little physic went to the bed, grasping Aubrielle's wrist to take her pulse one last time. "The heart can tell us a great deal about a person's health," he said. A few seconds was all he needed and he set her hand back down. Then he looked at Kenneth. "Oh, she took a fine beating, no doubt. No doubt at all."

"And?"

"And she'll need some time to recover, but I do not believe there is any permanent damage. She has a beauty of a bruise on her belly."

"But nothing serious?"

"Not that I can tell. Mind she doesn't strain herself, though. She must rest for a few days."

Aubrielle suddenly came alive. "But I cannot rest a few days," she insisted. "We are leaving for Glastonbury on the morrow."

"Pah!" the physic spat. "You'll be making no trips for some time, m'lady. You could do serious harm frisking about on the open road. Your injured belly might rip open and spout bright red guts all over the dusty trail."

He had said it so dramatically that Kenneth struggled not to smile. The look on Aubrielle's face was priceless; she turned positively red. Kenneth could sense the storm coming and hastened to remove the cause in the hope that it would blow over.

"As long as there is no serious damage, I am sure the lady will do all she can to regain her full strength," he said. "A good night's sleep will do wonders."

The physic gathered his two boxes, handing one to the toothless wench hovering near the hearth. "I shall be back tomorrow to check on the lady."

"Very well."

"Mind she doesn't get out of that bed."

"She will not."

Kenneth walked the old man to the door. Aubrielle heard it close softly. She was exhausted, in pain, but all she could think about was the fact that she would not be leaving for Glastonbury tomorrow. It was an agonizing disappointment; damn her aching cheek and gut. It would seem that whenever she came close to achieving her dream, something always prevented it. She was coming to think that perhaps she was never meant to go.

"Go to sleep, my lady," Kenneth was still in the room. "I shall stand watch this night, have no fear."

He'd been so silent that she had assumed he walked out with the physic. Aubrielle's sea-colored eyes found him in the dimness of the room.

"If you are here, then I most certainly will have no fear," she said quietly. "I thank you for your courtesy, sir knight. Your comfort has been invaluable."

He dragged the chair up to the bed and sat. "'Tis no courtesy, my lady. You are my betrothed, after all. 'Tis my duty to protect you."

Somehow that wasn't the answer she had wanted. As it was earlier in the evening, Aubrielle was behaving as if there was something more than mere obligation between them. She was feeling untamed emotions and struggling not to.

"Of course," she muttered. "'Tis your duty."

Kenneth heard it in her voice. There was a longing. It terrified him and pleased him at the same time.

"Aye, a duty and a pleasure," he said quietly. "I am truly sorry that I was not here to protect you against this brutal assault."

"It was not your fault."

"But I should have escorted you to your chamber. I should have made sure you were safe before leaving you."

"The attack happened inside my chamber, sir knight. You would not have come inside my chamber and escorted me directly into my bed. There was nothing you could have done."

He sat there a moment in thought. Aubrielle watched his handsome face in the firelight, the edgy ticking of his jaw. She sensed that there were heavy matters on his mind.

"May I ask you something?" she asked.

He looked at her. "Anything."

"Are you comfortable with this betrothal? If you've had time to think the matter through and have decided against it…"

"What would lead you to believe that?"

"Nothing in particular. But we must face facts; we hardly know one another. What we do know of each other has been, well, violent at times. I am not the easiest person to get along with. Everything happened so quickly yesterday that if you've changed your mind, I would understand."

He just sat there and looked at her, his elbow against the arm of the chair and his chin in his hand.

"Have you changed your mind, my lady?"

"No."

"Are you sure?"

"I am sure."

He un-propped his chin and sat forward. "Then I shall have you know that never, at any time, have I questioned my decision. I am looking forward to this marriage."

It was a sweet thing to say. Aubrielle couldn't help the smile on her lips. "You are?"

"Of course. I shall have the most beautiful wife in the whole of England and all men will envy me my good fortune. How could I not look forward to it?"

"But what about the earldom?"

"I could not care less about that. You are the prize."

She had the most wonderful, giddy feeling. But her smile faded. "If that is true, why do you ignore me whenever we are in public? It seems to me that you are ashamed somehow."

He gave her a gentle, reproving look. Her hand was still resting at the edge of the bed and he picked it up, holding it between his two enormous palms. Ever so tenderly, he brought her fingers to his lips and kissed them.

"Not at all," he murmured. "But I understand why you would feel that way. I have thought of almost nothing else for the bulk of the evening. All I can tell you is that it is important that I project a certain image for the soldiers. They fear and respect me, and in the minds of men, any show of compassion or kindness will be construed as weakness."

Aubrielle understood, somewhat. "Are you afraid that they would think that a female had you by the throat?"

He grinned, patting her fingers. "Something like that. There is nothing more pathetic than a man who is controlled by the whims of a woman."

"I see," she said softly. "Then you do not intend that my whims should control you."

"As I said, polite requests will always be honored. I am not sure a whim would come as a polite request, but a piercing whine."

He was smiling as he said it. She pretended to grump. "Is that what you think? Have you ever known me to whine?"

"Indeed, no," he said firmly. "From what I have seen, you have two distinct moods. The first is to fight like a wildcat, and the second... well, the second is right now, when you are as sweet as a soft summer rain and twice as nice."

It was the most touching thing anyone had ever said to her. Aubrielle felt as if her heart swelled so that it was close to bursting from her chest. At that moment, she felt closer to this stranger than she had ever felt to anyone in her life and her carefully guarded control slipped peacefully away. She was being reckless and didn't care.

"When I was a small child, I can recollect climbing into my father's bed and lying against him where it was warm and safe," she murmured. "He would hold me in the night, singing songs and telling me stories. I have not felt such peace nor safety since that time. But when I look at you, even though I have not truly come to know you, I think that perhaps I could feel that peace and safety once again."

His features softened. "I would hope so, my lady. I will certainly do my best to make you feel that way."

"Then would you do something for me now?"

"Anything."

"Would… would you lay here with me until I fall asleep? I fear that I need that comfort and safety now, and I would be most grateful if you would do this for me."

It was a bold request, but Kenneth didn't care. Removing his boots, he climbed into bed beside her. Aubrielle was under the coverlets and Kenneth lay on the top of them. The little dog was happy for the company and licked his face a couple of times before he could set it on the floor. Alone in the bed with her, he rolled Aubrielle onto her side, away from him, being very careful not to exacerbate her injuries. When she was settled, he pressed his massive body against her backside, his arms enfolding her tenderly. Her head ended up cradled between his shoulder and neck, his mouth against the side of her head.

"Sleep now, my lady," he murmured. "You are safe. I swear that I will never let anything happen to you ever again."

She twisted her head back so she could look at him. Kenneth realized too late that it was an extraordinarily dangerous position, for she was far too close. She looked as if she were going to say something but he didn't give her the chance. The heat of the moment was upon him, and he could do nothing but surrender to a force stronger than anything he had ever experienced.

His mouth came down over her lips, soft at first, but persistent and hard within a matter of seconds. A big hand came up to her throat, holding it gently but firmly, forming a vice that held her head still while he ravaged her mouth with his lips and tongue. When he should have been well aware of the impropriety, he could only think of how sweet she was.

It didn't help that Aubrielle hadn't pulled away from him, shocked at his indecent behavior. In fact, after a moment's indecision, she had responded to him admirably. He was aware of her hand on his face, her mouth tasting his lips just as he was tasting hers. He was unaware how long he kissed her: it seemed like an eternity, yet it hardly seemed long enough. He could have kissed her for the rest of his life and have never grown tired of it.

His lips left her mouth and moved over her face, kissing her nose, her undamaged cheek, her forehead, and her chin. He even kissed her little ear that protruded so delightfully. It was an extremely tender gesture. There was nothing about the woman that wasn't delectable, and he wanted to taste it all. He was so swept up in his mounting passion that it was a dreadful shock of reality when he put a hand on her torso and she gasped in pain.

"Christ," he breathed. "I am so sorry. I did not mean to do that."

Her lips were red from his stubble. In fact, he had nearly rubbed her raw with it. "I know you didn't," she could see how badly he felt. "I forgot about that, too."

He wiped the moisture off her lips and smiled apologetically. "I am sorry for all of it. I do not know what came over me. Perhaps… perhaps I should reclaim my chair."

"Why?"

"Why? Because lying here… with you… well, I am afraid my control is somewhat lacking."

He was already rising from the bed and Aubrielle grasped his arm. "Where are you going?"

"To sit in the chair."

She clamped on to his arm and refused to let go. "You'll do no such thing. You promised to lay here with me until I fall asleep and I intend to hold you to that promise."

He lifted an eyebrow. "But you do not understand. If I lay back down here, then I cannot guarantee that will not happen again."

"Let it, I say."

He looked at her, curiously. A smile grew upon his lips. "My lady, I cannot…"

"And do not call me 'my lady' when we are in private. You will call me by my name."

"As you say. Then you will call me by mine."

She nodded shortly. "Now that we have that established, come back to bed. I am cold and tired, and wish to sleep."

"If I start kissing you again, I may not stop. And you'll certainly not get any sleep."

She looked him squarely in the eye. "If that was meant to frighten me, it did not succeed."

"Is that so? Then if I tell you that I might rip off all of your clothes and ravage you, is that sufficiently frightening?"

"No."

"No?"

"No," she said firmly. "And I shall tell you why."

"Please, by all means."

"You are to be my husband, are you not?"

"Indeed."

"Then by practice if not yet by law, we are already married, are we not?"

He thought about that. "For all intent and purposes, we are."

"So if I wish for my husband to lay with me, then it is perfectly proper. If he wants to ravage me, then it is his right to do so. Is this also not so?"

He fought off a smirk. "It is not as simple as you make it sound."

She tried to sit up, but groaned when her body refused. She lay on her back, her knees bent, hands on her stomach. Her face was a mask of misery. "Now see what you have done?"

"What have I done?"

"You are arguing with me when you should be comforting me."

He gave up. "Oh, very well." He lay back down beside her. "Christ, I shall do anything if it will shut you up."

She grinned triumphantly as he gently gathered her into his warm embrace once more. She snuggled back against him, perfectly content, perfectly happy. Kenneth had one hand on her forehead, stroking her hair.

"Kenneth?"

"What is it, Aubrielle?"

She giggled. He could feel her. "I think a woman has you by the throat."

He growled. Rolling over, he clamped the hand that had been on her forehead over her mouth. At the same time, his heated mouth found her sweet little earlobe and he suckled it furiously. It tickled like mad in an erotic, happy sort of way. Aubrielle's screams of delight and frustration were for naught, muffled in the palm of Kenneth's massive hand.

ଓ

"KIRK IS A massive place," de Gaul said. "But she keeps her gates fairly open. It should not be difficult to enter."

Camped in the woods two miles south of Kirk, the group of murderers cooked snared rabbits over an open flame. Brother Grendel sat nervously by the fire, listening to the sounds from the haunted forest surrounding them, wondering how all of this was going to end. If he could escape, then he could make it to Kirk and warn Lady Aubrielle. But he was watched closely, always, and escape was not an option.

"We've been here for two days," another man said. He had a patch over an empty eye socket where once rested a carved wooden eyeball. "We've seen enough. When are we going to move?"

"Patience, Athelred," de Gaul said. "We must move carefully. Barging into a heavily armed fortress will only get us killed. We spoke of a plan last eve, if you recall."

Athelred nodded, chewing on a rabbit leg. "I remember. We pose as travelers looking for lodgings for one of our sick men. But who is going to be the sick one? I do not want a surgeon to operate on me!"

"The surgeon will not operate on you," de Gaul said impatiently. "But custom dictates that the lord of the castle cannot turn us away if we are bearing a sick man. They undoubtedly cannot turn us away if we harbor a priest, but I cannot take the chance that somehow Lady Aubrielle might become cognizant that Brother Grendel is in her midst. No, we cannot allow that. He may spill our purpose."

De Gaul winked boldly at the friar, who simply turned away. He was repulsed by all of it. Grendel listened to them bicker. Theirs was a weak plan, but it would get them into the castle if only for a couple of days. That would be all they needed to find Lady Aubrielle. These were clever men, frightening men. They wanted the scroll, more desperately now than ever before.

"We move on the morrow," de Gaul took a long swig of wine. "Thomas, you'll be the sick one." When the man he indicated raised a loud protest, de Gaul waved his cup in the air. "Break his leg! Make it good and bloody! And give Athelred a knock on the head that will ring his bells. They'll get us into the castle!"

The men roared their glee and the hapless Thomas was left to fight a losing battle. Somewhere in the darkness, a healthy bone was snapped and a hard head received a hard knock upon it. Grendel cringed, praying the rosary over and over, praying that Aubrielle Grace de Witney was amply protected.

He could do nothing more now than leave her in the hands of God.

CHAPTER SIX

AFTER THE GIGGLING, the tickling, and more heated kisses that had stiffened Kenneth's loins into a rock-hard appendage, Aubrielle had fallen asleep to his warm breath against her neck. She was exhausted and, as much as he wanted to delight himself with her all night, he knew that was not in her best interest. She was new and exciting, something to explore, but he reminded himself that soon they would be married and he could spend the rest of his life exploring her. He stopped his attentions long enough for her to calm down and drift off to sleep.

Unfortunately for him, it was a mental struggle to remove himself from her bed. He did not want to leave, but he had more pressing concerns at the moment. Everett and Reid would be waiting for him, as would Lucius, and he was determined to get to the bottom of what had happened to Aubrielle. He did not relish what he would discover, concerned as to how he would react. The woman seemed to have the power to disrupt his normally rock-steady control.

But disengage himself he did. The gray dog, having ended up on the floor when Kenneth lay upon the bed, was placed back near the pillow. Strangely, he felt some comfort with the dog watching over Aubrielle. The little animal had proven to be something of a protector to her.

He looked at the dog and put his fingers to his lips in a silencing gesture. The dog wagged its tail happily, but lay down obediently as if he understood Kenneth's command. Kenneth grabbed his boots and hastened from the chamber. The toothless servant was outside of the door, sleeping on a pallet, and he gave strict orders that the lady was not to be disturbed. He did nothing more to ensure her security, confident the perpetrator was still asleep in the knight's quarters and under close guard.

He pulled on his boots and descended the dark, treacherous stairs to the main living level. The great hall was dark, the dogs near the hearth snoring in loud unison. There was a smell of smoke and must in the air. Making his way out into the dead of night, he saw that there was a weak light emitting from the knight's quarters.

Everett, Reid and Max were sitting around a well-used table with a pitcher of ale between them. A single taper lit the cramped little room, hardly big enough for more than a few men at any one time. Kenneth entered the room, startling the men from their quiet conversation.

He looked at Everett. "Did you wake him?"

Everett sighed heavily. "He's in such a drunken state that I doubt the Last Judgment would wake him. You know how he is when he gets like this, Ken. By morning he'll remember nothing."

Kenneth stared at him, reading his thoughts. Sometimes he and Everett were so in tune with one another that words were not necessary.

"It was his hose, wasn't it?"

Everett nodded slowly. "Aye. He's missing a nice little patch right above the ankle."

After a long moment of silence, it was Kenneth's turn to sigh heavily. He wiped a weary hand over his face and took a seat next to Max. The squire poured him a cup of ale and left the table. He knew he was not invited to the conversation that was sure to follow.

Kenneth took a long, healthy drink of ale, attempting to organize his thoughts. There was much to consider now that any doubts he may have harbored were erased. Everett and Reid regained their seats, watching him expectantly.

"Drunken stupor or no, he must be punished," he finally said. "It matters not that he is our captain. His offense is punishable by death."

Reid had been at Kirk longer than any of the knights, save Lucius. He knew their captain well and was probably the best one to analyze the situation.

"He's never liked her, you know that," he said quietly. "Not since he first met her and she chastised him in front of her uncle. I do not even recollect what it was about, but that set the tone. The Lady Aubrielle seems to know that she can gain the upper hand with him because he hasn't the strength to stand against someone of her caliber. Deep down, he's a weak man with a weak character. He has achieved his status in life by gaining political favor rather than by deeds or actions. The lady knows this. Though he is the captain of a mighty army, that woman sees him for what he truly is."

Kenneth listened carefully. Reid was a wise man and he respected his opinion. "Be that as it may, his assault cannot be tolerated and I care not for the reasons behind it."

"They are reasons nonetheless." Reid knew that Ken was an inordinately hard man with little division between the right and wrong of a situation. He sought to lend more of a balance to the man's decision. "Ken, the man got drunk, acted out his frustrations, and will have no recollection come the dawn. Do you really want to kill him for that?"

"What I want is not at issue. He attacked the Lady of the House."

"Understood. But I also believe you must consider that he was not in control of himself when it happened. You've known Lucius long enough to know how he is when he gets drunk."

"Do you defend what he did, then?"

"Of course not. I am simply saying that he didn't know what he was doing. He was too drunk to know."

Kenneth pursed his lips. He didn't agree with Reid's view. "Then what would you suggest? That Lady Aubrielle simply dismisses him from her service and leaves it at that?"

Reid lifted his eyebrows. "He might consider death preferable in that case," he said. "Lucius has worked hard to achieve this post. He is close to retiring. A dismissal will scar an otherwise good career."

"Christ, Reid, he scarred his good career when he attacked the Lady of Wrexham," Kenneth raised his voice in emphasis. "The law says that he should be put to death and you know it. He made the choice to ruin his career, unconscious though it might be. No one forced his hand in this."

"True enough," Reid said. "But if he is dismissed, he will see it as the Lady Aubrielle replacing him with you. He already thinks that you have gone behind his back to marry her in an attempt to gain his post."

Kenneth scowled. "Is that what he thinks? The man is insane."

"We all know that, Ken," Reid could see that the idea genuinely distressed him. In fact, this was the most passionate conversation he had ever had with Kenneth. "It simply happened to be you. Had any of us been placed in the same position you had been ordered into, she might have offered the earldom to us. It just happened to be you."

"And there is something else you should probably consider," Everett entered the conversation. "The last thing you need is for a disgraced Lucius de Cor to go to London and spread lies about you. It would scar your reputation."

Kenneth knew that Lucius was politically savvy enough to do that. "I ruin him, so he ruins me."

"Exactly. And the worst part is that he would actually believe it. There is no knowing what he would tell others, particularly those in position of command and influence."

Kenneth didn't fear damage to his reputation. But somewhere in the back of his mind, he was feeling guilty, though he wasn't sure exactly why. Lucius de Cor had always been kind to him. When he first came to Kirk, the man had been more than helpful. Maybe, unknowingly, Kenneth had somehow driven him to this. But what Reid and Everett said was true; Lucius had been a political player, not a hard-core warrior. Certainly, he would ride to battle and show a good amount of bravery at times. He was also a decisive captain. But he used Kenneth like an attack dog, to control the men and carry out his commands with an iron fist. There had been times when Kenneth had carried out duties that Lucius had taken credit for. Kenneth had not let the man's actions bother him, for he was merely the second in command and not interested in glory. He was interested in being the best knight that he could be. Lucius had taken advantage of that, and now, it was Kenneth who had the power. Lucius was understandably threatened.

"Then what would you suggest, Reid?" he finally asked. "You have known him longer than anyone. I will take your advisement."

Reid toyed with his cup. "If it was me, I would simply send him away. For as long as he remains, he will always be some manner of a threat. He can be a force to reckon with and that is a worry that you do not need. He's attacked the lady once; next time, she might not be so lucky."

Kenneth thought on that. "Send him away, but not dismiss him?"

"Send him away under pretense. Make it a job of import that will keep him away for a while. Hell, send him to London on a shopping trip. My suspicion is that once he is off and traveling, he'll not want to return. He'll resign himself, with honor, and we'll be done with him."

Kenneth considered the advice; it was sound. "Then I will invent a pretense and Lady Aubrielle will deliver it to him when he wakes from this binge. However, for the rest of us, his departure will leave a hole in the chain of command. Reid, 'tis only logical that you assume his position. Everett, you'll be in charge of the field troops, and Bradley will be in charge of the fortress personnel."

"What about you?" Everett asked. "If Reid is our new captain, then…?"

Kenneth fiddled with a crack in the table, a faint grin playing on his lips. "My good knights, I have the most difficult job of all. It will be my solemn duty to rule an earldom and keep Lady Aubrielle in check in the process. Anyone care to switch positions with me?"

Reid snorted into his cup. Everett stroked his chin thoughtfully. "She is a pretty piece of work," he said. "It might almost be worth it."

Kenneth's grin broke through, so rare that none in the room could remember when last they saw it.

"So she has you smiling, does she?" Reid prodded. "Pray tell us what she has done to warrant this from our stoic leader?"

"Let me say that she has proved to be a challenge and leave it at that." Kenneth didn't want to tell them any more than he already had.

He didn't want to look like a silly, besotted fool, which he was already dangerously close to doing. "A challenge isn't always necessarily a bad thing."

Reid held up his cup. "Then a salute to Lady Aubrielle," he said. "Long may she be a challenge to you."

Kenneth lifted his drink in response. "And God help me to live through it."

Everett snickered as he drank the toast. Kenneth drained his cup. It would have been a good night to sit and drink with men he could easily consider his friends. Still, he was not one to let people close to him, not even men he trusted with his life. He was ignoring the fact that Aubrielle was rapidly becoming an exception.

Making sure Everett was posted at Lucius door until the man awoke, he excused himself to go about his rounds before turning in for the night.

☙

WHEN HE RETURNED to Aubrielle's chamber, everything was as he had left it. Aubrielle was sleeping like the dead, the dog still lay by her head, and the fire in the hearth burned low. Kenneth stood a moment, watching her in slumber, enraptured by her beauty. He was still having difficulty accepting the turn of events over the past few days.

Not wanting to disturb her by climbing back into the bed, he sat down in the chair near the head of the bed and watched her sleep. He was still too edgy from his conversation with his knights to sleep. There was much on his mind. The dog stood up, stretched, and plopped off the side of the mattress. He watched the beast trot over to him and sit by his foot, wagging his tail. Kenneth cocked an eyebrow at the dog, finally breaking down to pet its head. There was such a surreal peace to the moment that it all seemed like a dream to him. Never in his wildest thoughts could he have imagined himself finding contentment seated beside a slumbering woman, petting her dog. But content he was, in spite of everything.

Before he could completely settle in for the night, there came a soft rap on the door. Kenneth rose to answer. Everett stood in the hall, dressed in armor.

"The sentries have spotted something," he told Kenneth. "You should come."

"It's the middle of the damn night, Everett."

"I am aware of that. But neither danger nor enemy stops for no one, not even the black of night."

Kenneth quit the chamber without another word said. It was an hour or so before dawn, the eastern horizon turning pale shades of purple and pink as they crossed the bailey and mounted the narrow turret stairs to the battlements. The walls of Kirk Castle were massive things, measuring up to twenty-five feet thick in some parts. Protection had never been a problem. Kenneth took his position on the wall as Bradley debriefed him on the latest intelligence. Since Lucius was still passed out and unable to tend to his duty at the present, Kenneth was in charge.

A large party had been sighted skulking in the shelter of the woods to the southwest. The initial sighting had been made just after midnight and Bradley has sent out a couple of scouts. The scouts had been swift and stealthy, and had returned a short time ago with news of a war party in the trees.

"Retaliation for Dinas Bran, perhaps?" Kenneth was always amazed that someone would have the gall to lay siege to Kirk. "They must not have had their fill of battle, then. We shall be happy to accommodate their request." He turned to Bradley. "Prepare for battle, Trevalyn. We have a busy day ahead of us."

Bradley had been up all night, but with the scent of war upon the wind, he was as alert as anyone. He was a seasoned knight and well acquainted with the drill that was part and parcel to siege preparation. As he handled the battlements, Everett went to rouse Reid. There were many arrangements ahead of them. A strange sense of excitement, one that was a part of their knightly blood, was in the air.

Kenneth went to the knight's quarters to don the garments he wore beneath his armor. His plate protection was stored in the armory, a large room on the second floor of the gate tower. It was his next stop with Max, and the squire helped his master dress. Kenneth's armor was more fitted than most, specially aligned pieces that fit together like a precise puzzle and left little room for intrusion. He'd had it specially made in London.

Helm under one arm, he and Max made their way back to the knight's quarters. Kenneth wanted to see if Lucius was anywhere near a coherent state. Upon finding the man snoring in his own vomit, Kenneth decided that a battle was no place for the captain. It was a disgusting spectacle, but he had seen it before. This was nothing new.

Promptly as the sun peered over the eastern horizon, the attackers let out a barrage of flaming arrows. If the Welsh had one particular battle talent, it was their deadly crossbows. Several found their way between the grates of the portcullis and rooted in the wooden gate. The majority sailed over the wall and wrought a deadly path into the bailey. Kenneth was barely missed by one up on the battlements; a few soldiers in the ward were not so lucky.

Bradley had joined Kenneth on the wall. Far below, they watched the enemy arrange loose lines and approach the walls.

"This bunch looks more organized than those fools we battled at Dinas Bran," Kenneth commented.

Bradley hadn't been at Dinas Bran and could not comment. "I would wager that Dafydd is involved. His men have always shown a remarkable amount of discipline."

"And Dafydd is not afraid of throwing a volley at us."

"Surely he can't be thinking to invade Kirk. He's tried before and failed."

Kenneth shook his head slowly, watching the approaching lines. "This is an action designed to rattle us. He's angry that we overran Dinas Bran. This is no invasion force, I assure you, but we must be on guard today."

"Agreed," Bradley took a last look at the enemy lines. "I shall pass the word for the archers. Today will be a war of arrows, I should think."

"Tell everyone to watch their heads," Kenneth called after him.

The soldiers of Kirk were all business. The scent of battle was in the air and they inhaled the heady brew. Bradley organized nearly three hundred archers upon the walls and a group in the bailey, and the deadly projectiles flew over the walls into the approaching Welsh. They responded by releasing another shower of arrows, worse than the first.

Shortly after sunrise, the earth and air of Kirk was full of fire, smoke, and death.

ଓ

AUBRIELLE WOKE TO the smell of smoke. Rubbing the sleep from her eyes, she rolled over on the dog and was rewarded with puppy licks to the face. She giggled and struggled to get away from the happy kisses. With effort, she sat up, rubbing her sore belly. It was painful, but bearable, and certainly nothing like it had been the night before. A heavy, peaceful sleep had done her a world of good.

It took her a moment to realize that Kenneth was not in the room. Disappointment settled. She thought that he would at least be seated in a chair, patiently waiting for her to awaken. But she was quite alone in the chamber, save the dog. He wagged his tail happily when she looked at him. She patted his head and went in search of her clothes.

Rising from the bed was a strain. Her stomach muscles were bruised; in fact, her entire body was stiff and sore. Aubrielle tried to shake it off as she went for her massive trunk. Lifting the top with a groan, she began to rummage through the garments her mother had so carefully packed for her. She wanted to find something pretty so that Kenneth would find her pleasing to look at. She smirked at her foolish thoughts, laughing at the ridiculous idea of caring what a man thought of her. Then she sobered, feeling like an idiot, knowing that Kenneth's approval had come to matter something to her.

She pulled out a simple garment of burgundy linen and an equally simple matching shift. The bodice of the gown had laces that cinched up her waist as tightly as a trussed-up warhorse. They were front-laces and she was able to do it herself. She'd done for years without the aid of a personal maid and didn't feel the need to begin now even though Kirk had servants everywhere.

As she ran her horse-hair brush through her brown tresses, she caught another whiff of smoke. It was strong and distinct. Curious, she peered from the lancet window in her room. The window faced northeast, away from the main portion of the bailey and overlooking the green hills of distant Wrexham and Shropshire. The smoke was heavier here and she pressed forward, sticking her head out of the window to see if she could see anything below. She was startled to see busy men with weapons and loaded crossbows on the battlements.

It did not take a great military genius to realize that something was amiss. It occurred to her that the reason Kenneth had not been in her room at dawn was because there was a battle going on. It wasn't strange that she hadn't heard anything, considering the walls of Kirk's keep were several feet thick and she was four stories above the ground. She raced for her shoes, unable to find them until she looked under the bed and found them shoved beneath. Holding her aching gut, she fled the room.

She took the narrow stairs too quickly and nearly tripped. The serving wench, having heard the mistress, scurried down the stairs after her. The sounds in the great hall drew her attention first, and she was shocked to see a few dozen men lying on the cold stone floor, wounded, dead or dying.

The seriousness of what was transpiring began to settle. Aubrielle's heart was pounding in her throat, from revulsion and shock, as she observed the carnage. Her uncle's majordomo was tending a man near the wall; she caught his attention.

"What is going on here?" she demanded.

He was an old man, with white hair and a spry manner. He stood up from where he had been tending a man's wounded shoulder.

"An attack at dawn, my lady," he said. "The Welsh have come to rattle our cage."

Her expression was grave. "Why was I not notified before now? Why did I have to come down and discover this… this travesty on my own?"

"Sir Kenneth left word that you not be disturbed, my lady," the man said. "He said that you had had a difficult night and were ill."

Half of her was furious with Kenneth, but the other half of her understood his reasons. Apparently, no one knew that she had been attacked. She supposed that Kenneth had his reasons for not telling anyone, but she could not imagine what those reasons were. For the moment, she was speechless, and the majordomo watched her anxiously.

"Are you feeling better, my lady?" he asked her.

She had been staring at a man with an arrow through his thigh several feet away. The majordomo's question startled her from her morose thoughts.

"Indeed," she replied, wanting off the subject of herself. "I would like to help. Where is the physic?"

The majordomo pointed; near the hearth, Aubrielle spied Argus tending a man with a bone sticking out of his arm. Before she took a step, she passed a lingering glance to the majordomo; she'd seen him every time she had been at Kirk but realized that she did not know his name. She felt a bit ashamed she had never thought to care. Now he served her and she didn't even know who he was.

"What is your name?"

"Arbosa, my lady," he bowed his head.

"Thank you, Arbosa."

"My pleasure, my lady."

She made her way to the little physic. He was hunched over, struggling to set the broken arm. Small though he was, he had man-sized arms and hands, and considerable strength to go with them. She stood over the old man.

"I should like to help," she said. "What may I do?"

Argus looked up at her, somewhat surprised to see that she was moving about. He wiped his forehead with the back of his hand. "I thought I told you to stay in bed and rest, m'lady."

"Aye, you did. But I feel better and it looks as if you can use my assistance."

"I have enough help for now."

She lifted an eyebrow at him. "I can be of more assistance than the others, I assure you. I learned something of the art of healing at St. Wenburgh."

"This isn't the art of healing, m'lady; this is war."

"But I can help. You must let me."

The bone that Argus was setting snapped back with a sickening sound. Aubrielle wasn't as strong as she liked to pretend; she swallowed the bile in her throat. The little physic wrapped the limb quickly and efficiently.

"Do what you can, then," he said. "I shall not argue the point with you."

He moved on to the next wounded man and Aubrielle stood there a moment, gathering her thoughts. Though the sight of blood made her nauseous, she felt it was her duty to assist. She'd committed herself and there was no turning back. The toothless wench was still hovering near her and she sent the woman for hot water, ale, needle, thread, and whatever bandages she could find.

Aubrielle's indoctrination into the position as Lady of Kirk wasn't as she had imagined. There were no gracious heroics on her part. It was a brutal, revealing experience. The first man she tried to help had a belly wound that had his guts protruding from a hole in his side. She came close to fainting as she struggled to push the innards back into the stomach cavity and sew up the hole. The serving wench helped somewhat and Aubrielle was grateful to see that the woman had steady hands. In the end, she didn't think she had done a very good job of sewing, but the wound stayed closed and the guts, in. She would have liked to have stopped at that one but she could not. She forced herself to move on to the next injured man.

Thankfully, the next few were relatively minor. It gave her some confidence. Then, they brought a young archer in that had lost his footing and fallen from the battlements. He was alert, but had no feeling from the shoulders down. Argus took one look at him and consigned his fate to God; the man had broken his neck and death was imminent. The lad was so very young, and so very frightened. Never once, however, did he cry out or ask for help. She couldn't bring herself to abandon him even as the physic moved away.

"Where are you going?" she hissed to the little man.

He shook his head. "I cannot help him, m'lady. There is nothing to be done."

She grabbed the man by the arm to stop him. "Will you not even try?"

"Try what?" he asked. "His nerves are severed. The fall saw to that. He cannot move, his breathing will fail, and he will be dead before night fall."

Aubrielle was appalled at his lack of effort. "So you are content to simply do nothing and watch him die?" she demanded. "How can you be so cruel?"

Argus could see she was working herself up over something he'd seen too many times. "I am not being cruel, I assure you," he softened a bit. "There were times when I would spend all of my energy and knowledge trying to save those who cannot be saved. If I spend my time trying to save this lad, knowing full well that he will die in spite of my efforts, some of those around here who I do have a chance of saving may perish. 'Tis a tough choice, I agree, but I have to make the wiser decision."

Aubrielle let go of his arm and watched him shuffle off. Even though he made sense, she was sure he was wrong. The lad was alert and talking; surely, he must be salvageable.

But the youth's countenance was changing. Even though she'd only spent a relatively few number of minutes with him, she could see the transformation in his pallor. He had gone from a healthy pink to an odd shade of gray. Aubrielle noticed that his breathing was very erratic. It seemed to her that the young man was suffocating because of his injury. When the lad noticed that she was staring at him, he smiled weakly.

"With your help, I am sure that I will be well again, my lady," he said in a strangely weak voice.

Aubrielle forced a smile and knelt beside him. "I shall do my best," she said. "What is your name?"

"Halla, my lady," he replied.

"Is that Welsh?"

"Nordic, my lady."

"Then you are from the north lands?"

"Nay, but my parents were. Now they live here, at Kirk."

"In what capacity?"

"My father is a smith. My mother takes care of my daughter."

"Oh? What of your wife?"

"She has passed on."

He was struggling to talk, to breathe. Aubrielle could see he was fading. She felt a sense of panic; she could not allow the young man to die without attempting to help him. She had to help him breathe. Making a fist, she pushed it deep into his stomach. The boy exhaled sharply. Pulling her fist up, his lungs automatically inflated. She did it again and again, until the boy actually appeared as if he was gaining enough air.

He smiled gratefully. "Th-thank you, my lady."

She smiled in return. "That is the first time someone has thanked me for punching them in the stomach."

He opened his mouth in a silent laugh. "I feel… better."

Aubrielle could not see the long term. She could only see the short. He was alive now and she wanted to keep him that way. She continued to push on the youth's belly, helping him breathe. It took her completely out of circulation, as she was unable to help anyone else. The hours passed and she continued to push and release, push and release, only to be spelled by the serving wench who insisted that her mistress take some nourishment.

She had no idea how long she had been breathing for the boy. Even though her own muscles were screaming, she ignored them and kept pressing forward. She didn't even realize when the great room dimmed as the sun set, and the servants lit the fat tapers that would cast off a weak, smoky glow. The lad slipped into unconsciousness but still, she kept pushing. As night fell, the great hall became a spooky, pain-filled place.

She was exhausted but refused to give up. This was the long term she had not thought about. The lad hadn't been conscious for several hours but the serving wench seated by his head kept telling her mistress that his pulse was strong. Hair askew, arms and body aching, Aubrielle gradually noticed a pair of massive boots standing just off to the left of her. She had no idea how long they had been there; she'd never even heard them. She looked up, her silken tresses hanging in her eyes, to see Kenneth standing there.

He looked none the worse for wear. He just stood there, gazing down at her, with a strangely gentle expression on his face. Argus had told him everything when he'd entered the hall a few minutes earlier. Then he had just stood there and watched her. Never in his life had he seen a more compassionate act and it tugged at his heart to know what the eventual outcome would be, no matter how hard she worked to save him.

"Is the battle over?" she asked.

"For the moment," he replied.

His gaze moved from her to the boy and back again. She could read his thoughts. "He will die if I stop," she said.

He took a long, slow breath. Kneeling beside her, he watched her push and release, push and release. It struck him as the saddest thing he'd ever seen.

"Unless you plan to do this for the rest of your life, I am afraid he is going to die no matter what you do," he said softly. "It is his time, Aubrielle. Although your efforts have been heroic, you must let him go."

She slowed but did not stop. She was staring at the young man's face. "How can I?" she whispered. "His name is Halla. His wife is dead and he has a little daughter. If he dies, his child will lose both parents."

"War is cruel, on those who fight it and those they leave behind. I wish I could tell you that he will awake and hold his daughter in his arms once again, but he will not. He is slipping. Only your strength of will is holding him here. You must not be strong anymore. You must let him go."

A sob escaped her lips. She struggled against another one, but before long, she was weeping. Her pushing slowed to a complete stop. Kenneth pulled her up and swept her into his arms. He didn't care if his men saw him or not.

"You did your best, my lady," he whispered. "He would have died a much more painful death had you not made his last moments more comfortable."

She wrapped her tired arms around his neck and held him tightly, as if afraid she would slip off, perhaps follow the young man into the jaws of death. She'd seen so much of it this afternoon that she realized death was a very easy thing to come by. The years at St. Wenburgh had protected her from that reality.

Kenneth mounted the stairs and took her back to her chamber. Even when the door closed softly, he continued to stand in the middle of the room and hold her. Two days ago, he was holding this woman because he had been ordered to. Now he was holding her because he so very desperately wanted to. As he sat on her bed, his lips against her forehead, the day they had met seemed like a million years ago.

He reclined against the pillows. Aubrielle was limp and warm and soft, and he wished that he did not have his armor on. It must be exceptionally uncomfortable for her, but more than that, he wanted to feel her against him. He'd never in his life actually wanted to feel a woman against him for emotional reasons. But Aubrielle had awakened something within him that was struggling to be let loose.

The little dog lay beside them, his chin on Aubrielle's leg. She was so still and quiet that Kenneth thought she may have fallen asleep. He, too, was able to relax for the first time that day. But she suddenly sat up, startling both him and the dog.

"My castle," she said. "How did it fare in the siege?"

He smiled inwardly at "my castle". "No damage to report to the walls or stone structures. The flaming arrows managed to cause minor damage to the front gates and to some of the structures inside the bailey, but nothing that cannot be easily repaired."

She pushed the hair from her eyes. "And you?"

"My lady?"

She gestured at him. "Are you undamaged, too?"

He smiled faintly. "I am."

Now she looked serious, her sea-colored eyes boring into him. "This was my first battle."

"I see," he could have guessed that from her reaction to the wounded. "I would have never known. Your bravery was astounding."

She looked away, flattered, modest. She reached out to absently stroke the puppy's back. "Not very much, it wasn't. But I do thank you for your gracious lie."

His smile broadened. "If you haven't a taste for battle, I would not worry overly. They are few and far between out here."

"That's not true. The day I came here, you were returning from battle. And now, two days later, we have another."

"This is not the usual, I assure you."

She rose from his lap, pacing over to a long, thin table that held a pitcher and some cups. The dog jumped off the bed and followed her. She poured two measures of honeyed wine, handing one to Kenneth. He didn't like honeyed wine, but he took it from her anyway.

"You have been fighting battles for many years, have you not?" she asked him.

He nodded. "I saw my first battle at ten years of age. I was a squire and my master decided it was time to take me into battle rather than leave me at camp."

Her face tightened with concern. "But you were so young."

Kenneth's ice blue eyes grew distant with the memory. "My master served the earl of Cumbria, on the Scottish borders. My first introduction into battle was against none other than William Wallace himself."

Aubrielle had heard of the Scots hero. The monks used to speak of him and his blasphemous fight against the English.

"It must have been a fearsome experience."

"It was. Wallace's men fought and died for him like rabid dogs. If nothing else, battling the Scots taught me the true meaning of loyalty. I admired Wallace's ability to garner that."

"You admire a rebel?"

Kenneth looked at her, knowing she had only heard the English version of the battle for Scotland's independence. He had seen it all first hand.

"Wallace was a patriot," he said simply. "If England was under occupation, I cannot say that I would so easily accept it without putting up a fight. Wallace did what any good Scot would do; he resisted. But he was blinded by his patriotic ambitions. He did not have the experience to realize that he had neither the support of the Scottish barons nor the strength of arms to accomplish this against Edward Longshanks."

Aubrielle took a sip of her drink, sitting on the bed beside him. "But he died a traitor's death. He was captured and killed for his resistance. Though you admire a man's ability to earn his countrymen's loyalties, do you also admire the futility of his convictions?"

He sat there, gazing at her lovely face, his mind churning up memories he had long forgotten. "I admire the man's strength. His convictions would not have been futile had they succeeded."

"You speak as if you see nothing wrong with rebellion and treachery."

He set the cup aside, his manner calm and quiet. "My lady, I am as loyal to England as any man alive and more so. You see, when I was fifteen, my master, a knight by the name of Sir Bretton de Touvier, was sent to Scotland on a secret mission to rendezvous with another knight by the name of Sir John de Menteith. De Menteith's liege was the earl of Moray, a man loyal to England. I was present when de Menteith and my master, among others, captured Wallace under a guise of truce. I was also there when Wallace was drawn and quartered. I myself took his right arm to Newcastle-upon-Tyne, where it was mounted on the main bridge for all to see. It is something I shall always remember, etched into my memory as if it had been permanently burned there. I watched my master and those men loyal to Edward betray Wallace, who had come to them with trust. At fifteen, I was very impressionable. It is something I shall never forget."

Aubrielle's eyes were brimming with surprise and horror. She remembered thinking, once, how hard Kenneth was behind those ice-blue eyes, as if something horrible had happened to him once that still lingered, still hardened him. It was something he could not let go. Perhaps this was part of it.

"And you were a party to all of it."

He nodded. "I did what I was ordered to do and what needed to be done. So you see, my lady, my loyalty to England is beyond question. I have proven myself to the degree where the king himself prizes my services. When I said I admired Wallace's ability to garner loyalty, I simply meant that it is every man's desire to earn such devotion from his men. It has always been my desire to emulate Wallace's ability, no matter what the man's political allegiances."

Somehow, a light conversation had taken a heady turn. Aubrielle was amazed at Kenneth's past, one he spoke of frankly, without arrogance. Though she was more than curious, it seemed to her that he did not wish to delve further into that period in his life. Though he spoke openly, it seemed to her that deep down, talk of it disturbed him.

"Well," she sought to change the subject. "I can truthfully say that, as your wife, you will have my loyalty."

His grin returned. "Loyalty, aye. But will I have your obedience as well?"

"What do you think?"

He shook his head as if horrified by the thought. "I think that I am in a good deal of trouble."

She cocked an admonishing eyebrow. "Come, now, sir knight. We are not afraid of a woman, are we?"

He folded his massive arms across his chest, protectively. "Perhaps," he said coyly. "I would rather face a thousand battles like the one today than just one battle with you."

Her expression sobered. "And I would rather you not fight in any more battles at all. The thought of you lying wounded like those men in the great hall..."

She trailed off, realizing she sounded like a fool. She tried to rise, but he clamped a big hand over her arm and would not let her stand.

"Finish your sentence."

"No."

"Finish it."

She tried to free her arm, but it was useless. "I was going to say that the thought of you lying wounded like those men in the great hall fills me with enormous joy because by virtue of some great gaping wound, you'll cease to be a thorn in my side."

She said it far too dramatically to be convincing. Kenneth smiled at her, his grip on her arm loosening. But he did not let her go completely. He gave a good tug and she fell forward, against his chest. He enfolded her in his great arms, gazing down into her face as a mother would when cradling her child.

"Your concern is touching, my lady," he murmured.

His face was an inch above hers. Gazing into his ice blue eyes, Aubrielle found it difficult to breathe. She also found that his proximity loosened her tongue tremendously.

"After we are married, do you plan to go to war again?" she asked breathlessly.

"I am a knight. If there is a war that concerns me, then I must fight it."

"But… but what if I did not want you to go to war ever again? What if I'd rather have you here, with me?"

"You'd rather have me fighting a war here, with you?"

She scowled. "You are impossible! That is not what I meant and you know it."

He laughed softly. "I know it. But I want to hear you say it."

She growled in frustration. "Let me up, you baboon. I shall not say anything remotely nice to you ever again."

He snorted as she struggled. "You are not going anywhere, my lady. Would it help if I say it for you?"

"By all means, go right ahead. Make a fool of yourself if it suits you."

"Very well," he cleared his throat. "You were going to say that the past two days has seen you fall madly, hopelessly in love with me and you cannot bear the thought of my being killed in battle. You would, therefore, prefer it if I never go to war again and remain here at Kirk, safely confined within her massive walls."

She stopped in her struggles, looking at him with the biggest eyes he had ever seen. His smile faded.

"What? Did I say something wrong?"

She swallowed hard. "What if I told you that you said everything right?"

☙

"I DO NOT recollect anything," Lucius looked horrible. "Why do you ask?"

Reid and Everett had corralled the man into the great hall to access the wounded from the brief skirmish with the Welsh. He had been given a tally of twenty-two wounded and six dead. Lucius was less concerned for the battle he missed and the injured or dead men than he was for the pounding in his head.

"Simple curiosity, my lord," Everett passed a long glance at Reid. "We tried to wake you up for the battle, but you would not respond. We were simply curious if you remembered anything at all since last night."

Lucius ran his fingers through his dark, dirty hair. He coughed and spit onto the stones by the hearth. It was apparent that he did not wish to respond to their question.

"Where is Kenneth?"

"The lady took the battle hard, my lord," Reid said. "He is attempting to calm her."

Lucius gave them a wry expression. "He spends a great deal of time attempting to calm her, does he not?"

"He was ordered to, if you recall," Reid replied.

Lucius only grunted. Disinterested in the wounded in the hall, he quit the room and was proceeding to the door of the keep when he nearly bumped into Kenneth, coming down the stairs. Lucius stepped back, startled by his second's appearance.

"Christ, Kenneth," he put his hand over his startled heart. "I did not hear you coming."

Kenneth's gaze was characteristically icy. "I see that you are feeling better, my lord."

"Indeed," Lucius eyed him. "I hear our lady was disturbed by the battle. I trust she is feeling better as well."

"Being at a monastery the majority of her life has afforded her little experience in the brutal realities of the world," Kenneth replied. "She will recover."

Lucius looked up the steps, as if he could see the lady in her chamber beyond. "I suppose, as her captain, I should make my presence known to her this eve and assure her all is well."

"I have already done that, my lord," Kenneth said.

Lucius' manner cooled. "I am sure that you have, Ken. However, I am still the captain of Kirk's troops. I would like to tend the lady myself."

"I understand, my lord, but the lady has retired for the evening. Perhaps tomorrow morning would be a better time."

It was not a request and they all knew it. Lucius stared at Kenneth; it was an ominous glance. "Then perhaps my knights will gather in the knight's quarters so that we may debrief after this battle," he said icily. "That is, of course, if I may still issue such a command."

The power struggle was obvious now. Kenneth would not respond to the challenge. "You are the captain, my lord. Your commands will be obeyed."

Without another word, Lucius turned back to the dark, quiet cavern of the great hall. Reid, casting Kenneth a long glance, departed for the bailey. Only Everett lingered behind with Kenneth. When Lucius was out of earshot, he turned to Kenneth.

"He doesn't recollect a damn thing," he said quietly. "Worse than that, he is not the least bit concerned that we had a skirmish with the Welsh and he was not coherent enough to lead our defenses."

Kenneth's gaze lingered on the open door, the dusk outside. "I sense his commitment to duty is failing since our lord's death."

"And Lady Aubrielle's appearance," Everett put in. "It is as if I am watching a candle blow out; one moment the light is on, then comes a wind and it slowly fades to nothingness. Lucius is heading for nothingness."

Kenneth thought the analogy rather appropriate, but in his case, it was just the opposite. His candle was turning into a roaring flame by the appearance of Lady Aubrielle. "Then he is condemning himself. No one has pushed him to it."

"Perhaps; but he makes it clear that he considers you a threat. Perhaps he feels that you, in fact, are pushing him."

"I will clear the air with him, have no doubt. Meanwhile, he is not allowed anywhere near Lady Aubrielle. Is that understood?"

Everett was forced to agree. "Have you told her yet who her attacker was?"

"Not yet," Kenneth replied. "It is not something I intend to blurt out, and it's not yet been the right time to mention it. But she will know; she has to. We must get Lucius out of Kirk as soon as possible."

Everett nodded in concurrence. They continued their conversation out into the night. Shortly, a sentry entered the keep and mounted the steps, taking position outside of Lady Aubrielle's room.

଼

LUCIUS HAD NO idea why he had come back to the great hall that smelled of rot and dying men; he was supposed to be heading for the knight's quarters for the debriefing. All he knew was that he had to get away from Kenneth to clear his mind and he had ended up here.

Kenneth was attempting to destroy him; he could see that now. Never in his tenure at Kirk had he felt so much as a mild threat from the man. In truth, he had always felt empowered by him. Now, the addition of Lady Aubrielle had changed that. Lucius was forced to admit that his orders to Kenneth to watch the woman had started the wheels of his destruction in motion.

It was collapsing, his world. He could see it. And his knights were siding with Kenneth. He no longer enjoyed their support. When the earl was alive, Lucius had been able to hold the reins of power oh-so-tightly. The earl had trusted him. But the new countess, Lady Aubrielle, did not.

Discouraged, frustrated, he wandered deep into the hall, oblivious to the injured and dying around him. In his oblivion, he accidentally kicked a man with a broken leg. The man groaned, and Lucius stopped.

His deep eyes were hard. "Watch where you lie."

"Forgive, m'lord. This is where they put me."

Lucius' gaze lingered on him. He felt the need for a confrontation to exorcise his frustration with Kenneth. "I do not know you, and I know every man in Kirk's army. Who are you?"

"I… I am not a soldier, m'lord. I had an accident before the battle started. I was here to seek help when they closed the gates and sealed me in. My companion as well."

Lucius' focus traveled between the man with the broken leg and his associate with a huge knot on his forehead. They didn't look like typical soldiers, or peasants for that matter. They had an odd, dark look about them.

"Where are you from?"

"London."

"What is your purpose at Kirk?"

"We…we are traveling men."

"How do you make your way?"

The questions were coming rapid-fire, filled with suspicion. The man with the broken leg, Thomas from de Gaul's troupe, struggled to keep his answers even and deliberate. This was attention he had never expected and certainly did not want; de Gaul would be furious with him for being so conspicuous. His instructions had been to keep silent and watch for the lady. Now, those plans were quickly falling into jeopardy.

"We are hired by nobles for tasks they may require," he said steadily. "We are men of enterprise."

Lucius' gaze narrowed. "Mercenaries," he hissed. "I knew it. How did you get in here?"

"We are not mercenaries, m'lord, I swear it. We are honest men."

"Pah," Lucius kicked Thomas' bad leg again, asserting his dominance. "You are no more honest men than those idiot Welsh who attacked us. What do you want here?"

"I told you; my companion and I were injured and…."

"That's not true, at least, not the way you explain it. I know your type; you were probably set upon by your brother thieves and left to die. You are all a bunch of thieving, traitorous cutthroats."

"No, m'lord, I swear it."

Lucius stood over him, his dark eyes brimming with ill intent. Thomas knew that he was breathing his last, suspecting that the knight was about to run him through and throw him to the dogs. It was always thus with thieves and outlaws. He was disappointed they had been discovered so soon, yet death at the hands of the knight would be far better than death at the hands of de Gaul. He cringed, waiting for the inevitable blow; but then a strange thing occurred.

Lucius' expression had changed from one of suspicion to one of thoughtfulness. His body relaxed and his gaze moved between the two men, assessing them, determining if they were worthy of the thoughts he was entertaining. The longer he stood there, the more enlightened his expression became. He took a step closer and lowered his voice.

"Are you good at what you do?"

"I do not understand m'lord."

"Aye, you indeed understand me completely. I know what you are, you little fool. Do not deny it. You speak in riddles, just as you have been trained to do in order to survive. Now tell me; are you good at what you do?"

Strangely, the man with the broken leg sensed something other than murderous thoughts. It was an unexpected turn of events. He sensed an opening to possibly take advantage of.

"We are very good at what we do."

Lucius' expression continued to cool. "Do you take to the task of... eradication?"

"Animal, friend or foe?"

"Most definitely foe."

"And this would be a threat to your life, no doubt."

"Who said this had anything to do with me?"

"No one, m'lord."

Thomas held Lucius gaze for a long, heady moment. The playing field was suddenly leveled and the sides seemed to be equal. Thomas understood what the knight was saying and the knight's gaze was audaciously honest. Thomas sensed no collusion in an attempt to trap him, only a genuine sense of foul intent. The man he was staring at had a heart as black as death.

"Tell me what it is you need, and with whom, m'lord," he said quietly. "Will this accomplishment also include safe passage from this place once the task is complete?"

"Of course."

"No offense, m'lord, but how can we be sure?"

"I am Lucius de Cor, Captain of Kirk's army. You have my word."

"Then we await your instructions, m'lord."

"You shall have them."

"Aye, m'lord."

"One more thing."

"What is that?"

"If you mention this to anyone, I shall deny everything and kill you before you can move beyond these walls. Have no doubt."

Thomas smiled, his pale eyes glittering. "Men such as myself do not survive long in my business if we are untrustworthy, Captain. This contract is strictly private."

Lucius quit the hall some time later, congratulating himself on his excellent fortune. Only by pure chance did he happen upon the answer to his problems and he silently thanked God for directing him to the injured men in the hall. He was positive it had been divine intervention. God was showing him the way to save himself.

The next move was at hand.

CHAPTER SEVEN

THE DEBRIEFING AFTER the Welsh attack had been a nightmare. Lucius had been combative and defensive while Kenneth and the knights attempted to review the battle, the strategies, the force behind it, and the potential for a retaliatory offensive. The affair had gone well into the night. The siege review notwithstanding, it was reiterated between Kenneth and the other knights that Lucius needed to be constantly watched until they could send him away from Kirk. Under no circumstances was he to be anywhere near the Lady Aubrielle. Kenneth retired somewhere after midnight, resisting the urge to go to Aubrielle, thinking he needed to spend the night alone to more clearly organize his thoughts.

There was so much on his mind that he had no idea where to begin. He didn't know how long he lay there, staring at the ceiling, thinking of the last conversation he and Aubrielle shared. Never would he have imagined that she could have fallen in love with him. But she said that she had, and then she had gone to sit by the hearth and cry. Kenneth was so surprised that he had been rendered speechless. But he knew, without question, that he felt the same way about her. As insane as it sounded, he knew it was the truth. But he couldn't bring himself to tell her. He was terrified. So he had abandoned the chamber without another word and left her sitting by the hearth, weeping.

He felt horrible for running out on her. He wanted to go back to her, beg forgiveness for running off like an idiot, and tell her that he adored her. Aye, she was stubborn, belligerent, headstrong and opinionated, but she was also sweet, charming, intelligent, and compassionate. He had come to see the good in her far outweighed the bad. Even her bad qualities had their charm.

He knew he would never get any sleep unless he told her how he felt. To the Devil with his fear; if she was brave enough to confess her innermost feelings, then he should be brave as well. Most men viewed emotion as a weakness; in faith, Kenneth had never felt so strong. It was as if Aubrielle had planted something deep within him that fed his soul. She deserved to know.

It was a couple of hours before dawn when he finally rose, donned his heavy leather trousers, tunic and boots, and ventured out into the night. The moon was full, bathing the landscape in a ghostly glow. He saw Reid up on the battlements with the night watch and he gave the man a half-handed wave. Everything was peaceful, the Welsh having limped back over the border to lick their wounds.

Kenneth took the first step on the wooden stairs leading into the keep when a piercing whistle sounded from the wall watch. He paused, watching the men scurry to their posts.

Reid called down to him.

"Our messenger," he shouted. "Returning from Highwood House."

Kenneth moved for the gates as the massive wooden panels were slowly cranked open to the sound of grating iron chains. The portcullis was down and that, too, was laboriously raised. The rider, bearing the scarlet, green and gold of Wrexham, spurred his lathered horse into the bailey.

Kenneth knew the messenger; he had seen many years of loyal service. The man was clearly exhausted as he yanked the steed to a halt and practically fell from the saddle. Kenneth reached out to steady the excited horse.

"What is so important that has you arriving home in the middle of the night?" he asked. "Surely, not all the local inns were full?"

The man rocked unsteadily with fatigue. His uniform was dirty, his face lined with sweat even in the night air. "Nay, my lord," he replied. "I could not stop to rest. I bear important news."

"What is it?"

The rider took a moment to catch his breath. "I bear bad tidings, my lord. Highwood House is gone."

"What do you mean gone?"

"Destroyed by fire."

Kenneth's brow furrowed. "What in the hell happened?"

"I am not entirely sure, my lord. What few witnesses there were seemed afraid to speak. I could not locate any of the house servants at all. It seems that everyone has scattered."

An ominous sense of dread filled Kenneth. "What of Lady Graciela de Witney?"

"There were two corpses in the ruins, my lord. The villeins told me that Lady Graciela was one of them."

By this time, Reid had joined Kenneth. The two knights looked at each other as the news sank in. This was unexpected, to say the least. Kenneth finally turned away, his expression tight. Reid had never seen Kenneth in any mode other than one of complete control and it was disconcerting to see him react to something as ordinary as death.

"Are you sure it was Lady Graciela?" Reid pressed the messenger. "Did you see the body?"

The man shook his head. "One of the groomsmen told me it was her, my lord. I would not recognize Lady Graciela on sight, but the man showed me the hand of one of the corpses. It was unburned. Upon it was this."

He pulled out a pouch from his vest and removed a small ring. It was an uncut emerald, oval shaped, surrounded by diamonds. He handed it to Reid, who in turn, handed it to Kenneth. Kenneth stared at it until Reid spoke.

"I am sure the daughter can confirm if this belonged to her mother," he suggested quietly.

Kenneth sighed heavily, closing his fist around the ring. But the messenger wasn't finished with his report.

"There is more, my lords," he said. "Some of the peasants told me that before the fire, there were several strange men at Highwood House."

More intrigue peppered the pot. "Did anyone know of their purpose?" Kenneth asked.

"As I said, most I spoke with were afraid to speak of much more," the messenger replied. "But the groomsman seemed to think they were looking for something. Out of fear, he hid in the barn but overheard them speaking of a scroll."

For some reason, the word rang in Kenneth's head. A scroll. Something told him that whatever the strange men's purpose, Aubrielle might have some connection to it. Only she would have knowledge or possession of such a thing. Wasn't Aubrielle the type to have a scroll lying about, something she had collected from St. Wenburgh? It wasn't out of the realm of possibility. But what fiend would kill innocent people for something as simple as a piece of vellum? Unless, of course, it was a valuable piece. Perhaps one that contained important information….

He didn't like the thought in the least. The mere idea was enough to set him on edge.

"Did the villeins say that the men burned down the house and killed Lady Graciela?" he asked.

The messenger shrugged. "That was the inference, my lord."

Kenneth had heard enough. He turned towards the keep. Reid sent the messenger to the kitchens for some food and caught up to Kenneth.

"Do you want me to do this?" he asked.

They mounted the wooden steps to the keep. "Nay," Kenneth said quietly. "I shall do it."

"Are you well, Ken?"

"I am."

"Then I shall accompany you. From what we know of the Lady Aubrielle, she's likely to fly into a rage and put your eye out. You'll need protection."

Kenneth came to an abrupt halt, a harsh retort on his lips. It was a great effort to refrain and realize that all the knights knew of Lady Aubrielle was a poker to Everett's head and a head-butt to Kenneth's lip. They knew nothing of the soft, sweet creature he had come to know of the past few days.

"That is not necessary," he said. "I shall be fine."

"You are sure?"

"Aye."

Reid let him go, being astute enough to realize that his superior officer wanted to go it alone. There was something occurring between Kenneth and Lady Aubrielle, far more than St. Héver was willing to let on. This was more than duty. He'd heard about the incident in the great hall the day before, how St. Héver had swept her off her feet and carried her away. The entire castle had heard of it. Kenneth St. Héver was the last man anyone of them would have imagined to show any measure of kindness for another human being, and particularly a woman. It had to be lust and nothing more.

Little did Reid know that lust had less to do with it than he could have imagined. Kenneth wished it was only lust; it would have been easier to satisfy. He carried the ring up to Aubrielle's bower, pausing at the door long enough to dismiss the sentry. He stood there a moment in the dark, wondering if he should let her sleep and wait until morning to inform her of her mother's passing. But it would only be delaying the inevitable.

He opened her door silently. The room was dark except for the glow of the embers in the hearth. The little dog, lying on the bed, suddenly leapt up and ran to him, teeth barred and growling. Kenneth whispered something to the dog and it immediately settled. Then he patted the dog on the head, grateful for the vicious little sentry.

In her sleep, Aubrielle stirred. Kenneth went to stand beside the bed, gazing down at her beautiful face softly illuminated by the firelight. He was deeply sorry that he had left her earlier, afraid to say what was in his heart, confused that a woman so beautiful and wise should have feelings for him. After two days, how could they possibly know what they felt for one another? Kenneth only knew that he did feel, as surely as God had put him upon this earth.

He put a big hand on her forehead, stroking her hair. "Aubrielle," he murmured. "Wake up."

She stirred again but did not awaken. Kenneth leaned down, planting a gentle kiss on her slumbering lips. She tasted so good that he gave her another. With the third lingering kiss, she grew lucid enough to put her arms around his neck. She responded to him hungrily and Kenneth lost all sense of control.

His tongue plunged into her mouth and his arms went about her fiercely. He lifted her out of the bed and at the same time fell into it. Somehow, Aubrielle ended up on top of him and he held her tightly, one arm around her while the other hand snaked into her hair. He kissed her hard and furiously, his mouth moving all over her face, tasting every inch of her. When he moved to her neck, she gasped, and he rolled her onto her back. His heavy body half-covered her, half-smothered her into the mattress, but Aubrielle did not seem to care.

"Kenneth, my love," she murmured feverishly. "I thought you had left me forever. I thought you would never return."

He was kissing her collarbone, his fingers pulling back the top of her nightshift to allow him more skin to feast upon.

"Never," he growled. "I will never leave you, Aubrielle, for as long as I live. I swear it."

"I am sorry if I upset you."

"You did not upset me. You have made me the happiest man in the world."

In the darkness, she smiled sleepily, feeling his weight and warmth upon her. His fingers had unlaced her shift and had pulled it down to her waist. Her breasts, smooth and round and soft, were exposed. Kenneth's hot mouth moved down her chest and between the luscious swells before taking in a peaked nipple. Aubrielle gasped with the newness of it. He held her fast while his mouth worked its magic.

Aubrielle had never known the touch of a man. From loose-lipped servants, she had heard tales of sexual exploits, and from her mother she had been told of a wife's duty. But none of those tales did justice to what Kenneth was doing to her. As he suckled and touched, she felt gentle fingers flutter across her Venus mound. He stroked her carefully, acquainting her with his touch. She was nervous at first, but Kenneth's gentle attentions quickly eased her.

His mouth left her breasts and moved to her stomach. It had been so long since Kenneth had tasted a woman that his control was very fragile. He didn't want to frighten her, nor did he want to do anything they would both regret later, but the fact remained that he wanted her in the worst way. He tried to walk the fine line between propriety and his rights as her intended.

He lifted himself up, his lips on her neck. In the confines of his leather breeches, his engorged manhood strained to be released. He removed his hand from Aubrielle's warm, wet folds and unlaced his breeches. Soon the garment was down around his thighs and he brushed his swollen, demanding erection against her Venus mound.

He did not penetrate her. He was very careful not to. But he rubbed himself against the core of her womanhood, acquainting her with the feel of his heat. Taking her hand, he placed her small palm against his member so that she would know the quality of his flesh. Aubrielle felt his warmth and instinctively clamped around him. It was far too delicious a sensation and his hot seed erupted onto the mat of her soft, dark curls.

His enjoyment was overwhelming, but through the warm haze, he wanted her to know the same pleasures. It was only fair. Taking his sticky fingers, he gently fondled the throbbing little nub between her legs and a great fire burst forth in Aubrielle's loins that quickly exploded into a shower of stars. When the delicious waves subsided, she opened her eyes to find Kenneth smiling down at her.

"Did you enjoy that?" he asked huskily.

She was glowing. "What did you do to me?"

He kissed her, his nose nuzzling her cheek. "It is a pleasure that all women should feel but seldom do."

She thought a moment. Educated though she might be, she was

fairly naïve. "A woman's pleasure?"

"Aye."

It took her a moment to understand what he meant. Then she was genuinely surprised. "Is *that* what it was?"

He laughed softly. "Aye"

"You, too?"

"Absolutely."

She glanced down, looking at their bodies in various states of undress.

"Kenneth?"

"Aye?"

"Why… why did you not take your pleasure inside me, as a husband would?"

He wondered if he could adequately explain himself. "Do you know what you are saying?"

"If you do not want to, I will not force you."

He growled, low in his throat, running his hands up her torso and stretching her arms above her head. His great body lay atop her, his spent manhood rubbing against her pink folds.

"I want to more than you can possibly imagine," he whispered. "The more I taste of you, the more I want. But I do not want you to regret it."

"What do you mean?"

"We have but known each other a matter of days. We've only been betrothed a matter of hours. You may decide next week that our betrothal was the greatest mistake of your life and I do not want to take from you, in haste, that which is your most precious attribute." When he could see that his remark had upset her, he kissed her to quiet the protests. "I simply do not want to rush into anything, to accomplish this most intimate act in haste. What I did tonight, perhaps I should not have. But it was my intention to acquaint you with what was to come between us. You and I have the rest of our lives to become familiar with one another; I do not want lust to dictate our actions so hastily because the process of this discovery is new and exciting."

She gazed up at him, understanding that the man had a far more level head than she did. She felt ashamed. "You are right, of course. I did not mean to sound so shameless or brazen. 'Tis simply that… this feels so right, Kenneth. Do you not sense this also?"

"More than you know."

He was caught up in the tenderness of the moment. But the underlying darkness of his reason for his visit was becoming an increasingly persistent jab. He knew it was something he could no longer ignore and he hated to break the marvelous spell between them.

"You will forgive me for changing the subject, but I am afraid I must. I did come here for another reason other than to ravage you."

"What reason is that?"

He hated to tell her what he must. He struggled to find words that would be the least upsetting, as horrible as the news was. Shifting himself off of her, he took her in his arms comfortably, so that they were lying side by side. A big hand stroked her hair as he tried to maintain the warm ambiance. He hoped it would make it easier on her.

"Do you recollect that I told you I had sent a messenger to Highwood House to inform your mother of the earl's death?" he asked.

"Aye," she nodded.

He reached into a small pocket in his breeches where he had put the emerald ring. He held it in front of her face.

"Do you recognize this?"

She blinked, focusing on the ring. It was a second or two before recognition dawned. "My mother's ring," she plucked it from his fingers and sat up, examining it. "Where did you get this?"

Receiving confirmation of what they had suspected, his tone grew increasingly gentle. "The messenger returned this night and gave this to me. It seems that Highwood House was destroyed by fire somewhere in the past two days. Aubrielle, there is no easy way to tell you this and I pray you will forgive me for being tactless, but your mother was in the house when it burned. Her servants took this from her body for you to identify."

Kenneth waited for the eruption. He could only imagine what outpouring of grief he would be forced to contain. But she remained still and silent, staring at the ring. He wasn't sure she even heard him, so non-existent her reaction. He stroked her hair.

"I am so sorry," he said gently. "If there is anything I can do for you at this time, all you need do is ask."

She stared at the ring a moment longer. Then she shook her head and lowered her hand. It was then that silent tears fell in big splashes on her cheeks. She collapsed back on the pillows, sobbing softly into the linen. Kenneth continued to stroke her hair.

"I will go to Highwood House myself and retrieve your mother," he murmured. "We will bury her here, with her brother."

She shook her head, her voice muffled by the pillow. "Bury her with my father. That is what she would want."

"As you wish." He leaned over and kissed her temple. "If you would like me to leave you to your thoughts, I understand."

She grabbed his hand, holding it tight. "You promised never to leave me."

"Then I will not leave." She looked so sad lying amongst the linens. He pulled her gently up by the wrist and into his arms again. "Let me hold you for a while."

She didn't argue, nor did she resist. His power and warmth was more comforting than she ever imagined it could be. Her sobs had faded and she fell quiet with her thoughts.

"My mother and I were never particularly close," she said softly. "It is awful of me to weep for her because I must. But I am sad; she did the best she could, I suppose. I was not an easy child."

His cheek was against the top of her head. "I can only imagine what a terror you must have been."

Aubrielle tipped her head back to look up at him, her eyes moving over the strong lines of his face. There was so much power there. "Kenneth?"

"Aye?"

"You believe in God, do you not?"

He snorted. "Of course."

"Why do you laugh at the question?"

"Because everyone believes in God."

"That is not necessarily true. I have met a few people who question God's existence."

He lifted a disapproving eyebrow. "Probably scholars. They think they know everything and shall burn in Hell for it."

"That is Mankind's natural curiosity. 'Tis not a sin to question the existence of something we cannot see, taste or feel."

"You cannot see, taste or feel my affection for you. Do you question that as well?"

She shook her head. "I feel it right now with your arms around me. I taste it whenever you kiss me. I can see it when I look in your eyes. That," she winked at him," was not a suitable comparison."

He smiled, glad to see her humor wasn't gone completely. "Even so, you avoid the true issue. God is the reason for our very existence. We only exist to serve Him."

Her bottomless eyes gazed up at him. "Do you believe He has a hand in your destiny, then?"

"Without question."

"Did He plan that you and I would meet?"

"That has been preordained since the beginning of Time. Though I have never married and have yet to produce sons to carry on my name, I was never concerned. I knew the time would come as God allowed."

She was silent a moment, thinking. "I do not want you to think me blasphemous if I speak my thoughts."

"I will not."

She sat up, taking his enormous hands in her small ones and toying with his fingers. "As a child, neither of my parents stressed a strong obedience to God. Of course, we were pious people and attended Mass regularly, but my father encouraged me to explore beyond conventional means. When I was sent to St. Wenburgh, strangely enough, the Monks encouraged the exploration of science and philosophy as it did not pertain to the Church. I was well-read on Hinduism and Islam by the time I had seen my thirteenth year and have, therefore, always questioned the existence of God. But…," she gazed intently into his handsome face, "since the day I met you, I have had a feeling that God has had a serious hand in all of this. You have made me feel more and think more than anyone ever has, and you have been here in my time of need. This has all been so simple and so right. I cannot imagine that God did not plan for our lives to cross right now, right at this moment."

He tenderly stroked her hair. "Somewhere in my life I must have accomplished something tremendously good to warrant such an honor as you."

Aubrielle could only gaze into his eyes, hypnotized. This moment, when it should have been so dark, was filled with hope that she could not begin to describe.

But the hour was late and she was feeling her fatigue. She and Kenneth seemed to have run out of things to say to one another, yet it was not an uncomfortable silence. She could have gazed into his handsome face, unspeaking, all night.

"'Tis late," she finally murmured. "I suppose I should try to sleep."

He kissed both of her hands and got up from the bed. "We shall discuss my return to Highwood House come the morrow."

She let him tuck her in. He swaddled her up so tightly that she could hardly breathe. She started laughing and he was forced to loosen the linen.

"Be quiet," he said with mock sternness. "Go to sleep."

She dutifully closed her eyes, biting her lips in an attempt not to smile. Kenneth kissed her on the forehead but dare not kiss her anywhere else; that would only lead to temptation. She needed to sleep and he had duties to tend to.

Closing the chamber door behind him, he saw no need to post a guard with Lucius under watch. She was safe this night. Though he had come to her bearing tragic news, she had handled it as befitting a woman of solid character and he was proud of her strength. The more he came to know of Lady Aubrielle, the more he liked.

ᗧ

LATE AND DARK was the night. Athelred waited until the big blond knight left before contemplating making his move. Thomas was awake, sworn to watch for the return of the big blond beast and, in such an event, create enough of a commotion to warn his companion. Their plan was simple; it had to be. With a fortress this size, they had to be exceptionally careful.

Athelred's heart was beating loudly in his ears as he stood up, making sure he was unnoticed by the sleeping wounded. There were a few servants to tend the injured, but they were either sleeping or had moved out of the room. He kept to the shadows, moving along the wall and nearly tripping over a sleeping man. His heart beat louder still, wracked with anticipation. Reaching the entrance to the stair hall, he made a dash up the dark steps.

It was dark as a tomb on the third floor, making it difficult to see. Athelred groped the walls as he crept forward, glancing in the first door and seeing that it was dark and void of human habitation. There were a few lavish trappings on the wall and he guessed that it was the dead earl's chamber. Moving to the second door, he quietly lifted the latch.

There was a small fire in the hearth. In the bed against the wall lay a sleeping figure. The man's heart beat faster and he swore the lady could hear it. He was afraid it would wake her.

Entering the chamber, he made no noise. From his waistband, he pulled out a small dirk he had managed to slip past the physics and those who had tended his wounded head. It was a very small weapon, easily missed. But it would be enough to convince the lady that she must do as she was bade. He and his companions had come too far for their mission to fail now. He was halfway across the room, preparing to strike. His beating heart eased as his confidence grew, knowing the task was finally at hand. What the mother could not tell them, the daughter would.

But his confidence was shattered as something scuttled across the floor at lightning speed. He realized too late that it was a dog. The pup barked furiously, latching on to his ankle with razor-sharp teeth.

It was an unanticipated variable. The man howled, falling over at the shock and pain of it. Aubrielle, startled awake, was angry and terrified to see a strange man in her chamber. Never one to bask in indecision, she leapt from bed, racing to the fireplace for her ever-favorite poker. But she realized with horror that Kenneth had removed the poker after she had struck Everett with it. Yet it was of no matter; grabbing the ash shovel, she wielded it high above her head. The man saw it coming, dodging the blow and getting a hand around her wrist.

"I have come for the manuscript," he snarled. "Where is it?"

Aubrielle was terrified. She struggled to release his grasp. "I do not know what you mean," she grunted. "Let me go!"

His response was to dig his nails into her flesh. The dog was still giving him a fight and he was distracted by it. "Your mother played stupid as well and was rewarded with pain and death. Give me the manuscript and I shall be merciful."

Horror rippled down her spine. It was difficult to comprehend what the man was telling her, but comprehend she did. But the manuscript he was referring to had no meaning to her; she had many manuscripts and had no idea which one was valuable enough to kill for. But the larger horror was the implication of her mother's death. She was enraged and aghast at the same time.

"My… mother?" she hissed. "You bastard!"

The man's struggles with the dog were increasing. His grip on Aubrielle was slipping as a result. "Scroll of Munsalvaesche. Give it to me now or I shall make you wish that you had cooperated."

Aubrielle was so shocked that she almost lost her grip on the ash shovel. But her shock quickly fled, replaced by an enormous sense of self-preservation. She knew the man meant everything he said. Her mother had suffered for it. With a surge of strength, she managed to pull her wrist free. Hurling the shovel through the air, she brought it down on the man's skull so hard that a sickening dull sound echoed across the room. He instantly fell still.

A small dirk, deadly sharp, fell from his fingers and onto the floor. Aubrielle stared at the weapon, knowing it had been meant for her. Perhaps this was the same man who had attacked her in her room earlier, now returned to finish his job. Had she not kept the company of the little mutt, she would be as good as dead. Just like her mother.

Aubrielle let the ash shovel fall to the floor. Her body was beginning to shake at the seriousness of what had occurred. She went in search of something to cover herself up with, digging a heavy brocade robe out of her open chest. She pulled on the robe and tightened the sash. Her fingers were quaking and it was difficult to move them. She slipped her feet into her shoes next to the bed, picked up the still-snarling pup, and fled the chamber.

Scroll of Munsalvaesche. He had known she had it, but how? No one knew, except perhaps the monks at St. Wenburgh when they had discovered its absence. Aubrielle had spent so much time with it that she was the logical thief. The attacker had wanted the scroll so badly that he had not only tracked it to St. Wenburgh, but he had made enough of a concerted effort to discover the supposed thief and track her to Highwood House where her mother, not surprisingly, knew nothing about it. Ignorance had killed Graciela. *No*, Aubrielle thought with mounting sorrow. *My God, I did!*

Her only thoughts were those of escape. It was dim in the stair hall and she nearly tripped in her haste. The great hall was dark, full of sleeping wounded. It was creepy and fed her skittishness. Practically running from the keep, she made her way down the outer steps and into the bailey. It was empty at this time of night, a soft cold breeze upon the darkness. She could see a few soldiers near the main gate and she made way towards them.

She asked for Kenneth's whereabouts perhaps more harshly than she should have. She couldn't help it; she was frightened. One of the soldiers, an older man, escorted her to the knight's quarters. Aubrielle felt foolish; it was her castle and she didn't even know where the knights were housed. The soldier knocked on the door, an action that produced Bradley.

The short, husky knight usually had the night watch. This was his one night off. Surprised to see the lady of the castle, he quickly ushered her into the small, cramped room beyond. He disappeared down a dark corridor and in a matter of seconds Kenneth appeared.

He was in a tunic and dark breeches, wrinkled from slumber. He looked sleepy but was nonetheless very alert, especially at the sight of Aubrielle. She had been very brave, very strong in her actions, until she saw him. Now it was a struggle not to burst into tears.

"What's wrong?" Kenneth gently gripped her arms.

His touch felt so good, so protective. Her brave façade faltered. "A man broke into my room," she said. "He… he had a knife. The dog bit him and I was able to knock him on the head and escape."

His grip tightened, pure fury in his eyes. "Did he hurt you? Are you all right?"

She blinked away tears. "He did not hurt me."

Kenneth was on the move, pulling her along with him. "Brad," he growled. "Wake Everett. Bring him with you up to Lady Aubrielle's chamber. And send word to Reid upon the wall to lock down the castle."

Kenneth had no weapon of any kind. In his fury and haste, he had no doubt that his brute strength alone would be sufficient against any intruder. He would tear the man apart with his bare hands. Aubrielle struggled to keep pace with him, the little dog bouncing along in her arms. Above his own enraged thoughts, Kenneth could see that he was not making things easy on her and he quickly paused to sweep her up in to his arms. She threw an arm around his neck and buried her face into his flesh, her frightened tears wetting him. The dog licked his chin.

By now, the keep was in a mild amount of uproar. A few of the servants, still awake, had seen Lady Aubrielle flee the keep and they had alerted others. By the time Kenneth carried her into the keep, there were several servants huddling in and around the stair hall. No one had ventured to the third floor yet. Kenneth took the stairs without hesitation.

The upper floor was dark and cold. Before he entered the chamber, he gently set her on her feet. The dog slithered from her arms and raced into the chamber, growling. Kenneth followed the dog, watching the animal race around the room excitedly. He saw immediately that the room was empty.

Aubrielle timidly entered the room, hovering near the door. "Where is he?" she asked with soft urgency. "He was right there, next to my bed, the last I saw."

Kenneth crouched down, noting the small wet spot on the floorboards and the ash shovel laying a few feet away. He ran his finger over it, observing the reddish-brown color.

"Blood," he murmured.

Aubrielle had walked up behind him. She stared at the blemish on the floor. "I swear that he was right here when I left."

"I believe you."

She just stood there a moment, dumbly. Then she walked over to her bed and sat heavily, her movements lethargic and full of despair.

"My God," she breathed. "Does it never end at this place? Am I to be threatened every night of my life?"

Kenneth stood up. "Both times I have made the mistake of leaving you alone. Never again."

Aubrielle was unnaturally pale. She shook her head at him. "You cannot be with me every hour of the day and night."

"Perhaps not, but if I am not, then another can be. I have a stable of competent knights and soldiers at my disposal."

She looked at him. "And for how long do you intend this round the clock protection? A week? A month? A year?"

"I am sure that will not be necessary. We will find whoever did this,

Aubrielle. Have no doubt. You are quite safe here, in spite of your recent experiences."

Her response was to sigh heavily. She pulled her robe more tightly about her, gazing thoughtfully into the embers of the dying fire. Kenneth inspected the room just to make sure there were no more assassins hiding in the shadows. He went to sit beside her.

She was silent and distant. He put his big hand over hers. "Are you sure that you are unscathed?"

"Aye."

"Do you feel well enough to tell me what happened exactly?"

Her fear was beginning to subside, replaced by raging depression and guilt. She knew she should tell him everything but she was reluctant to, for many different reasons. She took a deep breath for courage.

"I was sleeping when he entered," she said quietly. "The snarls from the dog woke me. I ran to grab a weapon and picked up the ash shovel. He grabbed my arm and we wrestled before I was able to break free and hit him with the shovel."

"Did he say anything to you? Do you know who he was?"

"I do not know who he was," she said. Suddenly cold, she rose from the bed and wandered towards the fire, pulling her robe so tightly about her that she was nearly strangling in it. "Kenneth, I must tell you something horrible. I am having trouble grasping it myself."

"What is it?"

She paused before looking at him. "I am afraid to tell you."

"Why?"

"I fear that my actions have caused something horrible and that… perhaps you will judge me by them."

"You will not know the answer to that until you tell me what it is you have done."

He was right. Aubrielle squared her shoulders. "This man who attacked me in my room was looking for something. It is something I stole."

Kenneth's pale eyebrows lifted. "Did you steal it from him?"

"No."

"Then what on earth did you steal?"

She looked like a scolded child, humbled by the remorse that now wracked her. "In my latter years at St. Wenburgh, most of my studies were focused on the history of Christ and Grail lore. It was something that fascinated me and the monks indulged my interest. There was a manuscript, an ancient parchment called the Scroll of Munsalvaesche that held particular fascination for me."

"What is the Scroll of Munsalvaesche?"

Her expression warmed as she was suddenly transported into something that held great importance to her. "During the Dark Ages, a king by the name of Titurel, lord of Munsalvaesche Castle, wrote of the Holy Grail. It was supposedly housed within his castle. But it is more than simply the account of the cup of Christ. It is a true account of what Christians refer to as the Holy Grail and its current resting place. This manuscript is the reason that I must go to Glastonbury. It is the most amazing piece of literature of this or any lifetime."

Kenneth was silent, absorbing the information as he watched her go to the smaller of her trunks. She rifled through a considerable amount of clothing, shoes, and a few belts that ended up on the floor. He watched her pick at the lining of the trunk and carefully tear it away. He heard the material give. Once the lining was separated from the sides of the trunk, she dug deep and pulled forth a long, ocher-colored cylinder.

Kenneth's gaze moved curiously between the tube and Aubrielle's face. Her expression was not lost on him; the wonder and awe was obvious. She went to sit down beside him, holding the revered object up between them.

"This is the scroll." She unsealed the end of the cylinder and pulled forth a yellowed, brittle parchment. In spite of himself, Kenneth was very curious. Aubrielle carefully unrolled the script to reveal very deliberate, artistic writing. It was, in fact, a very beautiful piece. She began to read softly "Many brave knights have dwelled with the Grail at

Munsalvaesche … the Grail of the purest kind. If you do not know it, it shall not here be named to you. By the power of that Grail the phoenix burns to ashes, but the ashes give him life again."

He looked at her. "What does that mean?"

Her face, so pale minutes earlier, fairly glowed with excitement. "The secret, Kenneth. The Grail isn't a cup at all. It's something else."

He was trying not to be skeptical. "A stone?"

She smiled, so brightly that it lit up the entire room. "I really do not know. But when I find it, we shall know once and for all."

His skepticism was growing. "Do you mean to tell me that you have no idea what you are looking for, only that you must look for it?"

"Aye," she looked back at the scroll. "King Titurel describes it as a stone that gives life. Others have accounted it as a cup, of course, and the Gospel of Nicodemus even describes Mary Magdalene as the Grail. You see, no one really knows what it is. But nearly everything I have read on the subject, including this scroll, points to the Isle of Glastonbury as the Grail's resting place." She pointed far down towards the bottom of the brittle parchment. "Right here, do you see? 'That Munsalvaesche wants for its Grail, for the knights, the *aeterno defensor*, have taken it to *Insula Vitrum* to restore the health of the sleeping land'."

Kenneth knew his Latin; years of knightly training by priests had taught him as much. He translated the words. "*Insula Vitrum* is Island of Glass. And *aeterno defensor* is immortal protector."

She nodded eagerly. "Glastonbury has been known as the Island of Glass since the Caesars ruled our shores. Our ancestors, in fact, called it Ynis Witrin, which is the old language for 'Isle of Glass'. This scroll was written many centuries after the Romans ruled the earth. If an ancient king wrote of this, then surely there must be some connection. Surely the Grail, whatever it may be, is truly at Glastonbury."

Kenneth stared at the parchment, the faded ink, attempting to determine if she was certifiably insane or if the entire idea intrigued him. He had to admit that it was the slightest bit interesting, but his religious sensibilities kept him grounded. Regardless of what he thought, however, someone wanted the scroll bad enough to kill for it.

"Be that as it may, how did this man know you had the scroll?" he ventured. "I sense there are far greater forces behind this than just one random fool."

Aubrielle shook her head, her joy in the scroll somewhat dimmed. "I truly do not know. How he even knows of the scroll is a mystery to me, unless he was a student at St. Wenburgh as well, perhaps before I was there."

"That is possible. But to go back to the monastery to search for it and then to discover it is missing… if you stole it as you said you did, of all the students there, how did the finger point to you?"

"I was always studying it in the months before I left. It was never out of my possession. Perhaps they rightfully assumed I took it." Her eyes suddenly welled. "The man… he told me that he had asked my mother about the scroll. Kenneth, he killed her because she knew nothing. She did not know I had it. He thought she was lying."

"He said that?"

"Aye."

Kenneth looked at her, his mind whirling with new, deep possibilities. He did not like the fact that something dark and ominous was following Aubrielle, something he couldn't fight off. It was a faceless, shapeless evil. All of this revolved around her damnable obsession for Glastonbury and the Grail. He couldn't control her obsession. All he could do was guard her until the fixation found a satisfactory end. The more he looked at her, the more protective he became.

His arms went around her, pulling her close. "I am sorry," he murmured into her hair. "It was not your fault. You could not have known this would happen."

"But they killed her," she held him tightly, drawing on his strength. "She knew nothing, yet they still killed her. She must have told them I was at Kirk and now they have come to kill me and take the scroll."

Everett and Bradley appeared in the doorway, swords leveled, preparing for a fight. Young Max the squire was with them. When they saw Aubrielle and Kenneth seated calmly upon the bed, they lowered their weapons.

"Where is the threat?" Everett demanded.

"He was gone when we arrived," Kenneth mouth was muffled against Aubrielle's hair. "Is the castle sealed?"

"Aye," Everett answered. "No one has gone in or out for a few hours according to Reid. Now everything is locked down. Whoever attacked the lady is still inside the castle."

Aubrielle pulled herself from Kenneth's grasp; she did not want the knights to see her in a weak moment. Keeping her back to them, she went to her dressing table and pretended to busy herself. Kenneth could see her dabbing at her tears from the corner of his eye.

"Then rouse the senior soldiers. I want this place scoured from top to bottom for this man that Lady Aubrielle will very shortly describe to us. Anyone even remotely fitting this description will be placed in the vault for identification." He looked to Aubrielle, still at her table. "My lady? Are you strong enough to describe him to us?"

She turned to face them, tears gone, a brave front at hand. Whether or not she felt strong enough, she would nonetheless show them a collected soul.

"He was not a large man, perhaps slightly taller than me. His frame was slight, but he had strong arms. He will have dog bites on his ankle, as my little protector had a good grip on him." She paused a moment, trying not to shudder as she thought about the man who had killed her mother and very nearly killed her as well. "He also had a wound to his forehead, perhaps from a blow. It was very bruised."

"He will also have a wound on his head where Lady Aubrielle crowned him with the ash shovel," Kenneth looked to his men. "With that kind of damage, he should not be too hard to find. I will expect this man located by dawn."

Everett and Bradley quit the room, determined and professional to carry out the command. When they were gone, Kenneth looked at

Aubrielle once again. Her pale pallor had returned, drained from the evening's events. Describing her attacker had taken something more out of her.

"Perhaps you should try and sleep," he urged gently. "It will be some time before they have found anyone for you to look at."

She went towards the bed, not particularly sleepy, but physically exhausted. The scroll still lay upon the linen and she sat down, picking up the parchment as she did so.

"Do you suppose that all of this is my punishment for stealing this scroll?" she asked. "I fear God is angry at me for breaking his commandment."

He shrugged weakly. "I am not sure that God would resort to murdering your mother in punishment for the sin of stealing. I am more concerned with why someone would want it so badly as to kill for it. Perhaps there is more to that scroll than what you have told me."

She shook her head. "I have translated the entire parchment. It only speaks of the Grail and its location."

He didn't know what more to say to that. He thought perhaps to take a look at it himself since he could read and write Latin. Although he did not want to leave her alone, he wanted very much to be part of the search for her attacker. His sense of honor and his feelings for her dictated as much. But there was also a great deal of vengeance involved as well. Aubrielle sensed his thoughts and knew it was foolish for him to sit with her, idle, while his men turned the castle upside-down.

"I am sure the search would go much faster were you involved," she suggested. "I am sure a few soldiers outside my door would protect me quiet sufficiently. Besides, I have my champion right here."

They both looked at the little mutt, lying next to the bed. The dog's tail thumped against the floor.

"That pup is worth his weight in gold," Kenneth agreed. "This isn't the first time he has protected you." He took a long, last look at her lovely face. "Very well. If you insist I search, search I shall."

She smiled, weakly. Kenneth couldn't help himself from kissing her forehead, her hand, and finally her lips. The tenderness was so deep that his limbs tingled from the pure joy of it. He smiled warmly at her, stroking her cheek.

"I shall be back," he whispered huskily.

Aubrielle watched him go, too many thoughts racing through her mind. She was tremendously thankful to have such a man at her side. When she thought of their first meeting in the forest, she could have thrashed herself ragged for her behavior towards him. Little had she known what a large part he would play in her future.

Where she had thought moments before that God was angry with her, she was coming to think that God was rewarding her instead. Kenneth St. Héver could be explained no other way.

☙

THE LADY HAD packed a wallop, of that there was no doubt. Though she had been able to flee his attack, he had been fortunate enough to wake and escape the chamber before she returned with assistance.

Athelred staggered down the dark, narrow steps and back into the great hall where the wounded still slept. It was a clever cover, actually; perhaps no one would think to look for him with the injured. He was, after all, injured himself. First de Gaul had knocked him on the head, and then the lady had hit him. Even if he was spotted, no one would think anything of the massive lump that now covered most of his forehead. Never mind the fresh blood smeared across it. He was hoping the darkness would cover for him.

He lay like a stone on the cold floor of the great hall. As he had known, the lady returned some time later with the massive blond knight and the two of them made haste to the second floor. They were followed several minutes later by more knights bearing weapons. It wasn't long before the castle was roused for a search, though, as he had hoped, the wounded were spared. That did not, however, prevent the knights from walking through their midst. Especially the big blond knight; the man had a weighty presence. He could feel their stares inspecting him even though he lay on his stomach, his face to the floor. He was terrified someone would turn him over to look at him. But they passed by and moved on.

Relief swept him as the footfalls and voices faded. Time passed and he continued to lay there, unmoving, hardly breathing. He'd long since lost sight of the companion he had come here with, the man whose leg de Gaul had so gleefully broken. Now he could no longer concern himself with the man. He had to make another attempt at the lady, at some point, or his life would be forfeit. When the excitement of this night died down and the castle once again became complacent, he would find another way to strike.

Athelred had no concept of time as he lay there. It could have been minutes or hours. Eventually, he rolled over onto his back and lay staring up at the ceiling. The room around him was dark and silent. He lifted his head slightly, looked around, and lay back down again. He was sure he had missed the threat and was now at ease to attempt sleep.

The knight who had coerced him and Thomas into a murder plot was nowhere to be found, but he suspected the man would find them soon enough to rage over their failure. Fact was, he hadn't even been trying to kill her. He simply wanted to abduct her and the scroll and take her back to de Gaul. Only pure chance had seen the dark knight plot with him and his companion to kill her. God and the Devil worked in mysterious ways, whichever you chose to believe in. Personally, Athelred believed in Satan. He'd seen too much evil in the world to believe in a God.

Another attempt would have to be made, but not right away. The furor over this attack must die down before there was any further movement. Closing his eyes, he began to dream of another time and place that he and the lovely lady would resume their struggles. This time, he would win.

CHAPTER EIGHT

BY THE COMING of the cold, gray dawn, they had not found Aubrielle's attacker. They had several men in their possession that remotely fit the description, but none were exact. The frightened, gnarled group was herded into the vault to await their fate. Frustrated and exhausted from a fruitless night of the hunt, Kenneth waited until after sunrise to wake Aubrielle. He wanted to make sure they had exhausted all efforts before disrupting her. A sleepy-eyed lady appeared in the vault as the sun mounted the eastern horizon, but she could not identify any of the suspects.

The knights were sorry they had not been able to find her assailant. Everett was positively bitter about it. As brutal as the lady had treated him, still, he wanted to please her like a child constantly seeking parental approval. When Kenneth took Aubrielle back up to her chamber after failing to identify her attacker, the other knights regrouped to plot a fresh strategy with renewed determination; an attack on their lady while there were several healthy knights sworn to protect her was an attack on their honor. In a selfish way, there was more at stake than simply the lady's safety. They were better than they had thus far demonstrated.

The only knight who seemed to not feel that way was Lucius. He had not been told about the search initially. He had woken to the noise of the search in the bailey and had proceeded to coerce young Max to tell him what was afoot. He had forced himself upon the search, but it was apparent that he was indifferent. Captain of Kirk's forces or not, he had no stake in this. His stake had died with the earl. With Kenneth preparing to become the new lord and master, Lucius was fast retreating into his own world, one where he had no rank or position. And the more he retreated, the more dangerous he became.

No one was more aware of this than Kenneth. With the whirlwind of events over the past few days, he had thought to put it off sending the man along his way. In truth, he had hoped that Lucius would show a measure of strength and come to accept the change of events at Kirk. But the more he observed the man, the more obvious it became that he could no longer delay in carrying out his original plans. The sooner Lucius de Cor was out of the castle, the better for them all. Though apparently not tied to the assault against Aubrielle the previous evening, Lucius was nonetheless a credible and independent threat that could not be tolerated.

The matter of sending him away, however, meant confirming to Aubrielle who had initiated the first assault against her. Kenneth had thought to spare her the grief, but the decision to send the captain of Kirk's forces away would rest on her more than any of them. Without official power and title, Kenneth could do nothing. Aubrielle would have to make the decision.

In the bright of day, the harrowing previous night seemed far away. Aubrielle was feeling well enough to bark in her usual manner at the toothless serving wench, who went scrambling for the morning meal. She smirked as the woman fled the room and smacked into the wall in her haste. It was cruel to laugh, but it had been humorous to watch nonetheless. Kenneth cocked a reproving eyebrow at her, which she pretended not to notice. She felt better this morning than she had in days. While she rummaged sloppily through her trunks in search of something to wear, Kenneth stood formally and properly by the door. Though they were betrothed, still, his manner remained official in the capacity of her vassal as he stood in her bedchamber. There was business at hand. Until he could figure out how to strike a balance, switching easily between lover and professional knight, he would stay with what he knew best. Kenneth knew little else but formalities.

"There are many things to discuss, my lady," he said. "I would like a moment of your time when it is convenient."

She didn't look up at him, throwing mounds of garments on the floor as she searched. The pup jumped about in the clothing and snarled at it. "What kind of things?" she asked.

Kenneth saw irony in that question. "There is the matter of your mother, of course. There is the matter of your attack last night. There is the matter of our wedding. And there is another matter I have yet to mention to you but find that it must now be addressed."

She almost fell backwards yanking out a yellow brocade gown that was caught on something inside the chest. Kenneth repressed a grin as she stumbled backwards and almost ended on her backside. The dog, thinking she was playing a game, leaped around her excitedly.

"If you organized your things better, you might not come to personal injury whilst in your search," he suggested helpfully.

She inspected the garment. "You will keep your observations to yourself."

"Are you always so messy?"

"Do you always butt in where your opinion is neither asked for nor required?"

"Not usually. But this is a special case, I could not help myself."

She lifted an eyebrow at him. "My organization skills are none of your concern unless that was one of the items on our agenda today."

"God knows, it should be," he muttered, watching her frown. He came back at her. "But more to the point, your decision is needed on several matters, most of which I have listed. Therefore, when you are finished with your meal and dressing, I would appreciate your time and attention."

She shrugged, looking back at the dress. "As you wish."

"Then I shall leave you to your morning." He turned for the door. "Send for me when you are ready, my lady."

"I shall send for you now." She laid the dress on the bed. "You may eat with me and we will discuss your agenda over the meal."

"As much as that would please me, there is much that requires my attention. We did not find your attacker last night and that has me gravely concerned. I feel that my time would be better served heading the continued search."

She looked at him as if he were an idiot. "So you would leave me alone at a time like this? What kind of man would do such a thing?"

"A man who would protect his lady."

"You will do me more protection staying right here."

She had a point. Every time she had been attacked, he had not been there to aid her. He sighed in submission. "As you wish."

She smiled triumphantly and he could see that it had all been a ploy to manipulate him into staying. He could not say that he was entirely displeased. But he would exact a price for it. His formal manner dissolved as he moved swiftly across the room and took her into his massive arms. Aubrielle smiled at him, thrilled to be in his embrace. She had been hoping all morning that she would end up here. The warmth and sensuality of it was enough to embolden her, and she kissed him deeply before he could kiss her. Kenneth lifted her off the ground, holding her tightly against him as their lips met in a passionate tangle of flesh and sweetness.

"You surrender far too easily," she murmured against him.

He did not want to talk. He wanted to kiss her. Aubrielle responded eagerly until the door to her chamber creaked open. The toothless serving wench slipped in and Kenneth set Aubrielle on her feet, trying to be discreet about it, but the tale-tell lump in his groin spoke volumes of the events of the past several moments. He did not want ribald stories of their lust spread around the castle by foolish servants, at least not until they were properly married. He moved away from Aubrielle, claiming a chair next to the hearth and pulling it over to the table where the servant was arranging the food. Aubrielle, cheeks still flushed, sat down and ripped into the bread.

The dog jumped onto Kenneth's lap the moment he sat up to the table. He frowned at the animal but did not remove it. When the servant woman finished placing the food and quit the chamber, Aubrielle let out a hiss.

"I shall make sure that in the future no one enters this chamber without knocking," she said.

He grunted, inadvertently stroking the dog and then stopping when he caught himself doing so. "I will have a lock put on that door today. After we are married, it will no longer be an issue. No one would dare risk my wrath by barging in on us unannounced."

Aubrielle chewed thoughtfully. "I think that I shall move into my uncle's chamber today. Surely there is a lock on that door and, by all rights, it is now my chamber."

Kenneth nodded in agreement. He found himself hungry as he watched her eat and took a pear for himself.

He took a big bite of the fruit. "Would you care to discuss our agenda now or will it ruin your appetite?"

"We can discuss it now."

"I would like to leave for Highwood House by noon. Will you be ready to leave then?"

She stopped chewing. "I am going?"

"You told me to bury your mother with your father. I assume he is buried at Highwood House and I further assumed you would want to be present."

She slowly conceded. "Aye," she said quietly. "'Tis simply that… burying my mother brings back memories of my father's death. I think perhaps I was hoping to stay here and avoid facing the unpleasant realities of my parent's fate. But you are right, of course; I will go with you. But on one condition."

He had no idea what that could be. "And that is?"

"That after my mother's burial, we will go on to Glastonbury."

He should have suspected. She could read the reluctance in his expression and she pressed forward. "'Tis logical that we should, Kenneth. We will already be at Highwood House, which is several days travel from here. Glastonbury is another two days beyond. We will practically be there. Why would we not go?"

"So you view your mother's burial as just another opportunity to fulfill your quest?"

There was disapproval in his tone. "No," she said. "But as long as we are there, I thought…."

He just looked at her. Aubrielle thought that perhaps he was thinking what a petty, shallow woman she was. Hurt, she bolted out of the chair.

"Why do you stare at me as if I am a horrid creature?" she demanded. "I already told you that my mother and I were not particularly close. Would you have me explain to you that her abandoning me at Kirk four days ago was not the first time that she had abandoned me? Would you have me tell you that my mother was a mentally unstable woman who could not handle a child and the first time I can remember being abandoned was when I was three years of age and she left me with a trollop at an inn and told the woman to raise me as her own? Only when my father came looking for me was I returned home, only to have her abandon me again and again, sometimes with the nuns at the cloister in Kintbury and sometimes with complete strangers. The only way I was ever returned home was when my father would discover what she had done and went out in search of me. There were times when it took weeks for him to find me, but find me he did. After my father died, perhaps I wasn't so much running to Glastonbury as I was attempting to escape my mother. She never wanted me, Kenneth, whether she was abandoning me or whether I was trying to escape her. And I am supposed to grieve for this woman? How dare you judge me. You know nothing about my life."

She turned away from him, tears brimming. Kenneth sighed heavily, full of regret for anything wicked he might have thought of her. He should have known she would have her reasons. He stood up, put the dog on the ground, and went over to her.

"Forgive me," he said softly. "You are correct; I know nothing about your past life other than what you have told me. I should have suspected there was something more when you told me that you and your mother were never close. A great deal makes sense now."

She sniffled. "You have wondered why Glastonbury consumes me. It is because the dream of something better, of doing something beyond a mother who never wanted me. It was all that I had. Perhaps I thought I could win her love and make her want me. But now… now that will not happen. Yet my desire to go to Glastonbury is still as strong as ever. It is something inside of me that cannot go away. Perhaps… perhaps now I can make you love and want me if I do this miraculous thing."

He turned her around to face him, an expression of gentle rebuke on his face. "Do you believe for one moment that I do not already?" he asked. "Lady, you sorely underestimate my esteem for you. You are a beautiful, intelligent, strong woman and I am deeply honored to call you my own."

Her tears faded. "Sometimes I do not want to be strong. Just once in my life, I would like someone to be strong for me. And I would like to feel as if I am wanted and welcome."

He pulled her into his powerful embrace. His lips were against her forehead. "You are both wanted and most welcome."

She held onto him for what seemed like an eternity. Normally, when they came within any reasonable measure of close proximity to each other, there was a sexual pull that neither of them could resist. But this embrace was without the lust that usually accompanied such a tryst; this embrace was deeper, stronger, more emotionally binding. Aubrielle felt more wanted than she had ever felt in her entire life. At that moment, something deep within her ceased to be wild and unpredictable. Her soul felt settled and secure.

"Thank you," she whispered.

His response was to squeeze her tightly. But, as was usual when there were other matters at hand, Kenneth could not chase away the larger purpose. Some matters of fate were in need of being decided and while time was ticking away, the matters were not losing momentum. They were, in fact, growing.

"I truly hate to bring this up," he said, "and as much as I would relish standing here all day with you in my arms, there are some items that require your attention."

She sighed heavily, burying her face in his chest. "Can they not wait?"

"I am afraid not."

"Very well," she removed her face and looked up at him. "What is it?"

He smiled and led her back over to the table, seating her gently in her chair. He resumed his seat, wagging a finger at the pup when it tried to reclaim its spot on his lap. He threw a crust to the dog and settled it.

"Now," he began. "The most serious issue is something I have resisted mentioning. We have a problem with Lucius."

She rolled her eyes, resting her chin on her hand. "Lucius has been a problem since I have known him. What now?"

Kenneth cocked an eyebrow. "He is very bitter about the death of the earl and our impending marriage. And he has proven that he is very hostile towards you."

"I am well aware of that. The bruise he gave me is still on my stomach."

His expression cooled. "He is fortunate he is still alive for what he did to you."

"And I am, frankly, surprised to see that he is still walking about. I saw him yesterday in the bailey. Why have you permitted this man to move about freely with no repercussions for his actions?"

"He was drunk when he assaulted you," Kenneth tried to explain, thinking it sounded rather weak even as the words left his lips. "He does not remember anything. Lucius had many years of flawless service to the earldom before that night and we thought to take that into consideration. Exiling him will be enough punishment for a man of his rank and political ambition."

"So you are, in essence, telling me that he will not be disciplined for his crime."

Kenneth scratched his chin. He was coming to think that he had been right and Reid had been wrong when they had had this discussion about Lucius' state of mind the night he attacked Aubrielle. Being drunk was no excuse. At the time, Kenneth had not wanted to appear as if he would be punishing Lucius out of vengeance. Now, he felt foolish; vengeance or not, had Lucius attacked the earl, his sentence would have been severe. Aubrielle was no exception. She was, in fact, more of a reason to dispense severe justice than the earl would have been.

"What would you have me do to him?"

Aubrielle just looked at him, having difficulty understanding that he did not believe punishment for Lucius was appropriate. "You have turned the castle upside-down looking for the man who assaulted me in my chamber last eve. What do you intend to do to him when you catch him?"

"Execute him."

She smacked her hand, open-palmed, on the table. "So why is Lucius any different?"

Kenneth felt more and more like a fool. He realized he was on the defensive, a bad side to be on. He was in the wrong and he knew it.

"Aubrielle, you must understand. He is my captain and entitled to special consideration. This is not a normal situation in the least and I have been attempting to deal with this as fairly and as impartially as I can. He attacked the woman I adore, for God's sake. My instinct is to run the man through and take pleasure in his pain a thousand times over. But because he is the Captain of Kirk's army, I must take that into consideration and be particularly introspective and cautious in this matter. It is not as simple as it seems."

She bolted up, for the second time since sitting down to their meal. "I cannot believe my ears, Kenneth. The man could have grossly injured me and only by the grace of God did not. I will heal. But the fact remains that he viciously and maliciously attacked me. He must and will be punished just as anyone would be who laid a hand upon me. Are you so muddled by duty and twisted loyalty that I must think clearly for you?"

He stood up to face her. It was a slow, deliberate movement, full of threat and ominous power. Aubrielle could feel the weight of his mood, but she would not back down. She did not regret what she said in the least.

"You do not, my lady."

"Then why the lack of action on my behalf?"

"I have explained this to you."

She shook her head, slowly. "What you have told me is that you have greater concern for Lucius than for me."

"That is not at all what I said."

"You have made excuses for your weakness."

It was a sharp, bitter thing to say. She would have done less damage had she taken a dagger and cut out his heart. The worst part was that they both knew she was right.

Kenneth left the room without another word. Aubrielle stood there, hurt beyond words by his lack of action where Lucius was concerned. Discouraged, upset, she plopped back down in the chair, tears brimming in the sea-colored eyes. He had lied to her, she knew; all of his pretty words, his assurance of his respect and feelings for her, were lies. Had he truly cared for her, this matter would have been settled long ago. Just like her mother, Kenneth held her in small regard, too. By his actions, he said as much.

His half-eaten pear was near her hand. She hurled it across the room in frustration, watching it explode against the wall. Then she did what she always did when frustrated, hurt, or angry.

She escaped.

☙

BECAUSE OF THE commerce that was dependent upon the castle, Kenneth ordered the gates opened on a limited basis. There were heavy guards posted at the gates, watching everyone coming in and out of the castle. They had searched the castle thoroughly enough that he actually hoped Aubrielle's attacker would try to make a break for the gates. In a reverse of logic, he thought that if they could not go to the assailant, let the assailant come to them.

Later, in hindsight, Kenneth would curse himself for not being at the gates to inspect the people passing to and fro. He would have recognized Aubrielle, disguised in a heavy peasant cloak and carrying a huge bundle of reeds she had pulled from the fish pond near the castle kitchens. She looked like a dirty, frightened farm girl. It was, truthfully, a clever disguise and no one questioned the small young woman leaving the gates. If only Kenneth could have suspected she would resume her escape attempts, to know how badly he had hurt her, he could have been there to stop her.

But that was the furthest thing on his mind. He was obsessively focused on Lucius, to right the wrongs that he had created. Aubrielle had been correct in every way and he harbored a huge amount of guilt that he had allowed himself to treat Lucius with special consideration. He did not blame Reid in the least for his advice; the decision was his burden alone. Reid, in fact, did not say a word when they cornered Lucius in the knight's quarters. He obeyed Kenneth's orders flawlessly. When Lucius resisted, Everett seemed to take distinct pleasure in roughing him up. That seemed to provoke Lucius into more violence and Kenneth found himself subduing his superior officer.

They took the captain to the vault. Much to Lucius' discredit, he kicked and fought the entire way. What should have been a discreet arrest was a public spectacle and the whole of Kirk was in an uproar because of it. The gossip flew.

In the vault, Lucius loudly proclaimed his innocence. That was natural considering he did not remember anything about the attack. Kenneth had no doubt that the man believed he was wrongly targeted, a victim of his new lady's hatred. But when he started spouting insults directed at Aubrielle, the knights on the other side of the cell grate could see, without a doubt, how much bitterness and resentment their captain harbored against her. If there had been any doubts in their mind as to whom the culprit had been in the first assault, those doubts were erased.

There was no question in Kenneth's mind what needed to be done. He did not even offer it up for discussion as he had before. The knights knew that, at sunrise the next morning, Lucius would face his ultimate punishment for his attack against the Lady of Kirk Castle. Now it was Lucius' last night on earth and the knights vacated the vault, leaving Lucius to his own morbid thoughts.

ᘓ

THOUGH NO ONE knew the charges, rumors flew like wild fire on the cause and consequences of Captain de Cor's arrest. Some said that he had made an attempt on the new countess' life; other said that he had made an attempt on Kenneth's life. Still others said he had tried to desecrate the earl's grave in a fit of grief. No matter what the reasons, the fact remained that Lucius de Cor was now housed in the cramped vault of Kirk's gate-tower and the entire castle was in shock.

Shock faded to wariness and fear. No one had suspected there was trouble within the ranks, a worrisome thought now that the earl was dead. Perhaps the knights were embroiled in a power struggle. In fact, the reaction to Lucius' arrest was exactly as Kenneth had feared; the vassals of Kirk were unbalanced in the wake of Mortimer's passing and the added disruption of Lucius' capture only heightened the apprehensive ambience. Hearing Lucius' screams of protest as he was carried into the vault was as bad as it could have possibly been.

Eventually, the news reached the injured in the great hall. Athelred and Thomas overheard the servants and other soldiers as they discussed the captain's capture. Soon the whispers were picked up by the wounded, passed from man to man like a great dark secret. De Gaul's two men remained largely silent as the rumors flew, gleaning as much information as they could out of several different versions of the story. But one thing was for certain; it could a very bad situation for them both.

"De Cor," Athelred repeated slowly. "Isn't that…?"

"It is," Thomas hissed. "Perhaps they are on to his plot. Perhaps that is why he was arrested."

"If that is true, then he will tell them of us," Athelred's fear was evident. "We must get to him before he can point to us."

"How? He is in the vault."

Athelred thought a moment. He wasn't the brightest man, but he was devious. Fending for himself nearly all of his life had taught him that.

"I will go outside and watch the gatehouse," he said quietly. "Mayhap there will be an opportunity to get into the vault. Guards do not normally post inside the vault, but at the gatehouse itself. Mayhap I can slip past the guard."

"Go, then," Thomas was feeling his concern; he was reckless with it. "Release him or kill him, I care not. But he cannot name us."

Athelred nodded, cautiously slipping from the hall when he was sure there would be no one to see him. It wasn't an easy task, especially since it took him through the main entrance to the keep, but he managed to leave unnoticed because of the general chaos going on as a result of de Cor's arrest. No one was paying attention to a lone man. Driven by panic, he pushed forward.

The gatehouse was protected, but the soldiers were distracted. The knights had left to go about their duties, leaving less-professional subordinates to man the gatehouse and the main gates. Peasants passed in and out, vendors with daily produce and commoners from the nearby village transacting business within the massive walls. The soldiers, when they weren't talking about de Cor's arrest, were inspecting the surfs, and especially the women. When two of the guards focused on a particularly buxom woman, Athelred saw an opportunity to slide into the gatehouse and he swiftly took it.

The vault was surprisingly empty. A servant with a fat belly and little hair was on the narrow stairwell, refreshing the torches that lit the dank passage, but he said nothing as Athelred moved past him. At the bottom of the steps, Athelred slipped on the green slime that coated the stone and nearly fell on his face. Recovering swiftly, and hoping he wasn't followed, he ventured further into the dungeon.

De Cor wasn't difficult to find. He was still grousing in the cell to the left. Athelred clutched the iron bars.

"M'lord," he whispered loudly.

Lucius caught sight of him and rushed the bars. "You!" he reached the through the bars as Athelred stumbled back, out of his reach. "What have you told them?"

Athelred shook his head. "Nothing, m'lord. By what charge do you come to this place?"

Lucius hung on the bars, insane with fear and mistrust. But the dark eyes cooled as he struggled to gain control. "You've said nothing?"

"No, m'lord. I have not spoken to anyone. Neither has my companion. We've done nothing, I swear it."

Lucius' jaw ticked, spittle on his lips. He licked it away, the crazed look fading from his eyes. With both hands, he rattled the bars. "Then get the key, fool. Let me out of here."

Athelred looked around, but there was no key to be found. The bars, however, were on hinges and using an iron sconce he ripped from the wall, Athelred leveraged the grate so that the hinges disengaged. The bars were heavy and it took both Lucius and Athelred to lower them to the stone floor, carefully, so it would make no noise. Now that he was free, Lucius' panicked expression returned.

"I must get out of this place," he said. "You must help me."

"What would you have me do?"

Lucius thought quickly. He knew this place, and he knew the guards. He waved his hands in the direction of the stairs. "Go and create a diversion. Move the guards away from the gate. I must escape."

"How will I distract them?"

"Think of something, idiot."

The fat servant who had been refreshing the torches picked that moment to descend the stairs. Lucius grabbed the man and snapped his neck. Yanking off his clothing, he quickly swathed himself in the ragged clothes of the peasant. The final touch was to wrap the man's shirt around his head, covering his hair and partially covering his features.

He shoved Athelred in the direction of the steps. "Go, now. Do this for me."

Although Athelred's original intent had been to kill Lucius before he could tell anyone of their murderous plot, he was not a natural leader. He tended to follow orders because he was used to doing so, especially in de Gaul's legion. Now, Lucius was giving orders and Athelred would instinctively follow.

He raced up the steps, planning the diversion as he went. Lucius was behind him, his eyes open for guards or any other threats that might linger in the gatehouse. Athelred paused at the top of the stairs, motioning for Lucius to stay low. So far, it was still empty, but there was activity outside in the passage. He turned to Lucius.

"There are more of us in the forest," he whispered loudly. "If you make it out of here, run to the trees. You will find us to the south."

Lucius wasn't surprised to hear that. Bandits lingered everywhere outside civilized walls. "You will make it there, also. We must re-think our plans on the countess. Will your brethren be with us?"

Athelred lifted a bushy eyebrow; if de Cor only knew the truth. "Indeed they will. Perhaps… perhaps we will not kill the lady, after all. Perhaps we should simply take her for a prize. We have use for a lady like her."

"I care not. As long as she is removed from Kirk never to return."

Athelred was very good at playing a loud, loathsome drunk, just long enough so that the two guards watching the open gate had to physically pick him up and remove him. By the time they threw him out of the gates, Lucius was on the road leading from Kirk and putting more distance behind him with every step.

As long as she is removed from Kirk never to return….

The plan was taking shape.

CHAPTER NINE

IT WAS SUP before anyone had an inkling of Lady Aubrielle's absence. The toothless serving wench was the first to suspect it, and she passed the information along to the majordomo. The small, efficient man went to the lady's chamber, completely inspected it and the rest of the keep before racing personally to the knight's quarters. Much was amiss at Kirk these days and this latest event would only serve to stir the bedlam. Everett was the only knight he could find and the two of them went in search of Kenneth.

They found him in the armory going over the inventory of weapons lost during the brief siege against the Welsh two days prior. Historical ly, Kenneth tended to drown himself in duties when he was feeling particularly moody or frustrated. This afternoon had seen both moods. Inventorying the crossbows and hammers kept him from running to Aubrielle like a fool and begging her forgiveness. He was ashamed he had put himself in a position where such a thing was necessary. He wondered if she would ever forgive him. All he could see was the look on her face when she realized he had inadequately protected her and he knew it was something that would haunt him the rest of his life.

Everett's news drained the color from his face. They could all see it. Kenneth knew where she had gone, and he further knew that a search of the castle would prove futile. There was only one place Aubrielle would go. He ordered the chargers brought around and sent Everett to gather a small party of armed men. Without waiting for the search party, he mounted his charger and took off on his own.

His mind was whirling as he raced from the gates. He was fully cognizant that he was without his armor or weapons, but he didn't care. All that mattered was that he found Aubrielle before something horrible happened to her. He struggled to calm himself, full of fear and anger, and tried to think as she would. She was clever, he knew, and he further knew that once her absence was discovered that Kenneth would set out looking for her. She would not stay upon the open road. She would take to the woods.

He reined his horse off the road and into the bramble. It was the same area where he had first seen Aubrielle and chased her into the woods. He remembered the hunt, the head-butting, and the thought made him smile. It also made his heart ache for her more. He reined his horse to a halt just before entering the woods and dismounted.

He was trying to pick up her trail. He stood at the edge of the tree-line, looking for broken grass or anything that suggested a path into the woods. It was growing dark and he knew that, very soon, it would be impossible to follow any trail. His heart began to race. Everett and several men came up behind him and he admonished them to take care with the environment in case she had left a path to follow. The men spread out, and began to search.

Kenneth entered the woods, dark and spooky as night set. He could hear the others in the distance, hunting for a trail that was no doubt several hours cold. He tried not to let his mind wander, thinking of what could become of her and of how miserably he had failed her. Kenneth had never failed at anything in his life up until the past few days. Now, when it mattered most, he found himself inept. Odd how every measure of training, every battle he had ever fought with flawless dedication suddenly paled in comparison against Aubrielle's needs. If he could only excel at being a husband and father, it would be his proudest accomplishments. He wondered if he would ever have the opportunity to tell her.

"I wondered how long it would take before you came looking for me."

It was a soft voice from the shadows. Kenneth whirled in the direction of the sound, startled to see Aubrielle seated on the ground against an old, rotted tree. She was so well camouflaged that he would have walked right past her and never have known. As it was, his heart was in his throat, indescribable emotions of joy bubbling within him. But he just stood there, looking at her.

"Are you well?" he asked calmly.

"I am."

He couldn't help it; he emitted an enormous sigh, as if his entire body suddenly deflated of everything it held deep and strong within.

"Why, Aubrielle?" was all he could think to ask. "Why did you do this?"

She gazed up at him, her sea-colored eyes glistening in the light of sunset. After a moment, she patted the ground beside her. Kenneth walked over and obediently set himself down. He refrained from throwing his arms around her, fearful he would chase her off. All he knew was, at this moment, he was never more thankful for anything in his life.

"I suppose running off is my way of dealing with distress or sorrow," she said softly. "As I told you, running off has become a part of me, for many reasons. I run to escape, I run to seek out something. Glastonbury seems more and more to me as if it was just an excuse to escape situations I cannot control. 'Tis true, the Grail still means a good deal to me. It always will. But as I ran down the road and into the trees, it occurred to me that you mean a good deal to me, too. By the time I reached this very spot, I realized I could go no further. I could not leave you no matter what has happened."

Kenneth gazed at her, studying the lovely lines of her face, feeling his heart swell.

"My lady?"

"Aye?"

"Would this be an appropriate time to tell you what is in my heart?"

An expression of longing washed over her. "Aye, Kenneth, it would."

A great hand came up, cupping her sweet face. His thumb stroked a velvet cheek. "I have never known such terror as I have the past hour," he murmured. "To think you had gone filled me with a feeling of panic as I cannot begin to describe. I thought I had lost you."

She smiled wryly. "You lost me only as far as the trees. After that, I thought I would sit and wait for you. I knew you would come."

His smile faded. "I will always come for you. I will never leave you, and I will defend you to the death. What happened with Lucius…? I am a man unused to apologies, but in this case, I must. I was wrong. I was attempting to be fair and it only came across as indecision and weakness. For that, I beg your forgiveness. That is not a usual happening with me."

"There is nothing to forgive. I understand that you had your reasons."

"You are too kind."

He was humbled, uncomfortable. Aubrielle saw this. Rising to her knees, she put her hands on either side of his face and forced him to look at her. "Kenneth," she whispered. "Do you not understand that these past few days have seen an unexpected love for you blossom in me? No matter how much I would like to become angry with you, or bear a grudge against you, I cannot. I cannot hurt you that way, or myself. I would forgive you anything. Perhaps it is foolish of me, but I cannot help myself."

He stared at her, his ice-blue eyes melting into pools of warm, limpid water. He took her hands in his own, kissing them before calling out to his men.

"Everett!" he boomed.

Somewhere in the darkness, the knight responded. "My lord?"

"I have located the lady. Return to the castle."

Everett darted through the brush. They could hear him running towards them. He burst through some bushes, his brown eyes wide with surprise.

"My lady!" he exclaimed softly. "Are you all right?"

Kenneth didn't let her respond. He spoke to Everett directly. "Take the men back to the castle."

Everett had heard that tone before. It usually meant trouble, which he suspected the lady had enough of. He would wait and get the story at a later time. It was best now to obey.

They heard Everett calling out to the men as he walked away. Soon, the woods became quiet but for an occasional night bird. Aubrielle was still on her knees and Kenneth was still on his bottom. When he was certain they were alone, he looked at her.

"No one has ever said what you have said to me," he said quietly. "My entire life has been focused on duty and discipline. Emotions were not a part of that. In fact, I have done everything possible to ensure that emotions did not affect me at all. But when you speak to me… I feel your words as well as hear them. But I cannot believe that it has only taken a week for us to fall madly in love with each other. There is no logic in that."

She grinned. "Whoever said love was logical? It is a supremely illogical emotion that is more powerful than anything else on this earth."

He studied her features, looking deep into her eyes as if he wanted to say something. Finally, he just shook his head. "God knows, I find myself loving you. If this is weakness, then let me be weak."

He seemed baffled by the whole idea. Aubrielle put her arms around him because it seemed as if he needed it. Kenneth responded by drawing her closely to him, holding her so tight that he squeezed the breath from her. She could feel his mouth against her shoulder. It wasn't long before his lips began to move against her flesh.

"God, I do love you," he muttered as he feasted on her collarbone. "Swear to me that you will never do anything foolish like this again."

She closed her eyes, relishing the feel of him against her. "I swear it."

"I would have never stopped looking for you, do you realize that? I would have spent my entire life searching even when all hope was lost and my life was at an end."

Her head lolled back and his mouth moved up her neck. "Like Percival searching for the Grail."

He stopped and looked at her. "Does everything have a Grail connection with you? Even something like this?"

Her arms were wrapped around his neck, her face an inch from his own. "Do you not see it?"

"See what?"

"How you would have stopped at nothing to search for me until the end of your days?"

"Do you mean to suggest that you are my Grail?"

Her sea-colored eyes twinkled. "No," she whispered. "I mean to suggest that perhaps you are mine."

"I do not understand."

She cocked her head, attempting to formulate the answer that was suddenly abundantly clear.

"Think about it, Kenneth. Just as Percival and the knights of Arthur's court searched for that one thing that would make their lives complete, just as I have also been determined to search for it, perhaps I have been searching for the wrong thing. Perhaps, all of this time, I have been searching for you and did not even know it. Even as I look at you now, I sense completion now that we have declared our adoration of each other. The part of me that I thought the Grail would fill has been filled by you, Kenneth. I have been so… blind."

He smiled, touched by her words. "Were that true, my lady, I could ask for no greater gift."

They gazed at each other, a miasma of emotion enveloping them. Kenneth kissed her, a deeper and more heart-felt gesture he had never given. He devoured her, knowing at this moment that there could be nothing better in life. He had every intention of claiming her bodily at that moment. He could think of nothing else. But his happiness was the last coherent thought before something deep, evil and painful struck him twice, in rapid succession, squarely in the back.

The fog of emotion turned into an abrupt nightmare of reality. Aubrielle felt the physical strike from the first arrow as Kenneth's body shook violently. He pitched forward, enveloping her to protect her. A scream erupted from her lips as the second arrow hit and he fell to the ground, trapping her beneath him.

"Stay down," he commanded huskily. "Do not move."

She was in a panic to see how badly he was hit. "Let me see how terribly you are injured."

She tried to squirm out beneath his bulk but his massive arms held her fast. "No, Aubrielle," he murmured. "Do not move. I do not want you to be hit. Just… stay."

She stopped fidgeting for the moment, her eyes welling with tears as she gazed up into his white face. The seriousness of what happened was dawning on her.

"My God," a sob escaped her lips. "What have they done to you?"

He could only shake his head. It was a struggle for him to stay conscious. Horror surged through Aubrielle and she threw her arms around his neck, holding fast as if fearful that to let go, death would take him.

"Do not die, Kenneth," she wept earnestly. "Please… please stay with me. I shall tend you back to health, I swear it. Just stay with me, listen to my voice. We shall get through this, I promise."

After the shock of the attack wore off, Kenneth knew he was in trouble. He cursed himself for not having taken the time to don his armor, but it was a wasted regret. There was no changing his hasty decision. Many thoughts rolled through his head, of a life that could have been, of the cruel fate that had betrayed him, but he chased those thoughts away. He tried to focus on the present, his chances for survival, and Aubrielle's. He was far more concerned for her than for him.

The woods around them were rustling with danger. He could hear the enemy in the shadows, coming to claim the prize. He was in no position to stand up and defend her, but he could buy her time. He would gladly sacrifice himself if only to save her.

"Aubrielle," he muttered. "Crawl to the bushes and stay low against the bramble so they will not have a clear shot at you. Do you understand? Go back to the castle and get help."

"I will not leave you," she hissed at him. "I am not a coward."

"Leave me or we both die."

She twisted violently, pulling herself from underneath him. Kenneth thudded softly against the cold earth, his immense body limp and placid. Aubrielle was still lying on the ground, but she could get a look at his injuries now; two nasty arrows protruded from his back, one to the lower portion near his spine, and the other from his left shoulder. Blood soaked his shirt, and had spilled down onto her, she noticed. The sight was enough to make her physically ill.

But she swallowed the bile. Her female fits would do nothing to help him and she needed to stay strong. It was a struggle to think clearly.

"I am going to drag you into the bushes," she whispered, taking hold of his arms. "If I can hide you, then perhaps they will go away and leave us alone."

He shook his head. "No, leave me. Run back to the castle. Now."

She lifted an eyebrow at his tone, making sure he saw her. "You cannot order me about, Kenneth St. Héver. You'll do as I say."

He muttered something but she grabbed ahold of his wrists, ignoring his protest. She barely had one good drag on him when a figure stepped from the bramble, aiming a crossbow directly at her. Aubrielle froze, her eyes wide with astonishment.

It was almost too much to bear. Her shock cooled into simmering, deep-seated hatred. She let go of Kenneth, putting herself between the dark form and the wounded knight. It was a touching, sad gesture, like a mother bear trying to protect her young. Aubrielle had every intention of protecting him to the death.

"I always knew you were a loathsome, despicable creature, but even I didn't think you were capable of this." Her voice was laced with venom. "Why in the world have you done this? What is your excuse, you brainless, vile beast? Tell me now before I scream my lungs out and everyone at Kirk will hear me and come running. I swear to God I will cheer at your execution and take great pleasure in your agony."

Lucius lowered the crossbow. His features held no discernible expression. The fact that he had just launched two arrows into his second in command apparently held no meaning. In his opinion, it has been necessary and he had no regrets. As for the lady, he was used to the nasty words directed at him. But he had nothing to say in reply. There was no need. In this subversive game of politics that he played so well, he had bided his time and it had paid off handsomely.

"That day may come, Lady Aubrielle, but not today," he said as casually as he was discussing the weather. He eyed Kenneth and took a step towards him, but Aubrielle thrust herself into his path.

"Touch him and I shall kill you."

Lucius stopped his advance. "He was a fine knight. The very best. 'Tis a pity, really. You can blame yourself for this."

"Me?" she was horrified. "What have I done?"

"You led him into the forest." He smiled, without humor. "You have no idea how much trouble you have saved me this day. I really should thank you."

"For what?"

"For falling right into my lap. You are a stupid, stupid girl."

She ran cold, tears of anguish in her eyes. Having no reply, she turned to look at Kenneth, lying bloody and lifeless on the ground. She couldn't face Lucius any longer; she fell to the ground beside Kenneth, trying to shield him with her body.

"Leave him alone," she hissed through her tears. "Leave us both alone and be gone."

Kenneth could feel her soft warmth against him. His fingers grasped at her clothing. "Aubrielle," he murmured. "Get behind me, sweetheart. Let me…."

He was going to say "protect you". Through his haze, he realized that was foolish. He was incapacitated and they were both at the mercy of Lucius. He felt so completely helpless, so ashamed he had ended up this way. Aubrielle stroked his neck, his head; he could feel her soft kisses on his cheek and fingers.

"Do not die," she begged, tears dripping on his hand. "Please, Kenneth, be strong. Be strong for me. I love you so."

Lucius could only take so much. There was too much awry in his mind for him to process rational thought. At the moment, he truly blamed Aubrielle for Kenneth's injury, for his state as a fugitive and murderer. There were shadows lingering in the bushes and he turned to them.

"Take her," he said simply.

The bramble suddenly exploded. Men with weapons popped out from all sides. Aubrielle gasped with fright and grabbed the nearest weapon she could get her hands on. An old tree branch was a poor substitute for a sword, but she fought valiantly until the wood broke and one of the men grabbed her. Still, she continued to fight, to protect Kenneth, biting, kicking and screaming until they managed to get ahold of her and haul her away.

Kenneth, nearly unconscious, knew what was happening. He knew it, and felt it, with every inch of his wounded body. It only made matters worse that Lucius was behind it all. *Take her.* Once, Lucius had said those same words to him where it pertained to Aubrielle. Now the words had become lethal and revolting. He struggled to push himself up to fight, but his injuries were too great and his blood loss too much. It was impossible to do anything other than roll on to his right side, just in time to see four men pull Aubrielle, kicking and biting, into the trees.

If Kenneth had ever been close to crying in his life, now would have been the time. His vision was dimming and death beckoned, but still, all he could think of was saving her. He could hear her calling his name, screaming for him. He began to crawl towards the trees in a pathetic attempt to follow. He caught a glimpse of boots, but not much else. He knew that Lucius was going to kill him. It didn't matter how the man got out of the vault; the fact remained that he had, and he was going above and beyond what Kenneth had ever thought him capable of. He felt like an idiot for not having been more astute to the depths of the man's evil and slighted mind.

But Kenneth would not go down without a fight. And then he would continue after Aubrielle. Foolish as it was, he would not accept defeat, especially at the hands of Lucius de Cor. Not even Death could force that upon him.

As he struggled to push himself up into a sitting position to face an undoubtedly deadly battle, his vision dimmed completely and the world went abruptly silent.

The fight was over before it began.

CHAPTER TEN

IT HAD TAKEN all four of them to tie her up and put a sack over her head. Still, Aubrielle fought until she exhausted and bloodied herself. Her lip was torn where she had butted herself against someone's skull. She had bruises in places that didn't normally have bruises, but the biggest wound she had sustained so far was the gaping hole in her heart. Somewhere in the fighting and biting, she realized she had left Kenneth on the floor of the forest and that de Cor would surely finish him off. Then her struggles consisted of tears and hysteria in addition to the rest. She fought against them into the night, until her strength finally gave out and she could struggle no more.

Fatigue claimed her. So did despair. With Kenneth dead, she could not imagine what was left to live for. With the sack over her head and darkness surrounding her, she fell into a deep sleep, not caring what happened to her and praying she would never awaken.

But her prayers were not answered. She awoke to the sack being ripped savagely off her head. It was a startling movement, one that set her on edge in an instant. It was past dawn and they were in a clearing on the edge of a forest. Aubrielle didn't recognize any of it. The bright and beautiful day mocked her sorrow as a man dressed in black stood before her, inspecting her as one would inspect a brood mare. It was an unsettling feeling. The man was dark from the top of his soiled hair to the bottom of his worn boots and there were several other ragged men around her, all staring at her with malevolent eyes and pasty faces. She eyed each of them in turn, defiantly, daring them to harm her. At the moment, she had no plans of attempted escape. Without Kenneth to run to, there was no point. Life, at the moment, had no point.

There was movement next to her and when she turned to look, her defiance turned to shock. It was a face she knew very well.

"Brother Grendel?"

Grendel smiled weakly at her. He looked sick and thin, but it was still the same Brother Grendel she had known. "Good morn, Aubrielle."

She was thoroughly confused now. "What on earth are you doing here? What is happening?"

The brother attempted to comfort her but the man in black stopped him. "I will speak with the lady," he snapped. Grendel shut his mouth and the man focused on Aubrielle. "You are the Lady Aubrielle Grace de Witney, then."

She cast him a baleful glare. "What does that matter to you?"

"A great deal. In fact," he stroked his chin thoughtfully, "your mother told me that we would find you at Kirk just before we slit her throat and burned her body to cinder. I am glad to see that she did not lie to us."

If he was expecting a reaction, he was disappointed. Aubrielle already knew the fate of her mother and would not give him the satisfaction. With a supreme demonstration in control, she kept her expression from wavering.

"So you have found me," she said through clenched teeth. "Who are you? What is it you want of me?"

"Ah, she comes to the point and I like that," de Gaul said. His face quickly changed expression as his black eyes smoldered with intensity. "Since we know who you are, it is only proper that you know who we are. And since you are my prisoner, you cannot escape to expose us. My name is de Gaul. My men and I are known as *A Ordem do Anjo Preto.* We are The Order of the Black Angel and you, my lady, have something we want."

"I have never heard of your order."

"I am not surprised. Have you heard of the Templars?"

"Aye. But they were disbanded many years ago."

"We are their new order."

Her brow furrowed as she looked around. "But Templars were a helping order. As I recall, they took a vow of poverty but the order had grown so rich and powerful that King Phillip destroyed the order about twenty years ago."

"All is correct, as you say. The Templars had grown exceptionally powerful and the king of France, greedy. He only wanted what we had. There is no other excuse." De Gaul took a step towards her and crouched on the ground, eye-level with her. "My men and I have sworn vengeance on France. The king took everything we had and our resources are limited. We cannot raise an army to exact our revenge. The only thing that can help us is God himself, and in a vision, I was shown the way."

It was a fantastic story and he made it sound quite reasonable. But the flicker in the depths of de Gaul's eyes spoke only of insanity. "What way?" she was afraid to ask.

De Gaul smiled, a gesture that sent chills up her spine. "The Scroll of Munsalvaesche. I am told you know everything about it."

"What if I do? What use is it to you?"

"A great deal, my lady. The scroll gives the locale of the Grail. Whatever army holds this holy relic in its possession will be most powerful on earth. It will lay waste to whoever doubts or opposes it, especially heretics as King Phillip."

He wanted the Grail to seek his vengeance for what King Phillip had done to the Templars. Suddenly, it all became clear. All of the confusion, fear and death had been for a purpose. They wanted what she had also sought. She could see it, so clearly, without him having to further explain himself.

She rapidly considered her options. Clearly, she did not want to give up the scroll or tell them of its contents. She further suspected her life was not about to end if she did not tell him what he wanted to know. They needed her. She looked at Brother Grendel, surmising that, in their quest to locate the scroll, he had become an unwilling pawn. They had somehow traced it to St. Wenburgh and he had become involved. The poor man.

"What makes you think I do?"

"Your teacher has said you were fascinated by it and transcribed the entire scroll. He further says that you stole it from St. Wenburgh. If he has lied, then I will kill him right before your eyes."

She had no doubt they would kill him. They had no further use for him. One man, a thin figure in ragged mail, pulled out an enormous knife and made for the brother. Grendel gasped like a woman, putting up his hands to protect himself.

"Kill him and I shall tell you nothing," Aubrielle said quickly. "Spare him, let him leave in peace, and I shall tell you all that I know."

De Gaul stared at her a moment. A thin smile spread over his lips. "Anything is possible, my lady."

Aubrielle had a genuine fear for Brother Grendel. These men had killed her mother and had been in collusion with Lucius. She knew they were desperate.

"Let him go now," she said. "If I am what you truly seek, then let him go now, unharmed."

De Gaul made a show out of pretending to weigh his options. "What assurances do I have that you will tell us all we want to know?"

"My word as a lady. 'Tis all I can give you."

"Tell me now, all that you know, and I will judge whether or not that warrants the priest's freedom."

"Let him go, unharmed, or I will not tell you a word. Kill him, and I will not speak. Harm me, and you will never know. I am not afraid of you and I am not afraid of death. Do as I say. Release him."

De Gaul did not like to be ordered about by a woman; that much was evident. But he knew, simply by her manner and speech, that she meant what she said. He had no doubt. Without taking his eyes off her, he spoke to his men.

"Release the brother. He will receive no horse, no provisions, no protection and no weapons. The terms are to release him unharmed and nothing more. This I can do. If there truly is a God, then perhaps the Almighty will provide the rest."

One of the men untied Grendel's hands. Startled, he rose on unsteady legs and they pushed him away from Aubrielle. Her last vision of the priest was the man staggering into the trees. If the elements didn't get him, the thieves and bandits would. She was pleased for his freedom, fearful for his life. De Gaul grasped her firmly by the chin and forced her to look at him.

"Now," he said with the slightest smirk. "You will tell me; what does the Scroll of Munsalvaesche tell us about the location of the Grail?"

☙

IT WAS MISTY and warm, faint streams of light licking at his face. He could hear a soft droning in the background and gradually became aware of the voices around him. They seemed to fade and then grow strong again. And along with the sounds came a dull, throbbing pain that seemed to envelope his entire body. The brighter the light became and the louder the voices, the greater the ache. He felt like he was being born again, thrust out of the dark, warm canal and into the harsh world beyond.

"Look," he heard Everett's excited voice. "See here; he's moving."

Kenneth wasn't moving, exactly. But he did open an eye. It hurt to even do that, so he closed it again.

The startled physic scrutinized the movement, thinking that perhaps it was an unconscious reflex. But it looked real enough to his trained eye. Considering the wounds the man had sustained and the amount of time he had lain in the woods until he was found, it was a miracle in itself that he had survived.

"Sir Kenneth?" Argus lifted a closed eyelid again, inspecting the pupil. "Can you hear me?"

Kenneth's dry, cracked lips moved slightly. His tongue moved across them, with great effort, to moisten the flesh. "Aubrielle," he rasped.

Everett, Reid and Bradley were spread out in various posts around the musty chamber. They hadn't left Kenneth's side since he had been brought back to the castle three days prior. He had lingered near death for days. Now, they were thrilled and stunned to think that, perhaps, their liege would indeed pull through and they leapt up, hovering around his bed like eager children. The little dog, having slept on the floor diligently by Kenneth's side the entire time, now jumped up onto the mattress.

But Argus hushed the knights and put the dog back on the floor. He did not want his fragile patient disturbed. "Lady Aubrielle is missing, my lord. Can you tell us what happened?"

Kenneth had more pain than he ever thought possible and his muddled mind was having difficulty clearing the fog.

"Ambush," he muttered. "Lucius...."

The knights eyed each other ominously. Those two small words, as if Kenneth had known their question, told them what they had been waiting days to know. Everett hissed a curse and turned away, reviled. His mind was whirling with the succession of events leading to this moment; when their captain had escaped from the vault and Kenneth had turned up missing, they had no idea how Lucius had accomplished it. But he was their captain, a cunning man with connections and power, and it was not a surprise that he had an accomplice lurking about Kirk. They should have suspected and they should have kept a better watch on the vault. But they had been chasing after Lady Aubrielle at the time and thoughts of Lucius de Cor had faded from their minds for the time. It had been a grave mistake.

"Did Lucius take Lady Aubrielle?" Reid leaned in low against Kenneth's head.

Kenneth may have been mildly cognizant, but he was by no means out of the woods. The safety of unconsciousness was beckoning him once again. "Do... not know," he whispered. "There were others...."

Reid glanced at Everett, attempting to decipher what Kenneth was saying so he wouldn't have to say too much. "Others?" he repeated softly. "Ken, what others? Did you recognize them?"

Kenneth's ice-blue eyes closed. The exertion was too much. "West," was all he said.

He plunged into the fine waters of oblivion once again. Argus felt his pulse and lifted an eyelid before turning to the knights.

"That's all for now," he said seriously. "The man must rest."

"Is he going to live?" Everett demanded.

Argus was exhausted himself. He'd waited vigil for three days for the man in his care to live or die. "The man has been on Death's door for three days. He could cross the threshold at any moment, or he could just as easily return to the land of the living. Only time will tell us which path God has chosen for him."

Everett's expression told of his sorrow. His gaze drifted over Kenneth's enormous form, his broad back tightly bandaged where Argus had laboriously removed the two arrows. Kenneth had lost so much blood that they were positive he would die. But he continued to linger.

"He said 'west'," Reid said softly. "Did he mean that whoever has Lady Aubrielle took her in a westerly direction?"

"What else could he mean?" Bradley said from the shadows. "We combed those woods until not a leaf nor stone were left unturned. There were broken branches and footprints everywhere. Perhaps Ken saw them drag her off before he was hit."

"They hit him first," Everett muttered. "There is no way he would have allowed Lady Aubrielle to be taken had he been healthy and whole. If what he says is true, then Lucius fired two arrows into him to cripple him so that his way would be clear to abduct Lady Aubrielle. And one thing is for certain."

"What's that?" Reid asked.

"He wasn't drunk when he fired those arrows. He knew exactly what he was doing."

The situation was growing more sickening by the moment. Reid sighed heavily. "God's Bones," he growled. "It goes on and on. What has happened to this man we once called captain to turn him into such an evil monster? I cannot believe the appearance of Lady Aubrielle one week ago somehow provoked the man into madness, yet all evidence tells otherwise."

"This is my fault," Everett was despondent. "I should never have left him. He ordered me back to the castle, but I should have refused. I should have stayed to..."

"It wasn't your fault," Reid interrupted him. "We all share the guilt, Everett. Had we kept better watch on Lucius, none of this would have happened. The man knows Kirk like the back of his hand and we should have known he would have a way of escape from the vault. This is not your burden alone."

Everett was lost in his own world for the moment. "Do you know what it felt like to come across Kenneth with two arrows protruding out of his back, laying face-down against the earth? He must have lain there for hours before I realized he was missing. I should have known sooner. I should have been there!"

"Enough," Bradley snapped softly. "Had you not left Ken alone in the woods, Lucius might have killed you first on his quest to get at Ken. We can go over this a thousand times with a thousand different scenarios. But the fact remains that you cannot change the past. It is done. What is most important now is Ken's current condition. Argus has done all he can. The rest is up to God."

The quiet statement made them all look at Kenneth again. He was lying on his stomach, still as stone, his breathing labored. Argus' gaze lingered on his patient.

"If you are interested in my opinion," he said quietly. "I would worry less about Sir Kenneth and more about Lady Aubrielle. You must go after her."

Everett squared his shoulders. "I will go," he said firmly. "I will head west and not return until I find her."

"I shall also go," Reid said. "Brad, You are needed here. The command of Kirk is yours until we return."

Bradley nodded. "I will be here if Ken needs me."

"He loves her, you know."

Argus' tone was barely audible. The knights looked at him questioningly and he elaborated as if they were all deaf, dumb and blind to the truth.

"Sir Kenneth," he said. "He is in love with Lady Aubrielle and she with him."

The knights knew that. In the short time Kenneth had known her, those closest to him had seen an astonishing change. He had actually become human, though it was an imperceptible change to the inexperienced eye. Not strangely, Lady Aubrielle had become somewhat human, too. An amazing story was unfolding before their eyes. To see it come to this brutal end was beyond tragic.

"We shall do all we can to find her," Reid assured the old physic. "If Ken wakes again, make sure he knows that we have gone after her."

"But what about Lucius?" Bradley asked. "Do we assume he has her?"

"You heard Ken. He did not know. I can only surmise that if Lucius ambushed Ken, then he must at least have a hand in Aubrielle's abduction."

"Fair enough. But you did not answer my question. What are you going to do with him when, and if, you find him?"

Reid's jaw ticked. "There is no question. We are going to kill him."

ଓ

EVERETT WAS PACKING the last of his satchel when young Max entered his small, cramped chamber in the knight's quarters. The lad had been devastated by Kenneth's attack and had been further disappointed when told that he could not accompany the knights on their search for Aubrielle. When Everett saw him, he thought the boy had come to plead with him again.

But Max was there on a different mission. In fact, his face was pink with excitement.

"There is a man at the gates who says he knows of Lady Aubrielle," he said quickly. "You must come."

Everett shoved the last of the jerky into the pack. "No one knows she is missing, Max. Who is he?"

"He says he is a priest. He says that he has been three days in coming to us and knows of the men who hold her. Hurry!"

Everett didn't hesitate. He followed Max at a rapid pace from the knight's quarters to the guard house. Inside the massive gate, just this side of the portcullis, was a small room used by the gate guards. It was cold, cramped and uncomfortable at any given time of the year.

A very dirty, very pale man shivered on a stool against the wall, being watched by an armed guard. Everett walked up to man, sizing him up, wondering if he was a liar or simply crazy.

"Who are you?"

Grendel pulled his robe more tightly about him as if to protect himself. "I am Brother Grendel of St. Wenburgh," he said. "I bring news of the Lady Aubrielle Grace de Witney."

Everett sent the guard from the chamber. They had managed to keep news of Lady Aubrielle's abduction quiet for three days and were determined to maintain the secrecy. Those who knew of Sir Kenneth's wounds had been told a glorious story of his heroics, far from the truth. It was an attempt to keep life at Kirk as calm and normal as possible since the siege last week and the subsequent death of the beloved earl. The populace was still reeling from that; an abduction and attempted murder on top of everything would only serve to rouse fear and discord.

This man was a priest, which gave him more credibility in Everett's eyes. That and the fact that he did not have the look of a liar. Everett was grasping for any amount of hope at this point.

"What do you know about her?" he demanded quietly.

Grendel was quivering with fatigue, fear, exhaustion. "I know that she is in grave danger, my lord."

Everett grabbed him by his disheveled cowl. "How did you know to come to Kirk? Tell me who has sent you or I will kill you this moment."

Grendel recoiled. "I was held captive by the group that abducted your lady. I knew that she was taken from Kirk. I thought… I thought you would want to know her whereabouts and try to save her!"

He seemed genuine enough. At least Everett couldn't scare him into changing his story. He let go of the man. "Then where is she? Who has her?"

"A group with the foulest of intentions," the brother went on. "They are renegade Templars searching for the Grail. Lady Aubrielle has knowledge of a scroll that tells of its location."

Everett looked at Max; they were both slightly confused, more than slightly anxious. "You will forgive my bewilderment," Everett said. "This is all new information to me. Are you telling me that she was abducted because she has knowledge of a scroll?"

Grendel nodded his shaggy, dirty head. "Templars are an all-knowing, all-seeing sect of religious zealots. They have always been thus. They knew the Scroll of Munsalvaesche existed; a man by the name of Wolfram von Eschenbach told of a scroll written by King Titurel that spoke of the Grail's location. The scroll was taken from a castle in Catalonia and, from what I have gathered, the Templars traced the document across the continent to its final resting place at St. Wenburgh, where I am a teacher. Lady Aubrielle was one of my pupils. She had a special interest in this scroll, so much so that I believe she stole it from the monastery when she was discharged. The knights took me hostage and forced me to lead them to the Lady Aubrielle. They want her to tell them of the Grail's location."

"As described in this scroll?"

"Aye, my lord."

"My God," Everett breathed. "This is fantastic."

"Fantastic but true."

"But how did Lucius become involved?"

"Who is Lucius?"

"The captain of Kirk's army. He attempted to kill the man who was protecting Lady Aubrielle, thereby allowing your Templars to gain hold of her."

Brother Grendel shook his head. "I know nothing of this. But I know there were spies inside Kirk, searching for Lady Aubrielle. Perhaps somehow your captain came into contact with them."

Everett looked at Max as he filtered through the pieces of information. "And Lucius, already threatened by Lady Aubrielle's inheritance of Kirk and his general hatred of her, conspired with them to have her removed. Only Kenneth stood in his way, and when these spies somehow released Lucius from the vault, our captain showed his appreciation by attempting to kill Kenneth so these men could abduct Aubrielle." He hung his head in sorrow. "Good God, is this even possible that such a thing could happen?"

Max was young to hear of such treachery and betrayal. He was pale and visibly upset. "But why? Sir Kenneth has only served Sir Lucius with loyalty and dedication. Why would he try to kill him?"

Everett couldn't explain what he himself did not fully understand. He slapped the lad reassuringly on the arm.

"Who is Sir Kenneth?" Grendel asked.

Everett lifted his eyebrows; there wasn't an easy answer. "He is many things. Foremost, he is second in command of Kirk's army and betrothed to Lady Aubrielle. When he marries her, he shall become the 2nd Earl of Wrexham."

"And this Lucius, his captain, attempted to kill him?"

"Aye."

"But I do not understand."

"It is quite complicated, I assure you. Suffice it to say that even though Kenneth lies at death's threshold, all he has managed to speak of is Aubrielle. He only wishes for her safe return. And you say that she is unharmed?"

"She was well enough the last I saw her. But that was three days ago."

"Do you know where you last saw them?'

Grendel thought a moment. "I traveled the road that leads from Kirk for three days. I never traveled another. If you, therefore, retrace my steps for three days, that is the last place I saw her."

"Did they say where they were taking her, or what they planned to do with her?"

The brother nodded as if Everett had missed the entire point of the conversation. "They are taking her to the Grail, of course. The Scroll of Munsalvaesche tells of its location. Aubrielle knows where it is."

"And where is that?"

"Glastonbury."

ଓ

THE CANDLELIGHT WAS the only point of brightness in an otherwise black chamber. Kenneth didn't know how long his eyes had been open because it was so dark. But gradually, he realized he was seeing flickers of light and shadows of people across the wall. He blinked once, twice, and his arm twitched. It was numb from having been positioned above his head. The arm twitched again as he tried to bring it down.

"Ken?" Bradley's voice was soft. "Ken, are you awake?"

Kenneth's response was to take a long, slow breath. His body felt as it weighed a ton, and horrendous pain shot through his torso. But, strangely, he didn't feel as bad as he had the first time he had awoken.

"My arm," he muttered. "Help me…."

Bradley took hold and very carefully put his right arm down to his side. It was like lifting so much dead weight.

"Better?"

"Aye."

Argus' face loomed in Kenneth's line of sight. He looked frightful from days of no sleep, like a twisted little troll. "I fear this is a foolish question, but can you tell me how you are feeling?"

Kenneth tried to swallow, his throat dry and parched. "Compared to what?" he whispered. "Water, please."

Hearing his master's voice, the little dog jumped up on this bed again and licked Kenneth's chin. This time, Argus didn't remove the beast as it settled contentedly near Kenneth's head. Bradley grabbed at a pitcher of cool water, almost spilling it off the table. Argus took the cup from the knight lest he slop it all over the patient.

"I am going to have Bradley move you so you can better drink," he said. "This may hurt a bit."

Kenneth tried to brace himself, but nothing compared to the reality of movement for the first time in days. When Bradley grabbed hold of his massive shoulders and pulled him slightly on to his left side, Kenneth thought he was going to pass out. But he held his ground, his face a sickly white color, as Argus held the cup to his lips. He was able to drink nearly the entire contents. When Bradley rolled him back on to his stomach, Kenneth couldn't help the grunt that escaped his lips.

Argus took a cool, damp cloth and wiped his patient's face. "You are stronger than I thought, Sir Kenneth," the old man said. "By all rights, you should be dead. It's a miracle you have survived this far."

The cool cloth felt good. He closed his eyes as Argus wiped it over his shoulder and down the arm that was slowly regaining feeling.

"What of Aubrielle?" he rasped.

Argus looked at Bradley, who stepped forward so that Kenneth could see him. "Everett and Reid left two days ago," Bradley said. "They'll find her or die trying, Ken, I swear it."

Kenneth's response was to open an eye. The light in the ice-blue orbs was dim, but it wasn't out completely. The embers of life, of the old Kenneth, still burned.

"Last I saw her, she was being taken west," his voice was so soft they could barely hear him.

"We figured that out. But did you recognize the men who took her?"

"Only Lucius. Is there any sign of him?"

Bradley shook his head. "He is long gone."

"Perhaps with Aubrielle," Kenneth's expression took on a pained look. "There is no telling what he will do to her, if he has not already."

Another man came into Kenneth's line of sight. Bradley had him by the arm, pulling him toward the bed. He was a slight man, with thinning blond hair and a frightened look on his face.

"This is Brother Grendel," Bradley said. "He was a captive with the group of men who abducted Aubrielle. Aubrielle negotiated for his release and he came back here to help us. He told Everett and Reid everything he could before they went in search of her."

For the first time, some life seemed to come back into Kenneth's face. He gave the brother a second, more penetrating look.

"She is alive?"

Grendel nodded. "She is well, my lord.

"Is Lucius with her?"

"I have been told who this Lucius is," Grendel said. "I never saw the man. He did not travel with the group once they abducted the lady, of that I am certain."

That statement brought overwhelming relief. To know that Lucius did not have her, to know that she was alive and well, was an answer to his prayers. But the knowledge also brought on a host of new, desperate questions.

"God be praised," he muttered. "Then who are these men who hold her?"

Bradley pulled up a stool for the priest; the man looked as if he was about to collapse. Several days of fear, little food and almost no rest had taken its toll. His primary reason for being in the chamber was at Everett's request to provide last rites to Kenneth, which he had already done. Even though he was not yet a fully consecrated priest, he hoped God would forgive him. Sir Kenneth had been in a bad way and there was no one else to purify his soul.

"They are dangerous men in search of something Lady Aubrielle has knowledge of," Grendel said. "Did she ever tell you about St. Wenburgh?"

"Many times."

"I am a teacher at that place."

Kenneth took a long look at him. "I do not understand. What do you have to do with any of this?"

Grendel wasn't sure how to lead into this; when he had told Everett everything, he had been scared and blunt. But to a dying man, he was trying to be gentle. "Did she ever mention the Grail?"

"Many, many times."

"Then you know… of her desire."

"What are you leading to?"

"That the men who have taken her want her to guide them to the location of the Grail."

Kenneth was silent for a moment, digesting the information. His mind was not so muddled with pain and weakness that he could not put the clues together.

"Does this have anything to do with the Scroll of Munsalvaesche?"

"It does. Did she tell you of it?"

Kenneth sighed heavily. "She did. Then I can correctly surmise that the men who abducted her were also the men that murdered her mother in their quest for this scroll."

Grendel closed his eyes, briefly, reliving the horror of that event. He did not think he would ever be able to shake the vivid images.

"I can vouch for this, my lord. I was there and unable to stop them. But it wasn't the scroll they wanted as much as they wanted Lady Aubrielle. They knew she had studied it and was the best person to take them to the Grail."

Grendel proceeded to tell him the entire story, about The Order of the Black Angel and their purpose in life. He did not know the facts of Lucius' association with them, but added what he and the knights had managed to deduce. Kenneth listened, his ice blue eyes staring at the wall. He did not react to anything he was told. When Brother Grendel finished, the room fell silent and Kenneth continued to stare at the wall. Bradley and the brother exchanged glances, wondering if Kenneth had even heard anything of what was said. Other than his regular breathing, he was unresponsive to an otherwise explosive tale.

Kenneth's soft voice finally broke the stillness. "She said that she has always wanted to go to Glastonbury to search for the Grail," he said. "I doubt this is the way she wished to go. From what you have told me,

I have no doubt that those knights will keep her alive until they find what they are looking for. But after they have secured it, her life is forfeit. They will kill her."

"That is my feeling as well, my lord," Grendel said softly. "Murder is not unknown to them."

"Reid and Everett have been gone a day in search of her," Bradley said helpfully. "They will find her, Ken. You must have faith."

Kenneth's gaze drifted to the brother. "How many men would you say hold her?"

"About twelve, my lord."

Kenneth looked back to Bradley. "How many men did Everett and Reid take with them?"

"Fourteen men at arms."

"Against Templars?" Kenneth's voice was tinged with disbelief. "These men are seasoned warriors, hard to the bone and bred for battle. Reid knows this if Everett does not. Why did they take so few men?"

Bradley didn't have an answer. "This I cannot tell you, Ken. But they rode from Kirk armed to the teeth, I assure you."

Kenneth didn't say anything for some time. He remained unmoving, his eyes fixed back on the wall again in a trance-like state of distant thought. He sighed after several long moments, indicative of the heaviness on his mind, heart and body.

"I would eat something now," he said quietly.

Argus wagged a finger at him. "Broth and wine only. You cannot tolerate more."

"Then bring it. And bring something for the priest. He is close to collapse."

Grendel was grateful. Though the guard at the gatehouse had given him some bread, still, he could have eaten much more. It had been a long few days and he needed to regain both strength and sanity.

Argus fled the chamber in his quest for Kenneth's nourishment. Kenneth dismissed Bradley for the time being, knowing the knight must have surely been at his side both day and night. He looked like hell. When the chamber was empty but for Brother Grendel and himself, he shifted his pained body slightly so he could gain a better view of the priest.

"Now," he said quietly. "You and I will speak privately."

"What of, my lord?"

"Aubrielle. Tell me her true state when last you saw her."

Grendel thought a moment. "She was defiant and strong, as she always is. Her negotiation for my release was cunning."

"How was she physically? Did they hurt her in the capture?"

"She had a bloodied lip, but nothing more. She has been known to fight when provoked."

A faint smile creased Kenneth's lips. "Well I know," he murmured. His smile faded as he took on a distant look. "She is a strong woman."

There was something in his tone that made Grendel take a second look. He'd seen the expression before, though he'd never personally experienced the emotion usually associated with it. The man was in love. Knowing Lady Aubrielle as he had over the years, he wondered what kind of man would love such a headstrong, independent woman. Personally, he thought him somewhat foolish, but he would not argue with the influence of emotion. He found it rather touching.

"Would… would you like me to tell you of the Lady Aubrielle I have known?" he ventured. "I first met her when she was a child of nine years. I was a neophyte at the time, as old as the lady is now. Frankly, she terrified me."

"It is a trait she has."

"Shall I tell you of the time she brained Lord Wilcoxon of Ilsby because the lad stole her ration of bread? He thought he could get away with it because she was such a tiny little thing, but she exacted her revenge and then some."

A glimmer came to Kenneth's eye. "I think I have been waiting all my life to hear this story."

"I shall tell you that and more just like it. Of course, Monsignor punished her for her actions when he could catch her, but there were those of us who secretly admired her fortitude. She was like a lovely wild creature; we could not tame her, though we tried."

Something in his statement made Kenneth remember something Aubrielle had told him once; *if you are thinking of beating obedience into me, do not bother.* He remembered the scars across her shoulders. He knew that he should be bitter towards this priest for the brutality he represented, yet he found himself unable to complete the cycle because the man had come at great peril to help them find Aubrielle.

"I saw your attempts to tame her. They cover her back."

"I know. But they were not of my doing, my lord. In fact, on more than one occasion, I prevented even more than what she already has."

Kenneth didn't push. He sensed the man was telling the truth. Moreover, he was in no position to punish him for past sins or send him away out of anger. He needed him at the moment, as the last person who saw Aubrielle alive.

"I would hear your stories now."

"As you wish. But if you ever tell her that I told you, I shall deny it to my grave."

"If she finds out you've told me less than kind things about her, the grave may come sooner than you think."

Grendel grinned. He liked this man.

CHAPTER ELEVEN

ONE OF THE men had given her a dirty, worn cloak to protect her against the cold. They had taken her with nothing but the clothes on her back, in the heavy yellow brocade gown she had been wearing for almost a week now. The thin sleeves were torn and the voluminous skirt was soiled to the core. She used to love the garment; now she hated it. There were spots of Kenneth's blood on the hemline and she fingered the stains on a regular basis in a bizarre comfort ritual. The gown reminded her of the darkest moment of her life but as much as she hated the article of clothing, she knew she would never be able to part with it. Part of Kenneth was on it and she would keep it forever.

The darkness of time and space were passing in a blur; they carried no meaning to her. Several days of travel saw her and her captors on the outskirts of Bristol. It would be at least another four days to reach Glastonbury. At a quickened pace, they were covering nearly twenty miles a day. In Gloucester, they had stolen a horse for Aubrielle, so at least she was riding alone and no longer with de Gaul.

The weather was improved during the day even if the nights were cold. The black knights kept a tight watch on Aubrielle, always keeping her in the center of their group and making sure to steer clear of cities, crowds, and people in general. They didn't want her raising an alarm, and they themselves were used to staying well out of sight. The Templars had been an increasingly reclusive order during the last years and were conditioned to remain hidden.

De Gaul selected an area well away from the road in which to camp for the night. Since they did not want to draw attention to themselves, there was never a fire. Aubrielle was given whatever they could scrounge to eat; berries, roots, and the raw fish they caught in the streams. It was horrible fare. She had gagged on more than one occasion. De Gaul had promised her more decent provisions once they reached Bristol, for apparently he intended to steal it. Aubrielle had heard him talking with some of his men about raiding food stores. She didn't care, nor was she hungry for any of his ill-gotten gains. She was so numb, emotionally and physically, that nothing in the world mattered to her.

Her bones were cold in spite of the warmth of the day, and she was filthy from travel. At sunset, de Gaul planted her squarely in the center of their encampment so she could be easily watched. Being the summer season, the men scavenged about and were able to find ripe apples and pears for their sup, and soon she was up to her ankles in offerings. Aubrielle had to admit that they attempted, as best as murderers could, to see to her needs. Cleaning two of the apples off on her skirt, she ate them in quick succession.

"You are hungry this eve," de Gaul came up behind her. "That is good. You need to keep up your strength."

Aubrielle wouldn't look at him. She tossed the cores to the ground beside her and pulled the dirty cloak around her shoulders. De Gaul crouched a few feet away from her, toying with stalks of grass.

"Bristol is over the hill," he said. "You shall have meat and bread tonight."

She glared at him, gave a heavy sigh of disgust, and looked away. She had been intent on giving him the silent treatment for the past few days so he would know how much she hated him. De Gaul snorted softly.

"You are welcome." His gaze moved over her soiled clothing. "I shall also try to find you something clean and suitable to wear."

She forgot her plan of not speaking to him. "You'll not touch this dress. I will not take it off."

"But it is torn and dirty. Surely you would like something warmer and cleaner."

"I do not want anything warmer or cleaner. I want this dress to be a constant reminder of what you have done to me. I do not know you, nor have I ever harmed you, but still, you are driven to murder those closest to me to destroy my life. Let this dress remind you of that, always."

De Gaul considered her words. "Your mother was an unfortunate casualty."

"Is that what you call it? Then what was Kenneth; a necessary one?"

"He was an obstacle."

"You had Lucius kill him," she snarled.

"The man you call Lucius was a fortunate happenstance. He hated your companion and was quite willing to help us."

Aubrielle had known that all along, but it was still sickening to hear it. She fought off her grief, but pieces slipped through and her anguish was apparent. "At what price?"

"Oh, there was no price, my lady," de Gaul said casually. "He provided his services for free."

"I do not understand."

"He did it for the pleasure of it."

It was a stab to her heart. More anguish became apparent. "Where is he?"

"This, I am not sure. But he did mention paying the king a visit."

No doubt to tell the man lies of Kenneth, and of Kirk in general. Lucius would do such a thing to protect himself and to find himself reinstated at some other post to finish out his career. He was ruined at Kirk; there was no one there now to refute his lies other than Everett, Reid and Bradley, but for the lower rank officers to speak against their captain, true or not, would be considered treasonous. Lucius was politically savvy and cunning, as always. He killed Kenneth and would now retreat to London, find favor with the king, and move on to another royal post.

The very thought disgusted her. Lucius would get away with murder. She struggled with her anger, her tears. "Kenneth was a strong, virtuous man with more integrity and compassion than you can possibly comprehend. He was perfect, and you murdered him as if he meant absolutely nothing."

"Some must be sacrificed for a greater good."

"There is no greater good," Aubrielle exploded. "You have done all of this killing to find a holy relic. You mean to use the Grail to destroy and destruction is never for the greater good. Do you really think God will allow you to carry out your plans?"

"God has destroyed, when necessary."

"But you are not God. And you are arrogant to assume that you can dispense retribution as He can."

Something in de Gaul's gaze hardened. "Do not speak to me of retribution. You know nothing."

"I know that God will punish you for what you've done. I pray every night that you will die a thousand painful deaths, as my mother and Kenneth did. I hope you burn in hell."

He lashed out, striking her across the face. Aubrielle fell back, her hand on her throbbing cheek. She watched de Gaul walk away, his strides long and angry. For a moment, she had seen her death in his eyes. It did not frighten her. She realized more that she wanted to see Lucius and de Gaul punished for what they did to Kenneth. She knew they had written her off, a foolish woman that would soon be dead. But she would not die so easily.

She wanted to live long enough to see them pay.

ꟹ

IT WAS THE morning of the seventh day after Aubrielle's abduction. Kenneth knew this because Grendel had told him. Otherwise, he had no concept of time. All he knew was that today was the day.

It began as any other day. He was awake before dawn, listening to the little dog snore at the foot of his bed. He'd been listening to that dog snore for days and it brought him comfort. It reminded him of Aubrielle. Slowly, he rolled onto his side. He'd been able to do that since yesterday and though the pain was agonizing, he was able to manage it. He used it to toughen him. It reminded him that he was indeed alive and that every day was seeing his strength return. Aubrielle was out there and she needed him to come and rescue her. He could not do that lying on his back.

Sitting up was another matter, however. Since it was apparent he was on the road to recovery, the day and night bedside vigil had stopped. Only Argus wandered in and out, a few times a night, to check on his patient. At dawn, the old man was asleep and Kenneth was able to struggle to a seated position on the side of the bed. The room was rocking and his body felt like jelly, but he was determined not to let it ruin him. There was so much pain it seemed to come from every corner of his battered carcass, but he knew from Argus that he only had two wounds, one to his lower back and one in his left shoulder. Strangely, it was the wound to his shoulder that hurt the most. His left arm was virtually useless.

Eventually, the room stopped swaying. He actually felt better to sit up and take the pressure off his chest and stomach. He gingerly stretched one arm and then the other, one leg and then the other. His blood began to flow. Feeling confident, he tried to stand up and immediately realized it may not have been the best of ideas.

His legs felt like they had the strength of a newborn colt. He stood for several minutes, determined not to sit again, absolutely determined to walk to the wardrobe and find some clothes. He was in the earl's chamber and knew there were still clothes in the wardrobe, at least enough to cover him so he could return to his quarters and retrieve his own.

He heard thumping on the floor and glanced down to find the dog at his feet, wagging his tail happily. Like the crowds in the lists during a tourney, he sensed that the pup was cheering him on. That flopping little tail was encouraging him. Foolish thought, he knew, but he liked to think it nonetheless. He took a couple of steps and the dog followed. He was able to make it to the wardrobe and retrieve breeches and a tunic. Garson had been a tall man, but hadn't nearly Kenneth's bulk. He had to sit on the bed to pull on the breeches, which were too snug, but the tunic was moderately acceptable. By the time he stood back up again, Argus was coming in for his morning rounds. One look at Kenneth and his eyes flew open wide.

"Sir Kenneth!" he exclaimed. "What are you doing?"

Kenneth was pale, but he was moving better than he had been initially. "It is my intention to retrieve my armor, my charger, and go after Reid and Everett."

"You are mad!" Argus hissed. "You are still a very sick man. If you go, you'll only do more damage."

"Be that as it may, I am going."

Argus did something then that, under normal circumstances, he would have never attempted. He grabbed Kenneth by the arms. "You are not immortal," he said. "You'll do your lady no good if you kill yourself in the attempt. You have a wound to the lower portion of your back that, by the grace of God, missed your spine, but the healing wound is still fragile. The wound to your shoulder is worse; it nicked a major vessel and it was a miracle that you did not bleed to death. You must allow yourself time to heal."

Kenneth's ice-blue eyes had lost none of their intimidation as he glared at the tiny old man. "I will heal. But the more time passes, the more Aubrielle slips from my grasp. She is alive and I intend to find her."

"Reid and Everett have already gone after her. They have several days head start. They will get to her before you can."

"I must go. If you cannot understand why, then I cannot explain it to you."

"I know that you are in love with the lady. That is no secret. But if you kill yourself trying to save her, everything will have been for naught. Your legacy, your memory, will seep into this earth to be forever forgotten and Lady Aubrielle's fate will be consigned to God. Would you waste so easily what has been given to you?"

For the first time since Argus had known him, Kenneth's rock-hard gaze softened. There was a vulnerability that he had never seen before.

"I am not attempting to waste anything, nor am I ungrateful for the blessing God has seen fit to give me. But I believe the fact that I did not die from my wounds to be a sign. I am living for a reason, and that reason is to save Aubrielle." A pained expression crossed his usually stoic face. "That irrational, headstrong woman means the world to me. I must go."

There he stood, with all of his frail human characteristics. The mighty Kenneth was finally showing what he was made of and Argus knew there would be no discouraging him. "Then I shall go as well. You may have need of me."

Kenneth didn't argue with him. He'd seen Argus in battle and the old man was as strong as the rest of them. Stiffly, he moved for the door with the physic at his side, making sure he didn't injure himself. The little dog brought up the rear.

"It is my intention to go to the knight's quarters, secure my gear, and retain thirty men at arms to accompany me to Glastonbury," Kenneth said. "I would appreciate it if you could find Bradley and have him prepare the men."

"I will. Anything else?"

"The priest. He will go with us to identify the men that hold her."

"Wouldn't want to charge headlong into the wrong nest of bandits, eh?"

Kenneth's mind was already preparing for the battle to come, envisioning victory. More than vengeance, he simply wanted Aubrielle back in his arms, safe and whole.

"I want to look into the eyes of the men who took Aubrielle from me," he said quietly. "Let there be no mistake. They will pay."

Argus' eyes glittered knowingly. "The price will undoubtedly be high."

Kenneth did not reply. They both knew the answer.

☙

SHE HAD WAITED until well after mid-night before making her move. Aubrielle had spent her entire life escaping one way or the other and was well-versed in covert tactics. She was cunning and smart, as her mother, father, the monks at St. Wenburgh, and even Kenneth had discovered on occasion. Though there were two men on duty, it had been relatively simple to slip past them and into the woods. Once inside the trees, she ran as fast and as hard as she could and never looked back.

She'd been planning her escape since sundown. She knew in which direction Bristol was and headed for the town. It would be easier to lose herself in the bustle of the big city. She knew that de Gaul would hunt her down and she had every intention of erasing her trail.

Nestled in Somerset, Bristol was a large town, much larger than most of the villages that were scattered over this section of the country. From her days at St. Wenburgh, Aubrielle knew that Bristol was near the sea; she couldn't see it, but she had been smelling it all day. She also knew it was about a day's ride to Glastonbury. To be so close to Glastonbury would have been maddening had she given it much thought. But all she could think of was returning to Kirk, to tend Kenneth's grave, and to assume her position as heiress to the earldom of Wrexham. Strange how she had never wanted any of it, but now with Kenneth gone, she somehow felt it an appropriate tribute to his memory. They were to share it together, and now she was to face her destiny alone. She would return to Kirk and take her place. It was what Kenneth would have wanted.

She ran until she could run no more. She could see the town ahead of her and outlying farms. She turned to her right and passed the first few farms. She didn't want to make it easy for de Gaul to find her. Randomly selecting a small, dilapidated barn somewhere closer to the town, she slipped inside.

There were a herd of goats, a cow, and a very old-looking horse inside. It smelled strongly of urine and hay. A small loft was above her and she was exhausted. There was no ladder, but a few pieces of wood secured against the wall provided access. Climbing the wood in her heavy, torn and wet dress was a feat, but she managed. The hay was piled up against the narrow side of the loft and she threw herself into it. Able to relax for the first time in a week, she drifted quickly to sleep.

It was bright when next she opened her eyes. She thought she heard voices and, even in her exhausted state, experienced a flash of panic. She found herself staring into two small faces and two curious sets of eyes. Quickly, she sat up, cowering back against the wall.

"Do not be frightened. We will not hurt you."

Aubrielle blinked her sleepy eyes, thinking maybe she was dreaming. The face was small but the features were clearly mature. It was also male, as was his companion. But the voice that came forth was strangely deep, yet squeaky in quality. It was a very strange combination. He held out an enormous hand.

"Please," the little man said. "Do not be afraid. We've been looking for you."

It took Aubrielle a moment to realize that these two little men were not within the norm. In a world where fairies and elves were readily accepted, she had never seen one and, therefore, did not believe in their existence. But these two small men could have easily been taken for those from the other world. Yet Aubrielle was practical; she had seen dwarfs before. Argus himself was a dwarf.

"I am not afraid," she said. "What do you mean when you say that you've been looking for me?"

The two little men could see that she was standoffish, suspicious. "I am Miach, and this is Lugh," the first man indicated his companion. "We have come to help you."

Aubrielle thought she was dreaming again. They made absolutely no sense at all. "What do you mean? Who are you, and how did you know I was here?"

"We were asked to help you," the second man, Lugh, said. "You are a *senhora do rolo de papel*, are you not?"

"I have no idea what you just said."

"The lady of the scroll."

It took Aubrielle a brief second of indecision before she shoved one of the little men aside and made haste for the wooden steps that led from the loft. The men hastened after her.

"My lady, wait," Miach pleaded. "We mean you no harm, truly. But you are the Lady and we have been asked to help you!"

Aubrielle kicked out, throwing Lugh back on his buttocks. "Leave me alone! I will not go back to him, do you hear? I will not go back!"

She had her hands on the first rung of the ladder. Miach caught up to her.

"Please, my lady," he pleaded. "If you leave now, he will find you."

She froze, eyeing the little men, terrified and bewildered. Miach nodded his head to support his last statement. "He is close. If you leave, he will find you."

Aubrielle's heart was racing and she fought her natural instinct to run. The little man's expression was sincere and she was inclined to believe him. "De Gaul?"

"You must stay here. Wait until darkness."

After several long, agonizing moments, she let go of the makeshift ladder. Taking a deep breath, she labored to calm herself and think rationally.

"Tell me everything," she said. "Who are you, really?"

"Miach and…"

She put up a quelling hand. "Lugh, aye, I heard you the first time. But why did you call me the Lady of the Scroll?"

Miach smiled as if she had asked the most rudimentary of questions. "Because that is what you have always been. We have always known you."

"Who are you?"

"You have always known us, too."

Aubrielle shook her head slowly, having difficulty following their cryptic words. "I do not know you, little man."

Before Miach could reply, Lugh spoke softly behind him. "That

Munsalvaesche wants for its Grail, for the knights, the *aeterno defensor*, have taken it to *Insula Vitrum* to restore the health of the sleeping land."

The color drained from Aubrielle's face. "How did you know that?" she whispered.

"We have been raised in this tradition, for thirty generations. We have been born to protect that which Christendom holds most sacred. We have known of your coming. We are here to help you."

"I do not understand."

"We are the *aeterno defensor*."

"The knights of Munsalvaesche?" Aubrielle repeated with disbelief. "I cannot consider that possibility. They are myth."

"Myths are borne from reality. Our kind has never died. We are the farmers of the field, or the smith, or the physic. We do not exist as we used to, as a collective group of knights. That day is gone. But when we are called upon, we amass once again to protect our legacy."

"So you hide?"

"We conceal. It has become necessary not to attract attention to ourselves, where once we were proud and open."

Aubrielle gazed steadily at the man. Perhaps there was truth to what he said. The knights of Munsalvaesche had been forced to evolve with the time, through the Dark Ages, into the age they now knew. There were those, such as de Gaul, who searched for the Grail with a darker purpose. But there had also been those whose purpose had been altruistic.

Slowly, she shook her head. "I cannot believe you."

"Perhaps not. But will you trust us?"

Aubrielle did not have much choice. These little men had found her and could easily alert de Gaul were they so inclined. "If you really are who you say you are, then prove this to me. Why did Arthur and his knights not find the Grail when they searched for it? Did the knights of Munsalvaesche somehow prevent this?"

Miach and Lugh smiled in tandem. "They had the Grail all of the time."

"What do you mean?"

"Do you not understand, my lady?" Miach asked quietly. "Throughout time, the Grail has always been one thing – the strength of mankind and the legacy of our future. Every age had their Grail. Our Lord Jesus was in possession of his Grail, the strength of his future and lineage. When Our Lord was crucified, the Grail came to Munsalvaesche and we protected her."

The last word in his sentence was not lost on Aubrielle. She repeated the word slowly. "Her?"

Miach nodded. "Think on your history, my lady. The Grail was indeed a vessel, but not an inanimate one; it was a living vessel. The original Grail was Mary Magdalene, for she gave Christ strength and continued his legacy. For Arthur, his Grail was Guinevere, only he did not realize it. He spent years searching for what he already had, if he'd only allowed her to achieve her potential. She was his life and legacy that was never to be. And you… you carry their destiny also. Every age has its Grail. That is why we are here to protect you."

Somehow, it all made sense. Anything she had ever read about the Grail, like pieces of a giant puzzle, were coming together in a logical fashion. She had once told Kenneth in a fit of emotion that he was her Grail; perhaps it had been the other way around. She had always known it wasn't an object, but something else. It never occurred to her that it was a human, and least of all, her. The mere thought that it might actually be true was overwhelming, beyond what she could possibly comprehend.

"Who told you I was here?"

"One of our order who was sent long ago to watch for you. Not directly, of course, but indirectly. He took his commission at Kirk Castle, always close enough to catch word of you from time to time. When you came to Kirk last month, we rejoiced."

Aubrielle stared at the little men. The name of their cohort came to her lips before she could think it. "Argus."

"Son of Nuadu Airgetlam of the healing order. He sent word to us that you were missing. He asked us to find you before harm befell you." Miach grew serious as he spoke. "We did not foresee the path your life has taken; the men who are after you are evil, my lady. They have caused much grief in the name of God."

Aubrielle's eyes filled with tears. Her hand covered her mouth, keeping the sobs at bay. She was having a difficult time coming to terms with what the little men were telling her.

"If what you say is true, then how did Argus send word to you?"

"There are many ways, my lady. People are not the only living creatures with a language. There are birds, crickets, the fish in the streams. All one need do is speak; then you must know how to listen."

She wiped her eyes. "Are you telling me that Argus told a bird that I had been abducted and the bird flew to you?"

Miach smiled. "Something like that. A note tied to the bird's foot will do just as well."

It made more sense now. The mysticism was still strong, but Aubrielle was coming to understand that there were more earthly forces at work. Yet the fact remained that these little men were here to help her, and she felt a sense of overwhelming hope.

"I… I just want to go home," she murmured. "My beloved… those evil men killed him. If for no other reason, I must go home to see that he is properly taken care of."

Miach's grin broadened and he took her small, cold hand in his big warm one. "I am told that a knight rides even now to save you. Perhaps your beloved was not killed after all."

It was too much to hope for. Aubrielle burst into soft sobs, squeezing the dwarf's hand thankfully. As she wiped her nose and listened to Miach's soft words of comfort, Lugh climbed to the wall of the barn, peering out from between the slats. There was activity outside, near the tree line in the distance. He hissed at the others.

"Stay quiet," he whispered. "I see men in the trees."

Aubrielle's tears instantly faded as she and Miach scrambled over to the wall. The slats were wide and they were able to gain a view of the trees in the distance. They could see movement and when Aubrielle was finally able to focus on a figure, her blood ran to ice.

"'Tis them," she hissed. "I must hide!"

"No, wait," Miach held her fast. He gave Lugh a shove on the shoulder. "Go and make a distraction."

Rapidly, quietly, the three of them hustled down the makeshift ladder to the ground floor of the barn. The goats, the cow, and the old horse looked at them curiously. Aubrielle kept an eye on the tree line beyond while Miach and Lugh collaborated. Finally, Lugh took Aubrielle's soiled cloak and threw it over his head. Taking the biggest goat out of the herd, he leapt upon its back and the beast bolted from the barn in terror. The last Aubrielle saw, Lugh was racing towards the tree line atop the back of a rabid goat.

"Come on," Miach pulled her in the opposite direction.

Keeping low, they ducked from the barn and made a dash towards a cluster of homes in the distance. Much would depend upon how long Lugh would be able to stay atop the beast and lead de Gaul and his men astray. Aubrielle ran like the wind, not daring to look back. Miach was fast on his stubby legs and she followed his rabbit-like dashes through bushes and over streams. It occurred to her at some point that he didn't look like any knight she had ever seen, especially a knight of Munsalvaesche, but she pushed the subject aside. She had to trust that he was leading her to safety and prayed she wasn't being naïve. She had no choice but to have faith.

There were farmers in their fields as the two of them raced through. Aubrielle's slippers were rags on her feet and she felt every rock. Her gown, in tatters, was gathered up around her knees. She ran until her lungs felt like they were about to burst from her chest. She could see Bristol in the distance like a beacon and she would not let it out of her sight.

Something whizzed past her head, clipping her ear. It was sharp and she winced, her hand flying up to her head. It came away sticky with blood. She could hear shouting and she almost collapsed in grief; she knew, without looking, that de Gaul and his men had somehow caught up to her.

Miach looked over her shoulder, noting she had slowed down. There was blood on her left ear, streaking down her face. He slowed down and took her by the hand, urging her on. Several yards behind them were men on horseback with crossbows, dark men in old armor.

"Run, my lady," Miach urged her. "Come on!"

Aubrielle was holding her injured ear. She was trying to run, trying to hold her gown so she wouldn't trip on it, sobs coming to her lips as she realized it was futile. She had never been a quitter and the concept was unknown to her, but she knew she had been caught. Discouragement set in. She feared what would happen to Miach.

"Another step and I kill you both!"

De Gaul's voice boomed over the field. Aubrielle and Miach came to a halt, turning to face the group behind them. The Order of the Black Angel was in pursuit to varying degrees, but Aubrielle saw no sign of Lugh. De Gaul reined his black, bloodied charger forward.

"A fair try, my lady, but your attempt was in vain," he smiled thinly. "Who is your companion?"

Miach held Aubrielle's hand tightly. "A stranger who sought to help, my lord."

De Gaul's dark eyes blazed at him. "That, little man, will be your undoing."

Without hesitation, he lifted the crossbow. Aubrielle cried out. "No!" she put herself between Miach and de Gaul. "He was only doing as I asked. You will not harm him."

De Gaul did not have a clean shot at him. Sensing this, the wicked knights flanking him raised their crossbows. There was no way for Aubrielle to protect the little man from all sides. She backed up, trying to use her slight form to shield him. She was terrified that they had come to a dead end.

She heard the sound of an arrow being launched, followed by a painful grunt. Shocked, Aubrielle watched as two of de Gaul's men took arrows to the chest and toppled off their steeds. Suddenly, The Order of the Black Angel was in chaos as arrows flew at them from all directions. De Gaul, momentarily distracted from Aubrielle, took two arrows to the chest in harsh succession and within seconds was a casualty on the ground.

Aubrielle and Miach fell to the earth so they would not become targets. To the northeast, riding hard from a cluster of dense trees, were a group of heavily armed men. Straining to get a look at them, Aubrielle saw the green and scarlet of Wrexham come into view. It was the most beautiful sight she had ever seen.

The Order was scattering, though a few drew their weapons to fight. Mostly, they ran. Aubrielle leapt to her feet and began running like mad for the men she recognized. She heard Everett before she saw him. He very nearly ran her over in his excitement. Dismounting his charger, he reached out just in time to catch her as she fell into his arms.

"Aubrielle," he held her so that she would not fall. "Are you hurt?"

"I am well." Suddenly realizing she was safe, she burst into sobs. "'Tis a miracle you found me when you did. They were about… about to…"

Her weeping overcame her and she was unable to continue. Everett soothed her. "The priest you sent to Kirk helped us find your path."

"Grendel found you?"

"He did. Thank God, he did. He told us of the men who abducted you. We rode as hard and fast as we could until we came across their encampment from last night. After that, we simply followed their trail."

It was a sweet, simple miracle. There could be no other explanation and Aubrielle's heart rejoiced. But an even greater concern came to mind.

"Oh, Everett," she gasped. "I saw Lucius shoot Kenneth. Did he… is he…?"

"He lives, my lady. On death's door, his concern is only for you."

It was too much. Aubrielle's emotions got the better of her and she collapsed completely in Everett's young, strong arms. He picked her up, a weeping, sobbing mess, and held her while she cried. He didn't know what else to do. Having come upon her when they did, he was fairly shaken himself.

Reid came thundering up, flipping up his visor when he saw that Everett had the prize. "Is she well?" he shouted.

"Well enough," Everett replied. "The lady needs food and a warm fire."

Reid peered at Aubrielle, dirty and tired in Everett's arms. "Praise to God," he muttered, crossing himself. "I truly had no idea what we would find."

Aubrielle's head suddenly came up, her pale cheeks streaked with tears. "Miach," she said.

"My lady?" Everett queried.

"The little man that was with me," her gaze moved over the field. "Where is he?"

The knights looked out to the field as well. Except for Wrexham men-at-arms checking the dead and injured, including de Gaul, there was no one else.

"I do not see anyone, my lady," Reid said.

Aubrielle pushed herself out of Everett's grasp, taking a few steps on weary legs in the direction of the field. Her eyes searched and searched but she, too, saw no one other than dead or dying members of the Order and Wrexham men.

"Where did he go?" she turned to the knights. "Surely you saw him with me. A little man, no taller than a child."

"I must say that my focus was only on you, my lady," Everett said. "If there was a little man with you, I did not notice him."

Aubrielle knew she had not hallucinated. She grew increasingly concerned. "There wasn't merely one, but two. Miach and Lugh. They tried to save my life."

The knights thought her ordeal was affecting her mind, but they did not want to upset her. "Perhaps they went back where they came from,"

Reid said gently. "Arrows and knights can frighten those not accustomed to such a sight."

Aubrielle almost told them that the little men were knights themselves, but she thought better of it. Miach has said they had learned not to attract attention to themselves. If they knew her, as they said they did, then they had to know how grateful she was for their help. She did not want to seem careless and not search for them to make sure they were safe, but she was feeling particularly selfish. Thoughts of Kenneth were looming heavily on her.

"Take me back to Kirk," she murmured. "I must see Kenneth."

For all of his plotting and scheming, de Gaul was left lying in a field, far from Glastonbury and far from the secrets of the Grail.

CHAPTER TWELVE

KENNETH STOOD BY the stream, watching the water skip over the rocks in its progression to the sea. His ice blue eyes were focused on the water, the faint strains of dawn's light glimmering off the surface. With every bubble, he could hear Aubrielle's voice. Gazing up at the sunrise in all its glory, it was incomparable to her beauty. His heart hurt so badly for her that it was affecting every corner of his being. With every day that passed, his hope that she would be found alive weakened.

The column of men was ready and waiting. They had traveled for almost four days solid, stopping only twice when Kenneth decided that the horses deserved to rest even if the men were disinclined to do so. Bradley had chosen only the most seasoned warriors to accompany Kenneth, men who were hard to the bone. It worked well in that respect, since Kenneth had no patience and even the slightest complaint or issue was likely to draw blood. Furthermore, since Kenneth's strength wasn't nearly what it should be, Bradley insisted on accompanying him as well. Kirk was locked down with a senior sergeant in charge, and there were no worries afoot.

"Ken," Bradley's quiet voice entered his thoughts. "The men are ready when you are."

Kenneth shifted on his big legs, his armor creaking as he did so. His reflections lasted a split second longer before he slapped his helm upon his head, the three-point face plate hanging open. Stiffly, for the pain in his back was still great, he moved for the waiting column.

"We should have seen Everett and Reid by now," he said. "We are just south of Gloucester. We should have crossed paths."

Bradley knew he was despairing. He'd seen it for five days now.

"Perhaps they've made better time than we suspected. Though we've ridden ridiculously hard for days, I have seen Everett keep up a punishing pace when called for. He knows how important it is to find Lady Aubrielle. You must have faith."

Kenneth didn't reply. He made his way to his charger, at the head of a column of Wrexham soldiers. Argus and Grendel were also there, waiting for him. Argus hadn't left his side since he'd been wounded, and still, even with the heavy riding, he maintained his post. On occasion it had been necessary to give Kenneth something for his pain. The wounds were healing well enough, but slowly. Kenneth mounted his muzzled charger and spurred the animal onward. The company of thirty heavily armed soldiers followed.

They rode south for about ten miles, passing a few farmers and traveling merchants as they rode. Kenneth had stopped noticing long ago the fearful expressions of those they passed; he was used to it. He expected it. On the outskirts of the berg of Stonehouse was a large tavern called the Hog Snout and Rolling Gut Inn. Kenneth only paid heed to it because of the name. It seemed to him that a tavern shouldn't have "gut" in the title. But he also noticed, as they drew closer, several familiar horses in the tavern's corral. His body tensed.

"What is it?" Bradley noticed his expression.

Kenneth reined his charger towards the two-story structure. "Wrexham horses."

Bradley's head snapped in the direction of the livery, noting the tethered horses. Several of them had the tale-tell nick on the neck, just above where the breast plate would rest, and he recognized two of the chargers without a doubt.

"Everett and Reid," he confirmed. "We have found them."

Kenneth held off half of the troop, ordering the other half to follow him to the tavern. The mood was tense, cautious, and his heart was thumping loudly in his chest by the time he reached the inn. He bailed from his charger, unsheathing his weapon before his feet hit the ground.

"Sir Kenneth!" Argus called after him. "Mind your wounds, man. They cannot take a pounding yet. Let Bradley take the lead."

Kenneth ignored him and the little physic leapt from his pony, gathering his own weapon. He thought it a rather strange way to protect his patient, but nothing was usual these days.

"Come along, brother," he said to Grendel. "We must have your practiced eye."

Grendel didn't want to climb down. Argus went over and pulled him off the horse. "I shall be no good in there," Grendel insisted. "'Tis best you leave me out here; I shall only be in the way."

Argus threw a weapon at his feet. "You would rather come in with us than have Sir Kenneth come out looking for you."

Truer words were never spoken. Grendel was a pawn in a much larger game, starting when de Gaul took him from St. Wenburgh. But he thought, upon reflection, that perhaps this is where God wanted him to be. Perhaps this was where he was needed, though he couldn't imagine how. Reluctantly, he picked up the sword and held it clumsily. He didn't like knives. Frightened of what was about to happen, he followed the men inside.

It was near the nooning meal. The great tavern room with its high ceiling was already clouded with smoke from the massive hearth. It smelled of old ale and urine, and the room was moderately crowded. Kenneth hadn't taken two steps inside when he heard a familiar voice.

"Ken!"

He whirled to find Everett and Reid, up from their table, moving towards him. He took three enormous strides and grabbed Everett by the collar.

"Aubrielle," he barked. "Have you found her?"

It was a hostile move, but Everett didn't back away. He could only imagine the extent of Kenneth's turmoil, as evidenced by his very appearance. By all rights, the man shouldn't even be out of bed much less functioning normally. Though he was pale, he still looked every inch the man with the terrifying reputation.

"'Tis good to see you, too," Everett lifted an eyebrow. "And before you can take my head off, you should know that we were returning to Kirk to tell you the news."

Kenneth didn't realize that he was nearly choking him with his grasp. "What news?"

It took both Everett and Bradley to peel Kenneth's hand off of the tunic. They both knew how strung-out the man was, and Everett wouldn't let him continue any longer with his anguish.

"Follow me," he said with a smile.

Kenneth truly had no idea what he was about to face, but he suspect that Everett and Reid had somehow cornered Aubrielle and her captors. His big body stiffened, preparing for the battle that was surely to come.

"How many of them are there?" he asked.

Everett was leading him up the stairs to the second floor of the inn. "Just one."

"One?" Kenneth repeated. "Christ, he must have Aubrielle in a precarious position. Is he heavily armed?"

"There are no weapons at all."

They were on the corridor of the second floor. There were three doors; two on the left and one on the right. Everett walked up to the door on the right and put his hand on the old iron latch.

"Perhaps you would like to take care of this personally."

He opened the door and stood back. Kenneth, his jaw set for battle, held his massive sword in a defensive position as he moved into the doorway. The oilcloths on the windows were drawn, giving the light that filtered in to the room an amber-hue. His trained eyes assessed the room in an instant; a table to the left and a large, lumpy bed about fifteen feet in front of him. Other than the furniture, there was nothing, and no one, in the room.

He looked at Everett, bewildered and frustrated. Everett merely smiled. "Look in the bed, Ken."

Kenneth's head snapped to the massive oak frame, shoved up against the wall. It occurred to him that within the lumps, there was something rhythmically breathing. He could see it rise and fall. Carefully, he entered the room, his weapon still leveled. When he reached the bed, he lowered his weapon and very cautiously pulled back the coverlet.

A familiar dark head greeted him. Aubrielle was sleeping like the dead, lying on her stomach with her face shoved into the pillow. Kenneth stood there a moment, disbelieving of what he was seeing. He had expected, at the very least, an enemy assault and strong resistance. But there was none. Aubrielle was asleep, quite alone, seemingly whole and sound. It all began to sink in.

He almost dropped his sword, but he managed to somehow hand it off to the nearby table. He didn't want to wake her, but his entire body screamed to hold her. He simply couldn't believe his eyes.

An enormous hand gently touched her sleeping head, moving the hair aside to gain a better look at her. She was rosy and peaceful. He took his hand away, realizing it was shaking.

"Where did you find her?" he whispered to Everett.

Everett was standing just inside the door; Bradley and Reid were behind him, all trying to gain a look at the lady.

"We found her abductors two days ago outside of Bristol," Everett was trying to keep his voice down as not to wake her. "Those we did not kill ran off. It was not much of a fight, certainly not what we had anticipated."

"Did you capture any?"

"There was no point, Ken. We had Aubrielle. I was only concerned with regaining her and taking her to safety."

Kenneth didn't know what to say. There were so many emotions rolling around in his head that it was difficult to define only one. As the door to the chamber closed softly behind him, he took a knee beside the bed, saying a prayer of thanks for her safe return. Eyes closed and head lowered, he was deep in the most heart-felt meditation he had ever given when he felt something on the top of his head.

Surprised, he looked up to see a sleepy face smiling back at him.

Aubrielle's fingers were ticking the top of his cropped blond hair. When their eyes met, Kenneth's response was to smile as broadly as she was. In that brief, warm instant, all of the words created by all of the poets in the world could not have adequately described the beauty of the moment.

"Greetings, my lady," he finally murmured. "Did you sleep well?"

She continued to run her fingers along the top of his head, moving down the side of his face as if trying to convince herself that he wasn't a dream.

"The last time I saw you, there were arrows sticking out of your back," she whispered. "Are you real or are you a ghost?"

His response was to kiss her hand reverently, inhaling the scent of her skin. "I am real enough," he said. "When I saw you lying here, I thought the same thing of you."

Aubrielle reached out and wrapped her arms fiercely around his neck. Kenneth enveloped her in his arms, all of the fear and terror over the past few weeks dissolving in an instant. When he felt her sobs against him, it confirmed to him that she was not a dream. Up until that moment he'd had his doubts. She was real and alive and well in his arms. He'd never been more appreciative for anything in his life.

Aubrielle pulled him over onto the bed. Their kisses of relief, of joy, were feverish and deep. There were tears on her face and he kissed them away. His gloved hands entangled themselves in her hair and he paused long enough to rip off the gauntlets and throw them to the floor. The plate armor quickly followed.

The kisses stopped as Aubrielle unlatched his breastplate and let it slip to the floor. She needed to feel him against her and not a cold piece of metal. More heated kisses came in between unlatching his greaves and unstrapping his scabbard. Aubrielle pulled his hauberk over his head, the heavy mail coat that he wore underneath the plate. When all of the metal was off his body, she pushed him to sit on the bed and straddled his lap.

They gazed at each other a long, heated moment, reacquainting themselves with one another. Then tongues plunged deep and Kenneth tasted her delicious mouth over and over. His hands moved down her back, across her belly and to her full breasts. Then they moved up to her neck, touching the softness of her skin, cupping the sweet shape of her face. Aubrielle was still weeping silently and he shushed her in between kisses, assuring her that all was well now. He kissed her hands and fingers, murmuring into her flesh how very much he loved her.

They were functioning on instinct as well as desire. Kenneth pulled his padded tunic off, exposing his broad chest. Aubrielle ran her fingers across his skin, feeling the soft, crunchy carpet of hair. She had given up the yellow brocade dress for a bath the night before and wore a shift of coarse linen that the innkeeper's wife had found for her. Kenneth removed it, kissing every inch of flesh that was exposed until the garment found its way off her supple body.

Aubrielle was nude but unaware of any shame. She was only aware of the joy in her heart, of Kenneth alive and well before her. He took her by the waist and lay her gently upon the mattress. Removing his breeches, he lay down next to her.

Kenneth stroked her cheek before moving to cover her with his massive body, aware of the pain in his back as he did so. It reminded him of the time he came so close to losing her, making this conquest particularly sweet. He resumed his heated kisses, his hands on her silky flesh, moving to stroke the sensitive place between her legs. He didn't waste any time. Now was the time to claim this woman in every way possible. Aubrielle shuddered at his touch, surprised at the newness, the boldness.

When he gently thrust a finger into her warm, wet recesses, she gasped with pleasure. Aubrielle had never known the touch of a man until she met Kenneth and had no idea what to expect. All she knew was that everything he did set her senses afire. A single touch from his hand brought about a thousand pinpricks of delight. She had been so terrified that she had lost him, and now in this moment of intimacy, she could not imagine going on without this man. More than the physicality of it, there was an emotional bond that was stronger than life itself. Her body trembled at the splendor of it.

Her thighs parted naturally for him, settling his substantial weight between them. When his stiff arousal pushed into her, Aubrielle didn't wince. Kenneth was very tender. He worked her gently, stimulating her natural juices, sliding deeper and deeper into her until he was fully seated. His mouth continued to suckle her lips and tongue, feeding the fire of desire burning brightly between them. When he began to move, gaining rhythm, Aubrielle wrapped herself around him, feeling every stroke against her virgin walls.

Her arms held him tightly and her fingers found the angry wounds on his shoulder. The flesh was hot and puckered, and she immediately drew her hand back. When she opened her mouth to apologize, he kissed her so deeply that she forgot what she was going to say. His thrusts grew harder, more determined, and the friction against her loins grew more and more heated. He ground his pelvis against her, creating motion and pressure.

His mouth found her earlobe and he suckled furiously. It was all Aubrielle needed to throw her over the edge into a spasm of pleasurable convulsions. Feeling her honeyed contractions against his member, Kenneth released himself in a blinding burst. Sweat and exhaustion covered them, but still he continued to move in her, feeling her wet love around him, until the waves of pleasure faded and a cloud of contentment settled.

All of the fear, pain and death of the past several days faded from their memories. Like a bad dream, the recollections vanished like a puff smoke. All that mattered was that, from this point on, nothing would ever separate them again.

Kenneth's lips remained on Aubrielle's forehead long after they had both fallen into a peaceful sleep that mortals can only dream of.

☙

IT WAS DARK in the room when Kenneth next opened his eyes. Instantly awake, he felt better than he had in days. He'd slept like the dead. Aubrielle still lay curled up in his arms and he gazed down at her, thankful that his memories of her had not been a dream. The sweetness of their reunion was still lingering warm in his veins and as he continued to gaze upon her, he felt a peace like nothing he had ever known. In so many ways, Aubrielle had made him feel things that he hadn't imagined to exist.

He kissed her forehead, watching her stir. It brought a smile to his lips. He kissed her again and ran a delicate finger along the little earlobe that stuck out so delightfully. She wrinkled her nose and batted at her ear. He laughed softly and gathered her up tightly against him. He held her for what seemed like an eternity of contentment.

Aubrielle finally stirred, scratching her head and smacking him in the nose in the process. Startled, she looked up at him.

"I am so sorry," she murmured. "Did I hurt you?"

He smiled down at her. "No, my lady, you did not."

She returned his smile, feeling so very warm and safe in his arms. "Did you sleep well?"

"The best I ever have."

"As did I," she snuggled against him. "'Tis dark outside. I do not even know what day it is."

He held her close, smelling the faint sweet clean scent of her hair. "I would suspect we have been asleep the entire day and into the night. Tomorrow is Sunday."

"I am famished," she mumbled into his chest.

"I suppose that is your way of telling me to get out of bed and fetch you something to eat."

"I haven't eaten much this past week. I would appreciate anything you can do for me in that regard."

His warm expression faded as the reminder of her plight invaded his thoughts again. She hadn't meant to remind him, but it did nonetheless. Memories of Lucius and the mysterious sect threatened to ruin his mood but he fought it. He tossed back the covers and she squealed as her warm flesh came into contact with the cold air.

"I shall go at this moment and see what I can procure," he said.

She yanked the covers back over her. "I am particularly fond of bread with butter and honey."

"Bread with butter and honey it is," he said as he picked up his breeches.

"And I also like candied fruits and almond pudding."

"I shall search for that as well."

"And beef or fowl. But no mutton. It always tastes old."

He paused as he secured his breeches, cocking an eyebrow at her. "Anything else, my lady?"

She matched his lifted eyebrow. "Aye, there is. I need my gown back. The innkeeper's wife took it away and I need some clothes. I cannot go out in public in my shift."

"Aye, General."

He bent down to pick up his boots, sitting on the edge of the bed to pull them on. Wrapped in the coverlet, Aubrielle crept over so that she was leaning up against him. It took him a moment to notice that she was inspecting the wounds on his back.

There were tears in her eyes as her fingers drifted over the larger of the wounds. "Oh, Kenneth," she murmured. "They look so… painful."

He took her hands away, shifting her focus to his face. He kissed her palms. "Having you taken from me was a thousand times more painful," he kissed her lips. "Not to worry, love. I am fine."

"But…."

He kissed her again to silence her. "If I can locate suitable clothing, would you like to come downstairs and eat in the tavern?"

As he'd hoped, her grief was distracted. "I would. I have always liked taverns. They are full of interesting people."

He grunted as he stood up. "They are full of half-wits, thieves and murders."

She watched him pull his tunic over his head. "Do you suppose that Everett and the others are still here?"

"I would wager so."

"I would like to leave for home as soon as possible."

"As you wish, my lady."

"And there is another thing."

He shook his arms as the sleeves of the garment settled. "What is that?"

"Do you still plan to marry me?"

He stopped in his tracks, turning to look at her. There was a queer expression on his face. "Why would you ask that question?"

"Because… with everything that has happened, I just want to make sure that you've not soured on the idea. Kenneth, do not look at me so; it is not a foolish question. I just want to be sure that it is what you still want."

He came over to the bed and went down on one knee. He took her hands in his big palms. "Aubrielle, the day we were betrothed, I considered you my wife. When I told you I loved you, you became my heart. When I took you last night bodily, you became my soul. I am incomplete without you. Aye, I still plan to marry you, as soon as possible. I will send a messenger tonight back to Kirk and have a priest ready and waiting when we return. Does this answer your question and ease your concerns?"

She smiled sheepishly. "It does."

"Then I do not want to hear that question again."

"You will not, I promise."

He kissed her hands and stood up. "Good. Now, give me a few moments and I shall return."

He winked at Aubrielle as he quit the room. She sat there for the longest time with a smile on her face, wondering how it was possible to be so happy. She thanked God for this moment in time and prayed that there would be many, many more just like it.

☙

AUBRIELLE'S YELLOW BROCADE gown was a total loss. The innkeeper's wife, a round woman with a red face, could not save it as much as she had tried. After conferring with Kenneth about Aubrielle's need for decent clothing, she confiscated a blue broadcloth surcoat and rough linen shift from her own daughter and altered it to fit someone of Aubrielle's approximate size. It took her very little time to do so and, when Kenneth finally returned to the bed chamber, he brought with him the garments, hose with hemp garters, and shoes that were a shade too big for Aubrielle's feet. Because he really couldn't be of much help to her in dressing, Kenneth left her with the innkeeper's wife to assist her and went back down to the hall where Reid, Bradley and Everett had been seated at a table near the hearth since leaving Kenneth with Aubrielle twelve hours earlier.

The clothes were clean and warm, and that was all Aubrielle cared about at the moment. She did not think about nor did she miss her fine dresses as the innkeeper's wife helped her cinch up the borrowed leather girdle that emphasized her slender torso and full breasts. The woman brushed her long hair with her own daughter's brush and plaited her locks into one long braid that draped over her shoulder.

With her clean clothes and full night and day of sleep, Aubrielle looked absolutely dazzling. Kenneth could think of no other words to describe her when she and the innkeeper's wife descended the stairs into the great tavern hall. He met her at the base of the steps and took her hand, tucking it possessively into the crook of his elbow and escorting her back to his table. The knights stood up as she approached, each expression radiating approval. Everett was positively giddy about it.

"My lady," he held out a chair for her. "'Tis good to see you looking so well."

Aubrielle took pity on the knight and smiled, a departure from her normally clipped attitude with him. The man had risked his life to save her and she would show gratitude. Besides, she was coming to like him just the slightest.

"Thank you, Everett," she sat down and the knights took their seats, with Kenneth to her right. She noticed the food on the table. "What do we have here?"

"Boiled carrots, beans and peas along with a wild turkey and more bread and honey than you could possibly eat," Kenneth said. "'Tis all for you, my lady."

Aubrielle clapped her hands in delight and helped herself to the fare. The knights conversed lightly between themselves, but they were mostly watching Aubrielle gorge herself on bread and fowl. She ate as if she hadn't eaten in months, which only served to darken Kenneth's mood. He finally stopped talking altogether and just sat and watched her.

The innkeeper's wife came up behind Aubrielle, her manner respectful and fearful at the same time. "Sorry to interrupt, my lady," she said. "But I have a delicious subtlety and thought you might like some."

Aubrielle, her mouth full, nodded emphatically. "I would."

"'Tis in the kitchen; I shall go and get you some."

Aubrielle didn't want to wait. She jumped up and gave the woman a shove. "I shall accompany you. I want a big slice."

Kenneth had to suppress his natural instinct of following her. It was a very difficult thing to let her out of his sight, even for a moment, but he forced himself. He could not go the rest of his life being her shadow.

"She truly looks none the worse for wear," Reid said. "How are her mental faculties?"

Kenneth watched her, standing over by the kitchens with the old woman. "Better than mine, I think. The only thing that seems to bother her is the wounds to my back. She has said nothing about her captors and I have not asked. She will speak of it when she is ready."

"Has she spoken of Lucius?"

"Not at all." He turned slightly, facing his knights. "But rest assured that it is not far from my thoughts. Lucius is out there, somewhere, and I intend to find him. He'll not get away with any of this."

"I will go with you, Ken," Everett said earnestly. "He may have tried to kill you, but he has affronted all of us. This is our fight, too."

"I appreciate your loyalty, but what Lucius did, he did specifically to hurt Aubrielle. For that, I consider the matter personal. I intend to track the man down and punish him myself."

"When will you go?" Reid knew he could not stop him and wasn't naïve, like Everett was, to think that they could accompany him.

"As soon as the lady and I are married, which will be immediately upon our return to Kirk," Kenneth replied. "In fact, have a messenger sent ahead to have a priest waiting for us."

"So you plan to leave within the week," Everett would not be cast aside so easily. "Where will we start looking? Does Lucius have family or connections he would seek refuge with?"

"He's in London."

Aubrielle's voice came from behind them. Kenneth turned sharply to see her standing a few feet away, a plate with a huge slab of milk subtlety in her hand. Her expression was taut. When she saw she had their attention, she resumed her seat beside Kenneth.

"De Gaul told me that Lucius had fled to London," she said steadily. "I suppose he is, even now, making a nuisance of himself to the king and pining for another prestigious post."

"Who is de Gaul?" Kenneth asked softly, feeling guilty that she had heard what was not intended for her ears.

"The man who captured me, the head of The Order of the Black Angel," she was speaking calmly, honestly. It was a cover for the intense emotions she was feeling. "If you are going to find Lucius, no one is going with you but me. We must do this. I need for the knights to stay and protect my castle."

Kenneth's expression was unreadable, though inside, he was raging. He was not about to get into a battle with her in front of his men. He kept his cool admirably. "We can discuss that later. For now, I would suggest that my knights get some sleep. We will depart before dawn."

Everett wanted to stay, but Reid and Bradley convinced him with various expressions that Kenneth's statement was not a suggestion; it was a command. The three knights rose and quit the tavern. Kenneth sat for a long moment after they had departed, toying with his cup, watching Aubrielle delve into her dessert.

"Aubrielle...," he began quietly.

"You'll not discourage me, Kenneth," she knew what he was thinking. "I am going with you, whether or not you like it. If you do not let me come, I shall follow you. You know I will."

He did not rise to her confrontation. It was far easier to deal with her calmly. "I do not want to endanger you. I have no idea how long I will be gone, or what perils I will face. I would rather know you were safe."

"And I would rather you not face this alone," she swallowed the bite in her mouth. She was fully prepared for an angry exchange but all that came forth were teary eyes. "You promised you would never leave me, Kenneth. You promised."

He reached out and took her hand, kissing her fingers as he so often did. "I am not leaving you, love. But I must do this. Lucius must pay for his sins."

She sniffled and he took the spoon from her hand, set it on the table, and pulled her over onto his lap. His big arms wrapped around her.

"I cannot take another separation," she murmured through her tears. "Where you go, I must also go. I cannot accept it any other way. It will surely kill me."

He sighed heavily, deep in thought. "Do not believe for a moment that this is easy for me," he kissed her ear. "But I must know that you are safe. If you come with me, I will be forever worrying about your welfare and my focus on Lucius will be lessened. Lack of focus in my profession is deadly."

"I will not be any trouble, I swear it," she wrapped her arms around his neck and held him tightly. "Please take me with you. We must find him together so that he may see the both of us, united as one, and know that he cannot defeat us."

"Aubrielle...."

"I need to resolve this as much as you do, Kenneth. He has attacked and offended both of us. You cannot deny me my vengeance, too."

He put his hands on her cheeks, gazing into her sea-colored eyes. He did not want to take her; that much was apparent. But she was so sad, and his heart so soft for her, that he could not deny her. He did not want to be separated from her, either.

"Very well," he reluctantly conceded. "But Everett will come with us. If something happens to me, I would have you well protected."

"Nothing will happen to you."

"Probably not. Even so, I want to ensure your safety."

"When will we leave?"

"As soon as we are married. And I will say one more thing and speak no more of it."

"What is that?"

"In my absence, you will obey Everett."

Her eyebrows flew up. "I would rather…!"

He held up a swift finger. "Obey him in my absence or you will not go. These are non-negotiable terms."

"But…!"

"Non-negotiable, Aubrielle."

Her face folded into a pout. "Define non-negotiable."

"The palm of my hand to your buttocks if you disobey. Is that clear enough?"

She was about to follow her nature and become belligerent with him. But she was learning quickly that playing on Kenneth's sympathies was the best way to achieve her end. She had spent far too much time fighting him uselessly. He was too strong, too clever, and at times far wiser than she. It was time to try different tactics in the skirmishes against Kenneth St. Héver.

Instead, she smiled sweetly and wrapped her arms around his neck, nuzzling against him. "But I am smarter and shrewder than Everett," she purred. What if he tells me to do something that I know is not right?"

Kenneth found her attention quite enticing, but he wasn't so blinded that he did not know what she was up to. He smacked her lightly on the backside and she yelped.

"Non-negotiable, my love," he murmured, kissing her on the cheek when she stuck her tongue out at him. "Now, would you care to retire to your room and get a few hours of sleep before we leave?"

She pouted like a child. "I slept all last night and most of today away. I am not tired."

"You will be, come mid-day tomorrow."

"But I do not want to sleep."

Kenneth smiled slowly. "Who says that we have to sleep?"

CHAPTER THIRTEEN

EXACTLY ONE WEEK later, the Lady Aubrielle Grace de Witney became Lady St. Héver, Countess of Wrexham, in the same chapel she had buried her uncle in three weeks before. Clad in an expensive gown of garnet-colored silk with golden threads, she stood next to her new husband and listened to the priest speak of marriage through God's eyes. Brother Grendel had assisted in the ceremony, making the comment that he never thought to see the day. Kenneth could not disagree and Aubrielle had declared her disgust with both of them.

It was a joyous day. All of Kirk and the surrounding village turned out for the wedding. A huge feast was planned for the peasants in the bailey afterwards. When the new earl and his countess exited the chapel, the crowd of well-wishers and revelers was enormous.

The feast went well on into the night. Kenneth and Aubrielle sat for a time in the great hall, surrounded by their knights and senior soldiers. Kenneth had sent word to his oldest and dearest friends Tate de Lara and Stephen of Pembury to attend the festivities, but both men were rooted to their homes due to pregnant wives and inclement weather. It had been a distinct disappointment to all concerned that they could not attend but Kenneth understood. As small consolation, Lord and Lady Chereleton of Powys Castle, Kirk's nearest allied neighbor, arrived late due to the swiftness of the ceremony, but they nonetheless arrived with a large entourage bearing gifts. Lord Chereleton was a large man with a loud laugh and he ate heartily throughout the feast. His wife was more interested in bestowing presents on the new countess.

What gifts they were. Kenneth, pulled away by the men to drink and talk, kept an eye on his wife on the other side of the great hall as she opened her wedding offerings. Lady Chereleton had brought pewter with semi-precious stones, fabulous material from exotic places, and other items of value. Aubrielle was a bit overwhelmed with the woman's attentions and fine gifts, feeling strange because she did not know the woman. But Lady Chereleton had known Lady Isobel, her aunt, and apparently felt it was her duty to take Isobel's place at Aubrielle's wedding.

When the gifts had been accounted for and placed in the center of the hall to be admired, the women stayed in a cluster around Aubrielle, making sure she was well fed with dessert and plied with wine. Aubrielle kept straining for a glimpse of Kenneth, but he was near the entry to the keep in a group of men and clearly occupied with congratulating himself on his marriage. She had never seen him drink, but today was an exception. He had imbibed quite a bit and was more animated than she had ever seen him.

She would have liked to have enjoyed her wedding feast with her husband by her side, but the guests seemed determined to keep them apart. There was a small group of minstrels inside the hall with the required dances being properly drilled, but outside in the courtyard, there was a large musical group and far livelier celebrating going on. She wished that she and Kenneth could slip away into it and leave the stuffy nobles in the hall.

Seated at the head table, Aubrielle was surrounded by Lady Chereleton and her ladies. They meant well, but their cloying presence was becoming annoying. Aubrielle really didn't know them and wasn't particularly interested in their dull conversations. Whereas Aubrielle could intelligently converse on nearly every subject, these women were limited to fashions, jewelry, and the best method to organize a kitchen. Just as she was hoping a lightning bolt would come out of the ceiling and strike her dead, thereby mercifully ending her boredom, she felt a tug on her sleeve.

Grendel was smiling at her. Cleaned and shaved, he looked like a new man. "If my lady will come with me."

Aubrielle didn't care why he was asking. She was desperate to escape. She took the priest's outstretched hand, excused herself from the chattering ladies, and followed him gladly away from the table.

"Brother Grendel, you are an answer to prayer," she said quietly. "I was about to go mad. Where is my husband?"

"He is the one who sent me for you," Grendel said. "Apparently, the men are determined to occupy his time as the ladies are determined to occupy yours."

They passed through the great hall, alive with guests and celebration. Everyone she passed lifted a goblet to her and she graciously thanked them. They entered the foyer, darker and quieter than the great hall, and Grendel took her into the small solar immediately to the left of the entrance. It was dark and quiet in there, too, but Kenneth suddenly reached out and grabbed her.

She laughed softly and threw her arms around his neck. He picked her up and twirled her around happily.

"Imagine," he said. "I had to send the priest to secure my own wife. I could not escape Lord Chereleton no matter how hard I tried. The man was as clinging as tar."

She giggled. "His wife is the same way. The woman means well but she had me bored to tears." She turned to Grendel. "Thank you, again, for giving me the opportunity to spend some time with my husband on the day of our wedding."

Grendel nodded graciously. "Now," he said. "Would you like to attend a real party?"

He motioned them to follow. Kenneth and Aubrielle exchanged glances but dutifully followed him. He took them outside, down into the massive bailey where the entire village of Kirk was celebrating with great bonfires and roasting meat. It was exciting and gay. Grendel took them past several groups of well-wishers, who upon seeing the wedding couple, loudly and happily toasted them. One burly man shoved a huge cup of ale into Kenneth's hand. Kenneth drained it to cheers and handed it back to the man.

In a sense, it was a night of awakening for Kirk and her vassals. All anyone had ever known of Kenneth St. Héver was his fearsome fighting reputation and that he was a favored knight of the king. He was frightening and imposing. But here, relaxed in the celebration of his wedding, the man was becoming human. Kenneth was already known for his fairness and wisdom; now he was adding humanity to that persona. The overall picture brought gladness to the earldom, confident that Lady Aubrielle's choice of a husband was the correct one.

Grendel led them over to the dancing. A large group of musicians played a lively tune and Grendel was the first one to sweep Aubrielle out into the cluster of dancers. Kenneth watched, a smile on his lips, as she shrieked good-naturedly to the lively dance. Grendel was quite a dancer and took her through her paces, once, around the dance area. When he came back upon Kenneth, he let go of the winded bride and handed her over to the groom.

"There," he said, proud of himself. "I have broken her in for you."

Kenneth gave the man a nod, a half-grin, and collected his wife in his arms. "My thanks. But now it is my turn."

He swept Aubrielle into the group of dancers. Seeing the happy couple whirling about, the revelers began to stand back and clap loudly. Kenneth was an excellent dancer and swept Aubrielle around and around until she was completely winded. She was laughing so much that she could barely breathe. Someone handed her a wreath of flowers and she made Kenneth pause long enough so that she could put them in her hair, completely covering up the pearl and garnet tiara she wore. With the flowers tucked behind her ears and a smile on her face, he'd never seen a more beautiful sight.

They danced well into the night. At times, the musicians played a slow ballad and Kenneth was content to hold her tightly as they danced at a lesser pace. Several times, he glanced up to the battlements, more out of habit than anything else, and saw Bradley and Reid up on the ramparts waving down at him. In truth, he felt better knowing they were watching over the crowd so he didn't have to.

After too much dancing, Aubrielle was thirsty and Kenneth found her a cool cup of ale. She drank it, making a face at the taste, but asked for more. He turned to pour her another draught but when went to give it to her, he discovered her missing.

A glance to the group of dancers saw her jigging with Max, his squire. Somehow the lad had found her in this writhing mass of people. Soon she was passed off to several of the men in attendance; one was a blacksmith, one was a metal worker, and then a host of other hard-working peasants. Each one took a twirl with the new countess and, out of the benevolence of his heart and the fact that it was a celebration, Kenneth allowed it. He knew it helped solidify the loyalty of Kirk's vassals by giving them a personal memory of their lord and lady. Besides, he saw no harm in it, fighting down his normally class-conscious protocols.

It was nearly dawn by the time Aubrielle asked to retire. She was absolutely exhausted. There was still much dancing and celebrating going on in both the great hall and the bailey, but Kenneth could see she'd had enough. The usual tradition of exhibiting the bloody marriage sheet on the night of the wedding would be a problem, so he and Aubrielle discreetly slipped up to their chamber on the third floor. They had converted the earl's old chamber into their own, making it comfortable with new linens and another new, larger wardrobe to accommodate Aubrielle's clothes. It was a comfortable place with a big lock on the door, as he had promised. Kenneth took her inside and threw the bolt, ensuring that this night, they would not be interrupted.

Aubrielle went straight to the bed and threw herself upon the mattress. The little dog, thrilled to see his mistress, left his luxurious pillow in the corner and ran up, licking her ankles.

"I could sleep for a week," she muttered.

Kenneth grinned as he unlatched his ceremonial armor, propping it up on the armor frame in the corner. He'd had it brought up from the armory for just this occasion. "You were quite lively tonight," he said. "In fact, I do not think I saw you sit down once from the moment we entered the bailey."

She mumbled something he couldn't quite make out. By the time he'd removed all of his armor and went back over to the bed, his bride was fast asleep, snoring softly into the coverlet. Laughing softly, Kenneth leaned over and stroked her dark head.

"Aubrielle," he whispered. "Sweetheart, do you want to take off your gown?"

She groaned something and continued to snore. With a smile on his face, he removed her shoes and let the dog lick her toes, just to tease her. But she would not react and he gently moved her legs over onto the mattress so she wasn't hanging off of it. He removed the remainder of his clothing and climbed into the bed beside her, gathering her up in his arms. She fussed a bit at being jostled, but settled down once she realized she was in his warm embrace. Like a cat, she curled up against him.

Kenneth spent his wedding night listening to his wife and dog snore.

~

"I DO NOT!"

"Aye, you do."

Aubrielle's eyes narrowed dangerously. "Kenneth St. Hével, that is the nastiest thing you have ever said to me. I do not snore!"

Kenneth was having a difficult time keeping a straight face. "There is no shame in it. Many people snore. Drunkards and half-wits, for instance."

They were sitting at the nooning meal on the day following the event of their wedding. Though most weddings could last for days, Kenneth had made sure to cut his celebration short for security reasons. This close to the border, he was uncomfortable with the castle wide-open and off guard. The great hall was still a mess, however, with a few drunken bodies sleeping off their inebriation in the corner. The dogs that were a permanent fixture in the hall were still prowling the room, looking for scraps. Lord and Lady Chereleton were nowhere to be found, leaving Kenneth, Aubrielle, Everett, Argus, Grendel, young Max and Reid to share the meal. At the latest turn of conversation, Everett was trying so hard to hold back his guffaws that his face was red.

Aubrielle, however, thought it no laughing matter. Dressed in a gift from Lady Chereleton, a pale blue gown with a matching blue topaz necklace, her manner was hardly as beautiful as her striking appearance. Her husband's latest jibe had her blood boiling.

"How dare you say such awful things to me, leading our vassals to think that I am a common, disgraceful creature," she seethed. "How dare you say all of this in front of them. You will apologize to me and tell them that it is not true!"

Kenneth was having a good time at her expense, but he could see she was truly outraged. He didn't need a fist to come flying in his direction, funny though his teasing might be. He backed down.

"Very well, madam, I apologize," he said sincerely. "It must have been the dog that I heard."

She was still scowling-mad. "You are evil. Pure evil, do you know that?"

"As you say, madam."

"And another thing," she leaned forward on the table. "Why does your head not hurt after all of the drinking you indulged in last night? My head is killing me."

"I do not know. I have always been able to drink and not feel any after-effects."

She frowned, resting her head on her propped-up hand. "There must be something wrong with you."

"I have been told that."

She made a face at him, continuing to pick at her meal. Her stomach was lurching and her head hurt, and she had no appetite, but Kenneth had insisted she try and eat something. He was quite well and his appetite was fine. He handed her a piece of bread with honey and butter on it but she refused. Inwardly, he was laughing at her foul mood.

"Now that the wedding is over and Kirk has regained a sense of normalcy, what does the future hold for Lord and Lady St. Héver?" Reid wondered aloud. "Surely our new earl has a litany of tasks ahead of him."

Kenneth wasn't accustomed to hearing himself addressed as the earl. But since noon yesterday, he had indeed acquired that title. It would take some getting used to. He shrugged his shoulders.

"It is my intention to go to London immediately to reaffirm my fealty to the king and to track down Lucius," he said.

"And then?"

He glanced at Aubrielle. "And then, I plan to have many healthy sons to carry on my name."

Aubrielle slumped her aching head against the cool table. "Perhaps when I am feeling better."

From across the table, Grendel watched her. "No more Glastonbury, my lady?"

She shook her head weakly. "There is no need."

"Not even to search out the knights of Munsalvaesche to thank them for their protection?"

The past week had seen Aubrielle divulge everything that happened while under de Gaul's control, including the tale of the knights of Munsalvaesche. She had, however, omitted the link to Argus. She did not want to jeopardize the man's position and she did not want her husband to be suspicious of him. Though Kenneth was dubious about her claims of the dwarf knights, Grendel was nonetheless convinced. Aubrielle was a dreamer, and an intellect with high ideas, but she wasn't a liar. If she said the knights of Munsalvaesche were still a living order, he believed her.

"No," Aubrielle's gaze found Argus, who met her eyes steadily. "I believe they know how grateful I am. There is no need to seek them out."

"Perhaps that is true," Grendel agreed. "But do you believe what they told you about the Grail? Being a living vessel, I mean. Perhaps they simply told you that to keep you away from the true prize. They are, after all, charged with its protection."

Her head came up from the table. "You have a skeptical mind, Grendel."

"I am a teacher. It is my duty to be skeptical and ask questions."

She gave him a reproachful expression, but it hurt her head to do so, and she winced. Kenneth tried to feed her bread again.

"I do not want any."

"Eat it. It will make you feel better."

"Do as he says, my lady," Argus said. "You need something in your stomach to settle it."

She made the pouting face again. "And do you think it would be too much trouble to give me something for my head? You are the castle physic, after all. Here I am, suffering with pain, and you've not even made the offer."

Argus sniffled, wiping his nose to disguise the smirk on his lips. "That aching head is a reminder to control your drink the next time."

"Maybe you can give her something to brighten her mood as well," Kenneth suggested.

"I fear nothing can help that, my lord."

"God help us."

Aubrielle stood up, bracing a hand against Kenneth's shoulder to steady herself against her throbbing head. "I think you are both horrible. If you've nothing better to do than harass me, then I shall go and tend to packing for our trip."

"We are not leaving this minute, love," Kenneth patted the hand on his shoulder; they had been giving her a rough time and he was rightfully contrite. "Go back to bed and sleep off your aching head."

"If not today, then when?"

"Perhaps tomorrow or the next day. I must make sure that Kirk is settled before I depart."

"Kirk is fine," she scolded gently. "Reid has command. The Welsh are quiet. What better time to go?"

She had a point. He rose along with her, motioning to his knights. "Very well, then. I suppose we should go about the rounds and discuss what is to be done in my absence."

Aubrielle snaked her hands around his big forearm, laying her cheek against his bulging bicep as they walked from the hall. Argus followed to give the lady something for her head.

It was a bitter willow bark brew but she drank it. Kenneth returned to their chamber a few hours later to find her sleeping. She had slept quite a lot lately. She hadn't quite recovered from her harrowing adventure with The Order of the Black Angel, but at least now, she had some peace. She was the same Aubrielle he had first met, only now without the pure antagonism in her manner. She was still feisty but with a sense of humor. Not only was he madly in love with the woman, but he liked her, too.

"Do you think what Grendel said was true?"

Kenneth had been preparing to remove his ceremonial armor from the corner and take it back down to the armory, but he stopped when he heard Aubrielle's soft question. He went over to the bed.

"What was that, love?"

"About the Grail and the knights of Munsalvaesche. Do you suppose they really told me that story about the living vessel to throw me off course?"

He pursed his lips in thought, sitting down on the bed beside her. "I think that you would be the best person to answer that question. I do not know much of the scroll, or of the legend, or of these knights. You would be the expert on that. What do you think?"

She sat up in bed, her lovely hair mussed. After a moment, she simply shook her head. "Grendel is no fool. He knows as much, if not more, about Grail lore than I do. I have a terrible suspicion that he may be right."

"So what do you want to do about that?"

She paused briefly, thinking. "It has always been their duty to protect the Grail. Knowing now that they are indeed alive and still active, I can't say that finding the Grail would be a simple thing. They have been guarding it for a thousand years. Perhaps… perhaps I should just allow them to continue doing their job and leave it at that. I do not need the Grail any longer, as I once thought I did. I have you. My quest is finished. What more could I possibly need?"

He reached out and stroked her soft cheek. "So you think you have finally found your happiness with me?"

Her features softened. "Oh, Kenneth," she wound her arms around his neck. "I know I have."

He kissed her deeply. "As I have with you," he murmured. "Nothing else in this world matters so long as I have you."

In the dim light of sunset, Kenneth laid his wife back on the mattress and made love to her. It was a sweet, stolen moment, ripe with exploration and ecstasy. He made discovery of every inch of her ripe, full breasts and devoured the flesh on her trim torso. She was still not completely comfortable with his mouth on her Venus mound, and he took special attention to familiarize her with the intimacy of his tongue against her pink flesh. He loved tasting every inch of her. When he finally penetrated her with his maleness, it was with more emotion than desire. Every thrust was a word of love, every withdrawal a song of adoration. Aubrielle responded in kind, whispering in his ear as he moved deep within her. She climaxed twice before he allowed himself release. After that, his strong embrace told her more than words or a touch ever could.

They stayed together, wrapped in each other, until the dawn.

☙

SOMEHOW, THE TRIP to London became a production. Instead of just Kenneth, Aubrielle and Everett, it had turned into the three of them, plus Max, plus Argus and twenty men at arms. Everett insisted that adequate protection was needed for the earl and his party and, not surprisingly, the new captain of Kirk agreed. Reid had even commandeered a wagon to carry the countess' trunks. Aubrielle had packed two large ones. When Kenneth had hoped to depart by dawn, he found himself building up a slow burn as his small trip to London turned into a large one.

Kenneth the Fearsome made a return. Reid could see it in his eyes but he would not back down with what he felt was a properly armed escort. When Aubrielle came out of the keep with her two large trunks, Reid had hoped to intercept her to tell her of her husband's foul mood, but he was too late. She walked right into it and he was unable to save her.

It came as Aubrielle was having her trunks lifted onto the wagon. Kenneth approached her from behind, dressed to the teeth in armor and weapons. His swift, silent appearance started her.

"Hello, my love," she said sweetly. "I believe I have everything I need, but I would like to ask a favor."

It was the wrong time to ask. Kenneth gazed down at her with an expression usually reserved for assessing the enemy.

"What is that?"

"Can I bring the pup? I hate to leave him behind. He is so attached to us and I have no idea how long we will be gone."

Kenneth's jaw began to tick and he did not immediately reply. Aubrielle looked more closely at him, noting his expression.

"What is wrong? Why do you look so?"

He reached out and took her gently by the elbow. "Walk with me."

"With pleasure. Where are we going?"

He didn't answer her until they were well out of earshot. It was just the two of them, standing alone in the kitchen yard. Wrapped in dark blue from head to toe, Aubrielle smiled up at him, unaware of his trouble.

"What is it?"

"This trip."

"What about it?"

The tick in his jaw worsened. "This is nothing as I'd planned. A trip for you and me and Everett to London has turned into a circus. Since when did I give you permission to take two trunks? Everett wants to take twenty armed men and Reid has insisted we take a damnable wagon to slow us down. And then there is Argus; who invited that old man? What do we need a physic for?"

His words weren't particularly angry, but there was hazard in his tone. Rather than argue, Aubrielle put her soft hands on his arms to ease him.

"My apologies," she said soothingly. "I invited Argus and Max. Max is your squire, after all, and I thought we might need Argus' services. You are, after all, going to London to confront Lucius. Do you think the man will lie down without a fight? What if he injures you? I need the very best physic for you should that be the case. I was only thinking of you."

He rolled his eyes at the ridiculousness of her statement. "Aubrielle, I cannot go to London dragging half of the Welsh Marches behind me. So in answer to your earlier question, no, the pup cannot come. He will stay here, as will the rest of you. I am going alone."

He turned and walked away from her. She ran after him, her attempt to be non-confrontational vanished. She ran fast enough and managed to plant herself in front of him to stop his progression.

"Do not even jest about leaving me behind," she growled. "I swear that if you do, I will not be here when you get back. I shall leave Kirk and you will never see me again."

He crossed his thick arms. "Do not threaten me."

"Do not threaten *me*."

She spun on her heal and made haste back into the keep. Kenneth stood there a moment, watching her until she disappeared into the great stone structure. A heavy sigh of regret escaped him. He walked into the keep after her.

By the time he reached their chamber, Aubrielle was sobbing furiously on the bed. He felt like an ogre and a fool, all at the same time.

"Stop crying," he ordered softly. "I am not trying to be difficult, but you must understand the greater picture. I cannot go parading into

London like a returning prince. To announce my presence is exactly what I do not want to do; if Lucius is there, it will put him on his guard. He may even make another attempt on my life before I can get to him. I need the element of subtlety and surprise, Aubrielle. I need for this to be a quiet, well-planned operation."

She sniffled into her hand. "You would leave me behind."

He went over to the bed. "No, love, I would not. 'Twas my frustration speaking. And since when do you become such a weeper? You have been crying at the drop of a hat ever since we returned from Stonehouse."

She looked up at him, shocked at what she perceived as his criticism. It only served to fuel her tears. "I do not know," the tears started anew. "I cannot seem to stop crying. All I want to do is cry."

"The Aubrielle Grace de Witney I first met would have rather put my eye out than cry."

"I can still put your eye out if you want me to."

He smiled, kneeling on the ground beside her and taking her into his arms. "No, sweetheart, I do not want you to," he kissed her cheek, her forehead. "Besides, I threatened to spank you every time you had a violent outburst. Perhaps this is your way of releasing your frustrations in a different way."

He took the kerchief out of her hand and wiped her face. He smiled at her, trying to coerce her into doing the same. But she was hurt and wouldn't respond, so he kissed her until the tears went away completely. Exhausted from their argument, she lay down on the bed to rest. In the back of his mind, Kenneth tried not to worry over the fact that she was, again, exhausted. All the woman seemed to do lately is sleep and cry. He was beginning to feel concern over her health, but he chased the negative thoughts away. Aubrielle was fine; she was simply still recovering from her ordeal.

ଓ

THE PARTY FOR London left the next day because Aubrielle spent the entire previous day in bed. Kenneth had grown increasingly worried and even had Argus sit with her while she slept just to make sure she was all right. The little physic examined her and insisted she was in fine health and certainly well enough to travel. Therefore, at sunrise the next day, Kenneth, Aubrielle and Everett set out for London.

Aubrielle didn't look fine. She looked pale and drawn. Riding atop her white palfrey, she kept pace behind Kenneth because his charger snapped at anything within range. Her palfrey was terrified of the big warhorse. Everett's horse was slightly less aggressive and he took position a few feet to the left of her.

She hadn't eaten anything all morning. Kenneth knew that because he'd spent nearly every moment with her since they had awoken. Kenneth sent Everett on ahead to keep watch on the approaching road while he made small talk with his wife, still riding behind him. They were making much slower progress than he had anticipated, but he didn't care at the moment. He was more concerned with Aubrielle's lack of color. Somewhere around mid-day, they found a nice spot beside a brook and stopped to share a meal.

Kenneth dismounted his charger and went to help Aubrielle off her palfrey. She stretched stiffly, arching her back to bring some life back into her tired body. Kenneth removed some bread, cheese and wine from his saddle-bags and spread his rain cloak out on the grass so that Aubrielle could sit down. She sat gratefully and accepted the small cup of wine he offered her. She sipped at it, watching a small rabbit with a fluffy white tail frolic a few feet away. Kenneth distracted her by handing her a piece of bread.

"I am not hungry," she waved him off.

Everett was a few feet away, listening to the conversation but pretending he wasn't. Kenneth continued to hold out the bread to her, patiently.

"Sweetheart, you did not eat this morning. Please eat something. You need to keep up your strength."

There was genuine concern in his voice. Aubrielle looked at him, reluctantly taking the bread. She tore off a piece, putting it in her mouth and chewing it as if it were made of sawdust. It was a struggle to swallow. Then she repeated the process. It was the most laborious thing Kenneth had ever witnessed. After the fourth bite, he shook his head.

"We are six hours out of Kirk," he said decisively. "You cannot go all the way to London like this. For your own good, I must take you home."

"No!" Aubrielle cried. "Kenneth, you promised that I could go!"

He stood up. "Aye, I did. But you cannot go like this; look at yourself, Aubrielle. You are pale and sick and you cannot eat. I will not allow you to continue."

She stood up, the ever-present tears in her eyes. "Please," she whispered. "I promise to eat. I will not be any trouble."

He put his hands on her shoulders. "Sweetheart, I am not trying to be cruel. But you are obviously ill. Why Argus declared you healthy, I do not know. You are clearly not healthy."

"But I am," she insisted. "Argus was right. I am not ill. Please... you cannot go without me. You promised we would never be separated again."

He touched her cheek. "Must we go over this yet again? I did indeed make a promise to you and I meant it. But your health is of the utmost importance to me. If it makes you happy, then I will not go to London until this illness you have has passed, I swear it."

"Then you will not go to London for quite some time."

"Why do you say that?"

She bit her lip. "Because Argus told me... I made him promise not to...."

He didn't like her tone. He lifted an apprehensive eyebrow at her. "What did you make him promise, Aubrielle?"

She suddenly looked frightened, grasping for words. Kenneth never knew it was possible for Aubrielle to be frightened, about anything. The very idea scared him to death. He grasped her firmly by the arms.

"Tell me, Aubrielle," he pleaded softly. "What did you make him promise? What is so awful that you made him promise not to tell me?"

She began to cry. More terror seized him. "Aubrielle, for the love of God, tell me."

She fell forward, into his arms. "Hold me," she whispered. "Hold me tightly."

Kenneth was beside himself. He cradled her against him, stricken with fear. What could be so horrible that she could not tell him?

"Aubrielle, please…"

"I do not want you to be angry with me."

"I will not, I swear it. What is it?"

"Promise me that if I tell you, I can still go to London with you."

"I cannot promise you anything until I know what it is that you are having such difficulty telling me."

She was silent for a moment. When she finally spoke, he barely heard her. "I am not ill. I am going to have a baby."

Kenneth thought he hadn't heard her correctly. It took several long seconds before her words registered. When comprehension dawned, he held her out at arm's length.

"You… you were afraid to tell me that you are pregnant?"

She wiped her damp cheeks. "Aye."

"A baby?"

"Aye."

He stared at her, wide-eyed. Then, Kenneth did something so unexpected that he startled both Aubrielle and Everett, still standing several feet away; he fell to his knees like a child. Wrapping his arms around Aubrielle's torso, he buried his face in her belly. Aubrielle gazed down at the top of his helmed head, stunned.

"Kenneth, are you all right?"

He nodded. "What are you doing?" she asked.

He didn't say anything for quite some time. When his head finally came up, Aubrielle swore she saw tears in his ice-blue eyes.

"I was speaking with my son, letting him know that he is most welcome."

She smiled timidly. "Then you are not angry?"

He appeared hurt by her question. "My God, Aubrielle, why would I be angry? How can you even ask that?"

She was starting to feel like a fool. "Because… because we just got married. We have never really talked about having children. You are so determined to go to London and find Lucius… I did not know if this news would be welcome at this time."

He was stunned, elated, having no idea how to express what it was, exactly, that he felt. "How could I not be happy? Though I had hoped we would eventually have children, never did I believe… Christ, Aubrielle, how could you think I would be angry about this?"

Her face turned into a pout. "Well, you do not have to become furious with me about it."

"I am not, sweetheart, truly," he hushed her quickly. Then he just stood there with an idiotic grin on his face. "A son. Truly?"

"It could be a daughter."

The thought did not distress him. "I could only be more blessed." He caught a glimpse of Everett, several feet away and pretending like he was inspecting the plant life. "Everett, did you hear? I am to be a father."

Everett looked over at them, grinning. "Congratulations, my lord. We suspected as much."

Kenneth's brow furrowed. "What do you mean?"

Everett wandered back over in their direction. "Any time the Lady Aubrielle Grace de Witney St. Héver would rather cry than throw a poker at you, something must be terribly amiss. And, of course, it helps when the physic cannot keep a secret to himself."

Kenneth cocked an eyebrow. "Marvelous. Everyone knew before I did."

Aubrielle reached out and took his hand. "Do not be angry. A baby is wonderful news, for everyone."

Kenneth could not have become angry had he tried. In fact, Lucius could have walked straight into his midst at that moment and he would have crowed the news to him, too. He stood there for several long moments, trying to collect his thoughts, struggling to focus on something other than his impending child. He'd always been inordinately good at concentrating on what needed to be done in the heat of battle. Though this wasn't battle, the news had certainly shaken him up.

"I would feel much better if you would return with me to Kirk," he said. "I do not believe traveling is good for you at this time."

"I do not want to return to Kirk. I want to go to London as we have planned."

"You must think of your health and the health of the child, Aubrielle. Jostling you about on miles of endless road will be very difficult."

"I am strong."

He could see that he wasn't going to get very far with her on the subject. He would have liked nothing better than to put his foot down and insist they return to Kirk, but Aubrielle had other ideas. Like an idiot, he found himself unwilling to be forceful with her in her current state.

"Please, Aubrielle," he kissed her fingers. "Let us return to Kirk. I want this child to be born healthy and I want you to be safe. This trip to London will be more difficult than you can imagine. This is not a pleasure trip."

"But Lucius…"

"Lucius will not slip from my grasp nor escape my revenge, I assure you, but the news you gave me moments ago has changed everything. Can you not understand that? My wife and child are more important at this time than seeking vengeance upon a man who will, at a time of my choosing, suffer his punishment by my hand. Lucius is not going anywhere. I will be able to find him now or a year from now. But you are what is most important to me at this moment."

She gazed up at him with her great sea-colored eyes. A bit of color had returned to her cheeks. After a moment, she shook her head in surrender.

"I cannot argue with you, as much as I would like to. You make far too convincing a point."

His eyes twinkled. "I am glad you see reason."

He took her by the elbow and gently led her back over to the palfrey. Before she mounted, she jabbed a finger at him. "You will not try to go without me while we wait for the birth of our child?"

"I will not." He helped her up on the animal. "But I would speak with Everett a moment."

He walked over to where Everett was gathering the reins of his charger. The knight had heard the majority of the conversation between the earl and his wife and knew Kenneth well enough to know that he had not given up so easily, no matter what he had said to Aubrielle.

"What would you have of me, my lord?" he asked Kenneth quietly.

Kenneth kept his voice soft so Aubrielle wouldn't hear. "Ride to London and gain audience with Edward. Tell him of the earl's death and my subsequent marriage to the heiress. Assure him that the Marcher lordship of Wrexham is in good hands and reaffirm our fealty to him. Then, you will find out where Lucius is. Edward will know; I have little doubt. Lucius would not make himself scarce from our king, but do not let Edward know why we wish to know of Lucius' whereabouts. If the subject of Lucius' departure from Kirk's service comes up, let Edward take the lead and see if you can find out what Lucius told him. Stick to that story if you can."

"And if I cannot discover what Lucius has told him?"

"Then tell him that, as far as you know, Lucius is still in the service of Kirk but had a personal matter to attend to in London. We are simply trying to find him to assist him if he needs it. Pretend you know no more. But above all, find out what you can about Lucius' whereabouts."

Everett's young face was grim with the seriousness of his mission. "Aye, my lord. I shall return as quickly as I can."

Kenneth watched the knight ride off. Turning back to Aubrielle, he could see that she was once again that pale, slightly greenish color. She had her kerchief to her mouth.

"Where is Everett going?" she asked through the material.

He walked over to her palfrey and checked the reins, the cinch on the saddle. He was being overly careful and he knew it.

"To London," he said casually. "He will return before Christmas."

"Why have you sent him on?"

"To announce our marriage, of course. We mustn't keep the king uninformed."

Aubrielle couldn't disagree. But she found that she was less and less concerned for London, the king, or anything else at the moment. The only matter of concern was her lurching stomach.

"Kenneth?" she asked quietly.

"Aye, sweetheart?"

"Can we please return to Kirk now?"

He smiled and kissed her free hand. "We may indeed."

He mounted his charger and the horses swayed in anticipation of turning for home. "Slowly, please," she begged.

He laughed softly. In fact, he couldn't remember ever being so happy, or having so much reason to laugh. He could not imagine that his life could have ever gotten any better, but the last few minutes had proven him wrong.

If this is what it means to be weak, then let me be weak.

CHAPTER FOURTEEN

Early July, 1334 A.D.

"WHY AM I not allowed in?" Kenneth's face was flushed and veins bulged dangerously on his temples. "If there is something amiss, then I must be on hand."

Argus was having a difficult time keeping the man at bay. "There is nothing amiss, my lord, I assure you. These things take time."

"Nearly twenty hours?" Kenneth was beside himself. "Her pains started yesterday, for Christ's sake. Why is this child not here yet? If something is wrong and you are keeping it from me, I swear to God that I will…"

"Threaten me all you like," Argus snapped softly. "It will not bring this child any sooner. And I can promise you that nothing is wrong. Give the countess time to bring this enormous child forth."

Kenneth scowled. Not usually a scowling man, it was an unusual gesture, indicative of his frustration level. He looked at Everett, at Reid, and noting their sympathetic expressions, struggled to calm. It didn't help that he could hear Aubrielle groaning from the other side of the door.

"Can I at least see her again? You chased me out hours ago because you thought the birth was imminent."

"I chased you out because you were more nervous than she was. You were not helping the situation."

"I shall behave, I promise. Will you let me see her?"

Argus lifted an eyebrow as if he didn't believe him. But he graciously gestured towards the door. Kenneth entered the dark, smelly chamber with the little physic tight on his heels.

It stank of peppermint and clove, a scent that was both overwhelming and invigorating. It was thought to chase off the death and disease often associated with childbirth. Kenneth went to the bed where Aubrielle lay upon her side, curled up as much as she was able to given her colossal belly. The midwife had given her something for the pain, but she was clearly uncomfortable. At this point, there was not much relief to be had. When she saw Kenneth, tears sprang to her eyes.

"Hello, sweetheart," he kissed her on the forehead, smiling bravely. "What? No child yet?"

It was a gentle tease, but she was in no mood for it. "I am so tired," she whispered. "I simply want this to be over."

He kissed her again, kneeling beside the bed. "It will be soon," he assured her. "Argus says the child is merely being stubborn."

"Then it must be male," she grunted as she rolled onto her back. She squirmed uncomfortably on the mattress. "I want to stand up. I must move around. I cannot lie here any longer."

Kenneth had seen much of this restlessness over the past two weeks. The child was overdue and Aubrielle's discomfort had been unbearable. It was difficult to sit and exhausting to stand. He glanced at Argus for approval; the old man shrugged weakly. Taking his wife by the wrists, he gently pulled her into a seated position. She grunted and groaned as he carefully pulled her off the bed.

She waddled a few steps across the floor, her hands against her lower back. The pain was running rampant down her hips and legs. "Please, God, let this be over soon," she begged softly. "I do not know how much more...."

A heavy contraction hit her and she doubled over. Kenneth held on to her, watching her face contort with pain. He had never been so frightened. She held on to him until it passed, loudly wishing she could drop the child on the floor and be done with it.

When the pain subsided, she stood as straight as she was able and continued walking with Kenneth in careful attendance.

"I am very proud of you, Aubrielle," he said softly. "You have shown such strength in all of this. I doubt there has ever been a stronger woman."

She cast him sidelong glance. "Cease your praise. I shall have none of it. I hate it."

He suppressed a smile; she was full of the devil and rightfully so. He did not blame her. Another contraction bent her over and she groaned loudly, panting until it eased. Kenneth could do naught but hold her through it all.

"That one was close on the heels of the previous pain," the midwife whispered loudly to Argus. "This child should be arriving momentarily."

"My lord," Argus addressed the earl with quiet sternness. "Put her back on the bed. We must take a look."

Kenneth gently led her back over to their massive bed. Aubrielle grumbled the entire way.

"Never again," she told her husband. "This will be our last child, do you hear me? Never again will I go through this."

"Aye, madam."

"Any talk of more children in the future and I will gouge your eyes out."

"Aye, madam."

"Do not mock me."

"Aye, ma… I am not mocking you, most assuredly."

As he helped her back onto the bed, she mumbled uncontrollably. "There must be an easier way for children to be brought forth. Why can I not hatch one as a chicken does? Why can I not lay an egg? Will someone please explain this to me?"

It took all of Kenneth's self control not to smile, mostly because she was serious and he did not want to upset her further. Aubrielle lay back on the mattress and Argus and the midwife went to work. The long skirt of her shift, damp and stained, went up around her hips.

After a brief moment studying his patient's state, Argus spoke quietly. "This child comes." He glanced at Kenneth. "You will wait outside, my lord."

"No," Aubrielle latched onto his hand and would not let go. "He stays."

Kenneth didn't particularly want to stay, but he didn't want to leave her, either. She was exhausted, frightened, and her thought processes were muddled. He stroked her forehead.

"I shall not leave, have no fear," he knelt down beside her. "I shall stay right here if you wish it."

Aubrielle's expression calmed as she gazed at him, drawing strength from his presence. He gave her such comfort, knowing that nothing awful could happen to her or the child if he were here. The next pain overcame her and she was able to bear down with a steadier mind.

Argus was supervising the midwife. He stood by Aubrielle's left leg, directing the woman.

"Take hold, take hold," he instructed firmly. "The child's head is large. He requires help."

The midwife had been delivering children for twenty years. She knew well her craft. When the large head popped forth, she turned it slightly to allow for the shoulders.

"Now, my lady," Argus said to Aubrielle. "With the next pain, push as hard as you can."

Aubrielle nodded, panting and spent. The next pain came and she grunted loudly, bearing down with all her might. It was unfortunate that she had to repeat the process several more times before the babe's large shoulders were able to make their way through. Kenneth had becoming increasingly fearful that the child was stuck until the babe, literally, popped forth. After that, Aubrielle gave another large push and the entire body slipped through.

Argus grabbed the baby and whisked it to the edge of the bed where neither Kenneth nor Aubrielle could see it. The air was silent when there should have been a baby crying and Kenneth was positive that tragedy had befallen them. After a small eternity, Argus gave the child a brisk rub across the feet and a thin wail pierced the air.

"My child," Aubrielle demanded. "Is it well? What is…?"

"Your son is fine, my lady," Argus wiped the baby off and handed it to the midwife. His old eyes twinkled at the alarmed earl and countess. "He is a big, healthy boy. No wonder he took so long to come. He is the size of a pumpkin."

Aubrielle started laughing and weeping at the same time. Kenneth felt so much relief that he nearly slithered to the floor with it. But he put his arms around his wife's shoulders and buried his face in her neck instead; it was all he could manage at the moment.

When he finally lifted his head to look at her, she wiped a thumb across his cheek. "Tears," Aubrielle murmured. "So the mighty Kenneth St. Héver weeps tears of joy. Remarkable."

He didn't care if he had tears on his face; it seemed like a foolishly inconsequential thing. "Thank you," he murmured, kissing her sweetly. "From the bottom of my heart, thank you."

Aubrielle wallowed in his adoration, feeling more joy and fulfillment than she ever knew possible. Kenneth kissed her, stroking her arm tenderly, before looking to Argus.

"Is she well?" he was trying to be delicate with his question. "The child… he did not injury her overly, did he?"

Argus was inspecting the afterbirth. "The mother tore somewhat, but that is to be expected. She must stay in bed and rest in order to regain her strength."

The midwife came forth with the baby, now screaming lustily. The woman presented the boy to Kenneth, who wasn't quite sure if he should take him. His expression was wrought with uncertainty.

"Hold him, Kenneth," Aubrielle encouraged softly. "He'll not break."

Kenneth held out two hands and the woman put the baby in his palms. He looked bewildered until he looked into the child's face; then, it was if the sun suddenly broke from behind the clouds. Kenneth's entire expression changed.

"Welcome, lad," he murmured into the red, yelling face. "We have been waiting a long time to see you."

Aubrielle held up her arms and Kenneth carefully deposited the child into them. He put a pillow behind her back, helping her to sit up. The new mother and new father gawked excitedly at their child. They didn't even notice when Argus and the midwife quietly slipped from the room. For the moment, it was only the three of them in the entire world.

"He is magnificent, Aubrielle," Kenneth murmured. "See how strong he is."

"He has ten fingers," she said. "I must see the rest of him."

Kenneth watched her unwrap the babe to gain a better look. "We have a problem, you know," he said. "The only name you were able to decide upon was for a female. I would not like my son to bear the name of Geniver."

Aubrielle touched the fat little arms, inspecting the soft, round belly. "There is a name I have always been fond of."

"Not Parsifal or Arthgallo or Gawain."

She smiled, remembering their many conversations about a male name. They could not agree. She ran through the names of Arthurian legend and Kenneth wanted to name a son something simple, like John. Aubrielle had declared her son to be too exceptional to bear such a plain name and they had been at an impasse for weeks. Now, they had to choose.

"Back when the knights of Munsalvaesche brought the Grail to Britain's shores, a kindly king allowed them to settle in Glastonbury. His name was Brennan. How do you like the name of Brennan St. Héver?"

Kenneth gazed down at the fat little boy with the loud voice. He could see that, in the warmth of the room, his hair was drying into a downy shade of blond. He never thought he would ever feel the way he felt now, at this instant, ever again. It was a magical moment.

"Brennan de Witney St. Héver it is."

CHAPTER FIFTEEN

October, 1334 A.D.

ON THE OUTSKIRTS of Preesegweene, several miles south of Kirk Castle, a large man in ratted, heavy clothing had been sitting at the same table in the same inn for two days. He paid his bill for food and drink, and had slept intermittently with his shaggy head lying on the table, and the innkeeper had left him alone.

His armor and clothing had once been fine. Now it was soiled with wear. His dark hair was dirty and unkempt, and he wore a beard that had not seen a razor in months. Even if the man had been recognizable, it was doubtful even his wife would have known him. Filth and desolation followed him like a cloud.

Outside the walls of the tavern, the air was mild with fall. The summer had been unnaturally warm and the early fall was still warm. These days were lazy and mellow, followed by easy evenings. The peasants were in the fields from dawn to dusk harvesting their crops, mostly rye that grew in this rocky soil. Peace was upon the land. But for the dirty man sprawled across the table, one would have thought all in this land were enjoying the benefits of a prosperous spell.

The sun set gently this eve. The innkeeper stoked the fire in the hearth, bringing light and warmth to the night. The traveler sleeping on the tabletop awoke long enough to demand more ale and bread. The innkeeper, a large man who had no difficulty sending undesirables upon their way, asked to see his money first. Angered, the man threw two gold crowns across the table and onto the floor. It was an enormous amount of money. With no more questions, the innkeeper delivered the fare.

"Tell me," the man said as he took a drink from his full tankard. "Kirk Castle. What has happened to her as of late?"

The innkeeper shook his head. "Nothing has happened to her."

"I mean news, man. What news of her?"

The innkeeper scratched his beard in thought. "They had a marriage in the late summer this past year. The heiress married."

A ripple of emotion crossed the traveler's face. "The heiress?"

"Lady Aubrielle."

The man didn't say anything for a moment. He was having difficulty concealing his astonishment. "And who is the new earl?"

The innkeeper warmed to the conversation, propping a leg up on the bench beside the traveler. "He is a fair and decent man. He used to be a knight for the good earl Mortimer. And he and his wife had a son this past spring."

"Wait," the man waved a hand at him. "Tell me about the marriage. A former knight married the lady?"

"Aye."

The traveler's dark eyes flashed, an ambiance of dread settling upon him. "What is his name?"

"Kenneth St. Héver."

The man's eyes closed for a brief moment. It appeared as if he was struggling with something deep inside of him, grappling with it. "And they had a son, you said?"

"A fat, healthy baby. I saw him, once, when the earl and his wife were traveling south. The whole town turned out to see the little poppet. He rode with his father and I heard that the countess had fits over it. Seems she wanted him safe in the carriage with her. But I say the lad's got to grow up some time, eh?"

The traveler grunted in response, shoving bread in his mouth. Then he took a long drag of ale, his movements sharp as if he were angry. He demanded more ale and spoke again whilst the innkeeper was filling his tankard.

"Has the castle seen any action?"

"No, no action. The Welsh have been quiet."

"So the castle is open?"

"As far as I know."

The man finished his ale and thanked the innkeeper for his time. He left the dark, smoky hovel and plunged out into the darkness of the fall evening. Roughly, he mounted his unkempt black destrier and galloped off into the night.

☙

"KENNETH, HE CANNOT chew. Have you gone mad?"

Kenneth grinned as he held a very small piece of beef up to his son's mouth. The baby sucked on the salty morsel. "He has eight teeth," he said patiently. "And, according to you, they are razor sharp. Better have him gnaw on a piece of beef than your tender breasts."

Aubrielle sat back in her chair, her cheeks red. Everyone at the table had heard her husband's remark and she was mortified by the snickers of Max, now a full-fledged knight. It was mid-evening, the remnants of a good supper and bottles of local wine scattered on the table. The hall was moderately full of senior soldiers, knights, and a band of traveling minstrels in the corner.

"You do not feed a baby beef," Aubrielle reached out and scooped her son out of his father's grasp. "I will feed him now with better things than that."

Kenneth let her take the boy, smiling at the both of them. At six months of age, Brennan was a round, healthy child with his mother's sea colored eyes and his father's blond hair. He sat up, rolled around, and was learning to crawl as fast as lightning. Kenneth and Aubrielle had to be well alert when Bren was on the prowl. Though it was common practice to bind children at this age to a bed or a chair, neither Aubrielle nor Kenneth could bring themselves to do it. Brennan was, frankly, never out of his mother's sight and very rarely out of his father's. It was clear to all at Kirk that the sun rose and set on the smiles and exploits of little Brennan St. Héver.

Kenneth stood up and followed his wife and son from the room. Whenever possible, he liked to be with Aubrielle when she fed their son. Since the day the child was born, Aubrielle would not entertain the concept of a wet nurse, and Kenneth found something innately serene about watching his son suckle. He had developed into such an attentive father that Aubrielle swore Kenneth would have fed Brennan himself were he physically able to do so. It was exceptionally uncommon for men to take any interest in child rearing, but Kenneth was proving to be an exception. He adored the boy.

Their large chamber was more a nursery than a master's suite. Brennan had his own bed, but half the time he ended up on his parent's. Kenneth closed the door to allow for some privacy as Aubrielle settled herself on a chair by the hearth and began unlacing her bodice. It was difficult one-handed and Kenneth took the boy while she exposed a luscious white breast. Brennan fussed until Aubrielle settled him against her nipple, and then he quieted and began to suck furiously.

She winced as the baby suckled hard. Kenneth knelt beside the chair, one arm around his wife's shoulders and a hand on the baby's head.

"Is he still biting?" he asked.

Aubrielle's contorted expression told him the tale. "He made me bleed yesterday. The sooner we wean him, the better. I fear I cannot take much more of this."

"Argus made him a special cup to learn to drink from. Perhaps we should try to use that more regularly."

Brennan bit down at that moment and Aubrielle yelped. The baby laughed and continued sucking. "There, you see?" Aubrielle said miserably. "He likes to punish me."

Kenneth couldn't help but smile at his son; it was really quite dastardly and amusing at the same time. "If you did not cry out, perhaps he would stop. He thinks it is a game to make you scream."

She shot him a withering look. "Let him bite you and see if you do not scream."

He nuzzled her neck, her shoulder, inhaling the sweet smell of her. "I cannot blame him. I like to bite you, too."

Chills raced up her spine as Kenneth's lips moved against her flesh. "Not now, Ken," she murmured. "You drive me mad with your attention."

He dutifully stopped and refocused on the baby. His face was positioned as such that Brennan could look up and see his father. A fat baby hand reached up, grasping Kenneth's nose and mouth. Kenneth pretended to bite the little fingers, much to his son's delight.

"He gets it from you," Aubrielle scolded gently. "You show him that biting is an acceptable behavior."

Kenneth smiled as the baby touched his teeth. He finally kissed the boy's head, kissed his wife's cheek, and stood up. Stretching his powerful body, he moved towards the lancet window, gazing out over his empire. The land was at peace for the moment, and Kenneth knew that he had never been happier. He'd never know there was such tranquility in the world. Yet there was much on his mind in spite of the serenity, items that he had not yet discussed with Aubrielle for fear of shattering the calm. He was so content with the moment that he did not want to alter it, for any reason. But it seemed as if it always came to moments like this, heavy things on his mind when times were still.

"What are you thinking?" Aubrielle's soft voice floated upon the air.

She had become quite adept at reading his mind. There wasn't much he could hide from her. He looked at her, his heart softening anew at the sight of her feeding Brennan. With a sigh, he leaned against the wall, collecting his thoughts.

"A few things," he shrugged casually.

"I can always tell. What is it?"

"Have you heard of Dolforwyn Castle?" he asked.

She nodded. "I saw the charter to Uncle Garson. It is one of our holdings."

He should have known she would have read all of the papers her uncle had left behind. They'd not talked much about their holdings or lands or wealth at all. Their conversations during the course of their marriage had, not strangely, focused more on each other, Brennan, and other items unrelated to the earldom. Kenneth knew what his holdings and responsibilities were and though Aubrielle wasn't particularly concerned either way, still, she was naturally curious and had educated herself on her inheritance. It simply wasn't something they discussed.

"Correct, as usual," his ice-blue eyes had long since lost their icy glare when it came to her; now, they twinkled. "'Tis a smaller castle about 40 miles to the south. We have always staffed it as an outpost, with about 50 men and a commander. But it is a strategic location, very important to England."

She shifted the baby to the other breast. When he settled down, she gazed up at Kenneth with a serious expression.

"Come out with it. What about Dolforwyn?"

He moved away from the window. "Do you recall the messenger that arrived a couple of days ago?"

She nodded. "From Powys. News of Lord Chereleton's death."

"That, and of other things. 'Twould seem that the Welsh have decided to take Dolforwyn for themselves and kill my garrison commander."

"Oh," Aubrielle's brow furrowed with sorrow over the news. But the more she looked at Kenneth, the more she knew what he was thinking. "You are going to retake the castle."

"I must."

She opened her mouth to say something, but a glance at Brennan showed that the baby almost asleep against her breast. She did not want to disturb him with the loud voices that were sure to come. Carefully, she lifted him into his small bed and tucked a warm blanket around him. Cinching up her bodice, she indicated for Kenneth to quietly follow her from the room.

They moved into the smaller chamber that Aubrielle had originally occupied when she had first arrived at Kirk. Kenneth could sense what was to come. They hadn't taken two steps into the room when she turned on her heel and faced him.

"You are the earl, for Heaven's sake," she snapped softly. "You have men to go into battle for you. You needn't risk your own life."

"It is my holding, Aubrielle."

"And you have people sworn to you to protect your holdings. Your responsibility is to the entire earldom, and part of that responsibility is to keep yourself safe from harm."

"It is my responsibility to take action against any and all who have threatened my earldom, including the Welsh. If I do not act, then they will think the new earl soft and weak. This is my first test as earl and I cannot fail."

She stood there, looking at him as if he were daft. "And what of Bren and I? What happens to us if you perish? You would leave us alone in this world, your wife and son whom you profess to adore? All because you must prove yourself to the damnable Welsh?"

He sighed heavily. "It is not about proving myself to anyone. It is about fulfilling my duties as the Earl of Wrexham."

"You did not answer my question. What about your responsibility to Bren and me?"

He met her gaze, his ice blue eyes undulating with thoughts and feelings. He reached out to take her hand, putting it against his lips as he so often did. There was no manipulation in the gesture, only emotion.

"No man could ask for a greater privilege," he said quietly. "You and Bren have given me more joy and contentment than I could have ever imagined to exist. There is nothing I would not do for you, or for him. However, before I met you, and before I was the earl, I was a warrior. I am still a warrior. What you ask of me now, Aubrielle… you ask me to be less than what I am."

Aubrielle stared at him. Then it was her turn to sigh heavily. She lowered her gaze and found the nearest chair. She sat slowly, bewildered and sorrowful.

"I simply do not want to lose you," she spoke so softly that he could barely hear her. "I came very close to losing you, once. It was the worst moment of my life. I swear that I would die if anything happened to you. I could not go on."

He went to the chair and knelt beside her. His big hand stroked her dark head. "Sweetheart, I understand how you feel. Believe me, I do. But a fear of death must not keep us from fulfilling our destiny in life. Does the fear of death in childbirth keep you from wanting a brother or sister for Bren?"

She shook her head. "Of course not. But that is life renewing itself and the risk is well worth the result. But for you to deliberately go into battle, when you know that every Welshman will be aiming his arrows at you… it terrifies me."

He kissed the side of her head, stroking her hair, hoping he could somehow comfort her. "I will do my best to stay clear of their arrows, I promise you. And I will do everything in my power to return to you and Bren safe and whole."

She turned to him, wrapping her slender arms around his neck. Their eyes met and they shared a tender moment. "I love you so, Ken," she murmured as she brushed her lips across his. "I would be lost without you."

He returned her kisses, gently. "And you are the heart that beats within me. I love you more than my own life."

The smell and taste of him made Aubrielle's chest hurt, the pain of separation manifesting itself. Tears sprang to her eyes at the thought of never knowing the joy of him again. She wrapped her arms tightly around his neck and buried her face against him, tears coming softly. He held her tightly, allowing her to express her fear. He only wished he could give her more comfort.

"Do not cry, sweetheart," he murmured. "I know your trepidation. I can only swear to you that I will do my very best to return to you and Bren."

She sniffled and tried to compose herself. "I suppose I must get used to this, as a warrior's wife. I was just hoping we could go the rest of our lives avoiding a battle."

"Believe me when I say that I would not go if I did not feel it absolutely necessary."

"When are you leaving?"

"I should like to leave on the morrow."

Her eyes widened. "So soon?"

"The sooner I go, the sooner I return."

She had nothing more to say. They were both well aware of the situation. Kenneth collected her in his arms and rocked her like a child. Aubrielle chased away the last of her tears as he set her on the ground. They had one night together before he left and she did not intend to spend it weeping like a fool. She offered him a weak smile.

"There are minstrels in the hall tonight," she said. "Perhaps we should go downstairs and enjoy the evening. Perhaps I shall allow you to dance with me."

He wriggled his blond eyebrows. "I think I have done enough dancing lately."

She scowled. "The last you danced with me was at our wedding."

"That was recent enough."

She made a face at him and he laughed. It was enough to cause her to playfully pinch him.

"Perhaps I am hoping you'll trip and break a leg and be unable to ride out tomorrow."

"Ah. Then I shall thwart your plan at every turn."

She cast him a long look. "We shall see, my lord."

He watched her saunter out of the door in front of him. "You are a wicked wench," he muttered.

"What was that?"

"I said I would rather sit on the bench… with you than dance."

The sea colored eyes blazed at him, but it was with humor. "You," she pointed a delicate finger at him, "are in a good deal of trouble."

"God help me, I know it."

She smirked and he chuckled softly, catching her hand and kissing the fingers. Leaving the toothless serving wench watching over the sleeping Brennan, Kenneth and Aubrielle made their way down to the hall and were enveloped by the mood of the glowing evening.

CHAPTER SIXTEEN

KENNETH FELT LIKE an idiot.

He found it ironic that Aubrielle had remained so stoic and strong at his departure to Dolforwyn Castle when he had struggled through it like a fool. She had smiled at him and bid a cheery farewell, taking Brennan's fat little hand and waving it at his father. Kenneth had been so crushed at the sight that it had manifested itself into barking orders and a brusque manner. To anyone that served under Kenneth, it was simply his normal battle mode. No one suspected that inside, he wept like a woman.

A weak, foolish, insipid bundle of raging emotion; that's exactly what he was. He cursed his inability to control his feelings. Riding ahead of his mighty army for the first time in the capacity of earl should have been a proud experience, but the satisfaction Kenneth should have felt was diminished by the ache in his heart. All he could see was Aubrielle and Brennan waving to him from the steps of the keep. He missed them terribly.

It didn't help matters that he couldn't shake the odd sense of foreboding that clung to him. He'd been feeling this strange sensation since yesterday but had refrained from mentioning it simply because he attributed it to Aubrielle's own fears. Something she had said, or perhaps her manner, had infected him. Now he was fearful, too, and he couldn't rid himself of the feeling. But it wasn't for himself, strangely enough. His fear was inexplicably for her.

Reid's shouting distracted him from his morose thoughts. He was bellowing to the wagons to keep steady pace, causing the wagon-masters to smack the hides of their big-boned horses furiously with their whips. Everett and Bradley were flanking the foot soldiers, keeping the marching rhythm quick and steady. Two siege engines were to the rear, with the wagons, pulled by several large heavy-labor horses.

Dolforwyn Castle wasn't particularly large and from what his intelligence had told him, the Welsh force inhabiting her wasn't particularly organized. Kenneth didn't expect much of a resistance. But he had brought most of his knights with him and nearly two thirds of his army, just to make short work of it. He had left Max in charge of Kirk with one hundred men and several senior soldiers, locked down and heavily guarded from the ramparts.

A few drops of rain pelted his face. He glanced up, noting the darkening sky. The rain increased and he lowered his visor to keep it from his eyes. He was eager to gain back his outpost and return to his family, eager to be done with this whole troublesome business. Whereas once he had looked forward to battles, now he realized that he didn't even want to go. There was more to life than fighting and dying; there was a dark-haired woman and a blond infant he adored.

"We should think about finding shelter for the night," Reid rode up beside him, his voice hoarse from shouting. "Our scouts say that we are only a few miles from Dolforwyn."

Kenneth nodded slowly, struggling with the distraction of his thoughts. "Have the men take to the trees and make camp. It is my intention to lay siege to my castle before dawn and have her secured by noon. Pass the word."

"Aye, my lord," Reid replied. "Do you realize that this is the first battle we've fought in fifteen years without Lucius?"

Kenneth grunted. "It had crossed my mind. It seems somewhat strange."

Reid looked off over the landscape. "It also seems somewhat strange that Everett was unable to discover what had become of him when he went to London those months ago."

"Indeed. The young king said that he had given him audience and that Lucius made heady demands for his service. Edward denied him and that was last anyone saw of him."

"A man like him would not have simply given up. He is somewhere, living off the good graces of another master. Or plotting to take over the world."

"Perhaps both."

Usually, discussion of Lucius enticed Kenneth into a strongly-opinionated conversation. But he was strangely silent today.

"Is anything the matter?" Reid finally asked.

"Why do you ask?"

"I have fought many battles with you. I know the tone of your voice and the mood behind every movement. I would venture to say that there are other things on your mind."

Kenneth didn't reply for a moment. Then, he emitted a long sigh; since knowing his wife, one thing he had learned was that it was acceptable, from time to time, to let his guard down with his closest colleagues. Aubrielle had taught him the virtues and comfort of such an action and Reid was probably the closest. He need not fear judgment from the man.

After a moment of attempting to find the right words, he simply shook his head. "I fear I have become a foolish old woman."

"Why?"

"Because I have a sense of dread like nothing I have ever known. Ever since yesterday I have felt this vise around my heart and I cannot seem to shake it."

"You fear for this battle?"

"Nay, not this battle. Not even for my safety. What I feel… it is for Aubrielle. I cannot explain even what it is that I am afraid for, only that it centers around her."

Reid shrugged, glancing up into the darkened sky. "It is your first separation from her and the baby, and not a pleasant separation at that. It is battle. Perhaps you are afraid you will never see her again, but I assure you that…"

"No, it is nothing as such. I feel as if Aubrielle is in danger somehow, although I know she is perfectly safe at Kirk. But then I think back to when she first came to Kirk and was attacked twice when I thought that she was also perfectly safe. Perhaps it was a mistake to leave her and the baby alone. Perhaps she was right and I should have sent the army on to Dolforwyn with my competent knights at the head."

Reid smiled. "Ken, the simple fact of the matter is that you did not want to leave your wife and child. And now you are creating phantoms in your mind that do not exist."

"Like I said, I feel like a foolish old woman."

"You shouldn't. You and Aubrielle are quite attached to each other. I should think your longing is only natural."

They rode together in silence for several long minutes. The rain grew worse as the sky darkened with weather and the setting of the sun. By the time the army pitched camp and settled in for the night, Kenneth was nearly in a panic. It was all Reid could do to hold him in camp. After sup, he lost the battle completely.

ঔ

WHEN KIRK LOCKED down, those who were caught inside the bailey were forced to remain. The smithy, a few villeins doing business with the kitchens, and some miscellaneous villagers had resigned themselves to a long wait. A few made up comfortable quarters in or around the stables, while still others sought shelter within the gatehouse itself.

Kirk was a massive place. It was easy to lose oneself. While the soldiers patrolled and the inhabitants went about their business, the unkempt traveler who had sought comfort and information at the inn in Preesegweene sat huddled in the shadows near the kitchen walls. Concealed in a cluster of ale barrels that had been recently offloaded from Manchester, he had been able to watch most of the action from his make-shift cave. He had watched the soldiers and knights assemble, departing at daybreak the morning before. He had heard some of the men speaking of Dolforwyn Castle and he recalled everything he knew about the place in his mind; the fortress had seen much action over the past fifty years between Llewellyn the Last and the Marcher lordship of

Montgomery. Garson Mortimer's grandsire had eventually commandeered it from the Welsh prince and it had been a Wrexham holding ever since. Aye, he knew much about the outpost, considering it had once been his job to know this, and more.

Lucius de Cor had returned home.

Kirk didn't look any different from the last time he had been within her walls. In fact, it appeared more prosperous than he had remembered. It was a strangely satisfying sensation to envision her great walls again, the massive keep, and faces of those he recognized in the ward. Aye, it was satisfying. And it was also a prelude as to why he had returned.

London had been unsatisfying. The young king, it seemed, had no use for old soldiers who were beyond retirement age. He had found himself at the bottom of the food chain, a once-important knight who was now hardly more than an object of distain for those more popular and powerful. He had spent months trying to work his way up the political ladder of favor, but it had been to no avail. Young Edward was not interested in him.

Worse yet, Kenneth St. Héver was god-like according to the king so the sly rumors that Lucius attempted to start about St. Héver were quickly quelled. Kenneth could do no wrong as far as Edward was concerned. Lucius' confidence had faltered, his spirits sank, and his mind had wandered between sanity and the muddied waters of psychosis.

Kirk had been the only home he had ever known. It was natural for him to want to return. He truthfully had no idea what he would find, but Kenneth and Aubrielle had not been in his thoughts. The last he'd seen of either of them had been enough to convince him that they had, long ago, met their deaths. To find them alive and thriving, to find himself foiled by them once again, was more than his fragile mind could take.

He hadn't formulated any plan in particular when he had arrived. But seeing Kenneth in his full glory as the earl, riding from the gates of

Kirk, had fueled a deep sense of bitterness and vengeance. The man had the gods on his side; that much was apparent. Lucius had suffered no such luck. When the main gates closed behind the departing army, the former captain's thoughts turned to the woman who had been the source of his downfall.

The Lady Aubrielle Grace de Witney St. Héver was somewhere in the keep he knew so well, living her happy life with no inkling of what lurked inside her prosperous walls. With the mighty St. Héver gone, there would be no one to protect her. Lucius had almost killed her once; aye, he had pretended not to remember what he had done to her those many months ago, but the truth was that he did indeed recollect his act. He knew what he had done.

Sneaking in to the castle had been easy. He'd served at Kirk for many years and knew every passage, every door. He waited until the sentries changed shifts before making his move through the postern gate, right before it was locked for the night. Once he was inside the kitchen yards, it was simply a matter of making his way into the keep. That was made simple through the kitchens and the trap door through the floor that led into the great hall.

The great hall didn't look any different than he remembered. It still smelled like dogs and roasting meat, and he took a moment to pause, remembering the glory he once enjoyed within the very walls of this chamber. Once, he had been in charge and men listened to him. He longed for those days once again. Making his way along the eastern wall towards the doorway that led to the stairs, he suddenly crashed headlong into an old servant.

The old man had his hands full of scraps and remnants from a meal. He hardly put up a fight as Lucius snapped his neck and left him in a heap in the corner. Lucius knew, however, that it would only be a matter of time before the body was discovered so he made haste to the staircase that led to the upper floors, knowing that was where he would find Aubrielle.

His mistake had been in not killing her when he'd had the chance. He would not make the same mistake again.

CHAPTER SEVENTEEN

"WILL YOU BE needing anything tonight, m'lady?"

The toothless serving wench folded the last of the swaddling she had washed earlier that day. Aubrielle had Brennan around his fat little body, holding him against her hip as she picked up his woolen night gown in preparation for putting him down to sleep.

"Nay, nothing else," she told the girl. "Just make sure the fire is banked before you leave."

The girl did as she was told and bid her lady a good eve. When the door shut softly, Aubrielle put the baby on the bed to change his clothes for sleep. Brennan did not want to lie still, however, and he squirmed and rolled around while his mother struggled to dress him. Aubrielle made a game of it as he fussed, finally able to secure the little leggings that kept his feet and body warm. Brennan sat up, grabbed the toe of one of the leggings, and promptly pulled it half way off.

Shaking her head, Aubrielle pulled the legging tight again. The little pup, having watched all of the activity from his perch on the pillow, took up the revolt and grabbed the other legging and pulled. Aubrielle found herself not only dealing with Brennan, but with the wily pup. Finally, she was able to control the disobedient pair and picked Brennan up, pretending he was a bird and flying him through the air until they both came to rest on the large sling-back chair that Kenneth had made for her. He was a man of many talents, carpentry among them. The baby fretted until she settled him down on her nipple.

"Hush, now," she said softly, rocking him gently as he fed. She gazed down at the baby, already half-lidded, thinking how much he looked like his father. Stroking the downy-blond head, her longing for Kenneth burst forth and she allowed herself the first moment to truly miss him.

She knew how badly he had felt when he had left that morning. She had seen it in his eyes. It would not have done any good for her to cry at his departure, so she put on a brave front, hoping that would ease his ache. He had been characteristically strong and controlled, but she knew it was a façade. Even as he left the gates, proud and strong, she could feel his emotions as she knew he felt hers. She had prayed all day that the glimpse of her husband as he left the walls of Kirk would not be her last of him alive.

Brennan quickly fell asleep and she disengaged him from her nipple and put him in his little bed. She was coming to be firm about having him sleep in his own bed even though Kenneth preferred the baby in their larger bed between them. It made it rather tricky when he made love to her. Not only was the baby between them, but oft time, so was the little pup. Still, Kenneth seemed to want his family as close to him as possible, always. Sometimes Aubrielle felt it was an almost desperate need. It was as if he was finally so happy, so content, that he didn't want to let any of it out of his reach for fear that he would wake up and it would all have been a dream.

With Brennan fast asleep, Aubrielle was finally able to relax. The pup, at her feet, hopped on the bed to watch vigilantly over the baby. She put her finger to her lips in a silencing gesture to the little dog as she quietly closed the door. The smaller chamber next door, where she had spent her first few days at Kirk, had found new life as a sitting room until they decided to turn it back into Brennan's nursery. There was mulled wine and a fire in that room and Aubrielle gratefully retreated to it.

It was peaceful and warm. But as she poured herself a cup of wine, she realized how very much she missed her husband. This was the time they treasured together, away from Kirk and duties and even Brennan. It was just the two of them, talking softly or making love before the fire. She took a sip of her wine and her longing for him deepened. She said another silent prayer that he would survive the battle at Dolforwyn and return to her whole.

She eased herself into a chair, gazing into the licks of flame and thinking back to the time when the Grail had been the most important thing in her life. In this very room, she had told Kenneth of her quest and of the Scroll of Munsalvaesche. She remembered the look on his face when she had first confided in him, and the thought made her smile. He had thought she was insane as well as blasphemous.

A soft knock on the door roused her; glancing up, she saw that it was Brother Grendel.

"Come in," she motioned to him. "Have some wine with me. I was just sitting here, thinking."

He moved into the room, his narrow face warm with a smile. "What about, dare I ask?"

She laughed softly. "Days past when the Grail seemed like the most important thing in the world to me."

"And those thoughts have changed?"

"Dramatically so. Do I even seem like the same person?"

Grendel shook his head. "You do not. I give Lord Kenneth all of the credit. He has done what I thought no man could ever do."

She wrinkled her nose at him. "Did you come for a reason or did you simply come to insult me?"

His warm smile broadened. "Max and I drew straws to see who would come to see how you were faring. With Lord Kenneth gone, we thought you might be lonely."

"I am well enough."

"Then if you do not need anyone to talk to, I shall inform Max that you are well enough and retire for the night."

"I always need you to talk to. But it is late and I encourage you to retire."

He gave her a wink and moved for the door. "Grendel?" she called after him.

He paused. "M'lady?"

"You aren't still thinking about returning to St. Wenburgh, are you?"

"Why do you ask?"

"Why do you think? I tell you every week that I do not want you to leave us. We need your guidance here. I want you to promise me that you will stay, forever."

He sighed. "God knows, the longer I stay, the harder it will be to leave."

"Then why do you stay?"

"Because I believe I am here for a reason. I do not know what that reason is yet, but there is a reason nonetheless. I do not believe God wants me to leave you yet."

"Why?"

"I cannot explain. But I feel that way."

They had this conversation almost nightly. They always said the same things to each other. Aubrielle bid him a good night and he gently closed the door. Grendel had become such an integral part of their lives over the past several months that she could not imagine Kirk without him. He had become teacher, counselor and friend to them all, filling a void they never knew existed. Without him, Kirk would become a less wonderful place. If she had to chain him to the wall, she was determined to keep him.

She drained the wine and continued to sit before the fire, daydreaming and then finally dozing. She had no idea when she actually became aware of movement in the room, but suddenly, she realized that she was not alone. Something was moving in the shadows, and it was moving for her.

Startled, she sat forward in her chair, her eyes wide and alert. The shape was like a phantom, weaving through the darkness, silent as the grave as it deliberately stalked her. She sat like stone, thinking perhaps it might leave her alone if she remained perfectly still. When it finally emerged into the soft light from the fire, Aubrielle thought she was hallucinating.

It was several long, painful seconds before she was able to speak.

"Lucius," she hissed.

He came to a halt, bowing to acknowledge her recognition. "Countess."

Until that very moment, Aubrielle thought she might be dreaming. But the sound of his voice sent terror coursing through her body. She bolted up, knocking the chair over. She knew instinctively that Lucius had only her death on his mind; she could see it in his eyes. There was no question why he was here; pleasantries were unnecessary and pitifully out of place. She would not ask his business, nor where he had been the past several months. All that mattered was that he was here, and Aubrielle was fighting for her life before the struggle even began.

"Where did you come from?" she demanded. "How did you get in here?"

"I had the run of Kirk long before you came. I know her well enough to slip in unseen."

She backed away from him, rightfully terrified. "Get out of here," she snarled. "Get out and I will forget I saw you."

He smiled thinly. "It took much trouble for me to come to this place, Countess. I have no intention of leaving."

Aubrielle began mentally sizing up her options; her beloved fire poker was behind him, against the wall near the hearth. She knew she could not collect it before Lucius would stop her. Other than the poker, the room contained very little that she could use to protect herself with. There were, however, heavy candlesticks to her right, somewhat behind her, that held fat tapers. They were the only items she could think of that even remotely resembled an implement of defense.

No time like the present; she wasn't about to wait for Lucius to make the first threatening move. His mere presence here was the first move. Whirling away from him, she snatched one of the solid iron candleholders and wielded it like a club.

"Get out of here, Lucius," she growled. "Get out before I take your head off."

Lucius took a step towards her. "Still the same, are you not? Like a mad dog. A malevolent, scheming bitch."

Aubrielle screamed at the top of her lungs. "Guard!"

Lucius broke for the door, throwing the bolt before anyone come to her aid. Aubrielle, meanwhile, had hurled the candlestick at him, clipping him on the shoulder. In the same motion, she raced for the fireplace and snatched the poker. Her plan of distraction had worked somewhat, for now she had some protection. But the look on Lucius face quickly cooled any strains of hope that she might have been feeling.

He looked like Death. Lucius snarled at her, unsheathing his large blade. It was old, worn, but could still do a significant amount of damage. Someone pounded from the other side of the locked door and Lucius seemed to come alive with malice and fury. He sensed his time would be short and he would not waste it.

He lunged the sword at her, knocking the poker. Aubrielle didn't back down, she swung the poker at his head, a move he deftly parried. Grunting with fright and exertion, she stabbed the poker at him again, jumping back out of his effective range as she did so.

"You attacked me once in this room," she said. "Like a coward, you assaulted me and I was unable to fight back. But I will certainly fight back now; do not think I will make this easy for you."

"I expect nothing less," he stalked towards her, leveling the blade. "'Twill make this victory that much sweeter."

Lucius wasn't stupid and, unfortunately for Aubrielle, he was rather good with a sword. He easily countered her moves, swinging the big sword at her head. With a second huge lunge, he narrowly missed her and she shrieked with surprise and fear, ducking low and dashing well out of his range again.

Aubrielle quickly realized that the only way to stay alive was to stay away from him and get to the door so that she could unbolt it. On the other side, she could hear male voices calling to her, the guards who had been on duty on the floor below. More than fear, Aubrielle felt an extreme amount of anger.

"Why did you come back here?" she half-demanded, half-begged.

"You were safe wherever you were, out of Kenneth's mind. Now he will kill you for sure and make certain your death is as painful as possible."

Lucius chopped heavily with the sword, disintegrating a small table that held the wine decanter. The table and the decanter shattered on the floor, creating tremendous racket.

"Certainly you know something of knights, my lady," he was beginning to breathe heavily, his insanity and activity becoming laborious. "You know that honor is everything. You destroyed my honor. I have come to get it back."

Confusion flickered across her face. "Destroyed it? You never had any to begin with. You are the most dishonorable, despicable person I have ever known. My uncle knew it, too, though he was too kind to do what he should have done long ago. He felt sorry for you when he should have thrown you to the wolves!"

He thrust the sword at her suddenly, catching her arm. It was enough to tear her sleeve and nick her flesh. "But he did not. He kept me as his captain, a title that you tore from me the moment you inherited your uncle's wealth. You had no right to do it. It was mine."

Blood stained her sleeve but Aubrielle didn't take the time to inspect the wound; she suspected the next one would be far worse if she wasn't more careful. "I did not want you as my captain because you are a worthless excuse for a man."

He paled, his movement slowing as he stalked her across the room. "You took every opportunity to demean me, to insult me. I never gave you reason."

"Your character was reason enough, Lucius. The only thing you ever demonstrated was that you could shamelessly flatter my uncle and gain his favor when it was to your advantage. You never stopped to think that it was perhaps good deeds he wanted more than your silver tongue."

"What do you know of gaining favor? You were born to it."

"You cannot blame me for that."

"And you cannot blame me for gaining favor the only way I can."

He thrust the sword at her again, banging against the poker. Aubrielle responded by swinging her weapon wildly until she clipped him on the cheek. Lucius paused long enough to wipe the blood away, chuckling softly when he saw it on his fingers.

"Good contact, Countess," he said. "But see if you can deter this."

He swung the sword to his right; when Aubrielle moved to counter it, he spun around and undercut her. The tip of the blade scratched right across her midsection, blazing a path several inches long. Aubrielle cried out in pain, falling away from him. He did not give her a chance to breathe, however; he brought the sword down again but she managed to lift the poker. The two weapons came into contact with one another at an odd angle and Lucius lost the grip on his sword. As it clattered to the ground, he dove for it along with Aubrielle and they both ended up on the floor.

Aubrielle was bleeding but had no intention of giving up. She wrestled with Lucius for the sword, but he grabbed her by the hair and pounded her skull a couple of times with his fist. Dazed, she lost enough of her momentum to allow him to reach his sword before she did.

Though her head was swimming and her body screaming with pain, Aubrielle refused to surrender. When she saw Lucius reclaim his sword, she scampered to her knees and threw herself in the direction of the bolted door. Lucius came up behind her and swung his sword at her, but she had felt his presence and rolled to her left, away from the blade of death. Lucius swung the sword again, this time hitting the wall and jamming it in the wood. In the moments it took him to yank it free, Aubrielle raised the poker that was still in her hand and hit him, with all of her might, across the back of the neck.

Lucius groaned and fell to his knees. Bleeding, in pain, Aubrielle swung the poker again and again, beating the man as he went down. On the fourth strike, however, Lucius reached up and grabbed the poker, yanking it out of her hand. Her impetus interrupted, Aubrielle was thrown off balance enough that she stumbled back and sprawled on the floor. Lucius threw the poker across the room, yanked his sword out of the wall, and took a step towards her. Now was the time to finish what he had come here to do.

That was when the door exploded.

Kenneth was standing where the door had once been. One look at his wife, in mortal combat with a man he should have killed long ago, and there was no stopping his rage. Kenneth leveled his weapon with both hands and brought a heavy downward parry at Lucius' raised weapon. The second violent blow had Lucius reeling. The third blow knocked the sword from his hand and sent him to the floor.

Lucius might have lost his blade, but he was no means weaponless; he dove under Kenneth's last and surely final strike, dislodging a small dirk from his belt as he did so. He was closer to Aubrielle than Kenneth was; he grabbed her by the leg before Kenneth could get to him and thrust the razor-sharp point of the dirk straight at her heart.

"Stop right there or she dies!" he rasped.

Kenneth froze. Although his features held no expression, the ice blue eyes were filled with horror. His gaze moved to Aubrielle; she was beaten and bleeding, her lovely face a horrid shade of white. She stared back at him with her sea-colored eyes, more trust and peace than he had ever seen reflected in them. She had put up a good fight; he could see it in her face. When she smiled weakly at him, forcing her bravery, he very nearly came apart. But for appearance sake, he held himself together.

Lucius jabbed her with the dagger. "Drop the sword, Kenneth. Drop it, I say!"

His sword fell to the ground. "Release her. This battle is between you and me, knight to knight. You shame yourself attacking an unarmed woman."

"I beg to differ," Lucius scrambled into a seated position, the dirk never moving from Aubrielle's heart. "My battle is indeed with the lady. Were it not for her, I would still be captain of Kirk's army and you, my friend, would still be my second. All would be as it should."

Kenneth's manner frosted as he struggled to maintain his control. "She is not the cause of your troubles, Lucius. You and you alone have accomplished that. Let her go and we shall speak again, as we did long ago when you and I were friendly. Let us settle this man to man."

Lucius could see the fear in Kenneth's eyes even though he tried desperately to hide it. He'd known the man too long not to recognize the change. The knowledge empowered him. "Are you afraid, Kenneth?"

"Not for myself."

"For your wife, then?"

"I am."

"Is it a gnawing fear, as if your entire life is in danger of being destroyed right before your eyes?"

"It is."

Lucius' expression hardened, the madness in his eyes evident. "Then know that I felt that since the moment Lady Aubrielle arrived at Kirk those months ago. I felt the fear that my life was changing before my eyes and there was nothing I could do to stop it. I want you to feel what I felt. I want you to know that terror that all in your life is on the brink of destruction and God seems to have turned his back on you. Do you feel it?"

Kenneth didn't want to respond. It only seemed to fuel his insanity.

"Do you feel it?" Lucius shouted at him.

"Do not *make* me feel it."

"Beg for her, Kenneth. Let me hear the mighty Kenneth St. Héver beg."

"I beg you to spare her. With God as my witness, I beg you with all my heart."

Lucius' malevolent laugh filled the chamber. "The man I once knew would have rather thrown himself on his sword than beg for mercy. Now, look at what this bitch has done to you. She has destroyed us both; my life's work and your extraordinary strength. She has weakened you, Ken. Now tell me that she does not deserve to die."

Kenneth wasn't sure which way to go with this line of thought; if he denied Lucius' ravings, it might drive the man to finish his deed. If he agreed with him, they might find a common bond again and he could end this without Aubrielle losing her life. His head told him one thing, his heart, another.

"She has not weakened me, much as she has not destroyed your life," he said evenly. "She did not order you to attack her, nor did she demand you ally yourself with thieves and criminals that would see me dead and Aubrielle come to ruin. You did that by yourself, Captain. No one forced your hand."

The twisted smile on Lucius' face faded. "I did what I had to do to survive as the tides turned against me."

"You chose to dishonor yourself and now you resort to murdering an unarmed woman. Will your self-sabotage and lunacy never end?" He held out his huge palm. "Give me the weapon, Lucius. Give it to me and I shall be merciful."

A growl rose in Lucius' throat, radiating from his body until it echoed off the walls. His body tensed as he prepared to thrust the dirk. In that split second, Kenneth could see what was happening and he knew he was too far away to stop it.

"No!" he suddenly bellowed in a completely uncharacteristic show of emotion. "Do not do it. Please; I beg you!"

Lucius' eyes were wild with madness. "I should have done this years ago."

"No!" Kenneth's voice cracked and he fell to his knees, hands outstretched. "Please; I shall do anything you wish. No cost is too high if you will only spare her life. Do not kill her; I beseech you."

Something in Lucius' expression flickered and the dagger, although pressed into Aubrielle's skin, only drew a thin red line. "Anything?"

Kenneth nodded firmly, his control shattered. "Anything you wish. I will move heaven and earth to do it."

Lucius liked that thought and it was clear he was considering it. But before he truly got the chance, something strange happened.

Brown robes enter the shattered doorway, like a specter that moved too swiftly for detection. It was an odd image, shifting, flowing, as it moved directly upon Lucius. In the wink of an eye, Lucius howled with pain and his body went rigid. Kenneth's startled gaze fell upon Brother Grendel as the man removed a very long, very sharp dagger from Lucius back. As he did so, Lucius collapsed onto Aubrielle's legs in the throes of death.

Kenneth regained his senses enough to swoop on Aubrielle, picking her up and kicking Lucius off of her in one swift motion. She clung to him and he to her. Never in is life had he known such terror, thanking God in the same breath that he had experienced those sensations of dread, strong enough that they had forced him to return home. It all became clear; God and the Fates had been trying to warn him. They had known something he had not.

With tears in his eyes, Kenneth looked at Grendel, still standing over Lucius with the knife in his hand. Aubrielle, bloodied and weak, also looked at the man who had just saved her life. It seemed that any words at this moment were sorely inadequate.

Grendel appeared to be in shock over what he had done. His gaze moved to the knife and, as if it suddenly repulsed it, he let it slip from his grasp. He looked at Kenneth and then finally to Aubrielle. A trembling smile creased his lips.

"As I said," he whispered. "God did not want me to leave you yet. Now, I think I can leave."

He quit the room without another word. Aubrielle, amazed she was still alive, amazed at the turn of events, buried her face in her husband's neck and wept.

Kenneth wept with her.

EPILOGUE

1356 A.D.

"KEN," AUBRIELLE WAS hissing at him. "What are you doing up here? Our guests are in the hall and await you."

Kenneth was standing in front of the long lancet window in the bower he shared with Aubrielle, the fall breeze blowing cool on his face. He gazed off across the countryside, watching puffy gray clouds dance across the soft blue sky.

He was dressed in pristine clothing, breeches that were of the softest leather and a linen tunic that strained across his massive chest. He simply stood there, his big arms folded across his chest, his ice-blue eyes distant.

Aubrielle looked at him curiously although she knew what his trouble was. He just didn't want to admit it. Quietly, she entered the room and shut the door.

"My sweet love," she made her way to him, wrapping her arms around his torso and giving him a gentle hug. "You must come down. You cannot avoid this."

Kenneth sighed faintly. He began to look uncomfortable. "I do not know if I can go through with this."

Aubrielle laughed softly, kissing his rough cheek. She gently ran a hand through his cropped blond hair, now gray at the temples.

"You cannot keep her your baby forever," she murmured. "Witney is seventeen now and a woman grown. Her groom is awaiting her in the hall and you cannot avoid this marriage. It is time."

He sighed again, roughly, and moved away from the window. Aubrielle let go of him and watched him pace, her powerful handsome husband who had only grown more powerful and handsome with age. She knew his moods, his thoughts, his heart. She knew that the marriage of his only daughter, his youngest, had turned him into an emotional idiot and he did not want to embarrass himself in front of his guests. Hiding in their bower was his way of avoiding the situation.

"I look at her and I still see that little girl with the curly white hair and pure blue eyes," he sat heavily on their bed, seemingly despondent. "I see that baby I first held in my arms, the toddler who would eat nothing but cheese, and the beautiful young girl riding her new red pony. I see all of these things; who is this young woman downstairs, eager to be wed? That is not my daughter."

"The pony threw her," Aubrielle reminded him softly.

"I know," he said, agitated, as his eyes came up to meet his wife's. "The point is, she is my baby, my only daughter, and I do not know if I can hand her off to another man. What if he does not take care of her as he should? What if…?"

"Then she will let him know," Aubrielle interrupted firmly, moving to sit on the bed next to him. "Ken, we went through this when it was time for her to foster. You did not want to let go of her then, either."

He looked away. "She went away."

"Aye, she went to foster with Stephen and Joselyn," Aubrielle pointed out. "They treated her like one of the family until you went to retrieve her six months later because you could not stand to be parted from her. Joselyn thought she had done something wrong and you spent days convincing her that she had not. Do you recall? You made the woman cry, Ken."

He pursed his lips regretfully, remembering that difficult time. "I did not mean to," he said. "She knows that. I just wanted my daughter back."

Aubrielle wasn't unsympathetic. She put her hands on his face, forcing him to look at her. "She will always be your daughter," she reassured him. "But she must become another man's wife. She must grow up and you cannot stop it."

Kenneth gazed into the face of the woman he loved more deeply than words could express. She had grown into such a beautiful, wise woman, more beautiful with each passing year. She was dressed in a dark purple surcoat, her lovely hair wrapped in a bun at the nape of her neck. The sea crystal eyes were just as bright, hardly lined. The more he looked at her, the weaker he felt until he eventually fell forward against her and captured her in his powerful embrace. Aubrielle held him tightly.

"You should be very proud," she whispered into his hair. "Bren and Evan have become powerful knights, like their father, and you have a beautiful daughter who is much sought after. You have had a very proud life, Ken. But, as with all things, it must evolve. Children grow up and we grow old. It is the way of things."

He nodded, his face pressed into her shoulder. "I realize that," he murmured, pulling his face from her flesh. "But Witney…."

A knock at the door interrupted him and Aubrielle rose to answer. A beautiful young lady with flowing blond hair and ice blue eyes was standing there, dressed in a pink satin surcoat with flowers woven her hair. She looked like an angel. Aubrielle smiled at her daughter.

"He is coming, sweetheart," she assured her. "We will be down in a moment.

Witney Grace St. Héver put a hand on her mother's arm. She glanced at her father, knowing his trouble. She had known for years what would happen on this day and she was prepared. At least, she hoped she was. Her father was a rather hard case.

"Please let me speak with him," she said, moving into the room. "Will you please wait for me downstairs?"

Aubrielle sighed faintly, kissing her daughter's cheek and closing the door softly behind her. Witney went over to her father, gazing down into his ice blue eyes. They were her eyes. She smiled timidly.

"Everyone is waiting for us," she told him. "Bren and Evan have already eaten half the food set out and they are eyeing the wine. You had better come and stop them before they ruin everything."

Kenneth shook his head. "Your brothers are in for enough trouble when their mother discovers what they've done," he said, his expression softening as he gazed up into Witney's beautiful face. "And you, sweetheart? How are you feeling?"

She smiled at her father and sat down beside him, taking his hand. "Excited," she said. "And sad. I do not want to leave you and Mama, but I am very excited to become Rhys' wife. Do not you like him, Dada?"

He held her hand tightly, looking at her little hand folded within his massive one and realizing he was close to tears. He felt like a fool. Witney sensed his turmoil and she kissed him on the temple.

"I love you, Dada," she said softly. "That will never change. You will always be my hero, the man I am most proud of. But I want my own family now, a husband and children. Even though I will become Rhys' wife, I will always be your little girl. I promise."

Tears filled Kenneth's eyes. He couldn't even look at his daughter, knowing she was slipping away and there was nothing he could do to stop it. It was a joyful moment but a painful one. He kissed her hand, his tears falling on her flesh.

"I remember when you were born," he murmured, wiping at his eyes. "It was a snowy night, very dark and cold. Your mother was overdue to deliver you and when she finally felt the pains, you came so quickly that we did not even have time to summon the physic. The next thing I realized, I was pulling a little pink infant from her body… and she screamed like a banshee."

Witney grinned, gently squeezing his hand. "Mama said you fainted."

Kenneth gave her his best glare. "I did not," he insisted. "I simply had to sit down because I was so startled. Never did I lose consciousness."

"Mama says they had to pick you up off the floor."

"I shall beat her severely for telling such lies."

Witney continued to giggle at him and he put his big arm around her shoulders, pulling her against him. He kissed her forehead, trying not to mash the white flowers in her hair.

"Yours is the first face I remember," Witney said after a moment. "I have a memory of you feeding me cheese. Do you recall?"

Kenneth nodded. "Indeed I do. You were not quite two years old and all you would eat was cheese. Bren would feed you, Evan would feed you, and I would feed you. You looked like a baby bird as we popped pieces of cheese into your mouth."

Witney smiled at the memory. "I love my brothers," she said. "They are good older brothers, don't you think?"

"The best."

Witney pulled away to look at him. "And I love you, too. Thank you for taking care of me, and for feeding me cheese, and for your kindness and wisdom that I shall remember as I raise my own children."

Kenneth's good humor faded as he gazed into her eyes. He had done his job; she was wise, responsible, cultured and poised. Now it was time for her to grow up, as Aubrielle had said. There was nothing more he could say to her. Gently cupping his daughter's face in his two enormous hands, he kissed her softly on each cheek.

"I suppose it is time, then."

She nodded, smiling bravely and trying not to weep. "It is," she whispered. "Please, Dada. You have to let me go."

Kenneth knew that. He nodded his head, once, and let go of her face, standing up and helping her to rise from the bed. He continued to hold her hand as she smoothed out her dress. He still saw a little girl before him and could hardly move past it. But he knew he had to.

"What do you suppose we should do if we go downstairs to discover that Bren and Evan have made a mess of mother's reception?" she asked, simply to lighten the mood.

Kenneth wriggled his eyebrows. "Get out of the way. Your mother will be bent on vengeance."

Witney giggled, pausing as Kenneth opened the door for her. She gazed into his eyes, her smile fading as her expression conveyed thousands of words her lips could not seem to bring forth. She had her father's strength, his ability to control her emotions, but at the moment, she was having as difficult a time as he was.

"Thank you, Dada," she murmured sincerely. "For everything; thank you."

Kenneth could feel the tears again but he fought them. "No prouder father has ever walked this earth, sweetheart," he whispered. "You are a beautiful bride."

Her bright smile returned and she turned for the stairs.

"One more thing," she said as she began to take the steps. "In six months when you are feeling particularly lonely and missing me, you cannot come to Rhys' home and demand to have me returned."

Kenneth lifted an eyebrow. "Perhaps not," he replied, holding her dress up so she wouldn't trip on it. "But rest assured I shall visit often to see how he is treating you."

She shook her head. "No, Dada," she said firmly. "Leave us alone for a while. I would like to get to know my husband without my terrifying father showing up at every turn."

"Once a month?"

"No!"

"Once a week?"

"*No!*"

"Can I at least come to visit when my grandchildren are born?"

She turned to grin at him as they came to the bottom of the stairs. "If you do not, I shall be very angry with you."

Kenneth was present when all four of his grandchildren were born, the last one claiming Witney's life in childbirth.

They named the baby girl Witney.

C3 THE END 80

AUTHOR NOTE

All of the facts used in this book are true; the Rig Veda exists as do the other things Aubrielle learned while at St. Wenburgh. She truly was well before her time when the extent of women's learning were things like languages, needlepoint and music. They weren't expected to know anything (really) useful. Ah, Medieval Women's Rights! And God bless Kenneth for putting up with her unconventional ways – he's a good man.

The Dragonblade Trilogy Series contains the following novels:

Dragonblade

The Savage Curtain

The House of St. Hever includes this novel, Island of Glass, and Fragments of Grace, which is the story of the Keir St. Hever.

Fragments of Grace

The Fallen One

For more information on other series and family groups, as well as a list of all of Kathryn's novels, please visit her website at www.kathrynleveque.com.

About Kathryn Le Veque

Medieval Just Got Real.

KATHRYN LE VEQUE is a USA TODAY Bestselling author, an Amazon All-Star author, and a #1 bestselling, award-winning, multi-published author in Medieval Historical Romance and Historical Fiction. She has been featured in the NEW YORK TIMES and on USA TODAY's HEA blog. In March 2015, Kathryn was the featured cover story for the March issue of InD'Tale Magazine, the premier Indie author magazine. She was also a quadruple nominee (a record!) for the prestigious RONE awards for 2015.

Kathryn's Medieval Romance novels have been called 'detailed', 'highly romantic', and 'character-rich'. She crafts great adventures of love, battles, passion, and romance in the High Middle Ages. More than that, she writes for both women AND men – an unusual crossover for a romance author – and Kathryn has many male readers who enjoy her stories because of the male perspective, the action, and the adventure.

On October 29, 2015, Amazon launched Kathryn's Kindle Worlds Fan Fiction site WORLD OF DE WOLFE PACK. Please visit Kindle Worlds for Kathryn Le Veque's World of de Wolfe Pack and find many action-packed adventures written by some of the top authors in their genre using Kathryn's characters from the de Wolfe Pack series. As Kindle World's FIRST Historical Romance fan fiction world, Kathryn Le Veque's World of de Wolfe Pack will contain all of the great storytelling you have come to expect.

Kathryn loves to hear from her readers. Please find Kathryn on Facebook at Kathryn Le Veque, Author, or join her on Twitter @kathrynleveque, and don't forget to visit her website at www.kathrynleveque.com.

Made in the USA
Middletown, DE
29 November 2016